THE SHERIFF'S SURRENDER

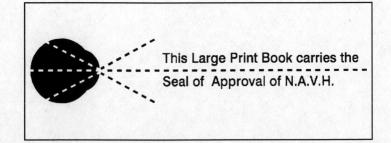

THE SHERIFF'S SURRENDER

SUSAN PAGE DAVIS

THORNDIKE PRESS

A part of Gale, Cengage Learning

GALE
CENGAGE Learning·

Detroit • New York • San Francisco • New Haven, Conn • Waterville, Maine • London

GALE
CENGAGE Learning®

LIBRARY OF CONGRESS CATALOGING-IN-PUBLICATION DATA

Davis, Susan Page.
   The sheriff's surrender / by Susan Page Davis.
      pages ; cm. — (Thorndike Press large print Christian fiction) (Ladies shooting club series ; #1)
   ISBN-13: 978-1-4104-4764-7 (hardcover)
   ISBN-10: 1-4104-4764-2 (hardcover)
   1. Shooters of firearms—Fiction. 2. Murder—Fiction. I. Title.
PS3604.A976S54 2012
813'.6—dc23   2012003241

Published in 2012 by arrangement with Barbour Publishing, Inc.

Printed in Mexico
1 2 3 4 5 6 7 16 15 14 13 12

To my first son-in-law, Tyler.
Thank you for taking such good care
of our daughter and grandchildren,
and for building great memories
with us in Idaho.

CHAPTER 1

Fergus, Idaho
May 1885

Gert Dooley aimed at the scrap of red calico
and squeezed the trigger. The Spencer rifle
she held cracked, and the red cloth fifty
yards away shivered.

"I'd say your shooting piece is in fine
order." She lowered the rifle and passed it
to the owner, Cyrus Fennel. She didn't
particularly like Fennel, but he always paid
her brother, the only gunsmith in Fergus,
with hard money.

He nodded. "Thank you, Miss Dooley."
He shoved his hand into his pocket.

Gert knew he was fishing out a coin. This
was the part her brother hated most — taking payment for his work. She turned away.
Hiram would be embarrassed enough without her watching. She picked up the shawl
she had let fall to the grass a few minutes
earlier.

"That's mighty fine shooting, Gert," said Hiram's friend, rancher Ethan Chapman. He'd come by earlier to see if Hiram would help him string a fence the next day. When Cyrus Fennel had arrived to pick up his repaired rifle, Ethan had sat down on the chopping block to watch Gert demonstrate the gun.

"Thank you kindly." Gert accepted praise for shooting as a matter of course. Now, if Ethan had remarked that she looked fine today or some such pretty thing, she'd have been flustered. But he would never say anything like that. And shooting was just work.

Fennel levered the rifle's action open and peered at the firing pin. "Looks good as new. I should be able to pick off those rats that are getting in my grain bins."

"That's quite a cannon for shooting rats," Gert said.

Ethan stood and rested one foot on the chopping block, leaning forward with one arm on his knee. "You ought to hire Gert to shoot them for you."

Gert scowled. "Why'd I want to do that? He can shoot his own rats."

Hiram, who had pocketed his pay as quickly as possible, moved the straw he chewed from one side of his mouth to the other. He never talked much. Men brought him their firearms to fix. Hiram listened to them tell him what the trouble was while eyeing the piece keenly. Then he'd look at Gert. She would tell them, "Come back next week." Hiram would nod, and that was the extent of the conversation. Since his wife, Violet, had died eight years ago, the only person Hiram seemed to talk to much was Ethan.

Fennel turned toward her with a condescending smile. "Folks say you're the best shot in Fergus, Miss Dooley."

Gert shrugged. It wasn't worth debating. She had sharp eyes, and she'd fired so many guns for Hiram to make sure they were in working order that she'd gotten good at it, that was all.

Ethan's features, however, sprang to life. "Ain't it the truth? Why, Gert can shoot the tail feathers off a jay at a hundred yards with a gun like that. Mighty fine rifle." He nodded at Fennel's Spencer, wincing as though he regretted not having a gun as fine.

"Well, now, I'm a fair shot myself," Fennel said. "I could maybe hit that rag, too."

"Let's see you do it," Ethan said.

Fennel jacked a cartridge into the Spencer, smiling as he did. The rag still hung limp from a notched stick and was silhouetted against the distant dirt bank across the field. He put his left foot forward and swung the butt of the stock up to his shoulder, paused motionless for a second, and pulled the trigger.

Gert watched the cloth, not the shooter. The stick shattered just at the bottom of the rag. She frowned. She'd have to find another stick next time. At least when she tested a gun, she clipped the edge of the cloth so her stand could be used again.

Hiram took the straw out of his mouth and threw it on the ground. Without a word, he strode to where the tattered red cloth lay a couple of yards from the splintered stick and brought the scrap back. He stooped for a piece of firewood from the pile he'd made before Fennel showed up. The stick he chose had split raggedly, and Hiram slid the bit of cloth into a crack.

Ethan stood beside Gert as they watched Hiram walk across the field, all the way to the dirt bank, and set the piece of firewood on end.

"Hmm." Fennel cleared his throat and loaded several cartridges into the magazine. When Hiram was back beside them, he raised the gun again, held for a second, and fired. The stick with the bit of red stood unwavering.

"Let Gert try," Ethan said.

"No need," she said, looking down at her worn shoe tips peeping out beneath the hem of her skirt.

"Oh, come on." Ethan's coaxing smile tempted her.

Fennel held the rifle out. "Be my guest."

Gert looked to her brother. Hiram gave the slightest nod then looked up at the sky, tracking the late afternoon sun as it slipped behind a cloud. She could do it, of course. She'd been firing guns for Hiram for years — since she came to Fergus and found him grieving the loss of his wife and baby. Folks had brought him more work than he could handle. They felt sorry for him, she supposed, and wanted to give him a distraction. Gert had begun test firing the guns as fast as he could fix them. She found it satisfying, and she'd kept doing it ever since. Thousands upon thousands of rounds she'd fired, from every type of small firearm, unintentionally building herself a reputation of sorts.

She didn't usually make a show of her shooting prowess, but Fennel rubbed her the wrong way. She knew he wasn't Hiram's favorite patron either. He ran the Wells Fargo office now, but back when he ran the assay office, he'd bought up a lot of failed mines and grassland cheap. He owned a great deal of land around Fergus, including the spread Hiram had hoped to buy when he first came to Idaho. Distracted by his wife's illness, Hiram hadn't moved quickly enough to file claim on the land and had missed out. Instead of the ranch he'd wanted, he lived on his small lot in town and got by on his sporadic pay as a gunsmith.

Gert let her shawl slip from her fingers to the grass once more and took the rifle. As she focused on the distant stick of firewood, she thought, *That hunk of wood is you, Mr. Rich Land Stealer. And that little piece of cloth is one of your rats.*

She squeezed gently. The rifle recoiled against her shoulder, and the far stick of firewood jumped into the air then fell to earth, minus the red cloth.

"Well, I'll be." Fennel stared at her. "Are you always this accurate?"

"You ain't seen nothing," Ethan assured him.

Hiram actually cracked a smile, and Gert felt the blood rush to her cheeks even though Ethan hadn't directly complimented her. She loved to see Hiram smile, something he seldom did.

"Mind sharing your secret, Miss Dooley?"

Fennel asked.

Ethan chuckled. "I'll tell you what it is. Every time she shoots, she pretends she's aiming at something she really hates."

"Aha." Fennel smiled, too. "Might I ask what you were thinking of that time, ma'am?"

Gert's mouth went dry. Never had she been so sorely tempted to tell a lie.

"Likely it was that coyote that kilt her rooster last month," Hiram said.

Gert stared at him. He'd actually spoken. She knew when their eyes met that her brother had known exactly what she'd been thinking.

Ethan and Fennel both chuckled.

Of course I wouldn't really think of killing him, Gert thought, *even though he stole the land right out from under my grieving brother. The Good Book says don't kill and don't hate.* Determined to heap coals of fire on her adversary's head, she handed the Spencer back to him. "You're not too bad a shot yourself, Mr. Fennel."

His posture relaxed, and he opened his mouth all smiley, like he might say something pleasant back, but suddenly he stiffened. His eyes focused beyond Gert, toward the dirt street. "Who is that?"

Gert swung around to look as Ethan

answered. "That's Millicent Peart."

"Don't think I've seen her since last fall." Fennel shook his head. "She sure is showing her age."

"I don't think Milzie came into town much over the winter," Gert said.

For a moment, they watched the stooped figure hobble along the dirt street toward the emporium. Engulfed in a shapeless old coat, Milzie Peart leaned on a stick with each step. Her mouth worked as though she were talking to someone, but no one accompanied her.

"How long since her man passed on?" Ethan asked.

"Long time," Gert said. "Ten years, maybe. She still lives at their cabin out Mountain Road."

Fennel grimaced as the next house hid the retreating figure from view. "Pitiful."

Ethan shrugged. "She's kinda crazy, but I reckon she likes living on their homestead."

Gert wondered how Milzie got by. It must be lonesome to have no one, not even a nearly silent brother, to talk to out there in the foothills.

"Supper in half an hour." She turned away from the men and headed for the back porch of the little house she shared with Hiram. She hoped Fennel would take the hint and leave. And she hoped Ethan would stay for supper, but of course she would never say so.

Chapter 2

From across the street, Milzie Peart watched two women enter the Paragon Emporium. She would make that her last stop before heading home. Libby Adams always let her warm up by the stove, and sometimes she let Milzie have a broken packing crate. Once the store owner had even given her a cracked egg.

She turned away, wishing she had enough money to buy something to eat. Her scant supplies at the cabin always ran low this time of year, but this spring had turned out worse than other years. Bitsy Shepard, who owned the Spur & Saddle Saloon, had given her a biscuit earlier and shooed her off, but it wasn't enough to fill her belly.

As Milzie pulled her woolen coat closer around her thin frame, a button popped off — the last of the metal, army-issue buttons. In the dusk, she saw it roll across the packed earth and under the weathered boardwalk that led to the Fergus jail. She went to her knees, heedless of the dirt grinding into her already filthy skirt, and stuck her hand beneath the edge of the walk. "Now where are you hidin'?"

A door opened, and she jerked her head up to see who was leaving the sheriff's office. A man hurried down the steps ten yards away, leaving the door wide open. Not Sheriff Thalen. Milzie couldn't make out his face in the dusk, but this man moved quicker than Bert Thalen. Not so broad through the shoulders either.

She expected him to come down the walkway, but instead he glanced her way, then slipped around the side of the building. She couldn't say she recognized him. He wore a dark coat and felt hat, like all the men hereabouts.

She shivered. Her joints creaked as she hauled herself to her feet. She would have to improvise a way to keep her late husband's old army coat closed — unless she could get the sheriff to lift the planks and retrieve that button for her.

She looked toward his office. The door still stood open to the chilly May evening. Bert ought to shut it. For the last fifteen years, Thalen had presided over the town's only jail cell. His office also held a desk and a woodstove. Smoke poured out the chimney. Milzie wasn't sure she wanted to ask his help, but she wouldn't mind warming her hands at his stove. Though the snow had been gone several weeks, the nights still dipped to near-freezing temperatures.

She shuffled to the jailhouse and winced as she slowly mounted the two steps. A whiff of cooking food tickled her nose. Baked beans. She peered inside. No one stood on ceremony with the sheriff of Fergus. You wanted something, you just walked in. Still, she hesitated, squinting into the dim interior. The outer room appeared to be empty, but she heard the fire sputtering in the box stove. Its heat felt good, and she eased inside, leaving the door open so she could see by the fading light that entered with her.

No one was in the cell — the barred door stood open. The sheriff must be in the back room. Or maybe he'd gone out and his visitor had missed him.

The tiny back room was smaller than the cell, with a bunk in it. The sheriff slept there if he had a prisoner, Milzie knew. He'd stayed there when he had her husband, Franklin, locked up for disorderly conduct years ago.

She edged closer to the stove. The warmth of the fire lured her, step by step.

18

"There now." She held out her chilled hands. Her knuckles ached as the delicious heat spread through her.

At the back of the stove, a pan of beans simmered. The smell nigh made her ribs rub together. Before she could stop herself, she grabbed the wooden spoon that rested against the edge of the pan and raised it to her lips. The sweet, hearty flavor filled her mouth and nostrils. Beans cooked with onions and salt pork, mustard and molasses.

She looked over her shoulder. Bert Thalen could walk in at any moment. Reluctantly, she set the spoon back in the pan and limped toward the doorway to the back room. If he was here, maybe he'd find her button and give her a plate of those savory beans.

A stick of split firewood lay on the floor near the doorway. She grabbed the doorjamb to brace against and stooped to pick it up. Her hip ached, and she straightened, panting. She caught her breath, trudged slowly to the wood box, and dropped the stick in. Sheriff ought to take better care of things.

Again, she limped to the doorway. If he was in there, he was sure being quiet.

Golden light from a small window in the

west wall of the building illuminated the room. The sun had just hit the horizon, and its last fiery rays streamed in, showing the empty bunk and a small stand with a bowl and pitcher.

Bert Thalen lay sprawled on the floor beside the bunk, staring up at the ceiling. His face was a horrible purple red. Or maybe it was just the reflection of the sunset.

Milzie took two steps into the room and stared down at the sheriff for a long minute. He didn't blink. A dark ooze stained the floorboards under his head. A large, shiny safety pin held his suspenders together on the near side. Milzie stooped and unclasped it. Her aching fingers resisted, but she managed to pin the front of her coat together where the last button had been.

She walked slowly out to the stove again and scooped the wooden spoon into the beans. The sheriff wouldn't be needing those.

CHAPTER 3

Libby Adams flipped the bolt of black bombazine over several times, spreading yards of the sturdy fabric on her counter. She could tell from long practice when she had laid out the four yards Mrs. Walker wanted. She could have cut it to within two inches without ever consulting her yardstick, but she measured it anyway, under the eagle eye of the mayor's wife. Mrs. Walker always bought dark colors and practical fabrics.

While Libby folded the cloth, Mrs. Walker browsed the notions counter, selecting buttons for her new dress. Her husband, meanwhile, hovered in the emporium's hardware section. The few groceries they had chosen were already tallied and waiting in a crate, but the mayor usually wound up cooling his heels while his wife shopped for her personal wants. He found rancher Micah Landry eyeing a posthole digger and greeted him with relief. Libby's part-time clerk, Florence Nash, was diligently restocking the cracker and candy jars. A housewife selecting soap and lamp oil was the only other customer at the moment. Well, Milzie Peart huddled near the box stove, but she seldom bought anything. Libby was tempted to ask her to leave. Her body odor, worsened by the heat, kept other customers away from the stove.

Mrs. Walker brought her sundries to the counter and placed a card of a dozen black buttons and a paper of straight pins on the folded length of fabric.

Libby smiled at her. "All set, ma'am?" She'd known Mrs. Walker for years. Their husbands had been friends in the old days. But the mayor's wife kept herself slightly aloof, and Libby never felt herself on an equal footing with Orissa Walker.

"You don't have any new silk floss?"

Libby tried to keep her smile from drooping. "Not yet. I've ordered a better selection, but these things take time."

She hoped her investment in expensive embroidery threads didn't prove a poor one. Only a few women in Fergus had time to fritter away on decorative arts, and she knew she might never sell all the skeins of fine floss she had ordered. Still, some of the girls who worked at the Spur & Saddle or the

Nugget were handy with a needle, and they all liked to add fripperies to their costumes. Libby shuddered when some of them entered the emporium wearing scanty dresses, but they were good customers. For them, she maintained one of Fergus's best-kept secrets: a supply of garish satins and sheer muslins stored in the back room. She had even special-ordered ostrich feathers, satin garters, and beribboned, glove-fitting corsets for Bitsy Shepard and her employees. Mrs. Walker would probably die of apoplexy on the spot if she saw the items that Libby procured for Bitsy. In the year and a half since Isaac's death, Libby had been forced to support herself, and that meant ordering merchandise that would sell.

The sleigh bells on the door jingled, and the door swung open. Cyrus Fennel charged in, bringing a blast of cold air. His gaze settled on the mayor's wife.

"Mrs. Walker! Is your husband here? I went by your house, but —"

"I'm here, Cyrus." The mayor stepped away from the wall of hardware. "You wanted to see me?"

Libby shivered. "Shut the door if you please, Mr. Fennel."

Cyrus glanced at her and hastily closed it. "I beg your pardon, ma'am. Charles, we have a crisis."

"What is it?" The mayor stepped closer, as did Micah Landry and the shopping house-wife. Florence paused with a handful of jawbreakers suspended over an open candy jar. Mrs. Walker eyed Fennel critically through her small spectacles.

Cyrus held the mayor's gaze. "Bert Thalen is dead."

Libby drew a sharp breath, and the others gasped.

"What happened?" Mayor Walker asked.

"I don't know. I was coming from Hiram Dooley's place, and I stepped in to have a word with Bert. He's lying on the floor in the back room of his office, dead as a plucked chicken."

"Oh dear." Walker fumbled in his pocket and produced a handkerchief, with which he dabbed at perspiration on his brow. "I suppose we'd better get someone to lay him out."

"You'd best come and take a look," Fennel said. "Thalen's the law around here, and there's no one else we can fetch to tend to him."

The mayor cleared his throat and glanced at his wife as he shoved the handkerchief back in his pocket. "Hmm. Well . . . I sup-

24

pose Hiram Dooley will make a coffin for him."

"But someone needs to take some kind of official notice that he's dead," Fennel persisted.

"We don't have a doctor," Mrs. Walker pointed out unnecessarily. Everyone in Fergus was painfully aware of the fact.

"It would take days to get someone up here from Boise," Landry said. "You'd best look at him, Mayor."

"Hmm . . . well, I suppose."

Fennel and Landry headed for the door. The mayor followed with slower steps. He glanced back at his wife. "You'd best stay here, m'dear. I shan't be long."

"Nonsense. I'm coming." Mrs. Walker wrapped her woolen cape snugly about her and walked away from the counter, leaving her purchases behind. "We haven't had a funeral in more than a year."

The Walkers and the housewife went out. Libby glanced over at Florence and said, "Or a wedding in twice that long." She tore a length of brown paper off the roll beneath the counter and wrapped Mrs. Walker's material and sewing notions. On the boardwalk outside, several people hurried past.

"Sounds like word's gettin' around." Florence screwed the lid onto the jar.

Libby felt a sudden urge to go over to Thalen's office. The mayor's wife was right about Fergus; the town had spent a dull winter. The sheriff's death was big news. Bert Thalen had been a friend of her husband's when Isaac was alive, God rest his soul. Besides, as owner of the emporium, she ought to get the details so she could tell her customers all about it. The store was empty. Milzie Peart must have slipped out while the others were talking.

"You mind the till," Libby told Florence. Quickly she took off her apron and grabbed her coat and bonnet.

A farm wagon approached from the north end of town, but Libby tore across the street before it came within hailing distance. A knot of curiosity seekers had gathered outside the sheriff's office. She sidled up to Gert Dooley.

"What happened to the sheriff?"

Gert glanced at her then turned her attention back to the office door. "Dunno. I was just dishing up supper for Ethan Chapman and Hiram when Griff Bane came pounding on the door and told Hiram he needed to get over to the jail 'cause Bert was dead. Hiram and Ethan are in there now with Griffin, the mayor, and Cy Fennel."

Libby nodded. Griffin Bane owned the

smithy and livery stable. Most likely the sheriff, a widower who lived alone just outside town, would be laid out over at the stable. Fergus lacked a lot of things besides a doctor, an undertaker being one of them.

The mayor came out of the sheriff's office and latched onto the handrail by the steps. His face held a greenish cast, and his knees seemed a mite wobbly.

"Folks," he called out, and the crowd went silent. "Folks, our beloved sheriff, Bert Thalen, has breathed his last. I've asked Hiram Dooley and Griffin Bane to take care of . . . what needs to be done. Funeral tomorrow at the graveyard, one o'clock sharp."

The people began to murmur. A few walked away, but more arrived, having just received the news or seen the gathering.

The mayor joined his wife on the walkway. "Well, m'dear, we need to retrieve our bundles from the emporium."

"Mayor, wait!" Cyrus Fennel hurried down the steps. "There's something else you need to take care of, Mr. Mayor."

Everyone halted, eager for more news.

Walker frowned at Fennel. "What is it, Cy?"

"Why, we'll need a new sheriff. I think you should appoint someone."

"Sheriff's an elected position," Gert called out.

Fennel's eyebrows lowered. "We can't leave the position open while we wait for an election. Can't go long without a lawman."

"You could appoint someone temporary-like," Micah Landry suggested.

Mayor Walker hooked his thumbs in his coat pockets and stood for a moment, staring toward the doorway. At last he said, "I'll take that under advisement."

The people let out their pent-up breath and shuffled away. Hiram Dooley and Ethan Chapman emerged from the office, and Gert advanced to meet them at the bottom of the steps. Libby followed on her heels.

"What happened in there?" Gert asked her brother.

Hiram shrugged.

Ethan said, "Not sure. Looks like he might have fallen and hit his head on the edge of his bunk. He's lying on the floor beside it."

"Tripped and fell?" Gert probed, frowning up at the tall rancher.

"Maybe." Ethan didn't sound convinced. "Coulda been heart failure, I guess."

"Bert was a strong man," Libby ventured.

Ethan glanced her way and nodded a greeting. "Miz Adams. He was gettin' along in years. Must have been well past fifty."

Closer to sixty, Libby thought, but she kept silent. Her husband, Isaac, had been fifteen years her senior, and he would have been fifty this spring. His friend, Bert Thalen, was several years older.

Gert persisted. "So somehow or other, he hit his head."

"All I know is, the mayor wants Hiram to build him a casket." Ethan clapped the gunsmith on the shoulder. "I'll help Griffin move the body over to the livery, and then I'll come help you."

Hiram nodded.

"That's it?" Gert asked.

"Well . . . I'd say someone needs to examine the body closer. Someone who knows what they're doing." Ethan gritted his teeth. "There's some blood on the floor, and it looked like he whomped his head pretty hard. Stove his skull in some."

Hiram nodded, and Gert eyed her brother critically, as though his silent opinion counted more than Ethan's.

"I did notice one other thing when they rolled him over," Ethan said.

"What was that?" Gert asked eagerly.

Ethan stuck his hand in the pocket of his Levis and pulled it out, then turned it over and opened his fist. A coin lay in his broad palm.

29

"A penny?" Libby stared up into Ethan's face, but he was looking at Gert.

"It was underneath him," Ethan said. "Probably doesn't mean anything."

"He might have had it in his hand when he died." Gert's forehead wrinkled.

Ethan nodded. "Might. And dropped it as he fell."

Griffin Bane appeared in the doorway. "Hey, Ethan, you ready? I can use some muscle here."

"Coming." Ethan shoved the penny back into his pocket and hurried up the steps.

Gert eyed her brother. "I suppose you need to see if you've got the right lumber for a coffin."

Hiram nodded, his lips clamped together.

"Well, come on then." Gert turned toward their nearby house. "Finish your supper first though. I'll put Ethan's plate in the pie safe until he comes back. If he doesn't forget and go home without his supper."

Brother and sister moved off, and Libby felt suddenly chilled. Full darkness had fallen, and she quickened her steps toward the emporium. Closing time had arrived, but if she stayed open, folks might come in to talk. The emporium made a good meeting place — not as good as the saloons, but a respectable place where decent women could gather. And when they did, they were apt to purchase an item or two.

Her speculation proved correct, and small groups of people wandered into the emporium over the next two hours, drawn by the lights. They leaned on the counter or clustered about the stove, debating the recent state of the sheriff's health and possible candidates to take over the office.

Libby sent Florence home at eight o'clock, and soon afterward, she locked the door behind the last lingerers. She locked her cash box in the safe in the back room. Heading up the stairs to her living quarters, she shivered. The apartment was cold, so she left the stairway door open to let some of the warmth up from the store. She set her lamp on the table and washed her hands. While she prepared her solitary meal, she thought about what Bert Thalen's passing would mean to the town. Her husband had respected him. Libby felt less secure just knowing Bert was dead. Cyrus Fennel had a point: Though Fergus was not a lawless town, it might become one if it had no sheriff.

When at last she lay down to sleep, she slid her hand under the pillow beside her — Isaac's pillow. The sheets were cool, but the polished wood of the Colt Peacemaker's handle felt the same as always. Solid. Dependable. Libby wished she knew how to handle the gun better. When Isaac was alive, she never worried about guns. Now she felt safer just having it handy. If someone broke in, she could point it at them. Chances were they'd listen to her. But maybe it was time she learned to load and shoot the big pistol.

CHAPTER 4

The mayor took center stage at the funeral the next afternoon. He spoke at length — too much length, Ethan thought — about Bert Thalen's contributions to the town. Ethan had pulled his hat off for the service, as had all the other men, and the wind cooled his ears to the point of discomfort.

"Bert was liked by everyone." The chilly wind caught Walker's thin voice, making it hard to hear at times. "When we came looking for gold back in '63, Bert Thalen, Isaac Adams, Cyrus Fennel, and I met up in the assay office. We immediately became friends. Bert was square. He always kept his word, and if another miner needed help, he'd lend a hand."

The mayor went on, but Ethan let his mind wander. True, most folks respected Bert, at least enough to keep electing him sheriff every fall for the last fifteen years. But he did have a temper. Thalen's ranch bordered Ethan's, and they'd ridden fence together several times. Ethan had heard Bert cuss and carry on when things didn't go his way. He liked his tobacco chaw, and he'd gotten set in his ways. But he was all right — better than most men would be if they wore the star.

Cy Fennel took the mayor's place at the head end of the grave, facing the crowd. Word had traveled fast, and most of the town's one hundred or so residents had turned out, along with a few outlying ranchers.

"I well recollect the first winter we prospected in these hills." Cy was putting on a bit of a folksy tone today. "My wife, Mary, and I homesteaded, but I spent a lot of time the first two years out on the claim I'd filed with Bert, Charles, and Isaac. The first winter, we got caught in a blizzard. We like to have froze to death. Cold! Wasn't it cold?" Cyrus shook his head. "Yup, those days it took a lot of grit to survive out here."

"It ain't no picnic nowadays," called Micah Landry, who ran a few cattle on his ranch out Mountain Road.

Everyone laughed uneasily.

"Yes, sir, Bert was a tough one." Cyrus nodded soberly, not focusing on anyone in the crowd.

He opened his mouth as though to speak again, but Mayor Walker called out, "Anyone else want to say something about Bert?"

"He was always a gentleman, and I never saw him drunk."

The crowd swiveled around to look at the speaker, Bitsy Shepard, who owned the Spur & Saddle Saloon.

"He encouraged me to keep the business after Isaac died," Libby Adams said.

Her voice was so quiet that Orissa Walker piped up with, "What'd she say, Charles?" No one had any trouble hearing the mayor's wife.

The murmuring increased, and Walker raised both hands. "Now, folks, quiet down. Let's have a psalm and a prayer, out of respect for the dead."

Griffin Bane stepped forward holding a worn, leather-covered book. His thick eyebrows nearly met as he opened it. If Ethan hadn't known him so well, he'd have thought Griff was angry. But he always scowled like that on somber occasions.

"Psalm 23," the blacksmith said. " 'The Lord is my shepherd; I shall not want.' "

A lot of the townsfolk recited the chapter along with Griffin, without the aid of a Bible — mostly older folks. The town had yet to acquire a church or a man to fill the pulpit and bury their dead. Some of them heard scripture only in snippets at funerals and such. For years, the only times Ethan had heard preaching came when he rode to Silver City or Boise.

Still, he didn't need every-week services to remember the verses he'd learned as a child. His mama had coached him for weeks until he could recite the Shepherd's Psalm and the Old Hundredth word perfect for his Sunday school teacher. But that was before they came to the ranch near Fergus.

" 'Yea, though I walk through the valley of the shadow of death, I will fear no evil,' " Ethan recited softly, along with Griffin and the others. " 'For thou art with me; thy rod and thy staff they comfort me.' "

He glanced over at his friend Hiram. While the gunsmith mouthed the words silently, his sister, Gertrude, spoke evenly, in unison with Griff. Only three Bibles were in evidence besides Griffin's. Libby Adams held hers open at the middle, while Orissa Walker clutched one close against her chest. To Ethan's surprise, Augie Moore, the bartender at Bitsy's place, also held one and followed along as Griffin read.

" '. . . And I shall dwell in the house of the Lord forever.' " Ethan hoped Bert had crossed into the house of the Lord. "Amen."

Griff clapped his hat on with one hand while flipping the Bible closed with the other.

Ethan started to put his misshapen felt hat back on, but Mayor Walker said, "Cyrus, would you lead us in prayer?"

Cy Fennel cleared his throat, and all the men dropped their hands back to their sides, holding their hats ready. Hopefully, Cyrus would have the sense to make it quick.

"Dear Lord, we ask You to take Bert into Your house and let him live in bliss forever among the angels. Amen."

"Amen," Ethan said firmly, though he wasn't sure they'd be rubbing elbows with the angels when they passed over.

As he at last pulled his hat low over his ears, the mayor spoke again.

"The ladies have laid out refreshments in the schoolhouse, but before we partake, there's a bit of town business we need to tend to. We'll try to keep it brief, but we need you all there. And I'm told we've got beans, corn cake, and dried apple pie, with sundry other delectables for when we're done. So get on over to the schoolhouse."

The crowd broke ranks, turning their backs swiftly on the open grave. Hiram and Griffin circled the mound of dirt at the foot end of the hole, where they'd stashed a couple of spades that morning. Gert Dooley stayed nearby, watching the people leave in an arrow-straight line for the schoolhouse.

"I can help." Ethan stepped up beside Hiram. "You two did all the digging this morning."

Hiram shrugged and dug the blade of his spade into the pile of loose earth.

"Thanks, Ethan. We'll be fine." Griffin hefted his spade.

"I don't mind," Ethan said. "Hiram, why don't you take your sister over to the schoolhouse? It's chilly out here. Gert would probably appreciate getting inside."

Hiram paused and looked uncertainly from Gert to Ethan and back. "You go on," he said at last.

Ethan shook his head and reached for the spade handle. Gert was a nice young woman, but he'd rather stay out in the cold a little longer than let the whole town think he was walking out with her. He'd decided long ago not to go down the courtship road.

Hiram eyed him for a long moment then handed him the spade and brushed off his hands. He turned and crooked his elbow for his sister, and they followed the others. Gert held her back as straight as a poker. A belated thought crossed Ethan's mind that he may have insulted her without meaning to.

He plied the spade vigorously, hoping the work would warm him up. May 5 ought to be warmer than this, but the distant mountains still held their snowcaps. Griffin labored silently with him. They had nearly leveled the pile when Gert came puffing back to the graveside.

"Ethan!" She pulled up, panting. "You're needed at the schoolhouse."

"What for?" He straightened and stared at her.

"Just come. Quick. Folks are getting impatient to eat." She turned away and walked back the way she'd come.

Now why had she asked for him and not Griffin? Ethan looked over at him, but the blacksmith merely shrugged.

"I never knew people in Fergus to keep the food back waiting for anyone," Ethan said.

"Mm. Like one pig waits for another." Griffin stuck his spade in the dirt. "Come on, we might as well see what the fuss is about."

They trudged together toward the rough log building on the edge of town. Fergus had a scanty school roll these days — seemed most of the children had grown up or families with young'uns had moved away. Isabel Fennel, Cyrus's daughter, kept school for fewer than a dozen pupils.

As they stepped into the schoolhouse and removed their hats, the warmth and smell of many people close together hit Ethan, but subtle food scents softened it. Griffin followed him through the small cloakroom into the back of the classroom.

"Here he is," boomed Augie Moore.

"Yeah, Ethan."

He looked toward the voice but couldn't pick out the speaker. From the front of the room by Isabel's desk, Mayor Walker spoke.

"Ethan, come on up here, please."

Ethan arched his eyebrows and put one hand to his chest as if to say, "Who, me?"

The mayor nodded. "That's right, son, come right up here."

Slowly, Ethan walked the aisle, feeling at least fifty pairs of eyes boring into him. People packed all the benches, and at least a dozen men stood along the walls. He stopped a yard from the mayor and stood still with his hat in his dirty hands. "Yes, sir?"

"Ethan, I'm appointing you as interim sheriff of Fergus until we have a chance to organize a proper election."

Ethan's jaw dropped, and immediately he

snapped it shut. No use looking like a fool, even though he felt like one.

Mayor Walker continued. "The people agree with me that you're the best choice for the job, so I'll just pin Bert Thalen's star on your coat, there, and —"

"Hold it." Ethan stepped back and threw one hand up as the mayor leaned toward him with the business end of the star's pin pointed at his chest. "I'm not sure I want that job, thank you."

"Nonsense. You've lived next to Bert for a long time, and you've helped him plenty. He even deputized you when he had to throw those ruffians off Cold Creek a couple of years back."

"That's right, Ethan," Cyrus said jovially from where he leaned against the log wall with his arms folded. "You're just the man for this job. Young, healthy, strong, and always on the right side of the law."

Someone started clapping, and the crowd took it up.

"Hey, Ethan! Speech!" voices called out.

He turned to face the crowd and held up both hands, in one of which he still held his hat.

"Folks, please."

"Let him speak!" The mayor couldn't seem to talk loudly without going shrill. The shouts subsided.

Suddenly all was as quiet as the moment after an owl screeches. Ethan swallowed hard.

"Folks, I dunno where this notion came from, but the truth is, I don't think I'm qualified. Besides, my ranch doesn't leave me time to perform official duties. The sheriff has to spend a lot of nights in town. I just can't do that."

"Hogwash!"

Ethan felt the blood rush to his face. That would be one of the stagecoach drivers. He was only in Fergus two nights a week. Did he even qualify as a citizen?

Cyrus Fennel again spoke up, and everyone looked toward him. "Now Ethan, it's only until we have time to sort things out and find someone permanent. But you meet all the requirements for the job."

"I do?"

"Well, sure." Cyrus unfolded his arms. "Besides the things I mentioned before, you don't have a family."

Ethan gulped. He surely didn't want a job where they wanted you to have no wife or kiddies to notify when you got killed.

"I —"

"And you served in the army."

Ethan's heart sank. The last thing he

wanted aired in public was his part in the so-called Indian wars six and eight years ago.

"You know how to shoot and how to act under pressure," Cyrus went on. "And you've got good horses and guns. The town wouldn't have to provide those."

Mayor Walker said quickly, "Of course, we'll pay you with that in mind. Same as we paid Bert. All the business owners in town will kick in."

Ethan frowned. "I don't want the people to have to scrape up money to pay me."

"You mean you'll do it for free?" Augie yelled.

"No, I didn't say that."

The room erupted in shouting and whistling.

The mayor picked up the stick his daughter used as a pointer during classes and tapped it on the desk. "Here, now. Settle down. Of course we'll pay the sheriff. It's a dangerous job."

"That's right," Cyrus said as the people calmed down. "Can't ask Ethan to leave off working his ranch anytime we need him without pay."

The mayor stepped closer and bent his neck back to look up at Ethan. "Truth is, I can't think of anyone else who's as well qualified as you are. Can't you help us out for a few weeks?"

Ethan looked out over all the faces — the rawboned ranchers and weathered old-timers, the resolute women and the young men determined to make a go of it in Idaho Territory. Hiram stared at him with gray blue eyes, his mouth in a straight line, offering no persuasion, merely waiting to see what his friend would decide. Beside him, Gert gazed at him with the same solemn eyes and thatch of straw-colored hair, but her plain face held an eager sympathy that somehow made Ethan wish he wanted the job. Gert worked hard, and someone ought to do something nice for her now and then.

He shifted his gaze. If he didn't watch it, he'd find himself a lawman out of sympathy. Sure, the women of Fergus were unsettled by Bert's death. He'd heard several asking this morning how the sheriff had died and if the town was safe. Did duty demand that he saddle himself with Bert's job just to allay their anxiety?

The faces of the women finally turned the corner for him. He wouldn't sleep tonight if he walked away from here knowing Gert and Bitsy and Libby Adams and Mrs. Walker and all the ranch wives were afraid. Most of them had followed men here with at least an implied promise that civilization would prevail in Fergus. Ethan couldn't let the whole town down.

He cleared his throat and looked at Mayor Walker.

The older man's eyes widened. "Well? What do you say?"

Ethan reached his hand out slowly, and the whole town exhaled as he took the metal star.

CHAPTER 5

All semblance of order disappeared after the mayor declared it was time to eat. Gert squeezed between people to get to the front of the room where the tables of food were set up. She found her apron and joined several other women to help dish up beans and stews.

People in Fergus had practical funeral customs. Women took food and aprons. Men took tin plates and cups and their appetites. After the deceased was laid to rest, an hour of good food and conversation followed, as sure as the corpse stayed in the grave.

Libby smiled wanly at Gert as she tied her apron strings behind her back. "Afternoon, Gert. What did you bring?"

"Four pies."

"Good for you. I hope there's some left for us."

They didn't converse much as they served

the long line of townsfolk, at least three-quarters of whom were men. Some of the ranchers made cheeky comments to the women serving the food. Gert noticed that they teased Florence, the young clerk from Libby's store, the most. A few made comments to Gert. A couple of men stared outright at Libby. Though most folks knew she wasn't looking to remarry, a few die-hards continued trying to impress her.

"Well, Miz Adams," one cowpoke from Micah Landry's ranch said with a grin as Libby plopped a large square of corn bread on his plate. "You look purty as a peach orchard today."

"Thank you, Parnell. I've never seen a peach orchard, but I'll take that as a compliment."

"It's a mighty purty sight, ma'am."

Libby chuckled. "Thank you. Next."

"Oh, wait," Parnell cried. "I was gonna ask if I could call on you, ma'am."

"No, thank you," Libby said. "Next."

Gert marveled that Libby could brush off a suitor so serenely.

Parnell huffed out a breath. "But —"

"Just move along, Parnell," said the next man in line.

Gert straightened her spine and dipped her spoon into the bean pot without meeting the man's gaze. Jamin Morell ran the Nugget, the new saloon in town. Gert held him personally responsible for the noise on the Nugget's end of the street on Saturday nights.

"Thank you, ma'am," he said.

"You're welcome." After he'd stepped over in front of Libby for corn bread, Gert sneaked a disapproving glance at him. His suit must have come from back East. The material was finer than what Libby stocked at the Paragon Emporium, and anyway, Gert doubted any woman in Fergus could tailor that well. His swirly-patterned silk waistcoat would be something to stare at if she didn't have to worry about him staring back.

Jamin beamed a toothy smile at Libby. "Good day, ma'am. That looks delicious."

Gert turned to serve the next man in line.

"Howdy, Gert."

Ethan's strained smile melted her heart. She could tell he'd hated to take the sheriff's position, but when he saw the need, he'd stepped up and accepted the duty. Ethan Chapman had to be the finest man in Fergus. After Hiram, of course, though her brother had slacked off on taking part in civic activities since Violet died. Before that, Hiram used to talk and even laugh with his customers. He'd squired Violet around town when she needed to shop, and he'd offered to help ranchers who were laid up. All that politeness and neighborliness had ended when Violet drew her last breath.

Well, no sense thinking about that. Right now the town's new sheriff was smiling at her.

"Congratulations, Ethan," she said softly. "I think the mayor chose the right man for the job." Of course, Cy Fennel did the actual choosing, and Mayor Walker had carried out his wishes, as always, but she would never say that to Ethan. It was fitting that he'd been chosen, no matter who orchestrated it.

He gritted his teeth. "I don't know about that, but it seemed someone needed to do it, and we wouldn't get any food until they did."

Ethan could always make her laugh. She loved it when he spent time with Hiram and coaxed a smile or two out of him as well.

"You'll do a good job." She ladled a generous serving of beans onto his plate.

"This your mess?" He nodded toward the bean pot.

"No, Annie Harper brought 'em. I brought pies."

He glanced down the tables toward where

49

the desserts waited. "I'll be sure and get some. I know they'll be good."

Gert was still smiling when she turned to the next in line — sour-faced Orissa Walker.

An hour later, she and the other women scraped out the pans and retrieved the biscuits and pie they'd hidden away to be sure they got something.

"I should get back and open the emporium," Libby said as she sank onto a bench.

"I could open for you, Miz Adams," Florence said. She sat down, balancing her plate and a tin cup of cider.

"We'll both go," Libby replied. "As soon as we finish eating and cleaning up."

"You've done enough," Gert said. "We've got plenty of women to clean up. If folks will remember to take their dishes, there won't be much to do anyway. Hiram will put all the benches back."

The crowd continued to thin. Bitsy Shepard and Goldie, one of her saloon girls, collected the four large pans in which Bitsy's contribution for the meal had arrived — sliced roast beef, a mess of succotash, a mountain of mashed potatoes, and a deep-dish dried pumpkin pie big enough to feed two dozen people.

"Thanks for sending all that food, Bitsy," Gert called.

Bitsy's gaze lit on her, and she smiled. " 'Tweren't nothing."

"Sure it was," Libby said. "Most folks hereabouts don't eat that well unless they go to the Spur & Saddle for Sunday dinner."

Bitsy flushed, which Gert thought a remarkable feat for a saloon owner of twenty years' standing. "I do thank you." She and Goldie hustled toward the door, their satin skirts rustling. Gert wondered if they'd chosen their least flamboyant dresses for the funeral. Bitsy's was a deep wine red, and Goldie's too-short green overskirt showed a ruffle of gold beneath and a scandalous hint of dark stockings.

Gert turned back to Libby and Florence. "Bitsy always thought a lot of Bert."

"Yes," Libby agreed, "but she'd have done the same for anyone in this town."

Libby took the prize for genuine sweetness, Gert decided. Some of the town's women wouldn't give Bitsy the time of day. But Libby always had a kind word for anyone — a ranch hand, a saloon girl, or the mayor's prim wife. She was more than passably pretty, too, with her golden hair and vivid blue eyes — the way Gert had always wished her own had turned out, instead of this scraggly hair the color of

51

dishwater and eyes like the smoke coming out of the chimney when Hiram burned greasewood. No wonder all the men in town hankered after the lovely widow. But Libby gently discouraged all who came courting.

Gert lifted her last forkful of roast to her mouth. Bitsy surely could cook, no denying that. Or maybe the rumors were true and Augie Moore did a lot of the cooking for her during the day, putting on his bartender's apron when the men began to gather after supper.

Libby stood. "If you're sure you don't need me . . ."

Gert shook her head and waved a hand at the nearly empty food tables. "Git. There's barely a thing left."

Her friend hesitated and looked around the hall. She leaned close to Gert's ear. "Have you heard anyone say for sure how Bert died?"

"Just what Ethan said yesterday. He hit his head."

"I can't help thinking about it and wondering."

Gert studied Libby's face. "You mean . . . maybe someone hit it for him? Nobody's said as much."

"Good. I probably worry too much." Libby turned toward the door. "Come on,

Florence. If we don't hurry, we'll miss some business."

As the two left the schoolroom, Gert's gaze drifted again to Ethan. He stood near the stove with the mayor and Cyrus. She wondered what Mayor Walker was saying so earnestly. To one side, Jamin Morrell sat sipping from a tin cup. He almost seemed to be listening to the men's conversation. Gert had no use for Morrell. He'd come to Fergus a year past and opened the Nugget Saloon on the opposite end of Main Street from Bitsy's establishment. Not that Gert approved of Bitsy's business, but compared to the Nugget, the Spur & Saddle was practically genteel. Morrell took a long pull from his cup, and suddenly Gert wondered if he'd sneaked a bottle of spirits into the schoolhouse.

After a moment, the two older men clapped Ethan on the back and left him. Cyrus went out the door, and Mayor Walker joined his wife and a couple who owned a ranch east of town.

Gert busied herself setting the few remaining pans closer together so she and Mrs. Landry could clear off one table. No sense letting folks see her making calf eyes at her brother's friend — the new sheriff, that is. She smiled to herself. Ethan might not be overly comfortable with his new position, but she couldn't think of a better candidate for the job. Not another man in Fergus could be as impartial and honest as Ethan Chapman.

"Hey, Gert."

She jumped and looked up to find the object of her thoughts looking at her with brown eyes fit to make a schoolgirl swoon.

"Ethan."

"Seen Hiram?"

"I think he went back to the graveyard with Griffin. They wanted to make sure the dirt got tamped down good."

Ethan nodded and turned his hat around in his hands, holding it by the brim. "Thought I'd ask Hi to go over to the sheriff's office with me. The mayor and Mr. Fennel think I oughta go over it to see if there's anything that will tell us more about Bert's . . . demise."

She nodded. "Hiram will go with you if you ask him. Just don't expect him to hold forth with his opinion."

Ethan actually smiled. "Right. He's restful, your brother." Still, he stood there, turning the hat round and round. "I guess I'll have to sleep in there some now."

Gert searched his face. Fatigue etched little lines like pine needles at the corners of his eyes, and his eyebrows drew together.

"I don't expect you need to stay there tonight. Bert only slept there when he had prisoners, didn't he?"

"I guess. But I'll have to make arrangements for someone to tend my ranch when I'm in town."

"Don't you have any ranch hands?" Gert asked.

"I had two last year, but I let them go in the fall. You know, Spin and Johnny McDade. Couldn't afford to pay them all winter."

She nodded. The two had ridden over from Boonville last summer, if she remembered right. Good, steady boys. "I expect they'll come back, now that it's warming up again."

"Maybe. If so, they'll watch things for me while I'm sheriffing, I guess." Ethan sighed. "Can't say I like this turn of events."

Gert laid her hand on his sleeve for an instant. "You'll do fine, Ethan. Just fine." She pulled her hand back lest he think she was being forward.

"Well, thank you kindly. Guess I'll go see if Hiram's done." He walked toward the door and clapped his wilted hat on when he reached it. As he half turned to close the schoolroom door behind him, his gaze again met Gert's, and he gave her a curt nod.

She stood looking at the closed door for a long moment until Mrs. Landry called, "Gert, is that Laura Storrey's dish?"

Ethan walked out of the school yard and looked toward the grave site. Sure enough, Hiram and Griffin were out there, filling in the last few shovelfuls of dirt. He took a few steps toward the graveyard, then stopped.

Since when did he need a friend to go with him into a scary, dark place? Not since he was a boy. Maybe it was time he faced reality. When his enlistment expired after the Indian wars, he had come back here looking for some peace and quiet. He minded his own business and worked his own land. Now the townsfolk wanted him to mind everyone else's business and make sure no one tried to mess with their property. Not Ethan's choice, not by a long shot.

But that seemed to be the hand God had dealt him. He frowned and pulled his hat off so he could scratch his head. Somehow it didn't seem quite right to think of God dealing him a poker hand.

"You understand, Lord," he mumbled. "It's what You gave me, I reckon. So I guess that means I have to play it out."

He sighed and turned back to the school

yard. He'd left his paint gelding tied to the hitching rail there before the funeral. Little did he expect when he'd left his ranch this morning to come home a lawman. He might never get that fence strung.

Scout stood with his head drooping, sound asleep.

"Hey, fella."

The paint whickered as Ethan untied the lead rope and stowed it in his saddlebag. He took out the bridle and held the bit up. The gelding smiled then opened his teeth enough for the curb to slip into his mouth. Ethan slid the headstall over Scout's ears and buckled the throat latch. He stood stroking the horse's long, sleek neck for a moment, knowing he was stalling.

At last, he tightened the cinch and swung into the saddle. Scout minced around toward the ranch. "Not yet, boy. We got one more stop to make." Ethan reined him the other way, toward the center of town.

The main street seemed strangely subdued in the waning afternoon. Half the buildings stood empty since the bust that had followed the gold rush, but usually folks were about this time of day. Ethan guessed they'd either had enough socializing at the funeral or had gathered in small groups indoors to keep discussing the recent events.

Scout's hoofbeats echoed off the facade of the three-story building that used to be a boardinghouse. Those were the days, when the miners poured into town to have their gold dust weighed and find a hot meal and a stiff drink. But the boardinghouse had stood vacant for nigh on ten years. Ethan had been only eleven when his family moved here, but the town's population had been at least triple what it was now. He remembered the time when three general stores served the needs of the hundreds of miners with claims in the area.

A few of the old buildings had been cannibalized for lumber, but most were still owned by someone who objected to such activity. In fact, a large proportion of the vacant buildings were owned by Cyrus Fennel. He'd bought up a lot of property, in town and outside it, when the boom collapsed. Cyrus kept saying the town would prosper again and then he'd make a fortune selling the storefronts and empty houses. And if anyone tried to steal lumber off one of his buildings, Cyrus put the law on them. Ethan wondered if he'd have to lock people up for pilfering boards. Lumber was in high demand here.

He came to the jail and pulled gently on the reins. Scout obliged by stopping. Ethan gazed toward the weathered building. No smoke puffed from the chimney, and from outside, the jail looked like one more abandoned house.

Scout shook his head and nickered.

"Take it easy, fella." The saddle leather creaked as Ethan lowered himself to the ground. He felt old today. He was only twenty-nine — at least, he thought it was twenty-nine. That or thirty. But he felt like an old man.

Was it because Bert Thalen was fixing to be an old man, and now Ethan had to take the old man's place? The town had always had an old sheriff. Ethan remembered Sheriff Rogers from back when he was a kid. Rogers had supposedly been the first sheriff, elected when the young town erupted with gold seekers. Then Rogers retired, back in '70, and the town elected Bert in his place. Bert had quit placer mining by then and taken up ranching. He must have already been over forty then.

Ethan tied his horse to the hitching rail and looked up at the gray sky. "All right, Lord, I guess I've got to be sheriff. But I don't have to be old, do I?"

He strode purposefully toward the jail, refusing to enter like a doddering oldster. He flung the door open. The dim interior smelled of ashes and scorched beans. A pan with crusted-on food sat on the cold stove. The door of the single cell was open, just as it had been yesterday. Inside, a wooden bunk was attached to the far wall, which had a small barred window. A straw tick and a chamber pot were the only other amenities.

Ethan glanced around the outer room. Across from the stove stood Bert's desk and a chair. In one corner, a stool sat beneath several posters tacked to the wall. Hanging from a nail was a large key Ethan assumed went to the cell door. A kerosene lantern hung from the ceiling. Another window — also barred — shed a little light on the surface of the desk. A few sheets of paper and a tin can holding a pencil lay on the scarred desktop.

He walked four paces to the door of the small back room. Bert's bunk — where Ethan would probably spend more nights than he wanted to — took half the floor space. On the bare board floor beside it, a dark, irregular stain marked the spot where Bert's smashed head had rested. A shelf held two cups, two tin plates, assorted silverware, a bullet mold, a can of kerosene, and a tobacco tin. In one corner, a mismatched china bowl and pitcher sat on a low stand, and near it on the wall, a grayish towel and one of Bert's flannel shirts hung from pegs.

Ethan felt the small room closing in on him. His ranch house, with two snug bedchambers, a loft above, and a huge, open kitchen and sitting room, would make three of this jailhouse. He inhaled deeply and recalled Gert's words to him at the school. He wouldn't have to stay here unless he had prisoners.

"Thank You for that, Lord."

Yesterday the old sheriff had lain on his back, here by the bunk, with his feet sprawled right about where Ethan stood. He stepped aside quickly, then gave himself a mental kick in the backside. He couldn't avoid the spot where Bert died forever. He'd have to sleep in the dead man's bunk.

"At least I can wash the bedding and clean up that bloodstain." He stepped forward, deliberately planting his boots where Bert's body had lain on the planks, and yanked the crazy quilt off the bunk. Beneath was only another straw tick. A small pillow covered with a linen case lay at one end, and he shook the pillow out and wrapped the case up in the quilt. Dust filled the air and set him coughing. If it ever warmed up outside, he'd empty out the tick and the pillow and fill them with new straw.

Bert probably never dusted or swept this place. Ethan had yet to see a broom, though there must be one somewhere. He walked back into the outer room, seeking the tools he needed. A bucket half full of water sat between the stove and the wood box. He hadn't noticed it before. He could get more water and scrub the floor in there. And if he couldn't find a broom, he could walk over to Hiram's and ask to borrow Gert's.

He opened the stove and stooped over the wood box. Plenty of kindling, but tinder seemed in short supply. He grabbed a split log and began peeling off slivers and placing them in a strategic heap in the belly of the stove. Over them he built a tepee of kindling sticks. Bert had left a matchbox conveniently on the back of the wood box. Ethan lit the tinder and blew to coax the tiny flames.

He eased the stick he'd taken the splinters from into the stove, then stretched to reach another log. As he started to put it in the stove, he looked at the stick and jumped back, dropping it. The firewood clattered to the floor, thunking his knee on the way down.

Ethan stared down at the stick of wood. Slowly he stooped and retrieved it. He held it up by one end, like he would a gopher snake by its tail. The dark blotch wasn't much — just a reddish smear on the edge of the light, rough wood. As he brought it closer and peered at it, he nearly gagged. A clump of graying hair was lodged in the dark spot where a sliver had split from the rest of the log.

"Ethan?"

He jumped and turned toward the doorway. Hiram ambled toward him, frowning. His gaze traveled to the firewood and back to Ethan's face.

"I found this in the wood box." It sounded stupid. Ethan stepped toward his friend and held out the split log. "See that?" He pointed to the dark patch and the hairs.

Hiram raised his eyebrows. He reached out and took the two-foot piece of wood by the other end.

"It must have been there last night when we took Bert out of here," Ethan said.

Hiram nodded. "Musta been."

"Yeah. Must have." Ethan swallowed hard. "Good thing we didn't build the fire up and toss it in the stove without noticing."

Hiram's eyes were plain gray in the dim light. "How come . . . ?"

"What?" Ethan tried to follow Hiram's thoughts as he studied the wood again.

"That's got to be Bert's hair and blood."

Hiram nodded again.

"I wonder if there were wood slivers in his scalp." The thought bothered Ethan. They should have paid more attention. "Someone hit Bert with that stick of fir."

Hiram eyed Ethan thoughtfully. "Not his heart."

"I'd say not."

Hiram pursed his lips and said nothing.

"If it'd been a woman, we'd have had the ladies lay her out," Ethan said. "They'd have changed her clothes and washed the body. They'd have cleaned the wound in the back of his head — her head. Oh, you know what I mean, Hi. They'd have noticed things."

The gunsmith nodded and scrunched his face up in distaste. "Gert said as much. Said we ought have changed Bert's shirt. But he was wearing his best one when he died."

"If we had, maybe we'd have looked closer. Did you notice anything odd about that gash on the back of his head?"

"Only that there wasn't any blood on the edge of the bunk where everyone said he must've hit his head."

"Yeah." Ethan walked over to Bert's desk and sat down in the oak chair behind it. "I guess I wanted it to be that way. There wasn't anything in the room that could have been a weapon. I didn't want to think someone did him in."

"Nobody wanted to," Hiram said.

"We could ask Griff. Maybe he noticed something."

"He'da said so."

Ethan nodded. Hiram was talking more than he had in years, but the things he said were small comfort.

"All right, what do we do? There's nobody to tell."

Hiram laid the stick of wood carefully on top of the desk so that the stained end stuck out off the edge.

Ethan rubbed the back of his neck. He hated being the sheriff. Less than two hours, and the job already scared him silly. Was a murder investigation his first duty? "All right, let's think about this. Maybe there's a U.S. marshal somewhere in the territory."

Hiram shrugged. "Boise, maybe?"

"Yeah. I'll send a telegraph message to Boise. That's good thinking, Hi. I'll ask who the territorial lawman is."

That settled, Ethan felt much better. He stood up. "Right. Let me finish building that fire. While the water for scrubbing the floor heats, I'll go to the telegraph office. Yeah. That's what I'll do." He looked at the stove. The door still stood wide open, and his little kindling pile was consumed. The flames had vanished, leaving the one split log forlornly smoldering.

He stepped toward the wood box, but Hiram put out a hand to stop him. "Go." Hiram reached down for another supply of kindling.

"Right." Ethan strode to the door and looked back. "Thanks."

CHAPTER 6

That evening, Ethan walked to the mayor's house. He'd sent his terse telegram. After that, Hiram had helped him clean up the jail, though they couldn't completely get rid of the blood stain on the floor in the back room. Gert had offered him a small rag rug the Dooleys had used by their back door for some time. It neatly covered the spot.

He'd ended up eating at Hiram and Gert's again. Ethan had to admit, Gert Dooley did two things very well: cook and shoot. He'd have to be careful not to wear out his welcome in her kitchen now that he'd be spending more time in town. The three of them had agreed over coffee and bread pudding that he needed to advise the mayor that he'd found evidence of foul play and initiated contact with the U.S. marshal.

The Walkers had a comfortable frame house on Main Street. It boasted a wide front porch and yellow paint, which made it stand out from all the weathered board buildings. Lantern light glowed through the checked curtains. Ethan knocked on the door, and a few seconds later, Orissa opened it. Her hair, as usual, was fixed in a high bun that seemed to pull her face up into a tight grimace.

"The mayor's not home." Mrs. Walker never referred to her husband as Charles. He was always *my husband, the mayor,* or *Mr. Walker.*

"Where might I find him, ma'am?"

She huffed her displeasure. "I'm sure I don't know."

Ethan took that to mean Walker was at one of the saloons. Where else would Fergus men go in the evening?

"Thank you kindly." He descended the steps and headed south on Main. The mayor being the mayor — and having to maintain his civic dignity — Ethan figured he would choose the Spur & Saddle over the Nugget.

As he passed a few businesses now closed for the night, some homes with lanterns glowing inside, and as many empty storefronts, the burden of his new office settled on his shoulders.

People complained about the noise and carryings-on at the Nugget. A lot. Would he have to wade through the drunks every Saturday night and attempt to keep order? Maybe he'd have a talk with Jamin Morrell before his first Saturday night as sheriff rolled around. It was only two days distant, which didn't give him much time to strategize. What did Bert do about the Nugget? Ethan always spent weekends quietly on his ranch, beyond the reach of the music and shouting, but he'd heard people talk about it. Miners and cowboys rode miles on Saturday to sample the offerings of the tiny town of Fergus.

He gained the boardwalk in front of Bitsy Shepard's establishment. The murmur of conversation reached him as he opened the door. Cigar smoke wafted through the air. The scent of a good dinner lingered, and the quiet atmosphere almost comforted him. A man could come here without embarrassment. He could even bring his wife, if he had one, on Sunday when Bitsy closed the bar and served a fried chicken dinner to all and sundry. Once when they rode fence together on opposite sides of their property line, Bert Thalen had told him that he was seldom called to the Spur & Saddle. Bitsy ran a tight ship, with Augie Moore as a competent bosun. Ethan understood that to mean that Augie didn't take any nonsense from the patrons.

Bitsy herself worked the room tonight. As Ethan entered, she stood next to a table where three men were seated. All were focused on Bitsy, who had changed her deep red funeral wear for a shimmering blue and silver dress with a plunging neckline. Other than that, the dress was quite modest, and Ethan tried to keep his attention on those other features. Even so, he nearly stepped on young Goldie, who carried a tray of drinks toward a table of card players in the corner.

"Oh, excuse me, miss." He jumped back out of Goldie's path.

"Don't mind if I do, Sheriff." Goldie gave him a saucy smile, and Ethan blushed to his hairline.

Walker sat at the table Bitsy graced with her presence, so Ethan turned in that direction, being more careful where he stepped. The room held a dozen ranch hands and miners, in addition to a handful of the town pillars. One of the pillars beckoned to him.

"Say, Sheriff, how are things in town this evening?" Cyrus Fennel called as he approached.

"Quiet so far, Mr. Fennel."

"Glad to hear it." Cyrus took a puff on his cigar and blew a stream of smoke toward the ceiling.

"Mr. Walker, I'd like to talk to you, if you've got a minute," Ethan said to the mayor, who sat on Fennel's left.

Bitsy smiled at the men. "Well, enjoy your drinks, gents. Bring you anything, Sheriff?"

"No thanks, ma'am."

She nodded and moved away, greeting the cowhands at the next table as though they were long-lost relatives.

"What is it, Chapman?" The mayor's shrill voice almost made Ethan smile. How many times had he imitated that tone to make Hiram laugh? The realization that he now answered to the mayor, when this morning he'd answered to no man, made his stomach churn. That and the cigar smoke.

"It's about Bert Thalen."

"God rest his soul," said Oscar Runnels, who ran a freight business consisting largely of several dozen pack mules.

"What about him?" The mayor cradled his glass between his hands and smiled up at Ethan as though he hadn't a care in this world, which he probably didn't, this far from Mrs. Walker.

"Well, I . . ." Ethan glanced at Cy Fennel and Oscar Runnels, suddenly wondering if he'd ought to spill all he knew in public. "Could I have a private word with you, sir?"

"Official town business at this time of night?" The mayor's voice escalated into a whine. "Just spit it out, Chapman. Is it about Bert's personal property?"

"No, sir. It's about . . . about how he died."

"Hit his head," said Fennel.

"That's right." Walker nodded vigorously, almost slopping his drink. "And we gave him a right good sendoff this afternoon."

"Well, sir . . ." Ethan saw that the miners and poker players had begun to take an interest in their conversation. He pulled up a chair and sat down so he could lean close to Walker and drop his voice. "It's true his head hit on something, all right, or rather, something hit his head. And I think I've found out what that something was."

The three men at the table stared at him. The others in the room had resumed their conversations, and Augie poured another round for two men leaning on the bar.

"Not his bunk bed?" Cyrus asked.

Ethan shifted his gaze to Fennel. The man's steely eyes made his neck prickle. Best to bring in the fact that Hiram could corroborate what he'd found. "No, sir. Hiram Dooley and I set out to redd up the jailhouse after the funeral, and we found a stick of firewood with blood and hair on the end of it, like someone had been smacked hard with it."

Fennel took a quick drink from his glass. The mayor continued to stare, but Runnels asked, "Where'd you find this here stick of wood?"

"Er, yes," Walker added.

"In the wood box beside the jailhouse stove."

The three sat in silence for a moment. Ethan waited for them to say something. He hadn't ever thought about it much, but Cyrus often seemed to speak when the mayor was addressed. Sure enough, he spoke next.

"If that was used as a weapon against someone, why didn't the person who used it throw it in the stove and burn it up?" Cyrus asked.

"That I don't know, sir."

"So, what are you going to do about it?"

Ethan gulped. He remembered Gert saying, 'I think the mayor chose the right man for the job.' But what did Gert know anyway? Guns and bread dough, yes. But law enforcement? She knew as much as he knew about tatting lace, which was nothing.

"I've sent a telegram to Boise," he managed. Fennel and Walker looked at each other.

"That's probably best," the mayor said grudgingly.

"Are they going to send a deputy marshal up here?" Cyrus again had the probing questions.

"I haven't heard back yet."

"I suppose we should inventory Bert's things," Oscar said.

"Yes, we should." Cyrus picked up his glass. "I told the mayor earlier that I went by Bert's place this afternoon to make sure his livestock was all right and there weren't any animals in the barn. His horse is over at the livery. The cattle will be all right in the pasture for a day or two, but we need to make sure no one steals them or the things in his house."

The mayor nodded decisively. "That's a good job for you to do tomorrow, Chapman. Take a couple of fellows with you and list everything of value." He turned to Cyrus. "Where's Bert's son living now?"

"Oregon City, I think."

Ethan cleared his throat. "I guess I can get an inventory made and send it to him. Peter Nash would have his address at the post office."

"Well, there's not much else we can do, is there?" Walker took a deep swallow that emptied his glass. He set it on the table with

a thump. "I need to get home, gentlemen."
He rose and donned his hat. "Sheriff, keep
me informed."

Cyrus and Oscar pushed their chairs back.
Ethan surmised the interview was over. As
Fennel pushed past him, he said, "Yes,
Chapman. If there's going to be federal law-
men coming here, we need to be prepared."

Ethan stared after them, holding his hat.
Didn't they care that Bert was murdered?
Weren't they anxious to have the killer ap-
prehended? They didn't seem worried about
anything except government men coming to
Fergus and upsetting their routine.

"So Bert's death wasn't an accident."

He turned his head. Bitsy stood at his
elbow, looking at the door where the men
had just exited.

Ethan wished Walker had let him tell him
in private. Too late now. Everyone at Bitsy's
place knew, and the news would be all over
town within an hour.

Libby hurried down the stairs Friday morning to let Florence in at the back door of
the Paragon Emporium. Punctual as usual,
Florence untied and removed her bonnet,
revealing the rusty red locks that clashed
with her rosy cheeks.

"Miz Adams, you'll never guess what

Myra Harper told me this morning."

Libby smiled as she headed for the counter. Her daily preparations for business would take most of the half hour that remained before opening time.

"You're probably right, Florence, so just tell me."

"The sheriff was murdered."

Libby stopped in her new high-topped, eleven-button calfskin boots and eyed her clerk cautiously. "Bert Thalen was murdered?"

"Well, sure. Not the *new* sheriff."

"I should hope not."

Florence giggled. "Me, too. Sheriff Chapman's a sight cuter'n Sheriff Thalen ever was."

Libby tried to scowl at her but failed. Ethan *was* a well-favored young man, and she supposed it was only natural for eighteen-year-old Florence to sigh over him, though Ethan probably had ten or twelve years on her.

"Now, Florence, don't speak ill of the dead. After all, you've no idea how Bert Thalen looked thirty years ago. Could be he was the handsomest man in the territory."

The girl giggled again as she hung up her bonnet. "I doubt that, ma'am. He was a nice man, but handsome he was not."

Libby sobered. "So, someone killed him? It wasn't an accident?"

Florence sidled up to the counter, puffed up with importance. "Myra stopped at the post office for her daddy's mail, and she asked Papa if he'd heard." Florence's father, Peter Nash, kept the post office on the family's front porch, and Florence was privy to a lot of gossip. "She said she had it from her father, and that he'd heard it from the mayor, who got it straight from Ethan Chapman last evening. Someone clobbered the old sheriff over the head with a stick of his own firewood."

Libby stared at her for a moment then swallowed. "I see." She leaned over so she could read the case clock near the front door. "Florence, I'm going to get the cash box out and run over to Gert Dooley's for a minute. You go ahead and get the ledgers out, and if Mrs. Harper brings eggs and milk around, pay her the usual rate."

She went to the storage room, opened the safe, and took the cash box out. She carefully put back most of the money, leaving only five dollars in change to start off the day. After closing the safe door on the rest, she carried the cash box out into the store and set it on the shelf beneath the counter. Florence had laid out the ledgers containing the regular customers' accounts and was now dusting the selection of housewares with a feather duster.

"I shan't be long." Libby tied on her bonnet and grabbed her gray shawl. She dashed out the back door and around to the alley between the emporium and the stagecoach office. A wagon rattled down the street, and a couple of people ambled along the boardwalk. She ran across and down to the Dooleys' house, set back from the street. Gert would be up and about her morning work. Libby hurried to the back door.

Gert answered her knock almost at once. She'd tied her pale hair back in a careless knot, and several strands had escaped and fluttered about her face. If Gert would just tend to herself a little more, she could be quite pretty, but she never seemed to care about the impression made by a crooked apron or untidy hair.

"Why, Libby Adams, what are you doing here so early?"

"I'm sorry, Gert. I hope I'm not disturbing you."

"Not at all. Can you take a cup of tea? Hiram's gone with Ethan Chapman and Zachary Harper to inventory Bert Thalen's belongings."

"No, really I can't. I'm glad to hear they're

78

looking after Bert's things. I just came to see if you'd heard the . . . well, I guess it's a rumor."

Gert folded her arms across the front of her apron. "A rumor?"

"Well, yes. That Bert was murdered."

Gert shook her head regretfully. "It's no rumor. That there is the honest truth."

Libby raised her hand to her lips. "Oh dear. I was afraid of that."

"My brother was at the jail yesterday when Ethan found what they're calling evidence. Someone cracked Bert across the skull with a stick of fir from his wood box."

Libby's stomach went a little twitchy, as though she'd drunk a glass of sour milk. "Are they sure?"

"Oh yes, they're certain."

"Well, I . . . I don't know what to say. Are we safe in this town?"

"Now, that's the question, isn't it? Ethan's got no idea who did it, which means it could be anyone."

"Anyone?" Libby licked her dry lips.

"Anyone at all." Gert nodded firmly, and another strand of hair slipped from her coif.

Libby raised her chin. "If I bring Isaac's pistol over here after closing time someday, can you show me how to shoot it?"

Gert arched her eyebrows. "Sure, I could.

What have you got?"

"It's his old Colt."

Gert nodded slowly. "Oh yes. A Peace-maker, isn't it? Hiram made a new walnut grip for that gun four or five years back."

"Did he? I don't remember. I never paid much mind to it when Isaac was alive."

"I'm surprised you haven't sold it by now." Gert eyed her with speculation in her gray blue eyes. "You might feel safer with something like that behind the counter."

"I sleep with it under my pillow." Libby flushed as soon as the words were out. Would Gert think her a ninny?

"Not loaded, I hope? If you don't know how to handle it, I mean."

"I had Cyrus Fennel check it for me after Isaac passed, to be sure it was empty. He offered to buy it, but I told him I thought I'd hang onto it for sentimental reasons."

Gert nodded. "Come by tonight if you want. We can shoot out back. Or we can ride out of town a ways if you want more privacy."

"Thank you, Gert. I appreciate that."

Libby bustled back across the street. Cyrus was opening the door of the stagecoach office and tipped his hat to her. Libby ducked down the alley and around the back of the emporium. Folks saw her as self-sufficient. Now she was one small step closer to being safe.

Chapter 7

"There now, hold it steady with both hands, and this time, don't jerk. Just squeeze gently." Gert gave Libby an encouraging smile and a nod.

"What?" Libby cocked her head toward her shoulder. "You had me put wool in my ears, and now I can't hear you."

Gert leaned closer and spoke with exaggerated enunciation. "Gently. Take it slow and easy."

Libby nodded and turned to focus on the target. Gert had hung a hank of knotted dried grass from a fir tree branch fifty feet away. She liked a bright piece of cloth or a slip of white paper for a target, but last year's crop of grass stood up free for the taking. The dry stalks were pale enough to stand out against a dark background of woods or a black rock.

Gert placed her hands on her hips and waited. Libby took aim, wavered, straightened her shoulders, and looked down the big pistol's barrel again.

"You're taking too long," Gert said.

"What?"

Gert sighed, leaned in close, and yelled, "The longer you wait, the shakier you'll get."

Libby raised her eyebrows and nodded, her lips parted as she considered the instructions.

"Put it down to your side," Gert yelled, pantomiming the action.

Libby lowered the pistol. It nearly vanished among the folds of her dark blue skirt.

"Now, when you bring it up, do it all at once, and shoot when you first focus on the target."

Libby nodded, but her eyebrows drew together and she looked far from confident.

"Like this," Gert shouted. She turned to face the target, drew up her pretend gun, raising her left hand at the same time to meet and steady her right. "Pow!"

She looked over at Libby.

"Did you hit it?" Libby asked.

Gert laughed and gestured for her to proceed. Her pupil was far too pretty and proper to be toting a Colt Peacemaker.

Libby inhaled deeply, held her breath, swung the pistol up, and pulled the trigger.

Mildly surprised that she'd carried through, Gert looked barely in time to see a fir twig flutter down. Libby hadn't hit the target, but she'd clipped the branch just below it.

"Good job." They both laughed.

Libby dug the wool out of one ear. "I've only got three more bullets."

"You shoulda brought more."

"That's all I had."

Gert frowned. "Don't you have more in the store?"

"No. I guess I should order more."

"Yes, you should. Don't you stock ammunition regularly in the emporium?"

"I wasn't sure what to order for this gun. Isaac used to do all that. Lately I just reorder what people are buying."

Gert grinned at her. "You're just too dainty to be true, Libby. The bullets for a Remington rifle same as Ethan uses will fit that pistol, right as rain."

A muffled shout drew Gert's attention toward the dirt track she and Libby had followed out from Fergus after supper. Cyrus Fennel, on his big roan, had pulled up at the edge of the road and hailed them.

Gert and Libby both stuck their fingers in their ears to ream out the wool.

"Did you say something?" Gert called to Fennel.

"I most certainly did. I asked what you ladies were up to."

"Just shootin'," Gert said.

"I see that. You usually shoot behind your brother's house, Miss Dooley."

"It's my fault, Mr. Fennel." Libby advanced toward him, holding the Peacemaker at her side between the folds of her skirt. "I asked Gert to give me a shooting lesson off where the whole town couldn't see. I guess we were close enough for you to hear us though."

"I was on my way home for supper and heard a few shots. Thought I'd check to make sure everything was all right."

"We're fine," Gert said.

Cyrus kept the rein short, and the gelding pawed the ground. The big man shook his head. "I'm not sure it's safe for you ladies to be out here shooting. What if I'd ridden up on that side of you?"

"You'da been foolish if you had," Gert said.

Cyrus glared at her. "Someone could get hurt. Miss Dooley, I know you're quite the marksman — or should I say markswoman? But still, you don't know who might be on the other side of those trees."

Gert puffed out a breath. Where to start? Anyone could see they fired only in the direction of a steep dirt bank that would catch all their lead. Yet he insinuated that he wasn't safe riding down the road behind them. Of all the nerve.

Before she could speak, Libby took two more steps, bringing her to within a few yards of the horse. "It's my fault. I heard Bert Thalen was murdered, and I wanted to be able to defend myself if need be, so I got out Isaac's pistol and determined to learn to use it."

He shook his head. "It doesn't do for nervous females to keep loaded guns. You could injure an innocent person. Why don't you let the sheriff worry about the killer, Mrs. Adams?"

Gert scowled. "What if the killer strikes again before the sheriff can stop him?"

Libby glanced at her and nodded.

"Oh, ladies." Cyrus sighed. "Let the men of Fergus worry about public safety. I'm sure Sheriff Chapman will find out what really happened to Bert. If he *was* murdered, it was likely by some miscreant he tried to arrest. That person won't hang around town waiting to be caught."

"Thank you for the advice," Libby said. "I do feel better knowing men like you are looking out for our well-being."

Cyrus tipped his hat. "Good day, ladies." He turned his roan and cantered toward home.

Gert looked at Libby. After a long moment, Libby's mouth skewed into a grimace. "Nervous females, my foot."

Gert smiled. "You've still got three bullets. And you've got more .44 cartridges back at the store, right?"

"I sure do."

"Then let's see if you can shoot that bunch of straw down, and then we'll go home."

That evening, Ethan slowly approached the Nugget. His palms sweated and his throat was a little dry, though it was chilly. He walked steadfastly, giving his sidearm a quick pat. His first visit to the Nugget had better not be on a rowdy Saturday night. Tonight would be bad enough. Best to show his face and let Jamin Morrell know he'd keep an eye on things regularly.

He hesitated before pushing the saloon door open. A sour rendition of "Camptown Races" plinked from the piano inside, and the fumes of tobacco smoke and liquor made him brace himself. Could his mama see him from up in heaven? He hoped not.

Although his purpose in entering the den of iniquity was innocent, Mama most certainly wouldn't approve.

He shoved the door open a little harder than was necessary, sending it flying back to bump the wall with a thud. Everyone in the Nugget swiveled and stared at him. The girl at the piano in the corner stopped playing and sat with her hands still poised over the keyboard.

Morrell had been leaning on the bar, conversing with a customer, but he straightened when he saw Ethan and smiled at him.

"Well, Sheriff. Welcome to the humble establishment."

Ethan cleared his throat. "Evening, Mr. Morrell."

"It's a quiet night tonight." Jamin looked over at the bartender, Ted Hire, who was wiping up a spill on the polished surface of the bar. "Ted, set up a glass for the sheriff." He turned back to Ethan. "What'll it be, Sheriff?"

Ethan stepped forward. "No, thanks."

"Oh, that's right." Jamin slapped his temple as if he were the most forgetful old codger in Idaho Territory. "You're on official business."

Ethan didn't contradict him, but they both knew he'd never darkened the door of the

Nugget since it opened last summer. Jamin probably knew he never drank liquor. Morrell was sharp. Ethan figured he knew which men in town imbibed and which didn't, and which ladies liked a nip now and then as well.

"Just stopping in to tell you to call on me if you need any help keeping the peace," Ethan said. His right eye tried to twitch. He stared hard at Morrell, determined not to blink.

"That's kind of you, Sheriff." Morrell pulled a gold watch from his vest pocket, consulted it, and put it away. "You're welcome here anytime. Mr. Tibbetts and I were just discussing how badly this town needs a doctor. Isn't that right, sir?" He looked to the dust-covered rancher leaning on the bar for confirmation.

"We sure do." Tibbetts upended his glass and drained it. When he set it down, the bartender refilled it without asking.

Ethan nodded. "Can't argue with you there." If they'd had a doctor when Bert was killed, the doctor could have looked at the dead man's wound and maybe known right away poor Bert had been murdered.

"A physician would be a fine addition to the community." Morrell settled again with one elbow resting on the bar.

"Need a bank, too," called a man who sat at a small, square table holding a half dozen playing cards in one hand. Ethan recognized him as one of Cy Fennel's stage drivers.

"Yes, indeed," Morrell said. "That's another thing that would help this town grow."

"How about a preacher while you're at it?" Tibbetts blinked at Jamin. "That's what my missus is always sayin'. We need us a preacher."

Jamin started to laugh then sobered. He flexed his shoulders. "Your missus may be right, Jim." His eyes narrowed.

Ethan wondered what the saloon keeper was thinking. When a town got a church and a minister, it usually forced restraint on its houses of entertainment. Surely Morrell didn't favor that.

Ethan glanced around. Besides Tibbetts and the poker players, only two other customers and the girl at the piano kept Morrell and the bartender company. The night was young, of course, but it gave him satisfaction to think Bitsy Shepard had kept the greater part of the saloon traffic despite the new competition.

Thoughts like that always muddled Ethan, since he knew deep down that any saloon was bad. As a nondrinking citizen, he'd avoided both and ignored their existence.

But as sheriff, he'd need to make his presence felt and even cooperate with the owners to keep things from getting out of hand. Saloons being legal, he had to live with the facts.

But that didn't mean he had to linger.

"Have a nice evening." He nodded to Morrell.

"Come again, Sheriff."

Oh, I will, Ethan thought as he strode toward the door. *I surely will.*

As the door swung shut behind him, he heard someone say, "I dunno if the new sheriff's man enough for the job."

He stood still for a moment on the steps, fighting the urge to charge back in there. But he wouldn't know who the speaker was, and besides, that wasn't the way to prove him wrong. Only time and diligence would do that. He walked on toward the jail.

On Monday afternoon Libby took off her apron and hung it behind the counter. Finally the air held the warmth of May and the promise of summer. She wouldn't need a wrap today. She'd chosen a large needlepoint handbag in which to carry her pistol and a supply of ammunition. She reached for a crisp green calico poke bonnet that would be perfect headgear for a spring day.

"Florence, I'll be back by three o'clock." Traffic in the emporium was always light after noontime, and her clerk could handle it without her.

"Yes, ma'am." Florence's hazel eyes held a hint of solemnity as she looked about the store.

Libby went out the back. She didn't like people to see her leave by the front door. The mayor's wife might try to go over and talk Florence down on prices, thinking she could get a bargain from the inexperienced girl. Libby smiled at the thought. For the first month of Florence's employment, Libby had made her repeat over and over before opening each morning, "Only Mrs. Adams makes deals with customers."

She lurked in the alley between the emporium and the stagecoach office until she was sure no one paid any mind to the foot traffic on her part of the street. As she dashed across the way, she noted smoke puffing from the jail's chimney. Ethan must be in his new office. He'd been sheriff less than a week, but he seemed to take the position and its responsibilities to heart. Already she'd heard complaints. When Ted Hire came in wanting some lamp oil, he'd mentioned how the sheriff had come into the Nugget three times on Saturday night and told the boys to keep the noise down. It put a damper on the usual hilarity, to hear Ted tell it.

At the Dooleys' house, she cut straight around to the back. Gert had already saddled the two horses she and her brother maintained. Hiram Dooley's Sharps rifle protruded from a leather scabbard on the saddle of Gert's dun mare, Crinkles. The other horse, Hiram's docile bay gelding he called Hoss, stood with his head drooping, eyes closed, and tail swishing now and then. His reins hung down from the bit, the only restraint Gert had used on him. That was about all the excitement Libby liked in a horse.

"Howdy," Gert called with a smile.

"Good afternoon. Am I late?"

Gert glanced up at the sky. "Not on my account."

"Are you sure Hiram won't mind if I take his horse?"

"No, he's got the mayor's rifle in. He'll be working on it all afternoon, I dare say."

Gert unhitched Crinkles and swung the mare's head around. "Need a boost?"

"Well . . ." Libby gathered Hoss's reins and moved him to an uneven spot in the ground, where she could stand a few inches uphill from him. She was able to lift her left foot to the stirrup from there. "I'll be fine," she called, but Gert led Crinkles over anyway.

"Forgot to put the stirrups up. Go ahead and mount. I'll run 'em up the leathers once you're on."

Libby swung up and threw her leg over, struggling to arrange her skirt and keep her bag from bumping Hoss's side.

"You ought to alter one of your skirts," Gert said. "It'd be easier to ride in."

"Oh, I know." Libby had ridden sidesaddle before she'd come west to marry Isaac Adams, but out here, the practice was out of fashion. She doubted the town of Fergus boasted a single sidesaddle.

Hiram's legs were a good deal longer than hers, and her toes slid out of the stirrups. In seconds, Gert had adjusted the straps. "All set?"

"Feels just right." Libby bounced on her toes, and Hoss swung his head around, fixing her with a reproachful gaze. "Sorry, Hoss."

Gert hopped easily onto Crinkles's back. Her divided skirt settled with modesty about her. Libby decided she would look at the pattern book when she got back to the emporium. Maybe it was time she had the practical Western version of a riding habit.

Gert gathered her reins and clucked. Crinkles set out at a swift walk. Libby squeezed Hoss. When he didn't move, she kicked him lightly, and he shuffled off in the mare's wake.

They ambled behind the row of houses and businesses that faced Main Street and soon were beyond the edge of town. Gert urged her mare into a quick trot, and Libby, with some effort, persuaded Hoss to keep up. They rode to a stream that gushed down out of the mountains on its way to the river. This time of year, the streams around Fergus looked as though they meant business, but by the end of July, most would be bone dry.

Gert led her up the ravine to a secluded spot between the hills, where she halted and jumped to the ground.

"Are we on Ethan Chapman's land?" Libby asked as she dismounted. She looked about for a place to tether her horse.

"Bert Thalen's ranch, actually, but he won't mind." Gert didn't seem to notice what she'd said about the dead man, or if she did, she hadn't considered it disrespectful. Libby liked Gert, but sometimes she seemed a little indelicate.

Gert looked at her. "Did you know that Ethan heard back from Bert's son?"

"No, what did he say?" Libby asked.

"He wants Ethan to sell off his livestock and keep an eye on the place until he decides what to do with it."

"Oh my."

"Griff Bane said he'll buy Bert's horse. Ethan thinks Micah Landry might buy the beef cattle." Gert added, "Don't worry about Hoss. He'll ground tie."

"Even when we start shooting?"

"Yes, he's too dumb to run away."

Libby let the reins fall and looked about. "It's beautiful out here. I should get away from town more."

"You can ride Hoss or Crinkles anytime," Gert offered.

"Thank you. Isaac used to keep a team and wagon, but I sold them after he died. Too expensive. I just hire freighters to haul stuff for me."

"It's an extravagance for us," Gert admitted. "Hiram and I like to be able to ramble around when the fancy strikes us, so we put up with these nags."

Libby pulled some small pieces of bright flannel from her reticule. "You asked for some scraps of cloth."

Gert's eyes lit. "Thanks. Those are perfect." She nodded toward a knoll a short distance away. "I'll set up the targets over there, and we can shoot from beside the stream."

Libby watched her easy gait as she went to prepare the mark. Gert walked like a boy, though she must be twenty-four or more. Libby could remember when she'd come all the way from Maine to help Hiram's wife, Violet, with her new baby. Or such was Gert's intention when she set out on the long journey. As soon as Violet Dooley had learned a baby was on the way, she'd sent a gushing letter, begging Hiram's little sister to come stay with them and help her keep house when the child arrived. Gert had gladly answered the summons.

She was sixteen when she arrived, of that much Libby was certain. Tall, raw-boned, and gangly as a colt. No one considered her a beauty. Gert had plain, honest features and a temperament to match. She probably could have married in those first few years here in Fergus. But she'd arrived to find her brother in mourning, with Violet and their sweet baby buried out near the schoolhouse. Gert had made it plain to all that she'd come to help her brother. Any young men who'd fluttered about the gunsmith's house soon learned she didn't intend to cook and clean house for anyone but Hiram. And so, eight years later, she still lived in her brother's home.

As she piled up a few stones and anchored a bright slip of cloth on top for them to aim at, Gert frowned in concentration. She wasn't homely, Libby told herself again. Some might say so if they saw her gritting her teeth like that, with worry lines creasing her brow. But Gert had potential. Libby wished she could coax her into the emporium when a new shipment of fancy goods came in from St. Louis. But it was the bar girls who hurried over in search of ways to pretty themselves up, not plain, honest Gertrude.

Gert finished constructing three targets at varied distances and walked back toward her. Libby realized she didn't have her gun out of the bag yet. She took her handbag down from the saddle and walked toward the stream. Gert went to Crinkles and drew Hiram's rifle from the scabbard.

"Ready?" She walked over to Libby's side with the Sharps resting on her shoulder.

"I haven't loaded yet," Libby confessed. "Go ahead and shoot a few rounds."

Gert shrugged as though it was nothing to her.

"That's a nice rifle." Libby nodded at Gert's weapon.

"Hi got it off a miner. He'd gone broke

on his claim and needed enough cash to get out of the territory. Someone told him the gunsmith might buy it." Gert shook her head. "Of course Hi gave him more than he should have."

"Your brother's got a soft heart."

"No, he didn't like the look of the fellow. I think he wanted to make sure he got far away from Fergus."

Libby laughed. "I hope he didn't give more than the gun was worth."

"Did I say that? He could have got it for less though." Gert swung the Sharps up to her shoulder.

Libby jumped at the sharp crack. To her, it seemed Gert fired as soon as the rifle reached a horizontal position.

"Sorry," Gert said. "We didn't plug our ears yet."

Libby reached into the depths of her reticule once more for a wad of wool. Within a few minutes, they were taking turns firing their weapons. Gert aimed at the farther marks while Libby shot at the nearest.

After firing six rounds in succession, Libby lowered the Peacemaker and exhaled in disappointment. She looked over at Gert and said loudly, "I'm just no good at this."

"I was watching. You're getting closer. Remember what I told you last time — aim, steady, squeeze."

"I thought I was doing that."

Gert lowered the stock of the rifle to the ground. "Load up again, and I'll pay closer attention, but I think you're improving."

Libby noticed a woman walking toward them from the direction of the road. "There's Mrs. Landry."

Gert swung around. "Sure enough."

"Hello," Emmaline Landry called.

"She lives out here, doesn't she?" Libby asked.

Gert nodded toward the nearest hill. "Yonder. Her man's ranch backs up against Bert and Ethan's spreads."

Emmaline trudged along holding her skirt up a few inches. She still wore her apron and had a smudge of flour on her cheek.

"I misdoubt my eyes. What are you ladies doing out here? I heard shooting like a battle and thought I'd better investigate."

Gert laughed. "No fighting, Mrs. Landry. We're just having a little target practice."

"Shooting? Whatever for?" The rancher's wife looked at Libby. "Now, Gert I can understand. But you, Miz Adams?"

Libby smiled. "Yes, ma'am. I've decided I no longer want to be helpless. Part of my husband's legacy to me was this pistol. After what happened to Sheriff Thalen, I thought it was time I learned to use it."

Emmaline's eyes darkened. "The other day, one of our neighbors had a bucket of milk stolen — bucket and all. Can you believe it? But what's that you're saying about the sheriff? We was at the funeral, and all I heard was he'd fallen and hit his head."

Libby looked at Gert, and Gert inhaled and pulled her shoulders back.

"Sheriff Thalen didn't bump his head," Gert said. "He was murdered, and that's the honest truth."

Emmaline's jaw dropped. "No."

Libby nodded. "I'm afraid so, Mrs. Landry. We've no idea who did it, and so I asked Gert to teach me to shoot. If anyone comes creeping around the emporium at night, I want to be ready."

"That's not a bad idea. Are you planning to do this again?"

Gert looked inquiringly at Libby. "Maybe. If Libby wants to practice again."

"Could —" Emmaline looked over her shoulder toward the road and back again. "Could I join you? Micah's got a shotgun I think I could handle."

"Sure," Gert said.

Libby smiled. "You'd be welcome. How about Thursday afternoon?"

"Suits me." Gert hoisted the Sharps onto

her shoulder.

"I'll be here." Emmaline caught her breath and lifted her skirts. "I'most forgot. I left bread in the oven. Thursday!" She ran for the road with her shawl and bonnet strings fluttering behind her.

CHAPTER 8

Cyrus Fennel was nearly sober when he entered the Nugget on Saturday evening. He'd already visited the Spur & Saddle, where he'd shared a drink with Oscar Runnels. The Nugget wasn't his usual haunt, but he wanted to speak to a couple of the men who worked for him on the stage line, and he had reason to believe he'd find them at Jamin Morrell's establishment.

He pushed open the door and squinted in the thick smoke. At a corner table, he spotted Ned Harmon and Bill Stout, one of his shotgun messengers and the driver he'd ridden in with that afternoon. The two were deep in conversation with Griffin Bane, the owner of the livery stable. Cyrus strode over to the table.

"You boys going to be in shape to take the coach on to Silver City in the morning?"

"What? We don't get our Sunday off?" Ned scowled up at him.

"Not this time. The Mountain Home coach broke down. Don't know when they'll get here. You'd best call it an early night and show up ready to roll at sunup."

"Sure, Mr. Fennel." Bill Stout looked up at him and hiccupped.

Cyrus turned and walked over to the bar. Ted Hire smiled a welcome and shouted over the loud voices and off-key music from the piano. "Mr. Fennel. What can I get you, sir?"

"Whiskey. And don't serve those two men any more tonight, you hear me? They've got to work tomorrow."

"Yes, sir, I hear you loud and clear." Ted set a glass on the bar and filled it.

A lull in the tinny music set off snatches of conversation.

"— twin calves, both bulls."

"— told the mayor that was hogwash."

"— ladies shootin' up a storm, out the Mountain Road."

Cyrus turned and homed in on the last speaker — a miner he'd seen before but couldn't put a name to.

Ralph Storrey, who had a small spread at the south edge of town, said, "Oh, that's likely Hiram Dooley's sister. She can shoot the whiskers off a gnat at a hundred yards."

"There was three of 'em," the miner said,

but the rest of his sentence was drowned out by a shaky rendition from the piano of "My Grandfather's Clock."

Someone jostled Cyrus's elbow, and he spilled part of his drink. He whipped around. A young cowhand stepped back and yanked his hat off.

"Sorry, sir. Don't pay me no nevermind."

Cyrus gritted his teeth. No point in making a scene over it. When he turned around again, Ted had already wiped up the spill.

"Let me refill your drink, Mr. Fennel."

When the girl finished the song, the card players were still discussing the female shooters.

"I say the women of this town don't seem to know their place," said a hardware salesman who had come in on the afternoon stage with Ned and Bill.

"That's right," Storrey grunted.

By now Cyrus had downed two and a half drinks, counting the one at the Spur & Saddle, and he thought the salesman showed a rare sense of propriety.

"I've got to agree with you, mister," he called out. "I saw a couple of ladies out shooting last week. Said they wanted to be able to defend themselves."

"Ha!" Ned yelled. "Ain't that what you got a new sheriff for?"

"That's right," said one of Micah Landry's cowpokes, who lounged at another table with the saloon girl now hanging over him. "Old sheriff died one day, and we got us a new sheriff the next."

"Well, them ladies don't seem to think much of the new lawman," said the miner. "Iffen they did, they wouldn't be out shootin' when they'd oughta be tendin' their young'uns."

The salesman nodded. "They should be home keeping house."

"My daughter Isabel would never go gallivanting around doing such things," Cyrus said.

"Well, you never know," drawled another cowhand. "She ain't got no man to keep house for but her father."

The saloon went as silent as a church.

Cyrus slammed his glass down on the bar. "What do mean by that, you jolt-headed lunk?"

The cowboy and three of his friends stood. Ted quickly scooped all bottles and glasses off the bar.

"What'd you call me?" the cowboy asked.

Cyrus squinted at him. This was no time to back down. "I said you're a —"

"Easy, now," Griffin Bane said, rising. All eyes swung his way. "You gents got no call to get riled up. If a few ladies feel safer knowin' how to fire a rifle, where's the harm?"

"I'll tell you where's the harm," Cyrus said. "They're like to blow somebody's head off while they're out blazing away at sticks and old bottles."

"The sheriff oughta put a stop to it," said Bill Stout. Cyrus wondered if he said it just to stay on his good side, but he nodded in Bill's direction.

"*If* the sheriff can do that," Ralph Storrey said. "I'm not so sure the new sheriff could handle a pack of gun-totin' ladies."

The young cowboy who had slopped Cyrus's drink laughed. "Yeah, he ain't got a woman. Maybe he's scared of petticoats."

"The new sheriff happens to be a friend of mine." Griffin's heavy words again cut through the bluster.

"Yeah? Well, he's s'posed to be a big Injun fighter, but I ain't seen him do nothin' since he come back to Fergus." Landry's cowhand glared at Griffin through the smoke.

Cyrus wondered, not for the first time, if pushing the mayor to appoint Chapman as sheriff was such a good idea. They wanted a man they could control, but Ethan was showing initiative, telegraphing the U.S. marshal on his own and patrolling the town regularly. If there was going to be real trouble . . . He reached for his whiskey glass, but Ted had moved it.

"Give me another drink," he snarled. Ted produced the glass from beneath the bar and poured while darting glances toward the men and the door.

Bane still stood glaring at the young cowboy. "Take back what you said about the sheriff, you buffoon."

"Make me."

"As for keeping the law in town," Cyrus began, reaching for his glass, "time will —"

"And speaking of the new sheriff," Ted shouted in his ear.

Cyrus jerked his head toward the door. Great. The one time he nearly lost control of himself, and that annoying young man they'd pinned a badge on had to walk in. The fact that he'd seen him half an hour ago at the Spur & Saddle, when he'd only imbibed one drink, wouldn't help now. He pulled in a deep breath. "Sheriff Chapman."

Ethan nodded gravely. "Mr. Fennel. I see you're making the rounds tonight."

Cyrus clenched his fists. "Just came to remind a couple of my men that tomorrow's a workday on the stagecoach line."

Ned Harmon jumped to his feet, swayed a little, and sat down again.

Bill Stout shoved his chair back and stood more slowly. "That's right, Mr. Fennel. We're calling it a night; ain't we, Ned?"

"Whatever you say."

Bill latched on to Ned's collar and pulled upward. "Come on. Let's get over to the livery and get some shut-eye."

"Hold it, boys," Griffin said. He walked over and stood deliberately in front of Cyrus. "If your men are going to bed down in my stable all the time, I think it's time we came to a financial understanding."

Cyrus felt his jaw twitch. If he couldn't see Ethan watching him with keen, dark eyes over Bane's shoulder, he'd have hit him. His drivers had sacked out in Bane's hayloft for years without any question of pay.

"It doesn't cost you a cent to let them sleep there," he said through his teeth.

"It's still my barn." Griffin's solid form didn't budge, and neither did his stare.

"I'm sure we can work this out, Griff." Cyrus managed a smile. "You know we've got no boardinghouse in this town anymore. The boys have to sleep somewhere."

"That's right." Ned raised one hand, as if what he said carried vast importance.

Griffin Bane still scowled at Cyrus. "Correct me if I'm wrong, but don't you own the building that used to be the boarding-house?"

"Yes, I do." Cyrus didn't like the quiet that bespoke the men's attention. This run-in would be all over town by morning. He'd better come out looking good. "If someone wanted to rent the place and open up the business again, I'd be happy to discuss it."

"Maybe you should put that daughter of yours to keeping a boardinghouse," the salesman said, and all the men but Cyrus and Ethan laughed.

Cyrus's eyes flashed. "My daughter is the town's schoolmistress."

"That right?" The salesman shrugged. "Beg pardon."

One of the bar girls swaggered toward Cyrus. "I'd like to keep a boardin'house, Mr. Fennel. You could set me up to run it for you."

Ted scowled at her. "Good thing Mr. Morrell ain't around to hear you say that. You just be glad you've got a job here."

"Where *is* Mr. Morrell tonight?" Ethan asked, looking around.

"He went to Mountain Home a coupla days ago. He ain't back yet." Ted shot a nervous glance at Cyrus. "I heard the stage broke down in Grand View. Likely he's staying there tonight."

"Yeah," Ned Harmon said dolefully. "They got a boardinghouse in Grand View."

"You insolent —" Cyrus drew back his hand but suddenly recalled that the person who had raised the topic was the sheriff. He lowered his hand and cleared his throat. "Well, I'll be heading home. You boys get over to the livery and hit the hay." He frowned at Griffin Bane. "Come by the stage office tomorrow and settle up with me. We'll discuss how much it's worth to let a squiffed messenger and a reckless driver sleep it off in your barn."

Cyrus clapped his hat onto his head and strode out the door. As he passed the sheriff, Ethan said, "Have a good evening, Mr. Fennel."

"Yeah," called the hardware salesman, "and you might want to think about that boardinghouse. It's mighty hard to get a room in this town."

On Sunday afternoon Gert forced herself to attack her overflowing mending basket. She and Hiram always spent Sundays in quiet occupations — no shooting or splitting wood. Occasionally Gert experienced vague twinges of self-reproach, not so strong as guilt, telling her that sewing didn't constitute a proper pastime for the Sabbath. But since they had no preacher to tell them so, the full weight of conviction eluded her, and she told herself that tranquil industry, performed away from the prying eyes of their neighbors, could not possibly cause one of weaker conscience to stumble.

Her brother sat near the window, patiently carving and smoothing a gunstock for one of the stagecoach line's "shotgun messengers," the men who kept watch on the Wells Fargo stagecoaches.

Gert groped the bottom of her basket for a darning egg, gasped when she found a needle instead, and jerked her hand out.

Hiram paused in wielding his sandpaper and cocked an eyebrow.

"Stuck myself." She sucked the injured finger. She'd always categorized sewing as a necessary evil. A few minutes later when she was sure she wouldn't bleed all over her project, she snatched one of Hiram's shirts from the basket. Buttons first. The darning could wait until she'd worked her way down the layers in the basket and prospecting for the egg was no longer so hazardous.

A knock at the kitchen door annoyed her slightly, as she'd just gotten her needle threaded. People dropped in at all hours to seek Hiram's services, but since he didn't like to talk to anyone, Gert was the designated door opener and greeter. She laid her mending aside with a sigh and rose. Her brother watched with mournful eyes as she walked across the room, but he never paused in rhythmically sanding the piece of walnut.

Gert swung the door open to the mild May sunshine and stared in surprise at her visitor.

"I want to join your club," Bitsy Shepard said.

"Club?" Gert tried not to be rude, but Bitsy's idea of Sabbath wear was one garter short of shocking, which made staring almost mandatory. Her deep blue satin dress, shot through with threads of silver, had been caught up over one knee with a rosette of ribbons to reveal a frothy underskirt of vermilion net. Though Bitsy wore a dainty hat with two bright feathers curled down over her left eyebrow, it didn't detract from the effect of her low-cut bodice. Gert cast a quick glance over her shoulder to be sure Bitsy was out of Hiram's line of vision. "Did you say 'club'?"

"Yes. I heard you have a shooting club for ladies."

The question of whether Bitsy would qualify to join any association for ladies barely grazed Gert's mind. It was the word

113

club that seized her attention.

"Oh, it's only me and one or two others. Mrs. Adams wanted to learn to handle her husband's pistol after Sheriff Thalen was killed, and then a couple of ranchers' wives joined us to practice loading and shooting, what with all the petty thievery that's been going on lately. It's not a club."

"I don't care what you call it. I want in." Bitsy's deep red lips quivered, and Gert realized two things. Bitsy was upset, and her lips matched her underskirt.

She glanced once more toward her brother's chair. Hiram, bless his heart, must have overheard enough to realize who had come calling. He'd taken his gunstock and sandpaper and retreated to his bedchamber. Gert inhaled deeply and stepped back.

"Would you like to step in for a minute, Bitsy?"

For the first time, Gert admitted a saloon girl to her home. Of course Bitsy was more than a saloon girl, some might argue. As owner of the Spur & Saddle, she was a businesswoman, the same as Libby Adams. Even as she thought as much, Gert knew comparing Bitsy and Libby was inherently wrong.

"Do you have a weapon?" she asked.

Bitsy hiked her skirts up even farther and

leaned over to disengage something from a loose pocket hanging between her petticoat and net underskirt. She straightened, tossing the dark hair back from her powdered brow, jeopardizing the stability of her hat. The feathers quivered next to her temple.

"I've had this since I was fourteen." She held out a pistol not much larger than the palm of her hand.

Gert stared at it for a moment. "May I?"

"Sure."

Bitsy surrendered it, and Gert walked over to the window to hold it up in the light. The beautiful little gun had a black walnut stock, smoothly curved into a bird's-head shape. The round barrel, only about three inches long, was flattened along the top. Silver fittings on the stock bore engraved swirls and the gun maker's name.

"I don't know's I've ever seen a genuine Deringer before." Gert held it tenderly and gazed at the big hammer spur and the low sight on the end of the engraved barrel.

"Oh? I thought they were pretty common." Bitsy stepped closer.

Gert looked up at her quickly. "Would you mind if I showed this to Hiram?"

"Well . . . no, I guess not. There's nothing wrong with it though. I just don't have any ammunition for it. Haven't shot it in years.

I figure it's time I brushed up my shooting skills."

"You're not the only one who feels that way."

"Well, with Bert being killed in broad daylight . . ." Bitsy choked a little, and Gert wondered just how close Bitsy and Bert had been.

"I think my brother would like to see this." Gert crossed to Hiram's bedroom door and tapped on the pine panel. "Hi? Can you come out and look at a pistol?"

A moment later, he opened the door a crack and peered out at her, eyebrows arched in skepticism.

"Miss Shepard's got a gun for you to look at."

Hiram opened the door a little farther and shuffled into the room, looking everywhere but at Bitsy. Gert stuck the pistol into his hand. He gave a curt nod in the general direction of their visitor without ever making eye contact and gave his attention to the gun.

Gert watched his face. She could tell by the way he inhaled slowly, his lips slightly parted, that he'd fallen in love. He cradled the weapon tenderly and examined it from both sides. He rubbed the cross-hatched lines carved into the butt and stroked the iron barrel — round at the front, octagonal where it fit precisely into the stock. He opened the lock and peered into the breach.

At last he looked up at Gert and smiled.

Gert touched his arm gently and turned to Bitsy.

"My brother says it's the real thing, made by . . ." She glanced back at her brother. "What was his first name?"

"Henry," said Hiram.

"That's it. Henry Deringer Jr. of Philadelphia. Most of the ones you see nowadays weren't really made by him, and they're not nearly so nice."

"Can I get bullets for it?" Bitsy asked.

Hiram nodded.

"It's a percussion pistol," Gert said, frowning. "Most of the newer ones they *call* derringers take cartridges. But I'm sure we can fix you up. If Libby Adams doesn't have what you need at the emporium, you can ask her to order it. I know she has powder, caps, and patches. Or you can make your patches. But it looks like a large caliber to me." She looked to Hiram.

He nodded. "Fifty-one."

"Ouch," Gert said with a smile. "You don't have a mold that size, do you, Hi?"

Her brother shook his head.

"What does that mean?" Bitsy took a step

toward them, and Hiram stood his ground but pulled his shoulders back a little.

"It takes an odd-sized bullet," Gert said. "Libby might have some lead balls that size, but I doubt it. Where'd you get fixin's for it before?"

"A friend brought me some. But that was in St. Joe, years and years ago. Like I said, I haven't used this since I came to the territory. I've . . . let Augie handle any roughnecks lately."

Gert shrugged. "Well, one way or another, we should be able to fix you up."

Bitsy eyed Hiram up and down, and this time he did step back. "Do you know anyone else in town with that size firearm?" she asked.

He shook his head.

"If anyone had one, he'd know it," Gert said.

"Maybe I should buy another gun." Bitsy raised a hand and brushed her hair off her brow, setting the feathers dancing.

Gert felt a soft touch on her sleeve. "What is it, Hi?"

He held the little pistol up and gazed meaningfully into her eyes.

Gert smiled and said to Bitsy, "My brother says, will you sell the Deringer? He'd like to buy it."

Bitsy blinked her artificially long lashes and turned her gaze on Hiram. "He said all that?"

Hiram's face flushed, and Gert suppressed her annoyance. Bitsy had lived in Fergus long enough to know Hiram rarely spoke the way other people did.

"Yes. If you're interested, he'll make you an offer. Maybe enough so you could buy a new revolver."

Bitsy smiled. "Sorry. I'd keep it even if I couldn't get the bullets for it. It was given to me by —" She stopped and shrugged. "Sentimental value, you might say."

Hiram nodded and handed the Deringer to Gert, though Bitsy was only two feet away. He turned and oozed back into his room, closing the door quietly.

Bitsy stared after him. She opened her mouth as though to speak and then shook her head. "Well, then, I need some bullets."

"Libby's closed today for the Sabbath," Gert said. "You can ask her tomorrow. If she doesn't have them, she can order them from Boise."

"All right, thanks. And may I shoot with you and your friends?"

Gert looked over Bitsy's colorful costume and knew she had to make the decision at once and not back down. What would Libby say? That was easy. Gert wasn't so sure about Emmaline Landry.

"Of course. We're meeting here tomorrow afternoon at two. We've been riding out of town so's people don't complain about the noise."

"Do I need a horse?"

Gert couldn't imagine Bitsy riding astride in one of her flimsy outfits. "Maybe we can get a wagon from Griff Bane this time. If you want to come regular, we'll work something out." She passed the small pistol to Bitsy.

"Thanks." Bitsy hiked up her skirt and stuck the Deringer in her pocket. "I should probably tell you, I'm not just doing this because I'm scared. I do have employees who can take care of me and my place if I need 'em to. But I heard Cy Fennel and some of the other men have been grousing about you and your friends taking up shooting."

Gert stared at her. "Mr. Fennel? What does he care?"

"He thinks it's not ladylike. And he's not just been saying it. He's been saying it over at the Nugget."

"Ah." Gert began to see the light. The saloon that comprised Bitsy's competition had begun harboring men who complained about independent women. She'd never considered Bitsy a friend, but in that moment, she felt a streak of sisterhood toward her. Anyone who disliked Cy Fennel must have other good points as well. "You're welcome to come shoot with us anytime. Anytime at all."

CHAPTER 9

Ethan took a quick ride around his pastures Monday morning. His herd of Hereford-cross cattle seemed to be doing all right, though he'd paid them little attention for the past week. He'd have to plant his garden soon and brand his spring calves. Then it would be time to cut hay, and his barn roof needed some work. His whole place would go to ruin if he didn't give it some care.

He looked around and with a sigh turned Scout toward the road to Fergus. He hated to head in to town again, but his conscience wouldn't let him stay at the ranch and feel comfortable. Someone in the town always seemed to want the sheriff's attention. Saturday nights had taken the starch right out of him, having to haunt the two saloons. And what about finding out who had killed Bert Thalen? He'd thought about it many times but seemed no closer to learning the truth.

At least they'd completed the inventory of everything of value in the house, woodshed, and barn, and gotten that in the mail to Bert's son. Ethan and Hiram had cleaned the food out of Bert's house, boarded up the windows, and put a lock on the front door to keep vandals out. So many details to consider. And the marshal in Boise was no help as far as the murder went. He'd sent word to carry on. What did that mean?

Ethan wondered what Mayor Walker would say if he told him he didn't want to be sheriff any longer. Maybe he should up and quit.

At midmorning he tied the paint gelding to the hitching rail in front of the jail. His gaze swept the main street. He was surprised to see Gert and Bitsy enter the emporium together. He'd never known Gert to socialize with the saloonkeeper. Not that Bitsy was a bad sort; she just wasn't . . .

The blood rushed to his cheeks. Bitsy was the type of woman his mother had taught him to stay away from. Gert, on the other hand, while neither wealthy nor elegant, was nevertheless a lady. What would bring those two together?

His curiosity got the better of him, and he crossed the street and edged through the door to the Paragon Emporium. Libby Adams stood behind the counter, showing something to Gert and Bitsy. Both seemed riveted by whatever it was she displayed.

Mrs. Adams's shop girl, Florence, kept busy at the far end of the store, arranging items on the shelves. Three or four other customers browsed, and Ethan decided he could imitate them and hear the ladies' conversation. He spotted a harness hanging on the front wall and hastened to stand near it, with his back to the counter.

"Yes, I can get a supply of lead balls for you," Libby said. "Are you sure you don't want to get one of the new cartridge pistols?"

Bitsy said, "Hiram Dooley seemed to think this was a well-made gun and would work fine."

"That's right," Gert put in. "And when you get the ammunition, we can test fire it for you if you like, just to make sure."

"All right. Let's order some lead then."

Bitsy's cocky laugh carried throughout the store, and a man who'd been reading labels on packets of garden seeds looked toward the counter. Ethan forced himself to study the tooled leather headstall on a bridle. That would look fine on old Scout.

"You know," Gert said, "you might want to lay in a few small pistols, Libby."

Ethan could hardly believe she'd said that. Since when did Gert tell a merchant what to order? He strained to hear her quiet tones.

"A gun like that isn't as accurate as something bigger would be," Gert went on, "but it sure would slip nicely into a lady's reticule. And if a ruffian gets too close, it'll blow a big hole in him."

Ethan caught his breath and forced himself to keep still, though he'd never in his life heard women calmly discuss blowing holes in ruffians.

"And it's the ones who get too close that you have to worry about," Bitsy said. "Ladies in this town are having to think about their safety."

"Might be a good idea to order some," Libby conceded. "I hate to order anything I can't sell, but I've had two women in here in the last few days asking me about firearms. I don't usually order new guns, but now and again someone will bring in an old rifle to trade for supplies."

"If you do decide to stock handguns," Gert said, "make sure you get ones with common-sized bullets. You don't want to have to order special ammunition for everyone in town."

"Sorry to put you out," Bitsy muttered.

"It's no problem," Libby said. "But I'd have some cash tied up in the stock if I started ordering new pistols. I'll think about it."

The man pondering the seeds had edged over next to Ethan, who recognized him. Zachary Harper farmed and ran a few beef on the south edge of town.

"Howdy," Ethan said.

Harper jerked his head toward the counter. "You hear that, Sheriff? Women talking about buying guns and bullets. You gonna let them do that?"

"Can't see why not," Ethan said.

Harper pulled back and scowled. "Why, if my missus wanted a gun, I'd take the back of my hand to her." He turned his stony gaze toward the cluster of females at the counter. "Those ladies don't have enough to do, that's what. And not a husband among 'em."

Ethan felt the blood rushing to his face, though he wasn't quite sure why. "Settle down, Mr. Harper. They've got a right to own firearms if they want, same as we do."

Florence finished her task and approached the counter, carrying an empty crate. The door opened, and Mrs. Walker entered.

"Gettin' a little crowded in here," Harper mumbled.

"Hello, Mrs. Walker," Libby called, and then, "Well, hello, Sheriff Chapman. Didn't see you come in. May I help you with something?"

"No, thank you, ma'am." Ethan touched his hat brim and hastily followed Harper outside.

Harper shuffled off toward his farm wagon. He'd climbed onto the seat before Ethan thought of what he *should* have said inside the emporium. Yes, he ought to have said that if those three ladies had husbands, they might not be so worried about their safety. Too late to say it now though. Harper had already turned his team toward home. Guess he'd decided to come back another time for his seed.

Ethan ambled across the street, still thinking about Gert and Bitsy egging Mrs. Adams on to buy weapons suitable for ladies. He paused to stroke Scout's flank and looked back across the street.

"Morning, Sheriff," Oscar Runnels called as he strolled toward the stagecoach line's office.

Ethan waved, still lost in thought. Instead of going to the jail, he took the path around the Dooleys' house, into the backyard.

Hiram sat on the rear stoop, meticulously spreading varnish on a gunstock. He looked up at Ethan with those innocent gray blue eyes.

"Hello, Hiram." Ethan stuck his thumbs into his belt. "Did you know your sister's over to the emporium with Bitsy Shepard?"

Hiram quirked an eyebrow and shrugged.

"Know what they're doing?" Ethan asked.

"Nope."

"They're telling Miz Adams what to order for guns and ammunition."

Hiram pulled an actual smile, as though he was proud of his sister.

Ethan eyed him cautiously. "I didn't know Gert was friends with the likes of Bitsy."

Hiram carefully set the gunstock on end, leaning it against one of the railing's slats where it wouldn't get knocked over, and stood. "She come over here yestiddy." He sighed and shook his head, a dreamy look on his face. "Purtiest little thing I ever seen."

Ethan stared at him in disbelief. "Bitsy Shepard? No, Hiram!"

His friend blinked at him and frowned. "No, not her." Hiram stooped and picked up the can of varnish and his paintbrush. "Miz Shepard's got a genuine Deringer."

"Whew." Ethan wagged a finger at him. "For a minute there, you had me worried. So what's this business about ordering guns for women?"

Hiram shrugged.

"Yeah, that's about the size of it," Ethan agreed. "Harper didn't like it though. He was in the store, and he heard 'em talking. He'll tell Cy Fennel, too."

Hiram leaned over the railing and spit in the grass.

"Yeah," said Ethan. "But Harper will do anything Fennel tells him to. I expect that's why he's on the town council."

Hiram said nothing, but his eyes had a way of speaking.

"What?" Ethan asked sharply. "You think I'm under Cy Fennel's thumb, too? Now you're making me mad."

Soft footfalls and the swish of a skirt caught his ear, and Ethan turned toward the path. Gert was rounding the corner of the house. She pulled up short and looked at Ethan, then Hiram, then back at Ethan again.

"What are you mad about?"

"I'll tell you. I'm thinking of turning in this badge, that's what."

"Why would you do that?" Gert breezed past him. Hiram stepped aside so she could enter the kitchen. When her brother started to follow, she glanced at the can of varnish. "Uh-uh. That goes in the barn."

Hiram ducked his head and went down

the steps. As he headed for the stable, Ethan wasn't sure whether to follow him or not.

"You eating lunch here?" Gert asked from the doorway. She was already tying on her apron.

Ethan cleared his throat. "Well, I dunno. I ain't been asked. And your brother thinks I'm letting Cy Fennel tell me what to do."

Gert's pale eyebrows drew together. "Did he say that?"

"He said plenty."

She smiled. "I'll just bet. You'd best go do your sheriffing business and come back in an hour. We'll talk over lunch."

Ethan looked down at his scuffed boots and nodded slowly. "Thanks, Gert."

"Anytime."

He turned to the path and plodded next door to the jail. It stood as empty as it had all week. What was the sheriff supposed to do all day, anyhow? Maybe he should have stayed out at the ranch, after all. Not for the first time, he wished someone would give him a job description. Yesterday Mrs. Storrey had sent her boy to fetch him because her neighbor's boar got loose and had rooted up her yard. The day before, Clem Higgins allowed Ethan should make his brother, Nealy, patch up all the windows he'd shot out of their cabin when he was drunk. Ethan wasn't sure he could force a man to fix up his own property, but he encouraged Nealy Higgins to do the right thing. Nealy, being a reasonable man when he was sober, had agreed to do it if Clem bought the panes. But really, was this how Bert had spent his days?

Ethan headed out into the street. The Mountain Home stagecoach rolled up before the Wells Fargo office. Jamin Morrell got out. The messenger hopped down and carried a wooden chest into Fennel's office. The payroll for the stagecoach line, no doubt. The town needed a bank. Fennel, Morrell, Bitsy Shepard, and Libby Adams all had safes in their places of business. Other people probably did what Ethan did and stashed their money in a cracker tin or under the mattress.

He strolled along the street, greeting people he met. Most replied cordially, and the crotchety mood Hiram had inspired began to dissipate. By the time he reached the Spur & Saddle at the south end of Main Street, Ethan felt much better. Augie Moore was heading into the saloon carrying an armload of firewood.

"Mornin', Sheriff."

"Mornin', Augie."

The street petered out into a trail across

the prairie. Ethan crossed it and ambled down the other side. Maybe tomorrow he'd stay out at the ranch. If anything serious came up, everyone knew where he lived.

He passed the mayor's house, the feed store owned by Mayor Walker, and two vacant buildings. The post office was next.

"Oh, Sheriff!"

He stopped and turned his head. Peter Nash, the postmaster, hurried out of his tiny office, the closed-in porch of his weathered house.

"This mail came for Sheriff Thalen, so I guess you should have it."

Nash shoved a rolled-up sheaf of papers into his hand.

"Thank you, Mr. Nash." Ethan broke the string that held the bundle together and unrolled it. Wanted posters. He stared at the first one, his mind racing. Maybe a known desperado had come to Fergus and murdered Bert Thalen. If nothing else, he should study these posters so that he'd recognize any of the criminals depicted on them if they rode into town.

He hurried back to the jail, where he spread the posters out on Bert's desk. Three train robbers and a horse thief. It seemed unlikely any train robbers would come to a town without a railroad. Unless they wanted a place to hide out. Ethan scowled and shuffled the papers. The horse thief looked awfully like the picture he'd seen of President Cleveland in the Boise paper.

He sat back and sighed. He was kidding himself if he thought one of these hooligans had sneaked into town, killed the sheriff, and left again without being seen. The wood box across the room sat innocently beside the stove. Ethan had placed the stick he believed to be the killer's weapon on the shelf in the back room, to be sure no one tossed it into the stove by mistake on a chilly evening. But really, what good would it do him to keep it? And what good would he do the town as a lawman? His chances of finding the killer looked pretty slim.

An hour must have passed, or near enough. He got up and trudged to the Dooleys' back door. Enticing smells hovered on the gentle breeze. Corn bread. Bacon? No, ham.

And something spicy. Oh, if Gert had baked a pie . . .

He shuffled up the steps and raised his fist to knock. Gert opened the door.

"Right on time."

She stepped back and let him in. Ethan slid his hat off and hung it on a peg next to Hiram's near the back door. Hiram already sat at the table, and Ethan took the place he customarily occupied when he ate here. Which was often. Come butchering time, he'd bring them a side of beef to make up for all the vittles he'd eaten with them.

"Ethan, would you ask the blessing, please?"

Alone at the ranch, he'd gotten out of the habit, but Gert always reminded him of more civilized days and places. He bowed his head, wondering if Hiram spoke the blessing when the two ate alone.

"Lord, bless this food and the hands which prepared it."

"Amen," said Gert.

Hiram's amen was spoken by his eyes only, but he plainly appreciated his sister's efforts.

"Now, what's this about you throwing down your badge?" Gert scooped a boiled potato out of the ironstone dish and plopped it on her plate, then handed him the bowl.

Ethan set the dish down between him and Hiram.

"I'm not doing much good as sheriff. The customers at the Nugget quiet down for a few minutes when I walk in, but overall, I'm not lowering the rate of alcohol consumption in this town."

"Can't expect to do that." Gert frowned

as she skinned her potato. "But if there weren't any sheriff, those rowdies might tear the whole town apart. You're a calming influence, that's what you are."

"Well, what about the murder?"

Brother and sister stared at him in silence. At last Gert said, "What about it, Ethan?"

"I'm not going to catch the killer. How can I? We've got no clues except for a bloody stick of firewood. Bert's dead and buried, and we've no idea who did it. What good is a sheriff who can't keep the town peaceful on a Saturday night, let alone solve murders?"

"Don't sell yourself short. You've only started the job. And I don't think anyone expects you to bring in the killer single-handed." Gert reached to the middle of the table and speared a slice of ham.

They ate in silence for a few minutes. At last Gert rose to fetch the coffeepot.

Ethan gave her a sheepish smile as she filled his cup. "Mighty good corn bread, Gert."

Her face lit up for a moment. "Thank you. I expect you'll feel better about your new job now that you've got a full belly. Of course, a piece of appleberry pie might tip the scales."

"What kind of berry is an appleberry?"

Ethan asked.

Hiram laughed aloud.

"Not an appleberry," Gert said. "It's a pie made out of dried apples and blueberries from last summer."

She bustled about for a moment and brought him and Hiram each a generous slice.

Ethan took a bite. The apples and blueberries went surprisingly well together.

Gert poured her brother's cup full of milk. "How about you, Ethan?"

"No thanks, just the coffee. Oh, and these are mighty good appleberries."

She snorted and resumed her seat at the table.

When they had finished dessert, she refilled his coffee and sat down again, watching him. Ethan took a sip from his cup and set it down. Gert had something on her mind. Like her brother, she would speak when she was ready. Unlike Hiram, she was often ready.

"Listen to me, Ethan Chapman. This town needs a lawman. Not just any man, but an honest and diligent man. I'm not just talking about the carryings-on at the Nugget. We've got a killer in Fergus."

The blunt statement jarred him. "Are you scared, Gert?"

"Maybe." She frowned and tossed her head. "Think about what would happen if you went over to the mayor's house today and gave him your badge."

"I expect he and the town council would appoint someone else to do the job."

"Maybe so, but who? What man in this town could do as well as you?"

"Seems to me anyone could. Besides . . ." Ethan shook his head. "Hiram here seems to think I'm Walker's puppet, or rather, Cy Fennel's."

"Why would he think that?" She didn't look at her brother but fixed her stare on Ethan.

"Just for agreeing to be sheriff, as near as I can tell. Because that's doing what they want. You know Hiram looks down on anyone who does what Fennel wants."

"Hogwash." Now Gert turned her ire in Hiram's direction. "You quit making Ethan feel useless, you hear me? We need him in this town. If you get him to feeling bad, he'll up and leave."

"That wouldn't be a big loss," Ethan said.

"Oh yes it would. It'd be one less decent man in Fergus. Don't you get all proud of your humility on me, sir. What would happen if we got someone like Augie Moore for our sheriff?"

"Augie?" Ethan stared at her, startled.

"Yes, Augie. I've heard it whispered that he'd be a good sheriff. He could knock heads together with the best of them — maybe better than some. But the man's got no morals; you understand me, Ethan?"

"Well, I . . ."

"Of course you do!"

He winced. "I reckon."

Gert nodded. "That's right. Now, I dunno if you can catch Bert Thalen's killer or not, but if I get my purse stolen and I need to go tell the law, I don't want to go to someone like Augie Moore about it. Or Jamin Morell or Zachary Harper."

"Well, if you put it that way . . ."

"I do."

"All right. I hear you." Ethan looked over at Hiram, who nodded. "Yeah, I hear you, too."

Gert crossed her arms and sat back in her chair. "Hiram apologizes for making you mad earlier."

"Oh?" Ethan glanced at her brother again.

Hiram gave a grudging nod.

"So. No more of this 'I don't want to be sheriff anymore' business." Gert picked up her cup and sipped her coffee.

Ethan hadn't felt so much a part of a family since he'd left home ten years ago to join the army and come home from the Indian wars to find his parents dead and buried.

"I still don't know why they picked me." Ethan shot a quick glance at Hiram. "And don't you say it's 'cause they can push me around."

"Partly it's because you've got no family," Gert said.

Ethan didn't like that thought, but it wasn't the first time he'd had it. Bert hadn't had a family either, other than his grown-and-gone son. Did Fennel and Walker want a lawman whose family wouldn't be destitute if he got killed?

"You're not needed at home all the time," Gert said.

"I have work to do at my place. I may not have a wife and young'uns, but I've got stock and a homestead."

Gert pursed her lips. "I reckon you do. Whyn't you post a bill on the jailhouse door saying the sheriff will be out to his ranch if needed."

"I dunno. Think folks would cotton to that?"

"Womenfolk do like having the sheriff within hailing distance," she acknowledged.

Ethan reached absently for his cup, but it was empty. Gert rose and brought the coffeepot over. She refilled his cup, and Hiram held up his for the dregs. Ethan took a swallow. The brew was strong and bitter now, and he got a few grounds in his swig. He grimaced and swallowed them down.

"I don't want to give up my ranch." He hadn't really meant to say it aloud, but it seemed it was either/or. Sheriffing or ranching.

"Don't," said Hiram.

When his best friend spoke, Ethan always listened.

Gert set the empty coffeepot on the sideboard. "Hi's right. This is a temporary job. Just do the best you can, at least until they hold an election and you know if you're going to keep on being the law."

"I could decline to run for the office."

Hiram shook his head.

Gert eyed her brother and said, "You're right again, Hiram. You may not be the best shot in town, Ethan, or the scrappiest fighter, but you're honest, and you're not afraid to call a spade a spade."

Hiram nodded.

Gert's eyes blazed as she gathered steam. "If I had to pick a man in this town who would stand up against evil when it came his way, I'd pick you, Ethan Chapman. So, no matter why the mayor picked you, I'd say he picked right." She scowled across at her brother. "You got anything to say, mister?"

Hiram shook his head.

CHAPTER 10

Milzie Peart rubbed her belly. Her root vegetables and flour had long since given out. She had a few lead balls for her husband's old rifle, but no gunpowder. She'd tried to snare a rabbit, without success. With only a quart of dry beans and a few herbs left, she knew it was time to make another foray into town.

The people in Fergus shunned her, mostly. Bitsy would maybe give her a bite. Or she could go through the trash heaps in hopes of finding something. And if Libby Adams would give her a few seeds, she could plant some sort of a garden and maybe harvest a few crops later on. She'd have died last winter if she hadn't put by so many turnips and carrots. When her cabin burned in early March, she'd been able to salvage only a few things and set up housekeeping in the cave that Franklin had shored up as part of his mining claim. Nothing good had ever come out of the cave, so since he died, Milzie had used it to store things.

After the cabin's ashes had cooled, she'd hauled the charred box stove step by step over to the cave's entrance. If it had been any bigger, she never could have done it. That was two months ago. She'd hung on to life by her broken, sooty fingernails since then, huddled up in the cave when she wasn't out foraging for firewood or something to eat. She'd sifted the ruins of the cabin and come up with a few things she could use — one blackened pot, a few nails and hinges, a fork and a tin cup. She'd even found a crock of sauerkraut that hadn't shattered and burned. That had kept her going for near a week.

What she wouldn't give for a mouthful of fresh beef now. Some nights she lay awake on the rock floor thinking about stew. Broth teeming with potatoes and onions and chunks of beef as big as hen's eggs.

Eggs. Sometimes an egg found its way into Milzie's pocket when she ventured about town. She kept away from the ranches with dogs. Lots of women in town kept a few hens, and on occasion she'd borrow an egg with no one's permission but the biddy's.

It had turned warm, and she didn't need Franklin's wool coat today, though she'd miss its deep pockets. A sugar sack would do for any bits she collected. She wound a raveling shawl that had once been blue about her shoulders and left the cave.

An hour later, she hobbled around behind the Spur & Saddle. Franklin had spent many an evening here. She wished she had a penny for every dollar he'd spent on drink. That would get her through a winter, it would.

Voices came from inside the kitchen. Likely that brawny Augie Moore was cooking. He was a good cook, but he didn't like folks to know it. Milzie smiled. Did he expect people to think Bitsy stood around all day in her fancy clothes hacking up chickens? And those little saucepots of girls who worked for her couldn't cook; you could bet on that. Nope, the barkeep did most of it.

She shuffled over to a small window and squinted against the glare of the sun. Sure enough, there was Augie, back to her, pounding away at a huge lump of brown dough. Rye bread, maybe. Just thinking about it set her to hankering for it. Over in the corner, another man hunched over a bucket into which he dropped potato peelings as fast as he could get them off the potatoes. He raised his chin to speak to

Augie, and she recognized him. Old Ezra Dyer. He used to have a claim on Cold Creek. Had he given up sluicing at last and moved into town? Maybe he'd bring the bucket of peels outside and she could carry some off. Men always peeled potatoes too thick. Likely she could make a good soup out of his leavings.

"Hey!"

She jumped. Augie glared at her, raising a floury fist toward the window. Milzie scooted back out of his sight. She'd best move along and come back later, when he was tending bar. That was the best time to forage for scraps at the saloon.

She walked down the street, keeping to the back side of the businesses, until she was certain she'd passed the mayor's house on the other side. Then she eased through an alley. Not many people were about, and she picked up her skirt and trudged across the street, winding up in front of the feed store. A couple of men lounged on the steps talking, so she didn't stop, but in passing she noticed where a bag of oats had spilled a little of its contents. Probably a mouse had chewed a hole in the sack. She could come back later and scoop up that handful of oats. It might grow out back of her cabin, where Franklin used to grow oats when they'd had a mule.

The emporium was the first building she dared enter. Like a shadow, she scooted away from the door and behind the racks of merchandise. Libby Adams and her red-headed clerk girl were at the far end of the store, where the yard goods and ready-made clothing were displayed. Milzie padded past a pile of flour sacks to a table heaped with canned goods. It would be easy to slip a tin of fruit under her shawl.

"May I help you with something today?" Miz Adams smiled. Her eyes sparkled a bright blue, even inside the store, where the light wasn't good.

Milzie straightened her bowed shoulders as far as she could. "Why, I was in town today, Miz Adams, and I wondered, would you have any extra seeds?"

"Seeds?"

"Yes'm. You know, to plant. A few beans, maybe, or squash."

"Oh. Well . . ." Libby glanced toward a shelf where neat little sacks and paper packets sat in an orderly array.

"I don't need much," Milzie said quickly. "I thought p'raps you'd spilled a mite when you was a-measurin' things out for some-one."

"Well, I might have something in the back

146

room." Libby nodded. "Yes, I think I might. Would you like to wait just a minute?"

"Yes'm, be happy to." Milzie hobbled toward the stove in the middle of the emporium. They hadn't built up the fire today, but habit drew her to the gleaming firebox. A couple of minutes later, Miz Adams came from the back room with something in her hand. Milzie eyed the twists of paper Libby held out to her.

"Here's a bit of carrot seed, and a few squash, and enough peas for a row."

"Thankee, ma'am." Milzie bobbed her head and put the paper twists into the sugar sack she'd hung at her waist. She shuffled slowly to the door.

Where next? She'd had no food yet. True, she'd got some seed. That was good, but it didn't help now. Milzie looked back up the street toward the mayor's house. No, she wouldn't try to forage in the mayor's slops, at least not in daylight. His wife would likely get the sheriff if she caught her. A vague notion entered Milzie's mind that there might not be a sheriff anymore. She'd seen Bert Thalen laid out dead and cold.

She walked slowly past the stagecoach office and saw Cyrus Fennel inside, sitting at a big desk. That was one man she didn't care to meet up with. She glimpsed the blacksmith shop on the next corner, and the livery stable beyond it. If she could slip in there, she might be able to sit down in the hay for an hour or two. She might even pick up some corn or oats from the barrels of horse feed.

A shortcut took her behind an abandoned store building, past the smithy, to the back of the livery. Used to be another man who ran the livery, back during the boom. But he'd gone away. Now the smith owned the livery, too. Like as not, he barely made a living from the two businesses nowadays, with the town's population so small.

Five horses stood in a corral munching hay. She hobbled past them to a path between two fences. In a second enclosure, four big horses stood in the shade. Probably a team for the stagecoach. The others looked like saddle horses, none of them too spirited. Must be the ones the liveryman rented out. Slowly she sidled up to the back door, beside the manure pile. It was partway open, and a wheelbarrow full of dung sat just inside.

Milzie peeked into the barn. Across the dim, hay-strewn floor, two men stood talking near the big front door, which was rolled wide open to the late morning sun. She recognized one as the owner. Bane, that was his name. His bushy hair stuck out beneath his hat brim, and his voice boomed and echoed off the barn rafters high above.

"Well, if you think you know who did it, you ought to tell the sheriff."

The other man, middle-aged and as wrinkly as the Idaho prairie, shook his head. "I don't know any better than you do. I'm just saying if Thalen was really murdered, the law ought to have found out who done it by now. And if Chapman wants to be the sheriff, he ought to do what a sheriff does."

"Which is?" Bane towered over the older man.

"He ought to find out who killed Thalen. People don't like to think we've got a murderer runnin' loose in this town. My wife hates to walk down the street to the emporium by herself anymore. She's right upset about it. Says the kiddies ought not to be walkin' clear out to the schoolhouse without a grown-up to watch out for 'em, in case the killer shows up."

Milzie slithered through the opening and along the shadowy wall. Harness and tools hung on pegs, and she tiptoed past them and around the end of a tall wagon tongue that stood leaning against the wall. To one side, a tie-up stall held several large barrels, and she figured they were full of grain. She slid into the small area and noticed an enameled cup and a biscuit tin on a shelf formed by the framing members of the stall. Curious, she moved closer and stood looking down at the tin. She used to buy Huntley & Palmer biscuits once in a while, back when Franklin was alive and they had a little cash to spend at the emporium.

She reached out and caressed the smooth green metal. The gold lettering and swirls formed a pleasing design. She was vaguely aware of the men's conversation as she opened the tin. The wad of paper money inside made her catch her breath. If Bane had that much cash money, would he miss the few coins in the bottom? Quicker than she could blink, the coins were in her little sack.

Sunlight filtered through a knothole and glittered off something else inside the tin. She smiled as she picked up a huge safety pin. Milzie stroked the smooth metal. The pin was open, and she stuck it through her shawl, then eased the cover of the tin shut. Her gnarled fingers were barely strong enough to squeeze the pin closed.

The men's voices seemed louder. Were they walking toward her? She ducked behind the barrels and hunkered down.

"I heard some ladies are starting to carry

pistols," Bane said.

"Tomfoolery." The other man sounded annoyed.

Milzie blinked, wondering if that was true. Maybe the schoolmarm could tote a gun to the schoolhouse to protect the scholars. She couldn't feature Miz Walker with one though. Maybe Bitsy Shepard. She was tough as two-penny nails. Milzie peered over the tops of the barrels. Assured that the men were still occupied, she thought she might sneak out the back without being seen.

"Well, I'd best get back and see if my wife's done with her shopping," the older man said. "Like as not, she's run up a bill I won't be able to pay till harvest."

Bane laughed and said good-bye, then turned toward the back of the barn. Too late, Milzie realized he'd probably come back here and finish the job he'd started of cleaning out the stalls.

The closer he got, the smaller she tried to make herself. She squeezed down and back into the corner, soundlessly contracting into a heap of rags. Bane grasped the wheelbarrow's handles and pushed it out the back door. She heard the *creak-thump-whup* as he tipped it up and emptied the contents at the edge of the manure pile.

When he rolled the barrow back inside, he took it to one of the stalls along the side of the barn and shoveled manure into it. Milzie relaxed. He had no inkling she was there. Maybe she could sneak out while he worked in the stall.

Furtively she crept out of the tie-up he used as a grain bin. Only a half dozen more steps to the door, and dark shadows masked the back wall. She took one step. Bane turned with a shovelful of manure, and she stiffened against the wall. A horse collar she'd bumped slid off its peg and thunked to the floor. Bane jerked his head up to stare, and Milzie dove behind the nearest barrel.

She heard his steps, cautious and stealthy. Her poor old heart raced. He was coming over here. If he caught her, he'd find the coins in her pocket and call her a thief. She held her breath. Maybe she could duck past him and out the door.

The barrel was shoved aside, and she jumped up, pushing past the huge shadow, toward the streak of light shining in the door. She forgot about the wagon tongue. Her foot caught it, and her shin connected, too. She sprawled in the straw and covered her head as the heavy thing fell.

Bane gave a gasp almost simultaneous

with the thud of wood on bone. The barn shook as the big man and the wagon tongue hit the floor together. Milzie scrambled over them. Her hand landed on the spongy expanse of Bane's stomach, and she yanked it back. The man wasn't moving.

She hesitated until he pulled in a long, shuddering breath. Relief swept over her. She hadn't killed him. Clambering over his massive body, she saw a knife lying on the floor just beyond his limp hand. He would have stabbed her if that wagon tongue hadn't hit him. She scooped up the knife and darted out the back door. The horses lifted their heads and stared at her. Milzie hobbled around the corner of the corral and flattened herself against the wall of the smithy, between it and the livery. She stood panting and listening for pursuit.

CHAPTER 11

Cyrus hustled outside as the stagecoach rolled down Main Street. The driver, Bill Stout, halted the team outside the office door in a flurry of dust. The shotgun messenger, Ned Harmon, jumped down and saluted Cyrus with a touch to his hat brim before opening the door of the coach.

Four passengers stirred inside. Good. Maybe the line would work its way out of the slump they'd had the last couple of years. More people were coming through Fergus this spring than usual.

"Mrs. Brice. Nice to see you back again." Cyrus offered a hand to the woman exiting the coach. "Watch your step. I trust you had a good trip to Portland?"

"Good to be home, Mr. Fennel."

"How is your daughter?"

"She's well, thank you." Mrs. Brice turned away to see to her luggage. By this time, two miners had climbed down.

"Good day, gentlemen," Cyrus said.

"Fennel," one replied with a nod. They went toward the boot of the coach for their kits.

"Thank you for taking the stage."

The last man out was a stranger. He eyed Cyrus as he straightened his jacket. "Is there an establishment in this town where I can get lunch?"

"We don't have a restaurant as such, but there are a couple of places where you could get a sandwich," Cyrus said. Again he thought of the abandoned boardinghouse. He wasn't about to set up one of Morrell's draggle-tails to run it, but maybe it was time to consider finding a couple or a respectable widow who could keep a few guest rooms open and serve lunch to the stagecoach passengers. To the customer at hand, he pointed down the street. "At the Spur & Saddle, they're apt to have a pot of stew on the stove. Or at the other end of the street is the Nugget, where it's strictly cold fare, and then only if you're lucky."

The man looked toward Bitsy's, then toward Jamin's.

"How long before the stage leaves?"

"Twenty minutes," Cyrus said. Ned had unloaded all the disembarking passengers' luggage. He signaled the driver, and Bill

155

clucked to the team. He'd get the horses to the livery so Bane could swap them out. Then he and Ned would wolf down a biscuit or two with a beer at the Nugget and be ready to drive out again.

The passenger checked his pocket watch and marched toward the Spur & Saddle. Cyrus wasn't sure he liked advertising the saloons. The men of the town had begun to polarize over Bert Thalen's death. Those who drank at the Nugget on Saturday nights seemed to think Ethan Chapman wasn't doing his job and should be replaced. Over at the Spur & Saddle, the men seemed more inclined to support Ethan and cooperate with him if he came up with a plan to catch the killer. Personally, Cyrus doubted the new sheriff had any desire to track down the murderer. But he seemed to be doing a fair job of keeping down the shooting and yelling at the Nugget.

Oscar Runnels approached along the boardwalk, carrying a leather satchel. "Am I too late for the stage?"

"Nope. They just went round to change the teams. You've got at least fifteen minutes. You buying a ticket?"

"That's right. I've got to go to Silver City today."

Cyrus went into his office and opened the

drawer where he kept the ticket books. Oscar pulled out his wallet, and they made the exchange.

"Good day for traveling," Cyrus noted.

Running footsteps thudded on the boardwalk outside. Ned Harmon caught the doorjamb and stood panting, blinking in at them.

"What is it, Ned?" Cyrus asked.

"Griffin Bane. He's layin' on the floor at the livery, out cold. We thought he was dead, but then he cussed, so he's not. But someone chucked him on the head a good'un and maybe robbed him."

"What's that?" Runnels asked. "Someone's hurt Bane?"

Ned nodded. "Bill's with him. I misdoubt he'll come to 'fore Sunday."

"What about the team?" Cyrus asked.

"Team ain't ready. They's still in the corral."

"That's not good." Cyrus pushed his chair back and grabbed his hat. "We've got to keep the schedule."

Oscar brought his fist down on Cyrus's desk. "What are you frettin' about the schedule for? Send that slacker to fetch the sheriff!"

Cyrus saw the good sense of that and barked at Ned as he strode for the door.

"Go round to the jail and see if Sheriff Chapman's there. If he's not, check Hiram Dooley's kitchen. Chapman's over there at lunchtime some days."

Ned bolted across the street. As Cyrus hurried toward the corner, he could hear Oscar panting along behind him. The stagecoach stood outside the livery, the tired team hanging their heads. Cyrus entered the big pole barn. Bill Stout was carrying a pail of water in through the back door.

"Where's Bane?" Cyrus called.

"Yonder." Bill didn't stop walking, and Cyrus met him beside the prone figure of the blacksmith. Without another word, Bill tipped the bucket and poured a quart or so of cold water in Griffin's face.

Griffin sat up spluttering and waving his arms. "Wha . . . wha— Hey!"

"You all right, Bane?" Cyrus asked.

The big man blinked up at him and rubbed his sleeve across his eyes. "My head." He clutched it and moaned.

Bill tipped the bucket again. When the first splash hit Griffin's head, he dodged to the side and swiped at Bill's kneecap.

"Quit that! I'm awake."

Cyrus extended a hand. Griffin grasped it and rose with a groan.

"What's going on?"

Cyrus turned toward the door, where Oscar had paused. Ethan Chapman and Hiram Dooley pushed past Runnels and skidded to a stop beside the three at the back of the barn.

"What happened, Griff?" Ethan put his hand on Bane's arm. "Are you hurt?"

"My head is killing me." Griffin put his hand up to the top of his head and pulled it away, holding his fingers up in the light that streamed through the back door.

"You're bleeding." Bill set the bucket down.

"I was attacked. Someone was hiding back there near the grain barrels. He jumped out at me and whacked me on the head with something." Griffin swayed on his feet.

"You'd best sit down," Ethan said.

"He needs to get the team ready." Cyrus cringed at the anger in Ethan's eyes. "I suppose Bill and Ned can do that." Ned had arrived behind the sheriff and Hiram and now stood panting between Cyrus and the timid Oscar Runnels, who edged closer to the group.

Hiram touched Ethan's sleeve then jerked his head toward the corral behind the livery. He marched outside.

"Go with Hiram, boys. He'll help you get the teams switched." Ethan looked toward

Cyrus. "Is Bill driving the next leg?"

"Yes. He and Ned are taking the coach as far as Silver City."

Ethan nodded. "All right, Griffin, what say you sit down and tell me what happened? See if you can remember anything else." He pulled a keg over, and Griffin plopped down on it.

"Too bad we ain't got a doctor," Oscar muttered.

"I couldn't see him very good." Griffin puckered up his face. "He musta been a big fella though. He hit me powerful hard."

"Bane must have been out cold for half an hour or more," Cyrus said to Ethan. "He hadn't even started to get the replacement team ready for the coach."

"I woulda." A belligerent gleam flashed in Griffin's eyes as he scowled at Cyrus. "If that robber hadn't jumped me, I'da had 'em ready and waitin' when your boys got here."

"Robber?" Ethan asked.

"Well, why else would he have attacked me?"

Ethan lifted his hat and scratched his head. "Maybe you'd best look around and see if anything's been stolen."

"That's a good idea." Griffin started to rise and sank back down on the keg. "Hoo, boy, I'm a little woozy."

"How many horses did you have in the corral?" Ethan asked.

"Horses?" Griffin swiveled to look out the back door and groaned again, putting both hands to his head. "Uh . . . the team of four in the corral on the west side and five saddle horses on the east. And old Sal in the front stall yonder, in case someone came in wanting a mount right away."

The men looked toward the stall nearest the front door of the livery, where they could see the back end of a chestnut horse. The mare stood placidly, swinging her tail now and then to brush off the flies.

Ethan walked to the rear door and perused the corrals. "Looks like all the horses are accounted for."

He stepped aside as Hiram came in, leading a big sorrel gelding.

"Hitch him right there, Hi." Griffin pointed to an eyebolt in the wall with a rope dangling from it.

"I'd best get back to the office and tell the passengers the stagecoach will be delayed a few minutes," Cyrus said.

He and Oscar walked across the barn floor and out into the sunshine.

"Crazy thing," Oscar said.

"Yes."

"Makes me a little skittish, what with old

161

Bert being killed in broad daylight a couple weeks ago."

Cyrus stopped and eyed Oscar for a moment. Bert Thalen and Griffin Bane had both been whacked on the head. What if the women were right, and the killer was still in Fergus? "You go back and see if they find out anything's missing. I'll tell the other passengers the coach will be right along. But don't you say anything on the ride. You hear me, Oscar? Folks will get unstrung if you spread rumors about killers attacking people all over Fergus."

"I wouldn't say anything like that."

Cyrus nodded. "I think we'd best keep this quiet if we can. Go back and see if the sheriff's found out anything."

After Bill and Ned rumbled off with the stagecoach, complaining loudly that they'd had no lunch and taking Oscar along inside the coach, Ethan turned to his friends.

"Now, Griffin, think carefully. How tall was the man who hit you?"

Griffin winced and scratched his chin through his beard. "He was hiding till I got right up close. Then he jumped out. I don't rightly know."

"You think he was as tall as you?"

"Could be. I was facing the light from the

162

doorway, and he was over there in the dark." Griffin looked up at him suddenly. "He smelled."

"Smelled how?" Ethan asked.

"Like a bear. Foul."

Ethan considered that. Maybe a trapper had come down out of the hills and thought to find some easy money in town. "You said your knife was taken. Anything else?"

"I keep a little cash in a box over near the feed barrels."

"What's it look like?" Ethan asked.

"It's a biscuit box. Green and gold."

Hiram had stood by in silence, but now he scurried to the corner stall and returned a moment later with the biscuit tin. Griffin took it and raised the lid. He grunted, staring at the contents.

"Looks like your money's there." Ethan nodded at the wad of greenbacks in the tin.

"No, there were some coins in the bottom." Griffin took out the small bundle of bills and frowned. "I had some change."

"How much?"

The big man shrugged. "Four bits at least. Not more'n a dollar all told."

"That's not much." Ethan scanned his face, wondering how seriously Griffin took the loss of a few coins.

"Why'd he take the change and not the

dollar bills?" Hiram asked.

"Good question," Ethan said. He hated to imply that Griffin's memory was spotty, but it did seem odd. "You sure you didn't take them out?"

Griffin nodded. "I just put them in there yesterday. And a horse-blanket pin." He looked down into the box again.

"Horse-blanket pin?" Ethan leaned over the tin once more. "Where is it?" He looked at Hiram, but he only shrugged. It seemed a strange item for anyone to steal. Ethan almost said as much but clamped his mouth shut. Griff might think he doubted his word. But it was odd. Deep down, Ethan figured he was mistaken. The pin would turn up, jumbled in the straw or tucked onto a shelf, forgotten.

Griffin stood slowly. "I sure don't feel like doing much this afternoon."

Without speaking, Hiram walked over to the half-cleaned stall where Griffin had left his wheelbarrow. He picked up the shovel and began to work.

"He's a good friend. You take it easy and let Hi help you out." Ethan looked up at Griffin. "You want me to do anything about this?"

"Not much you can do, I guess. I want you to find the robber, but I don't guess that will be easy."

Ethan looked down at the metal box again. "You don't have a safe, do you?"

"Naw. I don't have that much money lying around. I never have more than five or ten bucks. But still, if someone's sneaking around town stealing and killing people . . ."

"Some folks are scared," Ethan acknowledged.

"Those women who are shooting all the time," Griffin said. "You oughta put a stop to that, Eth."

"Why? If it makes them feel safer . . ."

"Someone's going to get hurt. Next thing you know, one of those ladies will get shot during one of their practice meets."

Ethan ran a hand through his thick hair. "I been meaning to ask Gert about that. I've heard folks talking, and I wondered how many women are involved. So far as I know, it's only a few."

"A few is too many."

Ethan noted that Hiram paused in his shoveling and looked toward them. He must have heard his sister's name mentioned. First there was the conversation Ethan had overheard at the emporium. Then Ted Hire at the Nugget had said Gert was rallying some women to learn how to shoot, and Ethan had wondered if it was so.

Gert was an odd girl. She wasn't all soft and stylish like Libby Adams, but she had a kind soul. She'd left her folks back in Maine to come help her brother and his family when they needed her. She fed a crusty cowpoke-turned-sheriff every time he showed up on her back stoop. And he'd seen her feed stray cats and give a man who couldn't afford to pay for Hiram's work a chance to split wood in exchange for a gunsmithing job. If she really had started teaching women to shoot, her motives were honorable. But he should talk to her about safety, if nothing else. The livery owner wasn't the only man in town grousing about it.

Hiram pushed a wheelbarrow full of manure out of the stall and trundled it past them. He stopped just inside the back door and stepped to the side near the grain barrels. In the shadows, he stooped and lifted a long wagon tongue and stood it up against the wall. He picked up a horse collar, which he hung on a peg.

Ethan brought his attention back to the injured man. "I'll look into it, Griff."

CHAPTER 12

Libby was aware when Milzie Peart entered the emporium. She didn't like to have Milzie come in and loiter. Customers didn't like it. At least it was warm enough now that they didn't have to keep the stove hot. The heat always magnified Milzie's stench.

But Libby couldn't run her off the way some did. She felt sorry for the old woman. As she measured out coffee for one of the rancher's wives, she tried to keep an eye on the stooped figure. Milzie had asked for seeds last time she was here. Libby wasn't sure she hadn't walked out with anything else. Usually she gave the old woman a little something to nibble on, figuring it might keep her from pilfering. If the other customers cleared out, she'd give Milzie the last few crackers from the nearly empty case beside the counter.

When the rancher's wife left, another woman stepped up to the counter. Libby smiled but again wished she could choose her clientele. One of the girls who worked for Bitsy at the Spur & Saddle smiled shyly back at her.

"Vashti." If that was really her name, which Libby doubted.

"Yes'm. Miss Bitsy said it's a good idea if we girls get ourselves a sidearm. She said you could help us."

"Oh. Uh . . ." Libby glanced around the store. Milzie was only a few steps away. "I have some small handguns." She took three from beneath the counter and laid them out for the girl to see, wondering if she shouldn't ask Vashti to come back Monday before she opened the store — or even tomorrow while the emporium was closed. But she hated to do business on the Sabbath. The shipment of pistols had arrived only yesterday with one of Oscar's mule teams, and she still could barely believe she was selling them like this. But what did it matter if the whole town knew she had stocked some handguns and would sell them to women? Word of mouth would probably bring her more business.

Vashti picked up the smallest one. Its pearl grips seemed to ripple as the light struck it. "I like this one."

"All right." Libby reached for the roll of

brown paper. "Let me wrap it for you."

"Thanks, but I'll put it in my bag."

Libby cleared her throat and glanced toward the door. Jamin Morrell was just entering. He nodded at her, smiling as he removed his hat.

"Good day," Libby said. "Can I get you anything, Mr. Morrell?"

"Carpet tacks," he said.

"Oh yes. Right over there near the nails." Libby pointed toward the hardware. She glanced around and saw that Florence was busy measuring ribbon for Mrs. Ingram "If you can't find them, I'll be over in just a minute."

Jamin nodded and headed for the hardware.

Vashti seemed to have shrunk into her silk shawl. She studiously avoided looking around toward the rival saloon's owner.

"Now you'll want some ammunition," Libby said in what she hoped was a smooth, professional tone.

"Is that the same size as Miss Bitsy's?" the girl asked.

"No, it's a smaller caliber, but it's a good piece."

Vashti leaned close and whispered, "I'm hoping Miss Dooley will teach me to use it."

"Oh." Libby tried not to let the smile slip. What had she started? When she'd gone to shoot with Gert on Thursday afternoon, they'd been joined by Emmaline Landry, Bitsy, and two other women. Word was getting around Fergus, and women were responding eagerly. She stooped and pulled out a box of cartridges. "It's fifty cents extra for the ammunition."

While Libby wrapped the box, Vashti dug into the ridiculously small satin pouch that dangled from her wrist. "My friend Goldie wants a gun, too. I'll tell her you've got some left."

A rancher carrying an ax handle and a tin of tobacco came and stood behind Vashti, ogling the young woman's back as he waited. Libby took her money and handed her the change and her package.

"I'll see you at the shooting practice on Monday." Vashti watched her, expecting a response.

"Uh, yes, I expect so," Libby said.

By the time she'd totaled up the rancher's purchases, Mr. and Mrs. Robinson had entered. Mr. went straight for the tools, while Mrs. made a beeline for the ready-made clothing. Morrell was still in the hardware, and Milzie had wandered to the far end of the store. Mrs. Ingram approached the counter with her notions and a bolt of muslin. Libby forced out another smile and told herself a busy store was a good thing.

"How many yards would you like?" she asked Mrs. Ingram.

"Six, please. Did you hear that the livery was robbed yesterday?"

Libby gulped. She didn't like to think about other business owners having trouble. "Yes, I did."

"They say Griffin Bane was attacked in broad daylight." Mrs. Ingram shook her head. "I'd think it would take a brazen criminal to attack a man as large as Mr. Bane."

"I . . . suppose so." Libby measured out the material. "Lovely and warm this morning, isn't it?"

More customers came through the door. A few minutes later, she looked up into Jamin Morrell's face.

"Oh, Mr. Morrell, I've neglected you."

"That's all right. You've been busy, and I found what I needed."

Libby glanced toward the yard goods. Several people browsed the merchandise, but Milzie was nowhere to be seen.

"Looking for the old woman, by any chance?"

"Well, yes." Libby fingered the lace at her collar. "I was going to give her some crackers."

"She left a moment ago." Jamin leaned toward her over the counter and lowered his voice. "You might want to check over your stock of safety pins."

Libby stared at him then looked toward the open door.

That evening, Gert walked slowly up the street toward the Walkers' house. She didn't really want to spend the evening quilting with a half dozen older women, but Orissa Walker had made a point of inviting her. The flying geese quilt would go to the Walkers' married daughter in Silver City. Libby had promised to meet her at the quilting bee, so Gert had agreed. She trudged along the boardwalk with her sewing basket — minus her overdue mending — on her arm.

Orissa welcomed her with a dour face and ushered her into the parlor. Isabel Fennel was the only other woman within twenty years of Gert's age. Where was Libby? She didn't ask. She figured she had to put in at least an hour without the risk of being thought horribly rude and becoming the subject of the quilters' gossip as soon as she left.

She settled in between Annie Harper and Isabel on one side of the quilting frame.

"How's school?" she asked Isabel.

"Not bad. We've another month. Then we'll break for the summer."

"I expect you'll enjoy a bit of a rest when the term ends."

Isabel's lip curled as she eyed her, and Gert felt her face flush. Was her face dirty? Why did Isabel look at her that way?

"I don't suppose I'll rest much this summer." Isabel bent over her needle.

Gert blinked. Had she just been snubbed? If this were Boston, she might just care.

"Do you know if the sheriff's found out who robbed the livery?" Mrs. Runnels asked as their hostess sat down in the chair nearest the door.

"No, I haven't heard anything new," Orissa said.

"Seems to me he ought to have arrested someone by now," murmured Annie.

Isabel humphed. "Ethan Chapman is incompetent. Father says he has no clues at all on Bert Thalen's murder, and now this. Why they picked him for sheriff, I have no idea."

"A poor choice to protect us." Mrs. Runnels jabbed her long needle down through the layers of the quilt.

A knock at the door summoned Orissa, and a moment later she ushered Libby into the parlor.

"Hello, ladies. I'm sorry I'm late." Libby smiled at the circle in general, but she gave a pert nod when her gaze rested on Gert.

"Sit right down, Elizabeth," Orissa said. "You can work on this part and stitch your way over to meet Bertha."

Libby slid into the seat between Orissa and rotund Bertha Runnels. She soon had her needle and thimble out, and the work progressed, along with the chatter. No one mentioned that the husbands of the married women present were probably out at one of the town's two saloons, knocking back whiskey. Instead, they focused on domestic topics. Gert let it flow around her as she made the boring up-and-down stitches.

She glanced across at Libby, who stitched industriously with a slight smile on her lips. She always looked as though she'd welcome an adventure. Funny, Gert thought of Libby as her own age, though the widow was probably eight or ten years her senior. Isaac Adams had been a friend of Cy Fennel and Charles Walker, but he'd married a younger woman. Libby never spoke to her of truly personal topics, but Gert had the distinct impression she'd loved her husband. She liked to think Libby had enjoyed some happy years with Isaac. Few of the married couples in Fergus seemed content. Rather, they survived.

"Gert, I can't say as I approve of this latest enterprise of yours," Mrs. Walker said.

Gert jerked her chin up and stared at her, unsure of how to respond.

Libby jumped into the silence. "If you mean the shooting club, I do."

"Club?" asked Annie. "What's this?"

Gert felt her cheeks flame, but Libby's musical laugh rang out.

"That's what some of the women call it. We practice shooting together two afternoons a week, and Gert instructs us. We're all learning to protect ourselves."

Orissa shook her head. "The mayor thinks it's nonsense."

"The mayor is on hand to protect his wife," Libby pointed out. "Some of us ladies have no husband or son or brother to defend us in time of need."

"Well, my father says it's dangerous, and someone's going to be killed by accident," Isabel said.

Gert scowled. Leave it to Cyrus to say that.

"We're extremely cautious whenever we shoot, aren't we, Gert?" Libby asked.

Gert looked up at her. Libby's rosy cheeks and gleaming blue eyes would qualify her for the girl on a soap advertising card. Libby smiled gently and nodded ever so slightly.

"Oh yes," Gert responded. Better to follow her friend's lead than to get upset and cause more talk. "We always follow safety measures."

"More than you can say for some of the men," Annie Harper muttered.

Bertha nodded, frowning. "I heard Emmaline Landry has joined."

"That's right," Gert said. "Her husband's out on the range a lot, and she wanted to know how to use a gun in case a drifter showed up at the ranch."

"She joins us on Thursdays," Libby put in.

"It's a wonder Mr. Landry lets her," Isabel said.

"She probably doesn't tell him." Bertha shook her head in disapproval.

Libby surveyed their project. "My, isn't this quilt coming along nicely?"

"Yes, we've made good progress." Mrs. Walker stood. "I think it's time for tea."

"Let me help you." Libby jumped up and headed toward the kitchen with Orissa. Gert wished she could make a graceful exit through the front door, but Libby had rescued her so kindly that she didn't want to leave her friend alone.

Right now all she wanted to do was get home and fix a bite for Hiram. She pictured him sitting alone in the front room, reloading cartridges for his rifle. Poor man. Loneliness had settled over him. She tried to be good company. She'd rather be sitting with her near-silent brother than with this bunch of cats. And without her, Hiram was practically helpless, though she would never utter such a thought aloud.

"Good coffee." Ethan raised his mug in Hiram's direction before he took another swig. "You make it?"

Hiram just nodded, but he smiled as he picked up his horse's bridle and a rag.

"I don't know what to do next," Ethan said. "Oh, not tonight. I know what I have to do tonight. Go over to the Nugget again and tell them to pipe down." He cocked his head to one side and listened. Was it his imagination, or could he hear loud music and laughter from the saloon? "It's what I should do about the crimes that's got me puzzled. What does a lawman do when he can't figure out who's committing crimes in his town?"

Hiram frowned and polished away at the leather cheek straps. "You've asked everyone if they saw anything."

"Yes, I think I've talked to every adult in Fergus, and a few of the children and horses."

Hiram laughed.

Ethan stretched out his long legs and sipped his coffee again. "Did I tell you Spin and Johnny showed up at my ranch on Monday?"

Hiram nodded and picked up a can of neat's-foot oil. He tipped it up, sloshing a little on his rag.

"They're taking care of the place while I loaf around town doing nothing." Ethan shook his head. "Useless, that's what I am." He looked around the Dooleys' comfortable kitchen. Did the plant on the windowsill and the bright tablecloth make the difference that marked this as a home?

"Do you think the same person jumped Griff as killed Bert?" Hiram asked.

"I've thought about it, and I can't begin to tell you. It would seem likely."

After a few minutes of silence, Hiram put the bridle aside and walked over to the cupboard near Gert's worktable. He returned with the coffeepot in one hand and a plate of ginger cookies in the other.

"Thanks. Gert make these?"

Hiram nodded and set two cookies on the table in front of his own chair and topped off his cup of coffee.

"Gert's a good woman," Ethan said around a bite of cookie. He'd almost said *girl,* but she wasn't a kid anymore. He chewed appreciatively. She knew how to bake. And shoot. And sew. And do a thousand other things. Hiram was a lucky man to have a sister so steady and diligent. And willing to keep house for him.

"She's all right."

That was high praise from her brother, as Ethan was well aware. He'd heard tell how Gert had come on the stagecoach to Boise, before it ran all the way to Fergus, and Hiram had driven over there to fetch her. She'd come three thousand miles of hard road, expecting to find Violet and a new baby to care for. Instead, Hiram had met her with the news that he was all alone now. That was back while Ethan was off in the army. And Gert had stayed. She'd grown from a lanky girl to a competent housewife — only she wasn't a wife.

"Has she got a name, other than Gert?" he asked. Somehow, he felt she ought to have a softer name, the same way he sometimes thought she ought to have a softer hairdo or a fancier dress.

"Trudy." Hiram sat down again and shoved half a cookie in his mouth.

"Trudy? Oh, of course. Gertrude."

Hiram nodded as he chewed. When he'd swallowed, he said, "Our pa used to call her Trudy."

They lapsed into silence again. Ethan pictured a little girl with flaxen braids tagging along after her big brother. That would have been in Maine, though, not out here. What did Maine look like? Lots of forest that came down to the ocean shore? Maybe he'd ask Gert someday. Hiram wouldn't string enough words together to give him a proper picture.

When his cookies were gone and his mug was empty, Ethan stood and stretched. "Well, Hi, thanks for the grub. Time to mosey."

"Watch yourself."

Ethan nodded and went out the back door, grabbing his hat from a peg on the coatrack. The noise from the Nugget hit him as he rounded the corner of the house. With a sigh, he headed north on the boardwalk, past the jail and the vacant boardinghouse.

"Trudy," he said to no one.

CHAPTER 13

Ten women showed up for shooting practice on Monday, counting Gert and Libby. Gert could barely trust her eyes.

"Where'd they all come from?" she asked Libby as they dismounted.

"Word gets around." Libby ground tied Hoss and took the Peacemaker from her saddlebag.

Gert hefted her Sharps rifle and walked slowly toward the waiting women. Bitsy and the two girls who served drinks and who knew what else at the Spur & Saddle had come in their short skirts and low-cut blouses. Emmaline Landry had brought her neighbor, Starr Tinen. Both wore faded housedresses with aprons tied over their skirts. Florence was there. Libby had given her the afternoon off, leaving Oscar Runnels's oldest boy, Josiah, who helped her unload shipments of new merchandise, to watch the store for an hour. And to Gert's surprise, Annie Harper and her oldest girl, Myra, had come.

Annie walked toward her with a sheepish smile on her face and an old shotgun resting on her shoulder.

"Hello, Gert. Will you take two more pupils? I told Myra about this club, and we both decided we wanted to learn to shoot."

Gert eyed her for a long moment. "You could have asked Mr. Harper to show you."

"I'd much rather learn from you."

"Pa's got no patience," Myra noted.

Gert nodded. She wouldn't want to learn shooting — or anything else — from an impatient man, and she'd seen Mr. Harper lose his temper over little things. What would he say when he heard his womenfolk attended the gun practice?

"Well, let's see your weapon. You got shells?"

"Only eleven. Figured I'd stop by the emporium for more on the way home."

Libby glanced at Gert. "I keep having to order more ammunition. It's a hot commodity in Fergus right now." She turned her lovely smile on Annie and Myra. "We're glad you ladies could be here."

"I had no idea how popular this shooting circle was." Myra turned wide eyes on Gert. "Miz Dooley, I've never fired a gun before.

You'll show me how to do it right, won't you?"

Gert looked over the cluster of eager women and pulled in a long, slow breath. She straightened her shoulders and smiled at Myra. "I surely will. But this is a lot of people. We'll take turns in an orderly manner. Everyone gather in close. First, let's talk about how we make sure none of us gets hurt while we practice." She looked at Libby and gave her a firm nod.

"Ladies," Libby called in her cheerful voice. "I didn't know how many of us there'd be today, but I've brought a small prize for the lady who shoots her personal best today." She held up an embroidered velvet needle book.

"Aw, now ain't that fine," said Emmaline.

"And if more than one of you qualifies, I'll bring extra prizes when we meet next on Thursday."

They murmured approval at Libby's promise. She was an excellent merchant, Gert noted, and would no doubt have all these ladies inside the Paragon Emporium ere nightfall.

An odd, unpleasant smell struck Gert's nostrils. She turned slowly. Another woman had come quietly down the path to join them.

"Mrs. Peart!"

Milzie grinned at her, revealing a gap where one of her front teeth had once resided. "Miz Dooley. Miz Adams. Ladies." She looked around the circle of faces a bit defiantly. "Mind if I shoot with you'uns?"

Gert eyed the Hawken rifle resting on Milzie's shoulder. With its heavy barrel and chunky stock, the gun would take down a grizzly with one shot if need be.

"This here was my husband, Franklin's, buffalo gun." Milzie lowered the stock to the ground and stood waiting. "I got some bullets for it, but no powder. Thought p'raps I could borry a mite."

Gert's stomach churned as she surveyed the old woman. Her heart did a little squirming, too. She tried to ignore the stench that hovered around Milzie. The other nine women were as silent as the school yard on Saturday, waiting for her to either cast Milzie out or . . .

She forced herself not to look to Libby for aid. This was a matter for the Almighty. *I think I hear You whispering in my ear, Lord.* She looked straight into the watery gray eyes.

"You're welcome here, Milzie. Show me what you've got for ammunition. We can help you with powder for today. But let me check your rifle over first, to make sure it's safe for you to fire."

Hiram jumped from his chair when Libby followed Gert into the kitchen. Libby hoped she hadn't embarrassed him by coming home with his sister after the shooting practice.

"Hello, Hiram. Gert said I'd best consult you before I place my next order for ammunition."

His soft, gray blue eyes widened, and his pale eyebrows rose. "Ma'am?"

Hiram didn't come into the emporium much. Libby seldom thought about him, but when she did, she pegged him as a quiet young man, probably about her age, who liked peace and solitude. In another time and place, she could imagine Hi Dooley as an artist or an inventor. Here in Fergus, he was the sad-eyed gunsmith.

Gert pulled off her bonnet and hung it on a peg near the door. "We've got all sorts of ladies coming out of prairie dog holes with odd-sized guns. Libby needs to know for certain what ones will take the same size cartridges. Then there's the odd ones, like Bitsy's Deringer. Annie Harper's got a shotgun —"

Hiram blinked, and Gert went on as if

185

he'd spoken aloud.

"Yes, Annie was there, and Myra, too. You know, her big girl. They both want to learn to shoot in case the killer comes around when Mr. Harper's away."

"Killer?"

Hiram's single word set Gert off again.

"You know what I'm talking about. The man who murdered Bert Thalen and tried to kill Griffin Bane. All the ladies in town are scared, and the men don't seem to be doing anything about it. Except for Ethan. I know he's trying to run down the killer, but so far, he hasn't had any luck. And the ladies are nervous, I'll tell you."

Hiram drew in a breath as though he would speak, but then he closed his mouth and shook his head.

Libby stepped forward and smiled. "So, Hiram, if you wouldn't mind, I'd appreciate your advice. Milzie Peart brought the oddest rifle today."

"That gun's the size of a cannon." Gert snatched her apron from a hook and tied it on. "You ever seen it? She said it was her dead husband's gun."

"Once. Big old Hawken." Hiram nodded as if he could see the thick barrel and heavy stock.

"That's right. And Milzie has no idea what

load it takes."

Hiram scratched his head. "That one can handle most any powder load. But you don't want to turn her loose with it, do ya?"

Gert had neared the cupboard, but her step faltered. She turned to face Hiram and brushed back a wisp of hair that had come loose and fluttered about her cheek. "I couldn't send her away."

Libby nodded. "I know how you feel. She comes into the store, and other people don't like it because she . . ." She stopped, feeling an unwelcome flush creep up her cheeks. Even though Milzie wasn't present, Libby couldn't bear to speak ill of her. "Well, she looks . . . unkempt."

"And she smells," Gert added.

"Well, yes."

Gert opened the cupboard and took out an empty pottery bowl. Her jaw dropped, and she stared at her brother. "Don't tell me you ate all those cookies."

Hiram ducked his head. "Me 'n' Ethan."

"Oh. Well, that makes it all right then." Gert slammed the bowl back onto the shelf and shook her head. "I'll tell you, Libby, since Ethan Chapman took the sheriffing job, I don't think he ever eats at home anymore."

Libby smiled as she watched Gert's jerky

movements about the kitchen. "Well, you're so handy to the jailhouse."

Hiram's eyes lit, and he nodded at her with a slight twitch to his lips. Libby nearly laughed aloud, but Gert kept up the injured air.

"That man eats twice as much as my brother, and that's the truth."

Libby started to speak but caught herself. *Perhaps he needs a wife.* That's what she'd wanted to say. But something about Gert's agitation told her this wasn't the time to tease. If Gert had feelings for the sheriff, teasing might cut deep, especially if Ethan didn't look at her in the same light.

Ethan hadn't showed an interest in ladies since he came home from the Indian wars. He'd seemed a normal, fun-loving young man before he went away, but now his face stayed frozen in serious lines. He kept to his ranch. Unlike a lot of former cavalrymen, he didn't frequent the saloons. The single women had hoped he'd enter the limited social circle of Fergus, but he'd disappointed them. Even Florence had sighed over him for a while, but she'd given up, declaring Ethan immune to feminine charms. Libby wasn't so sure. The fact that he and Hiram Dooley had drawn together made her think they understood their mutual sorrow. They could be friends without talking about Hiram's dead wife and baby or the Bannock War, or whatever it was that kept Ethan bottled up.

And Gert was in the middle of it. She probably saw Ethan more than any other woman in Fergus, and she saw him more often than she did any other man except her brother. Why shouldn't she have feelings for him? But if Ethan didn't wish to marry, Gert could expect nothing more than a broken heart. No, this wasn't the time to tease her.

Libby cleared her throat. "I've made a list of the women's firearms, Hiram. When I get back to the store, I'll inventory what I have for ammunition, but we go through a lot when we practice. The shipment I got last week is nearly gone already. I plan to order in a large supply. If you can give me a few guidelines, I'll make sure no one has trouble getting the proper cartridges again." She handed him a slip of paper.

Gert lifted the lid on the teakettle sitting on the cookstove. "Say." Her smooth brow wrinkled. "Where's my kerchief?" She touched her hand to her neckline, feeling inside her collar.

"You took it off out in the valley," Libby said.

"Yes. It was warm in the sun. I stuck it in the saddlebag. But when we put the horses up, I took everything out again, and I didn't see it."

Hiram shrugged and bent over Libby's list. His light hair spilled over his brow, and he pushed it back absently with almost the same gesture Gert used.

"Get this for Milzie." He pointed with his pencil to where he'd written the ball size and powder grains for the load. "The rest looks fine. But if you think some others might bring muzzle loaders, you may want to lay in some extra lead balls in a smaller size." He scrawled another note. "You usually have plenty of powder."

Libby nodded and took the paper. "Thank you. I've decided to go to Boise on the stagecoach and see about the order. When I send it by mail, they don't always ship exactly what I want."

"When are you going?" Gert asked.

"Maybe Wednesday, if Florence thinks she can handle the store all day. And now I'd better get back over there. Florence went ahead to the store alone, but she may need me."

As she turned to leave, she noted that Gert had set out a large mixing bowl, a crock of rolled oats, and another of brown sugar. She grabbed a small jar of cinnamon off the shelf. Unless Libby was mistaken, Hiram and Ethan would soon have a new supply of cookies.

CHAPTER 14

"Would you mind stepping over to the stagecoach office with me?" Libby asked the next morning.

Gert had come to the emporium for more brown sugar, but if Libby needed a favor, she allowed she had time. "If you like."

"I do."

Libby turned to Florence. "I'll be back in a few minutes." She reached for a smart blue bonnet that matched her store-bought woolen dress. Gert walked with her to the door as Libby tied the wide ribbons under her chin.

Once outside, Libby leaned close to Gert. "I don't like going over to Mr. Fennel's office alone."

Gert raised her eyebrows and pulled Libby to a stop near the wall of the store. "Does he . . . bother you?"

Libby smiled sheepishly. "Not really. Sometimes he comes out of his office and looks at me when I'm outside washing the front window or helping someone carry out their bundles. He stands on the boardwalk down there and . . . just watches. That's all."

"Think he's sweet on you?" Gert looked down the sidewalk toward Fennel's place of business. "He's been widowed nigh on three years now."

Libby grimaced. "To be honest, he came around once and asked me to take Sunday dinner with him at the Spur & Saddle. It was only a month after Isaac died, and I didn't want to. It seemed in poor taste for him to ask me so soon."

"Some folks remarry mighty quick out here."

"Yes, but . . . I don't *need* a husband. Isaac left me with a good business and a tidy sum of savings. Not that I'd say that to just anyone, you understand."

Gert nodded soberly. "That's one reason I stayed on with Hiram. So's he wouldn't think he needed to go looking for a wife to replace Violet."

"Poor man," Libby murmured. "He cared deeply for Violet."

"Yes, he did. And if he'd gone to baching it after she died, the women in this town would have inundated him with kindnesses he didn't want."

"Perhaps so. But . . . supposing someday he decides he *wants* to marry?"

"Then I'll move out. I could find employment, I expect. Or I could go back to Maine."

"Are your folks still living?" Libby asked.

"Yes. Our pa builds boats. That's where Hiram learned to use tools, in Papa's shop."

"That's interesting. But now he's out here where there's no call for boats."

"He likes guns. He likes anything mechanical, really. And if I ever thought he'd formed an attachment for a lady, I wouldn't stand in his way. I'd like to see Hi happy again."

Libby nodded. "I expect he feels the same way about you. If you decided to take a husband, I mean."

Gert huffed out a breath. "No chance of that."

"I don't know why you say that."

"Look at me. I'm just . . . just Gertrude Dooley, spinster. The gunsmith's sister, homely and drab."

"You're not homely, and you don't need to be drab." Libby could tell her words made no impression. She took Gert's arm. "If you ever need a job, come and see me. Come on, now. Let's get this done."

They walked the short distance to Cyrus's office. The sign WELLS FARGO CO. swung over the boardwalk. Fennel sat at the desk inside but jumped up when they entered.

"Ladies, welcome! How delightful to have you here. How may I be of service today?"

Libby stepped forward. "I'd like a ticket to Boise on tomorrow's stage, please."

"Happy to oblige." Cyrus turned to a set of shelves beside his desk and took out a ticket book. "Business or pleasure, if I may ask?"

"Business," Libby said.

"Ah. Scouting new merchandise for the Paragon Emporium?"

"You might say that."

Cyrus looked at Gert. "And are you riding along as well, Miss Dooley?"

"Nope."

He nodded and made out Libby's ticket. "That will be three dollars and thirty cents, please."

Gert winced at the amount, but Libby opened a small purse and counted out the money.

"I'll have a crate or two on the way back," Libby said. "Will that be all right?"

"So long as we don't have a coach full of passengers who have a lot of luggage." Cyrus stood and handed her the pasteboard ticket. "Will it be heavy freight?"

Gert laughed. "Not unless you call lead heavy."

"Lead?" Cyrus frowned at her.

"Well, I was thinking of picking up some braid and yarn, too," Libby said. "They're not heavy."

"Oh no, not at all. But . . . lead? Are we talking about bullets?"

Libby nodded. "I need to get some special sizes of ammunition. Some of my customers have found it hard to obtain bullets to fit their firearms."

Cyrus's face went stony. "For the shooting ladies?"

"Well . . . some of it," Libby admitted.

"I'm not sure I can let you do that."

"What?" Libby's face froze with her mouth open and her eyebrows lost up under the brim of her fetching bonnet.

"It might not be safe for other passengers for you to carry a quantity of ammunition over these mountain roads."

"That's ridiculous," Libby said. "People carry guns and bullets on the stagecoach all the time. It's expected of your shotgun messengers."

"Ah, but not cases of live cartridges. We don't carry kegs of gunpowder either. Too volatile. The stagecoach line has the right to refuse dangerous cargo."

Libby turned to stare at Gert, her mouth open and her lovely eyes wide. Gert had the distinct feeling she needed to help her friend out of this mess, especially since she was the one who'd mentioned lead.

"You've already sold her the ticket."

Cyrus glared at her. "That was before I knew what she was planning to carry on our coach."

Gert threw her shoulders back. "So you'll refuse to let her board the stagecoach?"

"She can ride to Boise anytime. She just can't bring back a large quantity of ammunition."

Libby held out one hand toward Cyrus. "Maybe I'll hire the freighter to haul it in. Though some of my customers won't be happy with the delay."

"Hogwash!" Gert stepped between Libby and Cyrus. "You're only doing this because you don't like us women out there learning to protect ourselves. You're one of those pigheaded men who thinks women should be home knitting and baking biscuits all day."

"I beg your pardon."

"Gert, dear, please don't overset yourself." Libby tugged gently on Gert's sleeve. "Please, we'll find another way to deal with this. Now, Mr. Fennel, if you'd kindly refund the price of my ticket —"

"We don't generally do refunds," Cyrus said.

"Of all the nerve!" Gert shoved Libby aside. "I've never seen anything so rude and stingy in my life. You're the one who won't let her bring her merchandise on the coach, and it hasn't been three minutes since you took her money. That is the meanest, nastiest thing I've ever — !"

"Morning, folks. Is there a problem?" A shadow darkened the door as the deep voice cut her off. Gert whirled and looked into Ethan's face. His brown eyes kept the gentle, coon-dog cast they always held, but his jaw tightened as he took in the scene.

"Sheriff, you're just the person we need." Gert grasped his arm and pulled him into the office. "Mr. Fennel says Libby can't carry a stock of ammunition on the stagecoach, and now he refuses to give her back the price of her ticket."

"Gert, really. It's nothing." Libby's face went scarlet. "It's only three dollars and thirty cents."

"But you bought that ticket in good faith not five minutes ago."

Ethan stepped forward with both hands raised. "Ladies, please." He stopped only a pace distant from Cyrus and looked him in the eye. "Mr. Fennel, what's the problem here?"

Cyrus's mouth drooped, and he reached for his pen. "I suppose I can make an exception this once and refund your money, Mrs. Adams. But I'll not have you transporting dangerous cargo on the stage."

Gert opened her mouth again, but Ethan caught her eye, and she divined from his expression that this would be a good time to keep silence. "I'll be outside," she muttered to Libby.

The bright sunshine nearly blinded her, and she wished she'd remembered to wear a bonnet. She'd thought she could get by without it on a quick run across the street to the emporium. Now, if she had a bonnet that matched her eyes, like Libby had . . . no, that wouldn't work. Gert's would be a lackluster gray blue, not at all attractive.

The fact that Cyrus had backed down when the sheriff appeared didn't appease her anger. Fennel wasn't the only man in this town who seemed to think women couldn't handle their own affairs and needed a man to tend to business for them. Men who thought that way found her and the ladies' shooting group offensive. Gert wondered if it didn't threaten their pride.

The men of Fergus somehow felt less heroic and manly if their women carried weapons. Well, in her book, the men of Fergus needed to show some evidence that they were capable of protecting their women and children. When they proved up, the ladies would be happy to back off and let them do all the defending and strutting they wanted.

Libby and Ethan came out of the office.

"You got your feathers smoothed down now?" Ethan eyed her doubtfully.

"Not hardly."

He shook his head. "You said some fighting words in there."

"He was being downright churlish to Libby."

"Well, now, that may be, but it's your opinion. The man's got company policies to deal with, but he made an exception."

"Exception!" Gert kicked at the bench outside the office and wished she hadn't. Her big toe smarted. "He's still mad at her because she wouldn't —" At that moment, Gert glanced Libby's way and took note of her stricken face. The widow had revealed Cyrus's advances to her in confidence. Gert's chest hurt as she realized how close she'd come to blabbing her friend's secret on the main street of town, in a place where Cyrus could probably hear every word she said through his flimsy office walls. She ducked her head. "Forget it."

"Yes, that would be best." Ethan's eyelids stayed halfway closed as he looked at her. Probably he meant for her to see he wasn't happy with her performance, but all Gert could think was how the sunlight threw elongated shadows of his lashes onto his cheek. Odd that she'd never noticed his eyelashes before.

She turned away swiftly and nearly bumped into Libby.

"Come on, Libby; let's go over to my house. I'll bet Hiram would make a run to Boise for you to fetch that ammunition. Let's give him the list."

"It can wait."

"No, it can't. We have practice again Thursday afternoon, and you've got three women with no bullets. How can they learn to shoot if they haven't got bullets?"

"Here comes the stage," Ethan said, and Gert raised her chin, looking down the street. Cyrus came to the door of the office, holding his gold pocket watch, and the three of them stepped aside in unison to allow him plenty of room on the boardwalk.

"Right on time."

As the stagecoach drew up in a whirlwind of dust, Ethan drew Gert back a step. Cyrus was now between them and the direct path to the emporium. If they wanted to go there immediately, they'd have to go out into the street, around the coach and team, or else elbow through the people now descending from the vehicle.

"Look," Libby hissed, and Gert stared toward the open door of the stagecoach.

Cyrus was helping a woman of about thirty-five climb down, and her gaze swept the street. Her crisp black traveling dress held the inevitable wrinkles and dust of the road through the valley, but her pleasant expression gave Gert a jolt of anticipation. The woman's hem nearly touched the boards underfoot, which bespoke an Easterner, but her dress was well cut from a serviceable fabric meant to withstand the rigors of the journey.

Behind her, a man disembarked. His bowler hat and worsted suit also pegged him as an outlander. He met the woman's gaze with a tired smile.

"Well, Apphia, we've made it at last."

"Welcome to Fergus." Cyrus extended his hand to the man. "I hope you had a pleasant journey."

Instead of the usual complaints about the rough roads and jolting coach, the man grinned. "Indeed we did, sir. I'm Phineas

Benton — the Reverend Phineas Benton. This is Mrs. Benton. We hope to make Fergus our new home."

Gert gasped. Mrs. Benton looked her way and smiled again. "Hello."

Libby leaped toward the woman, and Mrs. Benton held out her gloved hand. "I'm glad to see some civilized ladies live in town."

"My dear madam, you have no idea how happy we are to see you. I'm Elizabeth Adams, and I own the Paragon Emporium, behind you."

Mrs. Benton looked over her shoulder. "An impressive establishment, Mrs. Adams."

Libby turned and yanked Gert forward. "This is my friend, Gertrude Dooley. Her brother is a gunsmith, and Miss Dooley makes her home with him."

"Pleased to meet you, Miss Dooley." Mrs. Benton took her hand and bowed her head.

"H–hello." Gert tried not to stare at the woman. Even with a layer of travel dust, the dark hair that framed her face looked thick and glossy, and her warm brown eyes radiated sincere satisfaction.

Cyrus nodded toward Ethan. "This is Sheriff Chapman. Sheriff, may I introduce Mr. and Mrs. Benton?"

Ethan bobbed his head and briefly shook

hands with them. "Sir. Ma'am. Welcome."

"Are you a preacher?" Gert gulped as they all stared at her. Stupid thing to say. He'd told them he was a reverend.

Mr. Benton's laugh rang out and echoed off the facades of the empty buildings across the street, but his expression was not unkind. "Indeed I am, ma'am. That's why we've come here from St. Louis. Could one of you please direct me to a Mr. Jamin Morrell?"

"Morrell?" Cyrus's jaw sagged. "You want to see Morrell, Reverend?"

"Why, yes. I assume he's chairman of the pulpit committee. He's the one who invited us to come and minister here in Fergus."

CHAPTER 15

Cyrus was never one to let flies settle on him. He turned to Ethan and smiled. "Sheriff, I believe the mayor ought to be notified of this happy event. Would you mind stepping over to his house and telling Mr. and Mrs. Walker that a man of the cloth has arrived in town?"

In his attempt to carry out Cyrus's idea swiftly, Ethan practically fell over the Bentons' luggage. Within a couple of minutes, the mayor was pumping the reverend's hand and beaming as though he'd personally issued the call to shepherd the wayward flock of Fergus. Orissa Walker, her color high and her hat slightly askew, also welcomed the couple and insisted they retire to her parlor for refreshment.

"How kind of you," Mrs. Benton said.

"We should be delighted." Her husband held his bowler hat to his chest and bowed as though Mrs. Walker had lifted a burden from his shoulders, which she probably had. No doubt the minister and his wife had wondered where they would have their next meal.

Libby excused herself so she could get back to her store. As the Bentons bid the gracious widow good-bye, Cyrus heard Orissa whisper to Gert, "Can you run to Annie Harper's for me? See if she and Myra can help prepare a company luncheon in my kitchen?"

Gert nodded.

"We'll have the Bentons, the town council members, and of course the mayor and myself. If you're able to help, I'd be most grateful."

Gert made no commitments but scooted away on the other side of the stagecoach. Cyrus told the shotgun rider to carry the Bentons' luggage to the mayor's house until further arrangements were made. Nick Telford, the driver, gathered the reins and started the team toward the livery.

"Cyrus, you'll accompany us home, won't you?" the mayor asked.

"Certainly. But I need to take care of one small item first."

As the Walkers herded the new clergyman and his wife toward their home, Cyrus strode quickly down the boardwalk to the telegraph office. A quarter of an hour later he had his reply — Phineas Benton's credentials stood up. Such was modern-day America — pace for fifteen minutes, and someone in St. Louis considered your question and sent you an answer. He still wasn't sure how saloon keeper Jamin Morrell had managed it, but the Reverend Phineas Benton was the genuine article.

When Cyrus reached the Walkers' home, Oscar Runnels had already heard the news and answered the summons. He sat in the parlor drinking tea and inquiring about the Bentons' trip and whether they were related to the Bentons of Lewiston. The two other council members showed up soon after — Griffin Bane and Zachary Harper, whose wife presumably raced around the kitchen while her hostess sat languidly conversing with the Bentons. Someone was out there anyway. Pleasing smells emanated from the Walkers' kitchen.

After answering questions about their trip, Mr. Benton looked around at the assembly. "So, the church council is complete? I expected to see Mr. Morrell here."

The mayor shot Cyrus a panicky glance, and Cyrus cleared his throat. "Well, now, sir, that's a funny thing. You see, we didn't have a formal pulpit committee, or even a church committee or board of deacons. The men you see here make up the town council. We've hoped for several years to bring a minister to Fergus but were never able to do that. There is no congregation as such. That is, there will be, I'm sure, but you'll have to start from scratch, so to speak. And Jamin Morrell is . . . Well, I doubt he'll be one of the charter members."

"Oh?" The minister held his gaze with an innocent expression, and his wife also stared at him with raised brows. Cyrus wished he didn't have to break the news, but someone had to explain.

Mrs. Walker saved him the trouble.

"Jamin Morrell is the owner of the vilest saloon in town. He's a man of few morals, if any. Begging your pardon, Mr. Benton, but I cannot conceive of a reason why he invited you here." Orissa's wrinkled brow smoothed out again as she paused and dredged up a smile for the parson and his wife. "But we are all glad that you came."

The men chimed in with quick assents.

"I . . . see." Benton eyed his wife askance, and it was obvious that he didn't really see. "But . . . why did Mr. Morrell undertake to contact us?"

Cyrus set his teacup aside and leaned forward. "Mr. Morrell is a shrewd man, sir.

He knew the ladies — that is, the people — of the town wanted a church and a minister. It's my guess that he saw providing one as a way to gain respect in the town."

"You may be right," Walker said. "He's been trying ever since he moved here last year to get other folks to take him seriously as a businessman and a contributor to the community. He doesn't like being looked down on because of his profession."

Mrs. Benton frowned and turned to Orissa. "Do you mean to say that he would use us as a means of persuading people to look on him and his . . . business more favorably?"

"Why, I . . ." Orissa swiveled toward her husband. "I'm sure I don't know."

"Could be," Griffin Bane said. "Morrell runs a rowdy place over at the Nugget. Some folks wish he'd never come to town. Of course, others frequent his establishment." The blacksmith went red under his beard and glanced at Cyrus.

Cyrus returned his gaze steadily. The men of this town would stick together — and if no one started naming patrons of the Nugget, they'd be fine. He did wonder how the preacher's arrival would affect business in the saloons. Might keep the family men away for a few weeks. Bitsy would suffer more in that case than Jamin. But in the long run, people who were going to drink would drink.

"I see," Mr. Benton said again.

"You won't leave on account of Morrell being the one to ask you here, will you?" Zachary Harper asked. "You'll break my wife's heart if you pack up and go. She was all excited when she heard we had us a preacher at last."

Benton reached over and patted his wife's hand. She smiled tremulously at him.

"No, we won't leave," he said. "God works in mysterious ways, and we're here to stay."

Luncheon pleased all the diners and proved remarkably palatable, considering the amount of time the cooks had had to prepare it. Cyrus wondered if Gert Dooley and others in the neighborhood had brought over dishes they'd prepared for their own families.

"I'd still like to meet Mr. Morrell and thank him," Mr. Benton said.

"Why don't we ask the sheriff to show you around the town after lunch?" Cyrus asked. Inwardly, he congratulated himself on coming up with this brilliant notion. Chapman was polite and discreet, if a bit of a dolt. He could keep the Bentons busy for an hour while the mayor and council hashed over the unexpected developments. He smiled at Mr. Benton. "While you're gone, the council can discuss living arrangements for you and where you can begin holding services."

"You said there's no church building."

"No, there's not," the mayor said. "We do have a schoolhouse."

"We've got a dozen vacant buildings in town," Griffin said. "This used to be a mining boom town, but most of the people left after the ore played out. Why not use one of those empty buildings for a church? At least temporarily."

The suggestion bothered Cyrus, since he owned those buildings. No one would want to pay him for the use of one for worship services. On the other hand, Isabel hated having to rearrange the classroom after a community event. No doubt she'd be out of sorts if the council gave the minister permission to use her schoolroom for services. His daughter obeyed his decrees, but that didn't mean she wouldn't find subtle ways to make her displeasure known.

"Er, we can discuss the matter," he said quickly.

Six hours later, Cyrus wandered into the Nugget for a much-needed drink. Lately, if he went to the Spur & Saddle to drink, word got around. Why should the town care if he put a little whiskey back? He had a suspicion it was Bitsy's doing because he'd spoken out against the shooting club. For the last couple of weeks, she'd made snide comments every time he went in there. All right, if she didn't want his business, he'd take it elsewhere. The Nugget wasn't as quiet and comfortable, but at least he could have a drink there without worrying someone would count his refills and tell his daughter how many.

Jamin Morrell sat at a corner table with a couple of ranchers. When Cyrus entered, Morrell rose and headed over to the bar.

"Set up a whiskey for Mr. Fennel, Ted. He deserves a lot more than that for offering the new preacher free rent on a house."

Cyrus smiled, though it had irked him to no end when the mayor and the rest of the council had pressured him to do it this afternoon. Word of the decision had run through the town like a prairie fire, and now folks thought he was generous.

He'd argued with Charles, Griffin, and Zachary that if a preacher should be paid, so should a landlord. But he was the only one with vacant real estate in town. At last he'd agreed to give six months' free rent on one of his empty houses to the Bentons. If they didn't find other living quarters during that time, they could discuss a rental or purchase agreement with him.

"Not a problem, Morrell." His tone was more jovial than he felt. So long as the rest of the town never found out how bitterly he'd fought the free-rent proposal, he could play the hero as well as Jamin. "You deserve some credit yourself, persuading Mr. and Mrs. Benton to come to our fair town."

Jamin shrugged. "It was a long shot. That's why I didn't tell anyone. Didn't want to get the people's hopes up. But I knew someone in St. Louis who might know someone, so I sent off a letter."

"Well, we owe you a big debt. Been wishing we had a preacher for a long time." Not that he personally had wished it. He'd have to spend Sundays sitting through dull sermons now, but at least they'd have someone to perform weddings and funerals, and most of the ladies would be happy.

Cyrus sipped his first whiskey. He still thought there must be more to the story. Isabel and half the matrons of the town had nagged their menfolk for years to get a preacher for Fergus. The town council had written several letters to towns back East and even splurged on a newspaper ad in Boston, hoping to entice a man to come, with no results. But when Morrell got the idea, he asked a friend a favor, and presto — a bona fide, ordained minister showed up!

The argument over whether to use the schoolhouse for church services, build a sanctuary, or designate some other building a temporary church had lasted even longer than the one over housing the couple. Not everyone in town would attend church, and some didn't want to see the town subsidizing it. The council had discussed asking the members of the community for donations. At last they'd agreed that it really wasn't a town problem. The church members should bear the expense of a building to meet in. But since all the town pillars wanted a church and a minister, they would encourage the townspeople to contribute to the cause.

After much wrestling, Cyrus had agreed to open the old Jonnason Haberdashery building, between the jail and the telegraph office, for services. The people interested in having a church would clean it and provide seating. And a small rental would be paid to Cyrus from the church's offerings.

Mr. Benton had found this arrangement satisfactory, and Cyrus had left him after giving him and Mrs. Benton a tour of their new "church" and housing. Orissa Walker offered to let them stay at the mayor's house until the ladies got their new lodgings ready. She also promised to line up a bevy of local women to help clean both buildings. Griffin had offered to canvass the residents for basic furnishings for the new parsonage. All was accomplished so quickly that Cyrus's head spun — or perhaps that was partly due to the second and third glasses of whiskey Ted had poured for him. He still had the feeling he'd gotten the short end of the stick, but at least Charles and the others had agreed he should be paid for use of the haberdashery.

"The way I see it," Morrell now said, "having a preacher will help this town grow. The population dropped off after the mines played out, but it's still a nice little town. It will be even better with a few more businesses, a few more families. . . ."

A few more customers. That's what he was thinking, wasn't it? Cyrus nodded. "I like the way you think, Morrell. Well, mostly. You're a real businessman."

Now, if only the ladies of Fergus would get distracted by the cleaning frenzy and forget about their little shooting club. The very existence of the group peeved him. It wasn't right.

Maybe if he kept on the preacher's good side, he could bend his ear and get him to say something from the pulpit that would make the women see how wrong it was for them to be out shooting up the hillsides when they ought to be doing what they were doing this minute — cleaning and cooking.

A vision flitted through his mind of the town's ladies, led by the timid Mrs. Benton, lovely Libby Adams, and belligerent Gert Dooley, all marching toward the Nugget carrying axes and signs that read: DEMON RUM.

No. Not in this life.

"Ted, better pour me another."

"It's so nice of Hiram to do this for me." Libby totaled the columns of figures listing the amount of each cartridge size she wanted and her estimated cost.

"Well, with the new preacher coming and all, we need you ladies to stay here to help them get settled." Ethan smiled at her. "I think it's great that you've made a donation to start the church fund."

Libby circled her total and reached for the cash box. "I hope it will inspire others to do the same. The congregation needs to buy that building from Cy Fennel as soon as possible." She counted out several large bills. "I've wired ahead for a case of Bibles, too."

"That's a good idea. Folks will be wanting them, now that we're going to have church regular. I might even buy one myself."

"You don't have a Bible, Ethan? I'm surprised at you." Libby lowered her voice. "I hope Hiram doesn't mind carrying all this money."

"Griffin's going with him."

"Wonderful. But who will tend the livery?"

"He's got Josiah Runnels and Ezra Dyer ready to swap the stagecoach teams out. If anyone needs to have blacksmithing done, they'll have to wait."

Libby arched her delicate eyebrows. "I'm surprised Griffin would go to so much trouble. Loaning us a wagon and team was generous enough."

"Well, Griff isn't sure he approves of the shooting club, but he's starting to disapprove of Fennel. He may be doing it partly to make him mad."

"Ah." Libby nodded. "I'm afraid Gert's and my doings have caused people to take sides. I'm sorry about that."

"Don't be. You ladies are right to want more security."

Libby looked around as Florence entered the back door. "I don't like to trust this delicate an order to Oscar Runnels and his mule teams. They're slow, and besides, after what happened yesterday, Cyrus might forbid Mr. Runnels to do it for me. It's just as well Hiram and Griffin are willing." She handed him the money and her list. "Thank you, Ethan."

He nodded and stepped out onto the boardwalk. The sturdy freight wagon came down the street, with Griffin holding the reins and Hiram sitting beside him. They pulled up in front of the emporium, and Ethan stepped into the street. Two rifles lay at the men's feet.

"You two take care."

"We will," Griffin said. "If you don't mind looking in at the livery once or twice, I'd appreciate it."

"Maybe you can look in on Trudy, too," Hiram said.

"Trudy? Who's Trudy?" Griffin's bushy brows lowered, and he leaned away from Hiram, the better to stare at him.

Ethan grinned and ignored the question, hoping his face wouldn't go too red in front of the blacksmith. "I'll do that. Here's Miz Adams's list." He handed the cash over with it, and Hiram quickly stuffed both in his vest pocket and buttoned it closed.

"See ya tomorrow night." Ethan stepped

back up on the boardwalk and waved.

Griffin clucked to the horses and set off down Main Street, then turned his head again to stare at Hiram. "Who's Trudy?"

Ethan laughed and headed across the street.

"Sheriff!"

He stopped on the walk in front of the jail and turned toward the call. Micah Landry trotted up on his bay mare and dismounted.

"What is it, Mr. Landry?"

"My wife, that's what."

"Is she hurt?" Ethan's neck prickled at the anger in the rancher's voice.

"Not yet, but she might be soon. I've had enough of this shooting society."

"Oh." Ethan gritted his teeth and prepared to hear a passionate rant.

Micah wrapped the mare's reins around the hitching rail and stepped up on the boardwalk with him. "Emmaline is wasting two afternoons a week now, going out to yak with a bunch of misguided women and shoot off a passel of lead. Do you know how much ammunition she's used in the last three weeks?"

"I have no idea."

"Two boxes of shotgun shells, that's how much. I told her we can't afford a dollar a month for shooting practice. And what'll we

219

do when one of those women gets shot?"

"Easy, now. I'm sure they're being careful."

Micah balled his hands into fists "Don't tell me to take it easy. I want my wife back in the kitchen where she belongs. That's my gun she's using, and it's my money she's spending on shells."

Ethan swallowed hard and put one hand out toward Landry. "This is really between you and Mrs. Landry. She's not doing anything illegal that I can see."

"Well, there oughta be a law against it. Women shouldn't be able to take a man's gun without asking and shoot off his supply of ammunition. What if I want to go hunting and there's no shells left?"

Cyrus Fennel came down the sidewalk and ambled over to where they stood. "What's going on, Micah?"

"My wife. She's out shooting all the time with those other women. I'd like to take Gert Dooley and —"

"Watch it, now," Ethan growled. "Miss Dooley told me your wife asked to join them, not the other way around. It sounds to me as though you and Mrs. Landry need to sit down over a pot of coffee and discuss this in a civilized manner."

"We tried that this morning, and it weren't

220

civilized. Sheriff, you've got to disband that club."

Cyrus clapped Landry on the shoulder. "Now, Micah, have you told the missus you don't want her going to these club meetings?"

"I tried, but she just kept saying how much she enjoys getting out and talking to the other ladies. I says, 'How can you talk if you're all blazing away?' But she says she likes it and that she feels safer now that she knows she can hit a man if she needs to."

Cyrus's graying eyebrows rose. "Did you take that as a threat?"

Landry's jaw dropped. "Threat? No! What are you talking about? I never thought . . . Why, you don't suppose this is about women's rights, do you?"

"You just don't know with today's females. Bloomer costumes and the Women's Christian Temperance Union . . ." Cyrus shook his head, frowning. "I have to say I'm glad my daughter hasn't neglected her duties to join the shootists."

Ethan cleared his throat. "Gentlemen, I don't think you should take this too seriously. The ladies want to feel safe because they're left alone for long periods of time. They want to know they can defend themselves, that's all. Now, I have work to do.

Good day." Ethan tipped his hat and turned his back. He walked to the jail fighting the urge to look back.

CHAPTER 16

After the first Sunday service, Cyrus and Isabel left the new sanctuary just behind the Walkers. Pastor and Mrs. Benton stood at the door, shaking hands with the parishioners.

"Now you be sure and come over for dinner as soon as you're done here," Orissa Walker said loudly enough for all those still in the building to hear.

"Thank you," Apphia Benton said.

Her husband smiled and took Mrs. Walker's hand. "We'll be there shortly, my good woman."

Cyrus nodded at Mrs. Benton and shook the minister's hand heartily. "Good sermon, Reverend."

"Thank you." Phineas Benton's face barely contained his ear-to-ear smile. "And thank you again for your generosity, Mr. Fennel."

Cy left the building and put his hat on.

Isabel came out behind him.

"Are you coming straight home, Pa?"

"I may drop in to see someone for a minute. Go ahead and get dinner on though. I'll be right there." A month ago, he might have gone to the Spur & Saddle for his Sunday dinner, but Bitsy's venom was too much to face lately. He'd as soon eat at home. But first he wanted to stop by the Nugget. He went to the back door and knocked.

Jamin Morrell came to open it in his shirtsleeves.

"Well, Mr. Fennel, what brings you out?"

Cyrus nodded with a half smile. "Just thought I'd tell you, the church service was packed. But I think the reverend was disappointed that you didn't show up."

Jamin laughed. "It'll be a hot day in January when I start going to church."

He walked inside to a table in the corner, where he had writing materials spread out, and picked up a stoneware mug of coffee. "Just catching up on some correspondence and bookkeeping." After a quick swig, he set the mug down and slid a sheet of paper over the one he'd been working on.

Cyrus had glimpsed the salutation of a letter: *Dear Dr. Kincaid.*

"Why do you keep the Nugget closed

Sundays if you don't believe in religion?" he asked.

Jamin gave him a tight smile. "Everyone needs a day of rest, Mr. Fennel. If Bitsy Shepard wants to serve chicken dinners instead of taking a day of rest, let her. I doubt she makes much profit from it. I give my employees the day off. You can tell the reverend that if you want. He can do his business on Sunday, but don't expect me there."

Cyrus left him, noting peevishly that Morrell could at least have offered him a cup of coffee. Oh well, Isabel would have dinner ready at home.

As he walked, he pondered how he could bring the Reverend Mr. Benton over to his way of thinking about the shooting club. Dooley and Bane had driven all the way to Boise to fetch the ammunition Libby Adams had wanted to bring in on the stagecoach. On his visit to the emporium yesterday, he'd seen several new guns displayed. Those hadn't been there before. Oh, she'd ordered in Bibles, too, the hypocrite. Did she think that could offset the way she encouraged all those women to defy their husbands? Much as he admired her golden locks and sweet visage, he was glad he hadn't pursued an entanglement with Libby.

She would buck him all the way on both domestic and business matters, unlike his pliable and obedient daughter.

Maybe he and Isabel could entertain the Bentons for dinner next Sunday. If he could get the minister away from distractions, they could have a serious talk about a woman's place in society and how the shooting club was detrimental to the town and the congregation. Reverend Benton needed to understand the danger of an organization that prompted women to abandon their duties in the home.

Milzie set Franklin's Hawken rifle against the stone wall of the cave and carefully unwrapped her bundle. She had so few possessions she took great care to make sure they stayed in a safe place. The bundle consisted of her ragged shawl, for which she was thankful. That, with a wool skirt, one bodice she'd made from one of Franklin's old shirts, and a tattered nightdress, made up her entire wardrobe. She'd saved Franklin's wool, army-issue coat the night of the fire, and her shoes, but they were nearly in pieces now. Her stockings had long since worn through at the toes and heels.

The cave served her better as a home than it had as part of Franklin's mining claim.

He'd dug about inside for weeks, twenty years or more ago, hoping to find some ore, but without success. It only went back thirty feet or so into the rock. Frank had shored up the ceiling while he was at it and built a little shelf on one side of the opening, between two timbers. An old lantern hung above it. Her only furniture was a wooden crate she'd salvaged and used as a stool.

She peered at the jumble of items she'd brought back from her latest trip into town. The light streaming through the cave entrance revealed her new treasures, mostly bestowed on her by the ladies of the shooting club.

The bright red kerchief was a prize she'd almost passed up. She felt guilty as she stroked it. Miz Dooley likely would miss it, but it was so cheery, she couldn't walk off without it. And she could tie it about her throat when the weather turned cold again. She'd also picked up a few brass shell casings after the shooting practice. She wasn't sure what she would do with them, but they must be good for something. A bread roll and a clump of raisins — Bitsy Shepard had slipped her those, bless her heart. And Miz Adams had brought her a few crackers wrapped in brown paper. The final item was one she'd found when she cut behind one of the ranch houses on her way home: a button that looked all shiny in the sunlight, like silver. She held it up to the light. The design resembled a knot, cast in metal. She stroked it lovingly and placed it on the shelf.

The shell casings looked fine, next to her neat row of shining safety pins, including the big one from the livery. She raised her hand to her mouth and licked the spot on the back where she'd been burned in March, the night the cabin went up in flames. It didn't hurt much now, but the skin was still rough. She folded the red kerchief and set it next to the blacksmith's knife and the matchbox that held the few coins she'd found at the livery last week.

The shooting club was the greatest adventure she'd had in years. Franklin's Hawken bought her entrance into the company of the finest ladies in Fergus. True, she was reduced to "borrowing" ammunition to practice with. Libby or Gert brought her powder and lead for two or three shots each meeting. She was getting good at shooting, too. Under Gert Dooley's tutelage, her aim had improved dramatically. Milzie had visions of bringing down a pronghorn for meat someday. Wouldn't that be fine?

Her pitiful inventory mocked her. How would she survive with only these few things? But she'd made it through since March, and the warm weather was on her side. She'd planted the seeds Libby Adams gave her a couple of weeks ago. Already, feathery little carrots sprouted in the garden spot behind the charred remains of the cabin.

She would rest today and forage again tomorrow. Today she'd saved one lead ball for the Hawken. Somehow, she'd figure out a way to salvage a bit of powder next time and bring it home to the cave. And sometime soon, she would go hunting.

Gert drove the wagon to Bert Thalen's ranch on Monday afternoon with Libby and Mrs. Benton on the seat with her. In the back rode Florence, Annie, Myra, Vashti, and Bitsy. Libby had hired the wagon from the livery so that Mrs. Benton could attend the shooting practice in comfort.

When Gert reined in the team, six more women, wives of ranchers and miners, awaited their arrival. They swarmed around the wagon to greet the ladies from town.

"Ladies," Gert called, standing up on the wagon, "it gives me great pleasure to introduce Mrs. Apphia Benton."

Mrs. Benton smiled warmly and nodded

at the women assembled on the meager grass.

"Some of you met her yesterday at the church service," Gert said. "For those of you who may not have heard, she is our new minister's wife."

The women crowded in closer, and Emmaline reached up to help Mrs. Benton descend from the wagon seat.

After allowing a few minutes for greetings and chatter, Gert nodded at Libby, who raised her melodic voice.

"Ladies, if I may have your attention, please. Since our numbers have grown so, Miss Dooley and I have formed a plan for dividing the shooters into teams. Each team leader will be responsible for seeing that safety procedures are followed and that all targets and debris are cleaned up before we leave."

The women nodded and murmured their approval. With Ethan's permission, they continued to meet in a draw on Bert Thalen's ranch, but he had warned them that the site of their meetings would probably have to be moved if Bert's son sold the ranch or decided to come live on it.

"Before we name the team leaders," Libby said, "Miss Dooley has one other announcement."

Gert tried to smile, but her stomach lurched a little. She wasn't used to speaking to a crowd. "It has come to my attention that certain people in the town have given our group a name." The women waited in utter silence. Gert swallowed and went on. "They're calling us the Ladies' Shooting Club."

"Could be worse," Vashti said, and they all laughed.

Gert was able to smile then. "Yes, it could." She'd thought of several possibilities herself, none of them good. "I wondered if you would like to formally enact a resolution to take the name 'Ladies' Shooting Club.' That would make us an acknowledged organization."

"Acknowledged by whom?" Bitsy called.

Gert looked at Libby, a panicky dismay squeezing her innards.

"Why, by us, of course," Libby said, still smiling, and a ripple of amusement ran through the group. "And by all the kind gentlemen who have shown their support in various ways — the sheriff, Hiram Dooley, Griffin Bane, and others."

Annie called out, "The way I see it, if a man isn't carping about our shooting habits, he's on our side."

"What good will naming the club do?"

Emmaline asked.

Gert looked to Libby with a silent plea for her to continue. Libby rose to the occasion.

"As an entity, we can have a voice in the town. Miss Dooley and I thought the club might even approach the town council concerning safety. We could urge them to allow the sheriff to deputize men to help him patrol the town at night, for instance."

"Why couldn't we help with that?" Myra asked.

"Hmm, I'm not sure the town fathers are ready for that." Libby reached to squeeze the girl's arm and looked over at Gert.

Gert cleared her throat. "May I hear from those in favor of this resolution — to be hereafter known as the Ladies' Shooting Club of Fergus?"

"Aye," chorused the women.

"Any opposed?"

Blessed silence greeted her. "Thank you. The resolution is enacted. And now, I would like to institute a new tradition for the club. I'd like to ask Mrs. Benton to lead us in prayer."

"I'm delighted to be here with you as a part of this group." Mrs. Benton pushed a wisp of dark hair back beneath her bonnet. "Thank you all for your welcome. Shall we pray?"

The ladies bowed their heads — even Vashti, after Bitsy elbowed her sharply.

Half an hour later, as the teams worked smoothly through their shooting routines, Gert moved from group to group to give pointers on aiming.

In Emmaline's group, she heard Apphia say to Goldie, "Why of course you would be welcome at the church services. No one would turn you away from the Lord's work." The saloon girl eyed her dubiously.

When Gert reached Libby's team, her friend gestured for her to join them.

"I was thinking that perhaps on Thursday you could give us all a lesson in gun cleaning." Libby's blue eyes glinted with eagerness.

"Sure. That's a good idea." Gert looked over the orderly ranks of women and frowned. Milzie was hobbling away, past the row of tied horses and toward the road. "I gave Milzie her last bullet and powder load, but she's leaving, and I don't think she's fired it yet."

CHAPTER 17

Ethan stretched the wire tight while Johnny McDade pounded in staples to hold it to the fence posts. The bottom of the box of staples showed, and Ethan looked anxiously toward town.

"Sure wish that brother of yours would get back here."

"No doubt he's flirting with that red-headed gal at the emporium," Johnny said.

Ethan shook his head. Spin McDade, the older of the two brothers at nineteen, considered himself quite a ladies' man. Sending him into town on an errand was a risk, but he'd figured the two boys wouldn't get much done on the fence if he went, and he hadn't wanted to send the younger brother with cash. Of course, Libby would probably have opened an account for him if he'd sent a note, but Ethan liked to keep his debts cleared up. Credit could ruin a man, or so his pa had always said.

A few minutes later, Ethan saw a telltale plume of dust where the road ran behind some scrub pines. "Maybe that's Spin coming."

"We can hope." Johnny picked up the jug of spring water they'd brought along and tipped it back for a long swallow.

Spin and his horse appeared at the edge of the new pasture they were fencing — not that it produced much grass, but it would hold a few cattle while Ethan gave his north range a chance to recover from spring grazing. The leggy bay gelding cantered toward them.

"Hey!" Johnny waved his hat and grinned at his brother.

Spin pulled the horse to a halt and jumped down. "I got the staples. Miz Adams asked me to tell ya the shooting club will meet this afternoon."

"What's that?" Johnny asked. "Do we want to join this here club?"

Ethan laughed. "I don't think so. It's for women."

The two young men stared at him. They hadn't been into town much since they'd joined Ethan for the summer, and apparently they hadn't heard about the controversial new society.

"Some of the women in Fergus are learning to shoot. Since Sheriff Thalen was killed, they've wanted to learn to defend themselves. Mrs. Adams is just keeping me informed. They usually meet on Thalen's old property, not far from here, so don't you boys go riding over that way. They might blow your heads off." Ethan nodded toward Bert's land.

"I heard some shooting over thataway on Monday," Johnny said.

"Does Florence Nash go?" Spin asked. "I might want to join if she does."

"I told you, it's for women only." Ethan reached for the box of staples Spin pulled from his saddlebag.

"How much time did you spend following Florence around the store?" Johnny asked.

His brother smiled. "She's a peach. I might just need to ride into town with you Sunday, Ethan. She told me they're having church services now."

Ethan nodded. "You can both go if you've a mind to. Your ma and pa would be pleased, I'm sure." No doubt Spin would find his way onto the Nash family's bench that served as a pew, but that was all right. As big as he talked, Spin generally behaved himself, and Florence was a nice girl.

"You aiming to settle down?" Johnny stared at his brother in disgust.

"Maybe."

Johnny scowled and shook his head. "I never."

Ethan and Spin laughed.

"How about you, Ethan?" Spin asked in a man-to-man tone. "You ever think about settling down?"

Ethan grunted and pulled his work gloves on. "I consider myself settled."

"Aw, come on." Spin bent to help him lift and string the wire. "Don't you ever think about courtin' a girl?"

"No. I try not to."

"Why ever not?" Johnny asked, retrieving his hammer.

"I just don't want to think about getting married, that's all."

"Well, that Miz Adams is mighty pretty," Spin said.

"Hush," Ethan said, not unkindly. "Let's get this fence up."

"And there was another girl came into the store while I was there. Gert, they call her. Not so pretty as Miz Adams, but she seemed pert and likable."

"I told you to hush. Mrs. Adams and Miss Dooley are too old for the likes of you, and I told you, I'm not ready to settle. Now are you gonna work, or am I gonna have to pay you off and hire someone else?"

Ethan bent his back into the grueling work. When they'd strung the wire as far as he'd planted fence posts, he wielded the post-hole digger, and Spin followed, driving more posts in with a sledgehammer. Johnny chinked them with small stones when needed. By noontime, all three were drenched in sweat and ready for a meal.

As he wearily mounted Scout, Ethan considered the rest of his day.

"After we wash up and eat, you two can work on the barn roof." They wouldn't work so hard they suffered from it, but they'd make a little progress.

"You going into town?" Johnny asked.

"Reckon I should. Folks like to see the sheriff's face now and then."

He wondered if he could count on supper at Hiram and Trudy's. He smiled to himself. He'd taken to thinking of her as Trudy, and the more he cogitated on it, the better he thought the name fit her. He might even take her a little something as a token of his gratitude. But what? He wouldn't want her to start thinking like the McDade boys, that he ought to settle down. So nothing personal.

He thought back to when he'd left Fergus to join the army. He'd been only a couple of years older than Spin was now. Young, carefree, idealistic. That was before he helped chase the Bannocks all across the Idaho Territory and followed the Sheepeaters high into the mountains. Back then, he might have sparked a girl and dreamed of setting up to have a family. But now . . . now when he thought of families, he remembered the faces of the starving Indians they'd chased down. Memories of their skirmishes sickened him. And what woman would want to spend her life with a man haunted by wailing Sheepeater children?

No, a woman like Libby was better off on her own. She seemed content with her business and her friends. And Trudy? She had her brother to fret over. She didn't need another man whose past rose up to haunt him.

So that was that. He'd take them some beef when it came butchering time. But no flowers or candy for . . .

The image of Trudy as a little girl with flaxen braids flitted across his mind.

Libby sat up in bed, her heart pounding. She strained to hear. Something creaked, but the two-story building made its own noises when all else was quiet. Something different had yanked her from sleep.

She heard it again — stealthy footsteps in

the rooms below. She could barely breathe. Someone was in the back room of the store, where her desk sat and the safe huddled in the corner behind a stack of crates.

She slid her hand under Isaac's cool, undented pillow. The Peacemaker fit her hand like an old friend.

Her dressing gown lay draped over a chair, and she slid it on, tying it firmly about her waist, then picked up the pistol. Shoes would only betray her.

As she listened, the footsteps sounded again. The intruder had left the back room and gone to the main floor of the emporium. What was he after? Had he tried to open the safe? She took a trembling step and stopped to listen again. She heard quiet thumping and shuffling, then snapping. Three quick steps took her to the door. She turned the knob with excruciating slowness and pulled the door two inches inward.

With an eye to the crack, she squinted toward the staircase and saw a glow. He must have lit a lantern . . . or a candle. The glow flickered on the ceiling and walls over the stairs.

Smoke hit her suddenly, a roiling wave of it, and she gasped, which only sucked more into her lungs. She shut the door, not worrying about the sound it made. For a moment she stood groping for a reason. She'd had no fire in the stove downstairs for weeks, and she hadn't even lit her cookstove in the upstairs apartment tonight. How could there be —

The acrid smell reached beneath the door and choked her.

CHAPTER 18

Libby threw the door open and dashed to the top of the stairs, clutching the pistol before her. Smoke rolled up the stairwell. Pulling in a deep breath, she hurried down. The air seemed clearer at the bottom of the flight, though she could now see flames rising from a heap on the floor between the counter and the racks that held housewares and baking supplies.

She looked all around. No one moved through the thickening smoke in the big room. On tiptoe, she approached the site of the fire. Merchandise had been piled up in a mound — clothing, stationery, and seed packets. Combustibles. No hardware or pots. Things that would burn quickly. A sudden flare-up in the blaze drove her back several feet. Something had caught and sizzled. Lard, maybe, or bacon?

She laid the Peacemaker on a shelf and grabbed a wool blanket. The fire bucket always sat near the pot-bellied stove, even in summer. She shoved the blanket into it, trying not to slop the precious water. The heavy cloth soaked her nightclothes. She stood and carried it to the blaze. Choosing the part that burned most fiercely, she flipped the wet cloth over it, slapping at the fire and jerking her blanket back. The hot floorboards made the bare soles of her feet smart, but she couldn't stop. Several times she swatted at the flames and glowing embers. A flaring brand rolled toward her, and she lifted her robe and nightgown, jumping back.

She soaked the blanket again and returned to her task until the blanket began to smoke. The fire bucket was nearly empty, so she upended it on the fire and edged around the burning pile. She managed to squeeze past the end of the counter. The bucket of drinking water was nearly full. She picked it up and hurried back to the fire, coughing so hard she spilled some of the water. Aiming for the spot that persisted in burning the worst, she swung the bucket and threw the water on it. She jumped back, lest the swash throw hot embers on her.

The smoke thickened, and flames kept licking at the heap. More water. Libby ran through the storage room. The back door was unlocked, but she wouldn't think about that now. She ran to the rain barrel and scooped her pail full.

As she hurried back inside, sloshing water against her legs and again soaking the lower part of her nightclothes, she wondered if she should run for the nearest neighbors. But as she threw the full bucket onto the fire and a great deal of water ran off it and flowed across the floor, she decided she could put it out if she persisted. If she ran for Peter Nash or the mayor, the fire might grow beyond their ability to stop it.

She made three more trips before she was satisfied that the flames wouldn't leap up again. Exhausted, she leaned against the counter, panting. Her wet clothing was covered in soot, and she assumed her face looked as bad. She went to the front door and threw it wide open. What difference would it make now to leave the doors open? Already her domain had been breached.

Slowly she climbed the stairs and opened all the windows in her living quarters to clear out the smoke. Her feet were sore, but nothing worse than a sunburn, so far as she could tell. In her bedchamber, she lit the lantern and pulled the curtains. Dawn was upon her, and there was no point in going back to bed. She wasted no time but dressed carefully. Her hair would smell of smoke until she washed it, but at least she could scrub the soot from her face and hands. At last she felt presentable. Time to go for help.

She stopped partway down the stairs. The fire was out. Should she even bother her neighbors? The sheriff was the man she needed. A moment's thought, and she went out the front door, closed it firmly behind her, and dashed across the street and down the walk. The jail loomed still and dark, but already lantern light shone through the side kitchen window of the Dooleys' house. Libby hurried to the back and knocked softly.

Gert opened the door cautiously.

"Good morning! Forgive me for coming so early," Libby said.

"What is it? Is something wrong?" Gert's nose wrinkled as she threw the door wide and stepped back so Libby could enter.

"Yes. Someone broke into the emporium and started a fire downstairs. I was able to put it out, but I'd like to talk to the sheriff before I open the store."

"Oh, Libby! Are you all right?" Gert grasped her wrist and looked her over. "You're not hurt, are you?"

"No, I'm fine. I want to go back and start cleaning up right away. It's a mess, but I hope to open the store on time. Do you think —"

"Hiram's getting up. He'll go right away for Ethan. Maybe you should wait until the sheriff gets there to start your cleaning."

Libby shook her head. "No, I wouldn't be able to open on time if I waited. I want to get all the burnt stuff out and air the building well. I'm not sure how badly the floor is damaged, but if I can help it, I won't give the ruffian who did this the satisfaction of closing my business." Her voice choked, and Gert put her arms around her.

"There now. If some outlaw broke in and vandalized your store, you really oughtn't to be over there alone."

"He's gone now." Libby swiped at her tears, wishing she had strength enough to keep from crying. "Oh, Gert, why would anyone do this?" A little sob leaped out of her throat, and she put her hands to her face.

"Sit down." Gert led her gently to the table and pulled out a chair for her. "I'm fixing you a cup of tea as soon as I tell Hiram and get him on his way. Then I'll go over with you, and we'll do whatever's needed."

"You don't have to. You've got your own work to do."

Gert gave a little snort. "I've got nothing more important than fixing breakfast for a man who's capable of doing it himself."

Libby arched her eyebrows. Gert had never before implied that Hiram might not need her quite so much as she wished. "All right." She blinked back her tears and searched her pocket for a handkerchief.

Gert left the room and returned a moment later with Hiram on her heels. The gunsmith stopped in the doorway and eyed her mournfully. At last he spoke.

"You're all right, ma'am?"

"Yes, I am, Hiram. Thank you for asking."

"I'll go to the ranch for Ethan." He strode to the back door, grabbed his hat, and left.

Gert went to the stove and lifted the teakettle. "He offered to check through the store and your rooms, but I told him you'd rather he fetched Ethan. But I'm going with you, and no arguments. You might have been killed." As she spoke, she measured tea into a pot and poured hot water on it. Then she brought their cups to the table and pushed the sugar bowl toward Libby. "I don't expect you've eaten anything, have you?"

Libby shook her head. "But I don't want to lose any time —"

"Just a bite." Gert brought a tin box from

the cupboard and opened it to reveal several cold biscuits. "Leftovers, but with a little cheese, they'll go down. You'll be glad later that you had something."

Libby supposed her friend was right, though she barely tasted the biscuit and wedge of sharp cheese Gert placed before her. The tea comforted her.

"Thank you."

Gert put the last bite of her own biscuit into her mouth and stood. She reached to gather the dishes and carried them to the dishpan. "Come on, now. I'll take care of these later. Shall I bring my mop?"

"I've got everything we'll need in the store," Libby said.

Together they walked across the street and up the boardwalk. The early sunlight streamed down Main Street. Libby opened the door of the emporium and led Gert inside to the site of the fire.

Water had run over the floor, pooling in spots and draining through cracks between the floorboards in others. The pile of charred merchandise stank, and the air still held the strong, acrid stench of smoke.

"I'll prop both doors open," Libby said. "I've got the windows open upstairs." The storeroom had no windows to open. Isaac had designed the building that way on purpose, partly for security, and partly to give him more wall space for shelves and stacks of goods.

She took her broom, mop, and bucket from the back room.

"Maybe we should start with a shovel." Gert eyed the wet, ashy pile distastefully.

"Good idea. And I've got a wash boiler over there in the hardware section. We can fill it and carry it out back. I'll get Josiah to haul the trash off later."

"Right," Gert said. "Let's just get it outside for now."

Libby walked quickly to the apparel section and grabbed two pair of men's heavy work gloves. She took one to Gert. "Here. I don't think we want to touch that stuff without gloves."

They set to work, removing all of the ruined items. For twenty minutes they said little. Libby gasped when she recognized some of the wrecked merchandise — the remaining unsold Bibles.

"Wicked."

Gert peered over at the charred leather and paper. "Oh, Libby. I'm so sorry."

Libby sighed. "I've felt a little guilty, anyhow, making a profit from selling the scriptures."

"I don't think you need feel badly about

that. Folks in town were glad to get them."

Libby sat back on her heels and wiped her brow with the back of her wrist. "It could have been much worse. So much worse."

The sleigh bells hanging from the door jingled softly as Ethan brushed past them with Hiram close behind.

The sheriff strode toward them and halted, staring down at the stinking mess on the floor.

"This is where it happened?"

Libby nodded. "A pile of merchandise from all over the store — things that would burn easily. Cloth, paper. I'm guessing some lard to help it burn faster."

Ethan frowned.

Before he could speak, Libby said, "I guess you wish we hadn't started cleaning, but I want to open on time today. That is . . ." She faltered, looking to Gert for reassurance. "You don't think it's too smelly, do you? A lot of the other merchandise might be ruined from smoke. I wonder if the flour will taste like it. And the bolts of cloth — I suppose I could wash them if the smell won't air out."

"Let me look around for a few minutes, please, before you do any more," Ethan said. "Where did you put the burnt stuff?"

"Out back." Gert nodded toward the door

250

behind the counter as she pulled off her work gloves. "We made a heap behind the store and figured Josiah could take it away later."

"All right, but I'll want to look at it before he does. Mrs. Adams —"

"I think he burned nearly all the seed packets," Libby said absently, looking at her depleted shelves. "But it's late in the season. Most folks had got what they wanted for seed."

"Did you see the person who did this?" Ethan asked.

She jerked her head around to look at him. "No. I . . ." She was shaking. That was odd. She held her hand out before her, curious at the way it trembled.

Gert stepped forward and put her arm around Libby's waist. "We've been working hard. Why don't you come sit down in the back room while you talk to Ethan?"

"I'm all right." Libby pushed back a lock of hair and wondered if her face was all sooty again. "I didn't see anyone, but I heard someone walking around down here. I think that's what woke me up. Probably he was gathering the things to burn. I heard footsteps and thuds. It frightened me, so I got up and went to my bedroom door. Then I smelled the smoke."

"You put the fire out all by yourself?" Ethan asked.

"Yes. It . . . wasn't that big, but it put off a lot of black smoke."

"There was an empty lard pail in the junk we hauled out," Gert said.

Ethan nodded. "I'll have you show it to me later. Now, Mrs. Adams, think hard. You're sure you didn't see anyone?"

"No one."

"How do you think he got in?"

"The back door wasn't locked." She shook her head. "I know I locked it last night. I always do. But I suppose . . ."

"I'll look at it." Ethan knelt and examined the floorboards. "The fire doesn't seem to have burned through the floor, but it's charred here." He looked up at Hiram. "We could replace these three boards, couldn't we?"

Hiram nodded. "I can go get what we need right now."

"Oh, you don't —" Libby stopped. Hiram was already out the door.

"He'll fix it good as new," Gert said.

Libby looked toward the case clock. It was nearly six in the morning, and she had only two hours to get ready for opening. Florence would help when she arrived at seven thirty. Libby sent up a quick prayer of thanks that she'd put all the ledgers in the safe last night.

"If you could make me a list, I'd appreciate it," Ethan said. "You can do it later today when you have time. Put down anything that's missing from your inventory. And if you know it was in the fire heap, check it off. If you're not sure, and something was maybe stolen, let me know." He stood and walked around, peering under the tables and racks. He paused by a set of shelves that held blankets and linens. "Does this weapon belong to you?" He turned, holding Isaac's Colt pistol.

"Yes. It was my husband's. I brought it downstairs with me and left it there when I began fighting the fire."

Ethan brought it to the counter. "You'll want to put it back in a safe place before you open for business." He stood for a moment, looking down at the countertop. Then he looked up slowly. "Could you come here for a moment, please, ma'am?"

Libby walked over to stand beside him.

"Do you know how this got here?"

Libby looked down to where he pointed. Near the pistol on the otherwise bare countertop lay a penny.

CHAPTER 19

Ethan watched Libby's face as she looked down at the counter and spotted the coin.

"I suppose I could have dropped it there when I was putting the cash box away last night. You don't think the arsonist left it?" She reached for the penny.

Ethan touched her sleeve, and she stayed her hand.

"If you don't mind, I'd like to take it," he said. "I can give you another to replace it if your cash doesn't come out right."

Gert stood at Libby's elbow, staring at the coin. Her wide, gray blue eyes met his gaze. "You found a penny under Bert Thalen's body after he was killed."

"Yes." Ethan slid the coin off the countertop and tucked it into the watch pocket of his vest. He'd never owned a watch, but the penny would be safe there.

Hiram entered through the front door carrying a long board. Ethan looked it over. It was about the same width as the floorboards of the emporium. "You got more if this isn't enough?"

Hiram shrugged. "Thought I'd cut three short lengths off this. It ought to do."

"All right, I'll be with you as soon as I poke through the trash pile out back."

Gert stepped forward. "I'll show you where it is, Ethan. I'm sure Libby wants to straighten up the merchandise and start that list you asked her for. And maybe change her outfit before she opens for business."

Libby looked down at her rumpled and stained clothing. "If you don't mind, I'll do that next. Now that most of the filth is outside . . . although I suppose I'll be weeks getting rid of all the ash and dust." She looked around with a hopeless air.

"We'll help you," Hiram said softly.

"Thank you." Tears glistened in Libby's eyes. "I'd like to freshen up before Florence arrives." She turned and glided toward the staircase, hidden behind a partition that held tinware and kitchen utensils.

Ethan looked to Gert, and she pulled in a breath. "Come on. I'll show you the trash heap. You got gloves?"

He shook his head, and she picked up the pair Libby had discarded. "If these don't fit you, I'm sure she wouldn't mind if you took another pair from the store."

Ethan pulled them on and flexed his hands. "They're a little tight, but they'll do."

Gert stepped over the board. Hiram stood by the hardware table, sizing up Libby's selection of crowbars. Ethan followed her into the back room and paused.

"This is where she does her paperwork?"

Gert turned toward him. "Yes. And stores all the merchandise she hasn't put out yet."

"She's got a safe." He looked around for it.

"I think it's over there in the corner." Gert pointed beyond the desk and chair at the end of the room.

Ethan walked over and looked past the desk. A pile of wooden crates hid the corner from view. In the shadows of the window-less room, he could barely see. On the desk he spotted a fancy oil lamp.

"Mind lighting that lamp for me?"

Gert stepped to the desk, and he sidled around the stack of crates and ran his hand over the wall. As the glow from the lamp flared up, his hand touched cool metal. Gert came around the crates and held up the lamp.

"The safe looks fine," she said.

Ethan nodded. There was no evidence that anyone had tampered with it. So why had the arsonist broken into the store? Would they be able to tell if he'd stolen anything? Or had he just come to wreak havoc?

"Libby could have been killed this morning," Gert said softly.

His stomach lurched. "I thought of that. You don't think this lunatic's intention was to burn her alive, do you?"

"I don't know. He could have been more efficient, if that's what he wanted."

Ethan swung around to face her in the cramped space. "How?"

"He could have set the fire right at the bottom of the stairs so she couldn't come down. But no, he put it out in the open space in front of the counter, away from the walls. And he could have thrown more lard on it or dumped a couple tins of lamp oil. Down at the far end of the store, she's got at least a dozen cans of oil. He didn't even touch 'em. I only saw one lard pail in the pile that burned. It's like he wanted to make a lot of smoke and bother, but he wasn't intent on murder."

Ethan thought about that for a few seconds. "I think you're right. But that penny . . ."

"Yes. That's important, isn't it?"

He nodded slowly. "It must be. It's just like the other one."

Her eyes flared. "Exactly?"

"Yes. An 1866 Indian head cent. I saved the other one in a tin over at the jailhouse. I'll compare them, but I'm sure they're the same."

"He left you a message."

"Why do you say that? Whoever killed Bert couldn't have known at the time that I'd be the next sheriff."

Her brow furrowed as she puzzled over it. "Are we sure about that?"

Ethan caught his breath. "That's . . . reaching a little."

"I know, but —" She glanced over her shoulder. Ethan heard the sound of nails screeching as Hiram tore up the floorboards in the main room. "Just think for a minute. What if the mayor already had you in mind to replace Bert?"

"You're saying the mayor killed Bert?"

"No, I'm not saying that. But what if Cyrus did?"

"Cy Fennel? Trudy, are you loco?"

Her lower jaw dropped, and she stared at him. "What did you call me?"

Ethan gulped. "I'm sorry. I didn't mean you're loco." Why was she looking at him like that? He pulled off his hat and ran a hand through his hair. "Look, I'm sorry."

"You said that."

"Well, just forget about that, all right? We're talking about this criminal. There's no way he could have known. Even if the murderer was Cy Fennel — and I'm not saying it was, 'cause that's crazy — but even *if*, I still say there's no way he could know I'd take the job. Because I almost didn't."

"Why did you?"

He looked into her eyes and couldn't speak for a moment. The lump in his throat nearly choked off his breathing. He couldn't tell her he'd taken the badge because of her hopeful eyes. When had Gert-Trudy Dooley become the reason for the way he lived?

He broke the stare and let out a breath. "Look, right now we're talking about this fire, all right?"

"I thought we were talking about Bert's murder."

"No, *you* were talking about Bert's murder."

"Because of the penny."

Ethan shook his head. "Look, it's close in here with the smoke and the lamp and all. Let's go out back and look at that trash heap."

She set the lamp on Libby's desk and blew out the flame. "You know the same person did this as killed Bert."

"We don't have proof."

"The pennies are proof."

"No, they're not."

She stamped her foot and then scowled at him. "There's a connection."

"I'll give you that." He couldn't recall seeing her so worked up about anything, ever. The color in her cheeks and the spark in her eyes made his stomach gyrate, which rattled him more than finding the penny. He took her elbow and steered her toward the open back door. "Let's get outside where there's some fresh air."

The crisp morning breeze refreshed him better than a cool drink of water. Folks were stirring, and he could see Zach Harper, across three back lots and a field, walking toward his barn. Fergus was waking up to another day.

Ethan paused just outside the door and stooped to look at the latch and the jamb.

"Someone definitely tampered with this." He stuck his head back inside and squinted at the woodwork. Apparently Libby didn't use a bar on this door but trusted the brass lock. Her husband had probably installed it not too many years ago. "Let's look at the burnt stuff."

Gert walked ahead of him to a heap of smelly, charred refuse. She stooped and picked up a broom. The straws were coated in soot. "This is everything Libby and I hauled out. She didn't want to leave it in there, and I can't say as I blame her."

"No, me either." Ethan took the broom from her and used the handle to poke among the debris. He wished he could have seen it the way it was when Libby found it.

"They burned the new Bibles. That upset her." Gert's voice quavered, the first sign of vulnerability she'd shown. "We need to find out who did this, Ethan."

She looked up at him, and a tear shivered from the corner of her eye and streaked down her dirty cheek. He wanted to comfort her. Wanted to pull her into his arms so bad he could almost feel her head on his shoulder.

"Aw, Trudy."

She jerked her shoulders back. "Why did you call me that?" She stepped toward him with her hands clenched as though she would pummel him.

Ethan jumped back. "Hey, I'm sorry." He held up both hands, dropping the broomstick. How on earth had he let that slip out? "Your brother told me that your pa used to call you that." She stopped and considered his words, so he kept talking. "I guess I've been thinking on it some, about how it must have been when you were a girl. But I won't say it again, I promise."

Her lip twitched and she sniffed. "I don't . . . mind it."

"You don't?"

She shrugged. "Not so's you'd notice it."

"Oh. Well . . ." He studied her cautiously. Was she mad at him or not? Just because a woman said she wasn't upset didn't always mean it was true. He cleared his throat. "I'll do everything I can to find out who set the fire."

She nodded, staring down at the pile of refuse. "You can't deny that whoever did this was leaving a message. If not for you, then for someone."

"I'm not saying you're right, but who? What's the message, and who is it for?"

She bit her lower lip and shrugged. "I don't know what, but . . . for the town, maybe?"

CHAPTER 20

Tidying up the emporium and inventorying the merchandise proved time consuming, especially with constant interruptions from horrified patrons. News of Libby's misfortune had spread throughout the town, and it seemed everyone had to come in person to inquire about Mrs. Adams and see the damage. Most seemed disappointed that the industrious friends had helped Libby clean it all up and even replaced the burnt floorboards before the news got about.

"My oh my," Mrs. Walker wailed, surveying the clean new rectangle on the floor. "Why, Mrs. Adams might have burned to death if she hadn't woken up."

"That's right." Laura Storrey looked over the rearranged shelves. "Did she lose much merchandise? I hope that darling lavender silk I had my eye on didn't get burned."

"Let me help you look for it." Gert steered the woman toward the yard goods. Mrs.

Storrey bought six yards of the expensive material, which seemed none the worse for the smoke.

At the end of the day, Libby swayed on her feet as she closed up shop, and Gert determined that her friend must get some rest. That evening and the next morning, she gathered names of women from the shooting club who volunteered to give Libby a couple hours of help. Gert labored over her list the next morning, arranging it into a schedule. Myra helped her get the timetable to all the women.

Hiram presented the mayor's repaired rifle when she returned to fix lunch.

"Can you test this for me?" he asked. "I need to get it back to the mayor and then get over to the Bentons'."

Gert was more curious than annoyed at the interruption in her busy morning. Hiram rarely visited other homes. "What are you going over there for?"

"I told the parson I'd build him a stand to use until we get a proper pulpit made."

Gert put cotton in her ears, took the Winchester rifle out behind the house, and fired a half dozen rounds. When she finished, she saw Apphia coming up the path. "Here," she told her brother as she handed him the rifle. "Tell the mayor it shoots a little right of center. I expect he knows. Otherwise, it's fine. Now, I'm going over to help Libby. Mrs. Benton's going with me."

Hiram blinked at her. "No dinner?"

"On the back of the stove." She picked up the basket she'd packed to take with her and met Apphia at the back door. Together they stormed the emporium. Gert marched straight to Libby.

"You come upstairs with me for something to eat. Mrs. Benton will help Florence man the store for the next half hour. After that, we'll send Florence home for her dinner, and you shall have an hour's rest."

"Rest during the day?" Libby stared at her. "I can't do that."

"You can, and you will. We've got other ladies from the club coming in later, and we'll all take turnabout to help you mind the store and do any more cleaning and counting you need to do for the next couple of days. Annie Harper is bringing your supper over this evening at closing time."

Libby burst into tears. "Gert, I don't know what to say. You've been so good."

Startled, Gert patted her back awkwardly. "There now. Come on upstairs. You're worn to a stub."

Libby submitted after that, and Gert set out the stew and sourdough bread she'd brought over. For the first time, she sat down at Libby's kitchen table and ate lunch with her. She made sure Libby ate a full portion then tucked her into bed under the loveliest wedding ring quilt she'd ever seen. Libby's rooms above the emporium might have stood in a mansion. Had she brought the beautiful furnishings with her when she married Isaac, or had they ordered them one piece at a time over the years? Sometime when Libby wasn't exhausted, she'd ask.

Downstairs, Florence had shown Mrs. Benton the rudiments of adding a purchase to a customer's account, and Gert sent the girl home for her noon hour. She and Apphia did a brisk business.

After waiting on several townspeople and a couple of ranchers in succession, Gert caught her breath and looked around. They'd done all right, she and Apphia, though they were slow at locating some items people asked for. She'd gone to the right woman in time of crisis. The minister's slender, dark-haired wife carried on with stamina and dignity. At the moment, Apphia was talking to Milzie Peart over in the staples section. They appeared to be having a pleasant conversation.

Mr. Dyer came in just then.

"Well, Miss Dooley. I don't usually see

you here. Is Mrs. Adams all right? I heard she had some excitement yesterday."

"That she did, sir. She's fine, but she's taking a short rest. May I help you with something?"

"Maybe so. Miss Shepard needs sugar and potatoes. She says I'm not to bring home any punky ones."

Gert shrugged. "We'll do our best. You know how hard it is to get firm potatoes this time of year."

"I allow you're right. Just two or three months till we have a new crop though. I can hardly wait."

Gert smiled and took his basket from his hands. "This way, sir, and you can choose your own spuds if you wish."

While she and Ezra picked over the sprouting potatoes and chose the best for Bitsy's Sunday dinner crowd, Gert overheard a bit of Apphia's talk with Milzie.

"I do wish you'd come Monday after the shooting practice," she said. "We'll have tea, and you can tell me about your ranch."

" 'T'ain't much of a ranch," Milzie mumbled. "Since Frank died, 't'ain't much of anything. I put in a few vegetables though."

"Ah, you enjoy gardening. So do I."

Gert figured it was more a matter of

survival than a hobby for Milzie, but she said nothing. She silently applauded Apphia's courage in inviting the filthy old woman into her home. Maybe if all the women of the shooting club followed her example, they could influence Milzie to take better care of herself.

A few minutes later she took a broken candy stick from a jar on the counter and slipped it to Milzie. She was sure Libby wouldn't mind. Milzie shuffled out of the store with a gap-toothed smile.

On Monday the ladies gathered at Bert Thalen's ranch as usual. Milzie looked different when she arrived, and at first Gert couldn't figure out why. Then she realized the old woman had washed her tattered clothes. Her arms and face looked less dirt-encrusted, too, and Gert almost thought her hair was a shade lighter than she'd seen it before.

Of course. Today Milzie was invited to Apphia's for tea. Mrs. Benton had confided to Gert and Libby that she hoped she could convince Milzie to accept a gift of some new clothing. Gert wasn't sure the old woman would take new things outright and had suggested used items. After a moment's thought, Apphia had decided to offer her a

blouse she'd had for two years. Still serviceable, it showed a little fraying about the
cuffs. Libby had gleefully added a shawl that
had snagged on the wooden shelves, so that
it now had an imperfection. She'd entrusted
it to Apphia earlier.

"Tell Milzie I don't want to try to sell it,
since it's got that snag."

They'd decided that was enough for one
day. If things went well, the club members
could see that Milzie had a new skirt, shoes,
stockings, and underthings before fall. And
here she was, ready to go meekly home with
the impeccably groomed Mrs. Benton for
tea.

"I don't know how she lives all alone in
that cabin," Gert said, shaking her head.
She rummaged in Crinkles's saddlebag for
the three bullets she'd brought for Milzie.
She'd long since stopped expecting to be
repaid for them.

When their hour of practice ended, she
called the women all around her and praised
their orderliness and the improvement she'd
noted in their aims.

"I'd like to thank you all for your help
over the last few days," Libby said. "Things
are back to normal now, though we'll be
short of a few items in the store until Mr.

Runnels brings my next shipment from Boise."

Gert looked around at the sober faces. "Ladies, I've one more bit of business. As you know, there's been a rash of crimes in Fergus. Serious crimes. Murder, assault, arson. We've shown how we can support one another. I propose that we endeavor, as an entity, to help the sheriff foil the criminal who has been making mischief and striking in violence."

"What could we do?" asked Vashti. She looked almost wholesome today, without any cosmetics. The skirt she wore came down nearly to the tops of her smart tan boots.

"I'm thinking the biggest thing we can do is stay alert," Gert said. "Watch out for anything suspicious. And we could help prevent more crimes just by being watchful. We can look out for each other. Those in town can check in on one another during the day and the evening. Those outside town can call on each other more often to be sure no one's been attacked."

"And if something does happen, we can fetch the sheriff, like you did for Mrs. Adams the other day," Florence said.

"That's exactly what I mean. Let us help one another, especially the women who live alone or whose men are away a lot. Let's help each other stay safe."

Annie Harper began clapping, and the other women picked up the applause. Gert felt her face flush with the thrill of having an idea accepted and approved.

"Let's make a list then. Anyone willing to help out in ensuring safety for others, tell me and I will put down your name." The women crowded around, and Gert listed all their names but Milzie's. The old woman hung back, looking anxiously toward the westering sun now and then.

"We need to take this list to the sheriff and see if he can make use of our abilities," Gert said when she'd finished it.

"Would the sheriff be over to his house today, do you think?" Emmaline Landry asked.

"I passed him on the road on my way out here," said Bitsy, who had arrived a few minutes late.

"Then he's likely in town," Gert said. "Shall we go to him as a group? Those who live in town, I mean. I'm sure some of you ranch ladies need to get back home."

Milzie's frown grew more pronounced as they talked. Gert caught Mrs. Benton's eye.

"You'll excuse Mrs. Peart and me, won't you?" Apphia said. "We had made other plans for this afternoon, though we're more than willing to serve."

"Of course," Gert said, and Milzie perked up immediately. "And if you wish to ride back into town in the wagon with Mrs. Harper, she can drop you off right in front of your house."

Six of the fifteen women left for their scattered homes, and the rest rode their horses or the wagon back to town. Milzie smiled nearly all the way, swinging her legs off the back of the Harpers' wagon. At the new parsonage, Annie halted the horse, and Apphia hopped down.

"Here we are, Mrs. Peart." She reached up to help Milzie clamber down.

Gert waved to them. "Have a nice afternoon, ladies. We'll let you know what the sheriff says."

Annie flipped the reins, and the horse plodded on to the hitching rail in front of the jail. Gert jumped down and waited until Annie, Myra, Libby, Bitsy, Vashti, and Florence joined her. They were missing Goldie, who reportedly had taken to her bed with a catarrh, but otherwise, all the women who regularly attended had come to shoot today.

Gert smiled. "Ready?"

"Ready," they chorused.

She turned and led them up the boardwalk. If Ethan wasn't at the jail, she would feel pretty silly. They'd have to track him down. What if he was at the Nugget? Maybe Vashti or Bitsy would peek through the door to see. But he was more likely chewing the fat with Hiram.

Before they even reached the stoop in front of the jail, the door swung open. Ethan stood, tall, rugged, and flustered, in the doorway.

"Ladies! To what do I owe the honor?"

Gert cleared her throat. "Sheriff, we represent the Ladies' Shooting Club of Fergus, and we're here to offer our services in helping you catch the miscreant who is terrorizing our town and prevent further violence."

His eyebrows shot up. "Well, now." He looked them all over for a long moment then shifted his gaze back to Gert's face. "And what services does that entail?"

Gert gulped and took a step toward him. "We have some ideas. We also have a list of fourteen able-bodied women who can help in any capacity you see fit." She fished her list from her pocket and held it out to him.

Ethan leaned forward and took the paper from her. He perused it for a moment then looked up. "Would you like to come in, ladies? I don't have many chairs, but this seems like an idea worth discussing."

Gert couldn't hold back her grin as she glanced at the other women. Florence and Myra were grinning, too. Even Libby wore a restrained smile.

"I can see the sense of this," Ethan said a few minutes later. He'd let Annie Harper, as the eldest, have his chair and brought a stool and a short bench from somewhere in the shadows of the jail so four more women had seats. Vashti and Gert stood near the desk, and Gert had outlined her vague ideas of how the ladies could help.

"Thank you, Sheriff," she said. "We appreciate that you're taking us seriously."

"I can see that I'd be foolish not to." Ethan smiled. "Now, ladies, I know some of you have jobs, but if you're serious about this, your enthusiasm and energy can be assets to the town. I've noticed that several of the women on the list live a few miles outside town."

Gert nodded. "They couldn't do a lot, but they're willing to give a few hours a week."

"Good. Let's say Starr Tinen and her mother-in-law could check a couple of times a week on Mrs. Peart and the Robinsons — they're the last two places out the Mountain Road. That would be extremely helpful. I've pondered on how we'd know if one of the outlying ranches was attacked. I'd hate to think someone had trouble and no one knew about it."

"I've got an idea, Sheriff," Annie Harper said. "What if the Robinsons and Miz Peart had something like a flagpole where they could run up a signal? If the nearest neighbors could see their signal in the morning, they'd know the other folks were all right. But if there wasn't any flag flying, why then they'd know they needed to go and check on their neighbors."

"I like that idea," Libby said. "In fact, since the Paragon Emporium was attacked last week, I've wondered how I could get word out if I needed help again. I could hang a white towel out my bedchamber window each morning when I rose. Florence or Annie ought to be able to see it from their backyards."

"That's true," Florence said. "And if one morning I didn't see it, I'd run over to the store early to make sure you were all right."

Ethan nodded. "Good thinking, ladies. Let's set up pairs of women who can check on businesses in town. Look to see if windows or doors have been broken, for instance."

"Like my back door was broken in," Libby said ruefully.

"Exactly. They could check in on the elderly folks in town, too, to be sure they were all right," Ethan said. "And since the fire at the emporium, I've worried that someone is lurking about, waiting for a moment to do more harm where least expected. He might bother the school children on their way to and from the schoolhouse, for instance. If he wants to make mischief, there are plenty of opportunities."

Annie nodded. "It's a long walk to school for some. We could send two ladies in the morning to walk the children to school and have two more meet them when school's out. I'm sure their mothers would appreciate that."

"That's right. Of course, school will soon be out for the summer, but we could put this plan in motion until the term ends." Ethan looked at Gert and held up her list. "Would you help me work out the details, Miss Dooley? We can match up the pairs for their assignments, according to where the ladies live and the best times for them to carry out their duties."

"I'd be happy to." Gert felt her face flame, but none of the others seemed to notice. All were murmuring their approval and telling each other when their own most convenient hours to be on watch would fall. Gert met

Ethan's gaze. His dark eyes glittered, and his left eye twitched — almost a wink. His smile widened, and she found herself looking forward to working on the list with him. Perhaps over a piece of mince pie.

CHAPTER 21

Libby and Vashti waited outside the school-house for Miss Fennel to dismiss her class. They could hear the children reciting their lessons. Isabel's voice broke in as she spoke sharply to one of the Ingram boys. Vashti rolled her eyes skyward, and Libby smiled.

"I recall my school days with fondness, but something tells me this isn't Willie Ingram's favorite way to spend his time."

Vashti chuckled. "I never did more than three grades all told. We moved around so much, I never stayed in one place long enough to finish a reader."

Libby wondered how the girl had separated from her family and come to work at a saloon in an Idaho mining town gone bust. Vashti's enthusiasm for the shooting club had surprised her, and Bitsy had allowed her extra time off this afternoon to fulfill the duty Gert had assigned. Without her cosmetics and lurid costumes, Vashti might almost have passed for a schoolgirl herself. Libby doubted she was older than Florence Nash. The thought that wholesome girls like Florence and Myra Harper wound up working in saloons all over the country grieved her, but she had no idea what she could do to change that. Getting to know Bitsy and her girls through the shooting club had altered her attitude toward them.

The schoolhouse door burst open, and a handful of boys pounded down the steps. They paused and stared at the two women.

"Good afternoon, boys," Libby said. "We're here to see that you get home safely."

"Ha! That's a good one." Willie Ingram, his little brother, and Tollie Harper breezed by them and ran toward town. The girls and a couple of smaller boys emerged from the building at a more moderate pace.

Behind them, Isabel Fennel stopped in the doorway and eyed Libby and Vashti. "May I help you, ladies?"

"We've come to see the children home safely," Libby said.

Vashti nodded with vigor. "Sheriff Chapman assigned us this duty."

"What's that?" Isabel frowned and came down the steps.

Libby looked after the children, who had

gained the road and would soon be out of sight. "The Ladies' Shooting Club is taking on some civic duties, one of which is to ensure safety for the school children and women who live alone. Would you like us to walk you as far as your home?"

"No, thank you. That's not necessary." Isabel looked them over as though not quite sure what to do with them, especially Vashti. Libby wondered if she even recognized the saloon girl. Perhaps she was trying to place her.

"Well, your father's ranch is close by," Libby said. "If you're sure you don't want an escort, we'll go after the children."

"Thank you, I'll be fine." Isabel's upper lip rose into a little peak on the left side as she spoke, and she swept Vashti with a disapproving gaze.

So, she had catalogued the bar girl. Libby nodded and turned away.

" 'Bye," Vashti called and scurried after her, muttering.

"Did you say something?" Libby asked.

"I said, 'Fussy old bat.' "

"Oh!" Libby shot her a sideways glance. "We'd better hurry. The children are so far ahead of us, I'm afraid we won't do any good."

"We'd best tell their mothers what we're

doing, so they can tell the kiddies to wait for us tomorrow, no matter what that priggish old stick does," Vashti said.

"Yes," Libby said. "Er, I can inform the mothers."

"Can you? That's good, because I'll need to get ready for work soon."

Libby held up her skirts and kept pace with the saloon girl.

Milzie tried to hold the Hawken steady as she aimed, but her arms shook. Was it because the gun weighed so much, or because of the hunger that gnawed at her belly? The jackrabbit hopped a few steps farther. He blended in so well with the low brush that she could barely see him.

She braced herself and held her breath, lining the sights up with the ornery critter. But he hopped again. Now or never. He'd soon be out of sight. Milzie pulled the trigger and fell back from the recoil.

"Oof." She sat up, rubbing her shoulder. Must have forgotten to hug the stock up close like Gert had shown her. The rifle lay a couple of feet away. She hauled herself shakily to her feet and walked over to where the rabbit had been. Clean missed it. No surprise.

Oh well. According to Gert, if she'd hit it

with this load, she'd likely have blown it to bits anyway. She'd have been lucky to find any bits to put in her stew pot. She shook her head and trudged back toward where she'd stood when she fired. Now, where'd the Hawken got to? It was right here, wasn't it?

She peered all around at the grass and shrubbery. Nothing. She turned and looked toward where she'd seen the rabbit. Maybe she was a few steps this way. . . . Or had she stood farther away?

After twenty minutes, nearly ready to give up the search, she stepped on the gun's stock. The barrel lay all but invisible in the grass. Exhausted, she crumpled in a heap beside it. Better rest awhile before she tried to tote it home. Must be near a mile. And better stick to foraging. At the end of a day's picking through trash piles, she'd have more to show than she had today.

Gert had just hung up her dishpan after doing Tuesday's supper dishes when a frantic pounding came at the front door. Her pulse thudded. She glanced at Hiram, who sat at the table. He looked up from the new Bible she'd bought before the fire at the emporium.

"Who can that be?" she asked.

Hiram only raised his eyebrows. Gert wiped her hands on her apron and hurried across the sitting room to the seldom-used front door. She opened it, and Isabel Fennel all but fell in. Gert seized her arm to steady her. The schoolteacher stared at her, gulping in quick, shallow breaths.

"Isabel. Come in. Is something wrong?"

"I'm frightened."

Isabel's pale blue eyes looked bigger than usual in her pinched face. Her hairdo showed the wind had been at work during her short walk to town, and her shawl lay askew over her shoulders.

"Come sit down," Gert said. "What's happened?"

Isabel took the offered chair and put one hand to her brow. "Nothing, really. I shouldn't have come." She stirred as though to rise. "Forgive me for intruding."

"You're fine." Gert laid her hand lightly on Isabel's shoulder. Isabel had recovered herself somewhat and had thought better of blurting out her troubles. "I was about to make myself a cup of tea. Would you join me? My mother always made tea when things seemed a bit out of kilter."

"Well . . ." Isabel looked around the dim room toward the kitchen, where the glowing lamp illuminated Hiram at the table. "I

283

don't want to disturb you and your brother. I saw your light. . . ."

"You're most welcome, and you won't disturb us." Gert lit the small lamp on the side table and hurried to the kitchen before Isabel could change her mind. Her heart still pounded from the jolt of Isabel's interruption as she took down two teacups. The kettle steamed on the stove, and she quickly measured loose tea into the pierced tin ball and lowered it into her plain brown teapot.

Hiram watched her in silence for a moment then bent his head over the Bible. How could he be so calm when a woman who had never entered their home before came pounding on their door? That seemed to happen a lot lately — maybe he'd acclimated to it better than she had. Gert took a deep breath and fixed a tray with two cups, the teapot, and the sugar bowl. If Isabel asked for milk, she'd have to go out to the root cellar.

She carried the tray carefully to the sitting room and nudged aside a few of Hiram's tools so she could set her burden down on the bench beneath the window facing the street. "Do you take sugar?"

"No, thank you."

Gert hesitated but knew it would be impolite not to ask. "Milk? I have some —"

"Just black, please," Isabel said.

Gert exhaled and sat down opposite her with a smile. "Here you go. Careful, it's very hot."

Isabel raised her cup, blew on the surface of the liquid, and took the tiniest of sips. "Thank you."

"Now, tell me." Gert waited, wondering what had brought Isabel here. Cyrus Fennel's daughter had never sought out either of the Dooleys for company, though she was about Hiram's age. So far as Gert knew, she hadn't befriended Violet either, but preferred solitude or the company of the older women in town. She must have had a terrible fright to come here for refuge.

"I . . . I walked into town this evening looking for my father."

"Oh." Gert sipped her tea to cover her confusion. Apparently Cyrus hadn't shown up for supper at the ranch, which lay outside town, barely half a mile beyond the Nugget Saloon. "Did you look in the stagecoach office?"

"Yes, I went there first." Isabel swallowed and looked away. "He wasn't there. His office door wasn't locked, but . . ."

Gert nodded. She could guess where Cyrus was, but she didn't like to say it.

"I . . ." Isabel cleared her throat. "I

thought I'd stop at the emporium, but apparently I was a few minutes too late, and Mrs. Adams had just closed. As I came back along the boardwalk past the alley . . ."

"Yes?"

"There was a man in there. In the alley, I mean."

Gert put her cup down. "Just . . . loitering, or walking through the alley?"

"As I walked by, I noticed him leaning against the wall of Papa's office. He was in the dark, and I couldn't see his face, but he frightened me." Isabel shuddered.

"Perhaps he was waiting for your father to come back." Yet if the office was unlocked, why not wait for Mr. Fennel inside? It did seem odd. And Libby used that alley often to get from her back door to the street. What if the man was watching the emporium? Waiting for the emporium's lights to flicker out and Libby's apartment lights above to come on? There was a small window on that side in Libby's kitchen, Gert was sure. She'd seen it the day after the fire, when she'd eaten lunch with Libby. It overlooked the low roof and false front of the Wells Fargo building. The idea caused her pulse to take off again, though Hiram had repaired the back door of the emporium and installed a new lock and a sturdy bar as well.

Isabel leaned back in the chair, curling her fingers around her teacup. "I didn't like to walk all the way home alone. I thought of going to the Walkers', but I'd have had to pass the alley again, and . . . well, I looked across the street and saw your light."

"I'm glad you did," Gert said. "Isabel, you're welcome here anytime. And if you ever feel uneasy to be alone, I hope you will call on me or another of the shooting club women. We want to make sure all the women in this town feel safe."

Isabel took a sip of her tea and swallowed before she met Gert's gaze again. "Yes, Libby Adams and . . . and a girl came to the schoolhouse yesterday and again this afternoon to see the children home. Will they come every day?"

"Someone from the club will come all week, morning and afternoon."

"Thank you. Perhaps I shall accept the offer of walking with them tomorrow. Of course, school recesses on Friday for a month's vacation."

Gert nodded. "We'll come anytime you need us. The sheriff has approved our schedule of checking on people in pairs. If we can help you in any way . . ."

In the kitchen, Hiram's chair scraped the floor softly, and a moment later he stood in the doorway.

"Would you like me to fetch your pa, Miss Fennel?"

Isabel turned her head and stared at him. Gert suppressed a smile. She could almost hear her thoughts — *He talks!*

"I . . ."

"It's no trouble," Hiram said.

"I'm not sure where you'll find him." She looked down at the rug Gert had braided during her first long winter in Idaho Territory.

"This town's not very big. I'll find him."

Gert considered jumping up and telling him how Bitsy had revealed Cyrus's defection to the Nugget during the past few weeks but thought better of it. Hiram probably knew that, seeing as how Ethan stopped in nearly every day and told her brother all his official business.

Hiram went silently out the back door. Stillness settled over the house. Gert sipped her tea and cast about for a new topic.

"This shooting society," Isabel said at last. "Can just . . . anyone . . . join?"

Gert pulled in a sharp breath. Did that question have a right answer? After all, the club's members included several saloon girls and the new minister's wife; elegant Libby and slatternly Milzie. "We're open to just about any female."

"And do the women supply their own firearms?"

"Yes." They sat in silence for a long moment, and Gert scarcely dared breathe. Was Isabel interested in joining their ranks, or was she simply probing into something she found incomprehensible?

"I believe I should like to come next week after school is out."

Gert exhaled and reached deep for a smile. "You would be most welcome."

"I doubt Papa will approve." Isabel frowned and set her cup on the side table. "I could buy a small gun, I daresay. They can't be too expensive. And I've saved the biggest portion of my salary for more than ten years."

"I'm sure Mrs. Adams can help you find something suitable," Gert murmured. Indeed, Libby had educated herself over the past few weeks, devouring catalogs from gun manufacturers. She'd told Gert ruefully that she had to limit herself to make sure she didn't spend more time reading up on guns than she did studying the scriptures before bedtime.

Isabel met her gaze. "And do you instruct those who've never . . ."

"Yes, ma'am. We're bringing all the ladies

along to where they feel confident in handling their weapons."

"If you're sure no one will object, then I'll look forward to next Monday."

"Oh, absolutely certain. We meet at —"

The back door burst open and Cyrus Fennel strode through the kitchen.

"Isabel! What's the meaning of this?"

CHAPTER 22

Cyrus could scarcely believe that his daughter sat in Gert Dooley's parlor.

"I was worried about you, Papa." Isabel stood to face him.

Guilt and annoyance struggled inside him, and annoyance won. After all, Isabel had gone crying for help to the woman who had set out to make a fool of him. Gert had even gotten the minister to speak out in favor of the shooting club from the pulpit. Cyrus gritted his teeth and managed to keep his voice down. "It wasn't my intention to make you fret. We had some trouble with the harness on the stagecoach team this afternoon, and after I'd done with that, I stepped out to talk to someone."

"Is your business finished now?" Isabel asked. "I'm ready to go home, but it's dark now, and I don't wish to walk alone."

Was she trembling? Cyrus scowled at her. "I need to lock up the office."

Gert stepped forward. "Isabel saw a man hanging around the alley beside your office."

"So your brother told me. I'll check to make sure no one's lingering about."

Gert looked past him, and Cyrus realized Hiram had come in behind him and stood silently in the corner. The man was altogether too sneaky.

"Hiram, we should go check on Mrs. Adams," Gert said. "After what happened last week, I don't like the thought of a man loitering about beneath her windows when she's alone."

Hiram nodded.

"Well, Isabel, gather your things, and we'll head out." Cyrus looked at Gert and forced himself to do the right thing. "Thank you for helping her, Miss Dooley. And if you'd like, Isabel and I can check on Mrs. Adams."

"Yes," Isabel said, "and I'll tell her that I'll come around Saturday and look at those handguns she has for sale."

"What did you say?" Cyrus reared back and stared at his daughter.

"I'm joining Miss Dooley's shooting club, Papa. If you're going to be out evenings all the time, I need to know how to handle a gun."

Cyrus swung his arm back. "How dare —"

Gert pushed between them. "It's not *my* club. All the ladies together have made it a success, and now we're working with the sheriff to keep the town a little safer. To protect women and children from *violence.*" She spit out the last word and glared at him.

Cyrus's head spun. He hadn't had *that* much to drink tonight, but the room seemed to sway nonetheless. "Isabel!" He looked around and focused on her with difficulty. "I forbid you to join that society."

Isabel straightened her shoulders. "Papa, you always used to come home in the evening. Since Mama died, you've stayed in town a couple of evenings a week. Fine. But if you're going to make the Nugget your regular stopping place all week long and leave me alone at the ranch, then I need a way to protect myself. I will go to the shooting club."

She wrapped her shawl closer and stepped toward the front door. Cyrus's head felt as though it would explode. Never had his daughter defied him. Never! She'd grown from a sweet little girl into an awkward, plain young woman, and now suddenly she was more than thirty years old and a virago bent on humiliating him. No wonder she'd never had any serious suitors.

Isabel stepped toward the door, and Hiram scooted around to open it.

"Come, Papa," she said over her shoulder. "We'd best get over to the office and lock it up." She looked back at Gert. "And we'll go around and knock on Mrs. Adams's back door. Thank you for the tea."

"You're welcome," Gert replied. "I expect I'll see you both in church."

Cyrus stumbled down the front steps and followed Isabel toward the street, fuming. A dozen retorts fluttered into his foggy brain, but when he turned to look back, Hiram had closed the door.

"I didn't mean to call her Trudy, but it slipped out, and she got all ruffled and feisty." Ethan leaned his crossed arms on the fence of Hiram's corral. The moon shone down on Crinkles, Hoss, and Scout as they lazily picked mouthfuls of hay from the pile Hiram had thrown out for them.

"She doesn't seem mad at you now," Hiram noted, sticking a straw in the corner of his mouth.

"No, she got over it quick. I think it surprised her, and I promised I'd never say it again, but I need to be careful."

"How's that?" Hiram's gray blue eyes showed just beneath his hat brim.

"So's she won't get mad again."

"Huh."

Ethan loved Friday nights in June. The warm breeze flowed over them. The town lay peaceful, though he'd stroll around to the Nugget and the Spur & Saddle in an hour or so, just to make sure things stayed calm. Behind them, Gert clattered about in the kitchen, washing up the supper dishes.

"I sort of started thinking about her as Trudy." Ethan put one foot up on the bottom rail of the fence and waited for Hiram to comment. When his friend remained silent, chewing his straw and watching the horses, he added, "Shouldn't have done that. Now it's getting hard to think of her as Gert, and when I talk to her, I want to say Trudy."

"My fault."

"No, it's not."

"Shouldn't have told you."

Ethan sighed. "I've known you both a long time."

Hiram grunted.

"And sometimes I thought how hard she has it and how she ought to have things a little easier. Face it: life's hard on a woman out here. They work all the time, and for what? A lot of sorrow for most of 'em."

Hiram pushed his hat back and looked

over at him. "That why you never got married? 'Cause you didn't want to offer a woman a life of hard work and little to show for it?"

Ethan eyed him in surprise. Hiram seldom asked personal questions. "Well . . ."

His friend shrugged and looked away. "We're talking about my little sister."

"Are we?" Ethan asked.

"I thought we were."

Ethan considered that. Was this entire conversation about Trudy? He'd thought they were talking about frontier women in general, with Trudy as an example.

Gert. He meant Gert.

"I s'pose it is, partly. And partly because I never . . ."

Hiram swung around and looked at him with his eyebrows arched.

"I never felt worthy," Ethan said.

Hiram settled back down against the fence again, chewing and looking. Finally he threw the straw aside. "How's that?"

"Well . . . when a man offers a woman marriage, he's offering her his name and his property and his reputation."

"At least."

Ethan nodded. They agreed on that. Hiram had given the whole package to Violet.

"So he'd want to be sure he could offer something worthwhile. And . . . well, I don't feel I've got it."

Hiram sighed. "Are we talking about Gert now, or are you just philosophizing about what a crackbrained cowpoke you are?"

Ethan stood up straight. "Aw, Hi, I never thought seriously about . . . No. No, I'm not talking about Tru— about Gert. Just, you know, life in the territory."

"All right then. Just checking. Because if you were getting all addlepated over Trudy —"

"Gert. Her name is Gert."

"Right. But if you *were* getting addlepated over her, she'd be Trudy to you, wouldn't she?"

Ethan hesitated only an instant. "Fair enough."

Hiram nodded. "So. You're saying you're no better than a dirt clod, so far as your prospects for being a husband."

"That about sums it up."

"I couldn't agree more, but I'm afraid our reasons would be different."

"What's that supposed to mean?"

Hiram shook his head. "Tell me why you're disqualified from settling down and being a family man, and don't give me this 'hard life for women' malarkey. Their lives will be hard enough out here, whether you marry one of 'em or not."

"That's true, I guess." Ethan glanced toward the kitchen door. He could sure use a cup of coffee right about now, but this wasn't a conversation to have where Trudy could hear. Or Gert. Either one of them. He shook his head to clear it. "When I went away with the militia, I was young and idealistic. I was set to protect the settlers and save the territory. And to put those Indians on the reservation and make 'em stay there."

Hiram gazed off over the corral, but Ethan could tell he was listening.

"You know, my pappy tried to tell me there'd be days I wished I didn't go. Hi, there was things that happened. . . . I get all worked up just thinking about it, all this time later."

"Some things never get better."

"You got that right. But I'm telling you, if I'da known! The first skirmish I was in, over by Silver City — that went all right. I don't know as I even shot any Indians. I kept loading and firing, and . . . well, after a while, we'd won. But later on, after the excitement died down and we got out into the hills, chasing after them and half freezing to death and the other half starving, it wasn't nearly so palatable. The Sheepeaters were the worst. It was war, and I knew that meant there'd be some bloodshed, but it's a whole lot different when you get pinned down on a mountainside and the Indians set fire to the mountain below you."

"You never told me that."

Ethan shook his head. "We clawed our way out, but it's something you never forget. And it didn't make us feel like showing mercy when we finally caught up to 'em." Ethan pulled his hat off and threw it on the ground. He was shaking all over, even though it was warm. "Some things just ain't right, no matter which side you're on."

"I'm sorry, Eth. I saw a big change in you when you came back, and I knew you took it hard, but . . ."

Ethan let out a long, slow breath and stooped to retrieve his hat. "Is something wrong with me to feel so strong about it seven years later?"

"No. There's nothing wrong with you." Hiram's hand came down on his shoulder. "I expect you've gone before the Lord about all that."

"Many, many times."

"Well . . ." Hiram sighed. "If you did anything wrong, He's forgiven you. You do know that?"

"Yeah. I guess."

"God doesn't lie. He says He'll forgive us. He does."

Ethan nodded. "I've just felt so . . . I don't know. . . . Not just dirty. Corrupted. It wouldn't be fitting to tell a woman about the things I saw and did, but how can you live with another person and not tell them about things you think about so often?"

Hiram leaned on the fence again and spoke slowly. "I'm not saying it's a small thing, but if that's what's kept you from thinking of having a family . . . well, the right woman would understand and over-look the past, particularly knowing you'd confessed to the Lord."

"I s'pose."

"Oh, she would," Hiram said.

Ethan got the feeling he wasn't talking about a hypothetical right woman.

"Well," he said. They stood in silence for a moment.

The back door of the house opened, and Trudy called, "Hey, you two, your coffee's like to go bitter it's been simmering so long."

Hiram nudged him, and they walked toward the house together.

CHAPTER 23

"Thank you for going with me." Apphia Benton handled the reins capably as Gert settled onto the wagon seat beside her.

"I missed Milzie, too, at the club on Thursday. I hope someone's checked in on her, but I'm afraid we have to communicate in person until we all get telephones out here." Gert puffed out a breath.

"You told me she's been faithful at the meetings," Apphia said.

"Perfectly. I believe it's been good for her — and the rest of us, too. A lot of the members never see another woman for weeks at a time."

At the end of Main Street, Apphia clucked to the horse. The bay gelding loaned to them by Griffin Bane stepped out in a smart trot. Gert looked up at the sun. They'd be back in town before noon, and she could do her usual Saturday cleaning.

"I haven't been all the way out this road

since last fall. It's looking dry already, and we've barely passed the summer solstice."

"Yes, it *has* been dry," Apphia said. "I wondered if you usually have more rain this time of year."

"Some years." Gert pointed to a low house nestled between the brown hills. "That's the Landrys' place. You know Emmaline."

"Yes. Her whole family came to services last Sunday. I was so pleased."

"It surprised me, too. I didn't expect Micah to bring them."

"Well, I hope to get Milzie into church as well," Apphia said. "We had such a good visit on Monday. But then she didn't come Thursday. . . ."

Gert eyed her carefully. Could she have truly enjoyed serving tea to Milzie? Just the thought of inviting Milzie inside the Dooley house made her shudder. The smell would take as long to get rid of as the smoke stench in the emporium. Gert's limited acquaintance with the Bentons had raised her opinion of the clergy. Both Apphia and her husband seemed to have tender hearts toward the poor and the needy.

"I worry about her, too." Though her own concern might not be so pure-hearted as Apphia's, Gert spoke sincerely. She'd actually missed Milzie's snaggletoothed smile, and the three charges she'd prepared for the Hawken Thursday morning still rested in her saddlebag. "That's the Robinsons' house," she said a few minutes later. "I see Lyman out working his garden. Do you want to stop?"

"Perhaps on the way home. I confess I'm anxious about Milzie."

"That's fine." Gert waved to Mr. Robinson. He lifted his head as the wagon passed and waved his hat.

"How old are they?" Apphia asked.

"Both in their sixties, I'd say. They have a wagon and a mule, but the trip into town is a major undertaking for them. I don't know as they'd do it on a day they couldn't shop, too."

"That's a major drawback in the congregation. The parishioners are so scattered. My husband and I have tried to get around to all those who've come to services so far, but we've several ranches to visit yet."

"Milzie's is the last one out here," Gert said. "It's around that bluff, probably a good half mile from the Robinsons'. Maybe a mile. And they can't see each other's houses, so I don't know as the flagpole idea would work too well for Milzie. We couldn't expect her to climb up the hill every morning. Although her husband's mine is above the cabin."

"She told me about Frank's passing." Apphia shook her head. "I'm not sure how that woman has survived the years alone out here."

They rounded the hill that stuck out, blocking their view, and Gert looked forward, seeking the roofline of the cabin. Something didn't look quite right. She caught her breath and seized Apphia's wrist.

"What is it?" Apphia asked.

"Hurry. Her cabin's flat."

The horse trotted into what should have been the dooryard, but the only welcome they received was the view of a charred heap of ruins where the Pearts' modest home had stood for more than twenty years.

Apphia held the reins while Gert climbed down from the wagon and walked over to the burned-out cabin. Tears filled her eyes and choked her. How could she not have realized something was horribly wrong?

She stumbled back to the wagon and looked up at Apphia through stinging tears. "This isn't new. It's been awhile."

"But . . . where has she been living?"

"I don't know. Let's tie the horse and look around."

They walked slowly about the site of the cabin.

"She's started a little garden," Apphia said, stooping to pull a clump of grass from a crooked row of peas.

Gert spotted the root cellar, but it was empty. She turned slowly, looking over the valley. Apphia walked back to the ruins, shouting, "Milzie!"

"The mine," Gert called. Apphia turned toward her with her lovely dark eyebrows arched. "Up there." Gert pointed to the cave opening a short way along the hillside. Apphia walked quickly to join her.

"Do you think she could be in there?"

"Maybe. We should check. Franklin tried to mine it, but there wasn't much in these hills. I think he took a little gold out of the creek — that's what they lived on — but not the hillside."

They toiled up the path to the dark cave entrance.

"This would be a difficult walk for Milzie." Apphia turned to look back. "When she comes into town, does she walk all that way?"

"I expect so, unless she catches a ride with the Robinsons."

"It would take her a couple of hours to walk that far."

Gert nodded. "She shouldn't be out here alone. Especially with no house. I wonder when that happened."

When they'd approached to within two yards of the cave entrance, she stopped.

"Milzie? Are you in there?"

The wind ruffled her hair, but no one answered.

Gert stepped forward, her heart racing. "I hope there aren't any critters in there." She and Apphia stood in the opening, squinting into the darkness. "Look." Gert stepped into the cave and pointed to a heap of cloth on the floor.

"Is that a blanket?" Apphia asked.

"I think it's Franklin's old wool coat she wears in the winter." Gert looked around, spotting a few other items. "There's a lantern." She took it down and checked the reservoir. "No oil."

"Here's a candle stub." Apphia picked it up from a rude shelf between two framing members against the rock wall.

"I don't see any matches." Gert looked closely at the shelf. "If we come calling again, we'd best bring some, and some lamp oil or a few more candles."

"Do you really think she's living in this cave, poor soul?" Apphia's face softened as she took in the meagerness of Milzie's existence.

"She must be." Gert fingered the small

items on the shelf. "I wonder if she'd let us move her into town. She's so independent."

"But she's been accepting small gestures from the club members." Apphia opened her crocheted handbag. "I don't suppose we should be in here without her permission. I'll leave the gingerbread I brought for her." She took out a small parcel wrapped in a napkin and laid it on top of the coat.

"I hope animals don't get it before Milzie does." Gert spotted a covered crock on the floor and dragged it to the opening, where she could see its contents. She lifted the lid and sniffed the mass inside.

"What is that?" Apphia leaned closer.

"She's fixed a batch of camas root. Not much of that grows around here. She must have found a patch down by the river." Gert put the lid back and replaced the crock. "It's good nourishment, I guess. The Indians set a lot of store by it. That may be helping Milzie keep from starving."

"Poor thing. The town ought to do something. Do you suppose she *would* let us move her?"

Gert stared at her. "Well, ma'am, I don't know. And I can't think where you'd put her. You don't really have room in your little house, and . . ." She let her words trail off but couldn't repress a shudder. "I do feel sorry for her."

"Maybe the Robinsons could tell us when the cabin burned." Apphia pulled her shawl around her.

Gert took a last look around. "At least we know she's not in here now. But where is she?"

Milzie took her time Saturday morning, leaning on her stick as she walked across country toward town before the sun got hot. She stopped by the Higginses' cabin. Nealy and Clem weren't around, so she took a drink from their well and poked around the yard a little. They wouldn't miss the egg she took when they had at least three more that she left untouched in the chicken pen.

At the Landrys', she gathered the courage to knock at the back door. Emmaline opened it and promptly greeted her.

"Well, good morning, Milzie. Would you like a slice of corn cake? We've some left from breakfast."

Would she! After thanking the donor and devouring the food, Milzie ambled on until she was less than a mile from town. By then, her old legs didn't want to go any farther. She found a thicket to curl up in where she wouldn't be readily seen if anyone passed by. A good nap used up several hours. She awoke when a horse fly landed on her nose. The sun was high overhead, and she felt lazy. But she needed to get her stiff bones moving if she wanted to complete a foray into town and get home before dark.

Milzie knew every dump in Fergus. The trash heaps on the outskirts of town rewarded her.

At the pile belonging to the Spur & Saddle, she picked a large tin can to aid in her cooking and put it in her sack. A china cup with the handle broken clean off. Next, she found a good-sized shard of a broken looking glass. One of Bitsy's girls must be in for some bad luck. She frowned as she looked at her partial reflection. With a shrug, she wrapped the glass in a sheet of newspaper and stuck it into her bag.

She made her way down the back side of Main Street and paused behind the Dooleys' house. The gunsmith puttered about the place, but she saw no sign of Gert. Too bad. Milzie liked Gert, and she had a light touch with biscuits.

At the emporium, she had better fortune. Miz Adams greeted her with a smile.

"Well, Milzie, how are you? We missed you on Thursday."

"Had the grippe."

"Oh? I'm sorry to hear that. I hope you're

over it now."

"Middlin'." The truth was, clouds had rolled in on Thursday, and Milzie hadn't wanted to risk being caught several miles from home in a downpour. But that wouldn't sound like a very good reason to miss the shooting club.

Another customer entered the store. "Excuse me, won't you?" Libby asked. "Make sure you see me before you leave. I've got a little something for you."

Milzie wandered about the store for a good twenty minutes. Miz Adams had gotten in enough new bolts of cloth to cover a tabletop. Milzie surreptitiously ran her hand over them. The soft nap of the corduroy pleased her. Franklin liked corduroy pants in cold weather. They didn't itch like wool. It was too hot for summer, but wouldn't she love a skirt from that brown bolt for fall? Likely women didn't make skirts from corduroy though.

The flannels were even softer. She wanted to put her face right down and brush her cheek against the fabric.

"May I help you, Mrs. Peart?" Florence Nash, the red-haired girl, stood right next to her.

"You jumped me," Milzie said.

"I'm sorry."

Milzie looked toward the counter. Libby was handing a wrapped parcel to Oscar Runnels. No one else waited for her to tot up an order. Milzie ignored Florence and shuffled toward her.

"Oh, Milzie, I haven't forgotten you." Libby smiled again. She sure had a pretty smile. Her teeth were just as white as the bleached muslin bolts. She ducked down behind the counter for a minute then stood again. "I've been saving these for you." She placed a pair of knit stockings on the counter. "They came in mismatched. Can you imagine? See how one's a little larger than the other? I can't sell them like that. Could you use them by any chance?"

"Surely." Milzie reached out a shaky hand. Soft, whole stockings. "Thankee, ma'am."

Libby hesitated and looked about the store. "You know, it's time when I like to sit down for a minute. There aren't many customers, and Florence can look after things for a bit. Would you like to have a little refreshment with me in the back room?"

Milzie could scarcely believe it. Since joining the shooting club, she'd received invitations from the cleanest, nicest women in town — not to say the richest, necessarily, though Libby Adams probably qualified there — but some of the best. Tea with the minister's wife on Monday had nearly been enough to lure her into church. Hot tea with sugar and cream, little quarter sandwiches, boiled eggs, and cookies so small it took four to make a mouthful. Her mouth watered just thinking about it.

In the storage room, Libby let Milzie sit in the big chair by her desk. She took a cut glass bottle and two tumblers from a cupboard and poured each glass half full of red liquid. Milzie stared at the lovely swirling beverage.

"This is raspberry shrub." Libby smiled again. "It's my grandmother's recipe. I try to get enough berries every summer to make a good batch."

"It won't be long before the berries come on," Milzie said with what she hoped passed for a sage nod.

"That's right. This is my last bottle from last year." Libby sat down on a stool nearby and raised her glass to her lips.

Milzie lifted hers and smelled the liquid. It surely did smell of fresh raspberries. Her stomach clutched. Emmaline's corn cake was long gone. She took a sip. The sharp juice, sweetened, but not too much, slid down slicker than a greased eel. No fermentation. Miz Adams wouldn't offer anything like that, of course. Milzie gulped the rest and lowered her glass with a sigh. Libby's glass was still nearly as full as when she'd started.

"That's mighty pleasin'. Thankee."

Libby kept smiling but didn't offer more. "So you're feeling well now?"

"I am. You can expect to see me on Monday."

"Good." Libby stood in a swirl of challis skirts and rustling cotton petticoats. "Now, Milzie, I've put aside a few more things. Don't take them if you don't want to, but if you can use them . . ." She opened the cupboard again, put the ornate bottle away, and brought out a couple of tins. "A can of oysters and one of pears. Can you use those?"

"Oh yes, ma'am." Milzie opened her capacious sack, and the cans disappeared inside. "I do thank you."

Libby nodded. "You're welcome. I need to get back to the store now, but we've had a good visit today."

"Yes, yes." Clearly the hostess expected her to precede her back into the emporium, so Milzie went.

"Good day, Milzie," Libby said when they reached the store.

"Good day to you." Mrs. Walker was looking over the housewares, and she watched critically. Milzie made a deep bow to Libby. "I shall see you on Monday." She turned, chuckling, and walked as steadily as her tired old bones would allow toward the front door. Mrs. Walker's horrified expression was worth the aching feet she'd have tonight.

She made her way down the boardwalk, uncertain where to go next. Should she head for home? Her sack would grow heavy, and she might need to rest along the way. Maybe she would take a rest right now. She slid between weathered buildings and found a spot behind the smithy where she could lean against the back wall. Inside, the blacksmith was working at his forge. She liked to hear the *whoosh* of the bellows and the *cling-cling* of the hammer. She leaned back and closed her eyes. So far, she'd had a good day.

Sometime later, she awoke. The blacksmith had stopped working. A horse nickered, and she looked toward the back of the livery. The big, bearded man came out of the barn, leading a solid chestnut horse. He opened a gate and released the horse into a paddock with three others. The stagecoach must have come in.

She looked up at the sky. The sun would

set soon. She'd best get going. Already she doubted she'd be home before dark, but that didn't worry her much. The moon would be near full tonight, and the air would be cooler once the sun was down. She picked up her sack and headed back to Main Street.

As she passed one building, an open door drew her. It was an office. She looked up at the sign. Of course. Wells Fargo. This must be where Cyrus Fennel conducted his business. The coach was nowhere in sight. She peeked inside. A desk, shelves and cupboards, and a man crouched behind the desk, as though taking something from a low drawer.

She didn't care for Fennel, but he was rich. Maybe he would give her something out of respect for Frank, God rest his soul. Everyone else had been kind today. Why not see if the richest man in town felt generous?

She stepped forward. "Evening, Mr. —"

He looked up suddenly. Cold, angry eyes glittered in the dimness. The face beneath the hat brim wasn't right. Who was he? He stood, and she thought she knew, though why he should be in here . . . Maybe he worked for Fennel now.

"You!" He stepped around the desk toward her.

His harsh voice frightened her, and she backed toward the door. She fetched up against a wall instead, beside a small box stove.

Suddenly the silhouette of his hat and something about his nose sparked a memory. "You came out of the jailhouse the night Bert Thalen was killed."

His eyes narrowed, and he advanced toward her, his lips curled in a snarl. "You meddling old woman!" He reached for her.

Milzie tried to duck past him, but she was too slow, and he had her cornered between the stove and the wall. She dropped her sack of plunder and held her stout walking stick with both hands. Why was he angry with her?

He snatched the stick and tossed it aside as thought it were a twig. As his hands closed about her throat, she groped for something else — anything.

She grasped a poker and swung it up. He grabbed it and wrestled her for it. She stared into his eyes as they both stood clutching the sooty poker. He gritted his teeth.

"You should have stayed home, old woman."

He yanked the poker from her. Milzie shrank back against the wall and raised her hands before her face.

CHAPTER 24

Cyrus polished off his second whiskey and shook his head as Ted Hire raised the bottle to refill his glass.

"Not tonight, Ted. I'd better get on home, or Isabel will be beating the bushes for me." The Nugget was filling up anyway, and he didn't like to stay there on a Saturday evening. The noise at the saloon always mounted steadily after the sun went down. He'd rather go home and settle down in his comfortable chair before the fireplace. "I'll take a bottle of that good whiskey with me though."

As Ted bent to retrieve a fresh bottle, Cyrus pulled out his wallet. He settled his account and picked up the bottle — not as good as the stuff Bitsy kept. He'd have to speak to Jamin about that. He turned toward the door just as Ethan Chapman stepped through it. The noise level immediately fell.

"Evening, sheriff," said Nick Telford, the stagecoach driver. He had settled in early at a corner table and was playing poker for pennies with a few friends. An inveterate gambler, Nick had been known to lose his entire month's pay a penny at a time. Cyrus figured that was his business. Nick would win one week, and Bill Stout the next, and then Parnell Oxley. At least the currency circulated in the local economy.

"Howdy, boys." Ethan's gaze swept over the poker players, skipped quickly past the saloon girl carrying drinks to two cow hands, and landed on Cyrus. "Mr. Fennel."

Cyrus gave him a curt nod. He wished he'd have gotten away before Ethan walked in to see him carrying his bottle.

Jamin Morrell entered from the back room and called out cheerfully, "Well, Sheriff! How's life in the fair town of Fergus tonight?"

"Quiet so far. Doesn't look like you're having any trouble in here."

"Not a bit," Morrell assured him, though he hadn't been in the saloon at all for the last half hour. Of course, Ted probably would have fetched him in a hurry from out back or wherever he'd been if someone had started tearing up the place.

"Well, excuse me, gentlemen." Cyrus held

the bottle down at his side, away from the sheriff, and walked toward the door. "Have a pleasant evening."

He went out into the cooler evening air. The sun was low, and his long shadow stretched before him as he crossed the street diagonally. He continued up the boardwalk to the stagecoach office. Time to lock up and head for the ranch. He left his horse at the livery during the day, but lately his relationship with Griffin had seen some strain. He'd either have to confront the blacksmith or find someone else to house the stagecoach teams and his personal mount. That didn't seem practical. He reached the office and pushed the door open with a sigh. Griffin worked hard, but he had a stubborn streak. Too bad. It would be so much easier if he'd just go along with —

Cyrus stood still, staring at the dark heap on the floor beside the stove. What on earth?

Ethan left the Nugget and walked slowly up the boardwalk toward the jail. What now? He could relax for an hour or so then check the two saloons again. Drop in on Hi and Trudy? Didn't want to wear out his welcome. His discussion with Hiram last night had crossed his mind many times throughout the day. Had the time come to face up to the past and let go of it? That would mean thinking about the future, and he usually shied away from that.

Across the street and up half a block, Cy Fennel lurched out of his office, still holding the bottle of whiskey he'd carried at the Nugget. He must be drunker than Ethan had realized. He staggered to the edge of the boardwalk and retched.

Ethan paused, wondering what to do. Should he go get Cyrus and walk him over to the jail, where he could sleep it off? He'd leave the cell door unlocked, of course. But if he did that, Cy would be furious later. Maybe he should go to the livery, get Cy's horse, put him on it, and head him toward home. No, he might fall off halfway there and break his neck.

Cyrus straightened and looked about. He focused on Ethan and lifted his free arm.

"Chapman! Quick! Come over here."

Ethan blinked. He didn't sound drunk. He raised his chin and stepped into the street. *Lord, let me not have to mix it up with Cy tonight, please.*

He was only halfway across when Cyrus lunged down from the walkway and met him in the street.

"It's old Mrs. Peart!"

320

"What?" Ethan stared at him. Was the man right out of his befuddled mind?

"Millicent Peart. In my office. Go look."

Ethan struggled to make sense of that. Only one thing to do. He walked over and stepped onto the sidewalk. His boots thudded with each step to the office door. It was nearly dark inside. Before his eyes fully adjusted, he spotted a huddled figure on the floor near the cold box stove. It couldn't be. He stepped closer and stared down at her. Cyrus's words began to make sense. The poker lay beside her. He bent down and then stood up quickly. No wonder Cyrus had emptied his stomach. There'd be no question of how Milzie Peart died.

A shadow darkened the room even more. He swung around. Cyrus stood in the doorway, staring at the crumpled form on the floor.

"What happened?" Ethan asked.

"She was in here when I came over to lock up. Almost didn't see her."

"Can you light a lantern?"

Cyrus hesitated, and Ethan didn't blame him. The sight was bad enough in the gloom. When Cy reached for the kerosene lantern that hung over his desk, Ethan held out his hand. "I'll do it. You go 'round to

Dooleys' and fetch Hiram for me, would you?"

Cyrus's brow cleared. "Sure. I guess he'll need to build another box. Oh, matches are in my drawer." He nodded toward the desk.

When he'd left, Ethan stood still for a moment. *Lord, show me what to do. This is getting scary, and I've got no notion how to stop it. Please, Lord.*

Slowly, he moved around the desk and opened the top drawer. Sure enough, a box of safety matches rested inside. He lit the lantern and adjusted the wick. He had no reason not to look at Milzie again. Might as well get it over with.

He set the lantern on the edge of the desk, pulled in a deep breath, and turned toward the body. From the distance of three yards, the brutal destruction of her skull wasn't evident. He took a step toward her, bracing himself. Footsteps hurried along the boardwalk outside, and he paused. A moment later, Hiram appeared at the door. His gaze bounced from Ethan's face to the still body on the floor. He grimaced.

"Looks like someone took Cy's poker to her," Ethan said.

Hiram nodded and inched closer.

"I suppose we need to look her over a little better than we did Bert." Ethan forced himself to approach the body. Blood ran over the floorboards around her head. He knelt down, careful to stay out of it.

"Poor thing," Hiram said softly, crouching beside him.

"Where'll we take her?" Ethan asked. "Livery stable?"

"I sent Cyrus to ask Griff. Old Cy was white as my granny's Irish table linen, and he didn't seem eager to come back here."

"Understandable." They sat staring down at her. "I hear a good undertaker can fix a person up so's they look natural again," Ethan said.

"It would take a lot of fixin'."

"Yeah." Ethan swallowed back bile. "Maybe we should get an old blanket or something to put her on before we move her."

Hiram nodded. "Gert might help clean her up a bit."

"Don't want to ask her."

"Me neither."

After a long pause, Ethan said, "Maybe one of the older ladies?"

"We could ask."

Between Milzie and the door lay a grimy flour sack. Ethan leaned over and pulled it to him. Lumpy metal items clanked together. He opened it and peered inside.

"Cans and a wad of newspaper." He pulled out a pair of dark stockings.

Quick footsteps heralded a new arrival, and they both looked toward the door. Phineas Benton entered, panting and adjusting his waistcoat. "Gentlemen, can I be of assistance?"

Ethan stuffed the stockings back into the sack and stood slowly. "I don't think so, Pastor. This woman's good and dead."

"So Mr. Fennel informed me. He stopped at my house on his way to fetch the smith." Benton doffed his bowler hat and looked at the body with mournful eyes. "Is there anything I can do to help you, Sheriff?"

"Well, Hiram and I were just saying we should get a blanket or something to put her on and tote her over to the livery. We usually lay folks out over there because we don't have a . . . what you'd call a mortuary."

"Indeed," Benton said. "Perhaps I can find something, though most of our bedclothes were newly donated by the parishioners."

"Ask my sister, Gert," Hiram said.

Benton glanced at him and nodded. "Thank you. Shall I go now?"

"Please," said Ethan.

The preacher turned to go then looked back. "My wife will, of course, volunteer to assist the ladies who prepare the body for burial. I believe she was acquainted with Mrs. Peart, though I myself had never met her."

Hiram and Ethan exchanged looks.

"That'd be fine," Ethan said.

"Perhaps Mrs. Walker would help, too."

Ethan doubted that, but he said nothing.

"Gert will probably want to be there." Hiram looked down at the floor.

He was right; Gert *would* want to do a last service for one of the shooting club members and a senior resident of the town. Ethan still didn't like the thought of her seeing this grisly sight and handling the bloody corpse. "There's time to worry about that later. Just see if Miss Dooley can give us something to wrap her in, and we'll get her over to the livery."

"It shall be done." Benton tipped his hat and flitted out into the night.

Ethan looked at Hiram, whose lips twitched. "Yeah, he strikes me that way, too. A mite formal for Fergus, but his heart's good."

A moment later, Griffin arrived with Bill Stout and Ned Harmon, who had planned to sleep in his hayloft. The parson returned with a ragged old bedspread, and they began the grim task of transferring the body.

"Easy now," Griffin said as he carefully slid his arms under Milzie's torso. "Get that cloth under her head when I lift it."

Ethan was glad he'd wound up with Milzie's feet. He might have joined Ned outside vomiting if he'd taken the spot Griffin had. This wanton destruction of an old woman took him back to the atrocities he'd seen during the Indian wars.

Once Milzie's head was covered, things moved along quickly. The old woman wasn't very heavy. Bill and Griffin started carrying her out, but Griffin paused and shook his head.

"Just let me carry her, Bill," the big man said. "You come along and make sure the blanket ain't draggin' or nothin'."

Ethan called after him, "I'll be over in a few minutes, Griff." He turned back into the room. Phineas stood near the desk, his hat in his hand, with the air of a footman awaiting his command.

Hiram, however, knelt near the pool of dark blood.

"Ethan."

"What is it, Hi?"

His friend reached into his pocket and pulled out a jackknife. He opened one blade and bent low over the stain. Using the blade, he prodded at something resting in the blood.

"For your collection," Hiram said softly. He stood and wiped the small object on his shirttail then held it out to Ethan.

"What is it?" Benton asked.

Without looking, Ethan replied, "An 1866 Indian head penny."

CHAPTER 25

Much later that evening, Gert poured coffee for Ethan and Hiram at the kitchen table.

Ethan rubbed a hand across his eyes. "Thanks. Mrs. Benton will come after breakfast with Annie Harper, and you can all go over to the livery together to work on the body." When he glanced up at her, the dark shadows beneath his eyes stood out. A few weeks of sheriffing had aged him. "Are you sure you want to do this?"

"Of course. I wish I'd done more for her while she was alive. She never begged outright, but I could see she was hungry."

Ethan blew on his coffee and took a sip.

"Libby said she pilfered a few things from the store," Gert said. "She felt sorry for her and started giving her leftovers — broken crackers, dented tins, the last pickle in the barrel."

Hiram's eyes spoke to her with his direct

gaze and quirked eyebrows.

"You're right," she said. "I'd best tell Ethan."

"Tell me what?"

"Mrs. Benton and I drove out to Milzie's place this morning to visit her."

Ethan's brows shot up, but he waited in silence.

Gert cleared her throat. "We, uh, got a surprise. Milzie's cabin had burned flat."

"What? When did that happen?"

"No one seems to know. Milzie wasn't home, but we saw signs that she's been living in the cave up the hill where Frank tried to mine."

Ethan nodded. "I know the place."

"Well, she wasn't anywhere around, so we stopped at the Robinsons' on the way home. Lyman and Ruth said they didn't know. Can you imagine? They live that close to her, and they haven't been up to her place since last winter. Ruth's been poorly this spring, I guess. She said Milzie stops in now and again, and they usually give her something to eat. But when we told them the cabin was burnt, they seemed shocked. Lyman took on a case of guilt, saying he ought to have checked on her. But they'd seen her several times this spring, so they figured she was the same as usual."

"Too bad. I think your shooting club did more for her than anything." Ethan raised his cup again.

Gert went to the pie safe and took out the leftover flapjacks she'd saved. "I figure it had to happen in the night, and no one saw the smoke. The last Lyman could tell me for sure that he'd seen it standing was early February. You two want a pancake with jam?"

Ethan looked at Hiram before answering. When Hiram nodded, he said, "Don't mind if I do."

Gert put the plate on the table between them and took the jam pot from the cupboard. She gave them each a knife, and they set to work spreading the flapjacks with jam, rolling them up, and wolfing them down. She'd meant to save them over for Hi's breakfast with a couple of eggs, but no matter. These two had done a man's work this evening, and they deserved a snack.

Ethan ate three and then licked his fingers. "Sugar's good for folks who've had a shock."

"How shocking was it?" she asked.

"Worse than Bert. A lot worse. I hate to have you ladies see her like that."

Gert shrugged. "Someone's got to clean her up. I mean, you can't just bury a person all . . ."

"Her clothes are right filthy, too."

She sat down at the end of the table, with Hiram and Ethan on either side of her. "We should have done more."

Hiram scrunched up his face as though he'd eaten a mustard pickle. "Do more for someone else."

"That's a good thought," Gert said. "I felt like a hypocrite after Apphia and I saw how she was living."

"It's not your job to make sure everyone in Fergus is eating three square meals a day." Ethan's face flushed a bit, and he added quickly, "Though I'm grateful for the meals you've served this stray."

"Well, I think Hi's right that we can do more for other people. There's a lot of folks living hand to mouth around here. How long since anyone's seen old Jeremiah Colburn, for instance? He's got a flock of sheep on his place east of here, but I don't recall seeing him for a long time."

"I heard Zach Harper mention him the other day," Ethan said. "He'd come and wanted to trade three roosters to Zach for a hen. He gave him two."

"Well, good." Gert rested her elbows on the table and her chin in her hands. "I just hate to think of these poor old people dying alone."

Hiram drained his coffee cup and set it down. "Milzie wasn't alone."

Sadness swept over Gert, and a painful lump rose in her throat. "I've been thinking about it." She pressed her lips together and nodded. "I don't know what Milzie was doing in Cyrus's office tonight, but it could have been anyone who was attacked — anyone who went there at the wrong time. It could just as easily have been Isabel who was murdered."

Ethan frowned, and the lines at the corners of his eyes deepened. "Hiram told me about the other night when Isabel saw the man in the alley."

Gert wasn't surprised that her brother had told Ethan the tale. They talked a fair amount when she wasn't around, and Hiram took Ethan's new responsibilities as seriously as Ethan did. "What if she'd gone looking for her father tonight instead of that night?"

"Yes." Ethan turned his cup around slowly, as though studying its design. "I've kept an eye out since, for men loitering about in the evening."

Hiram inhaled deeply. "You think that fella might have killed Milzie?"

"I don't know. What do you think?"

Hiram set his jaw for a minute then

shrugged.

"Well, I have ideas about who killed Milzie," Gert said.

Ethan eyed her cautiously. "Plan on telling me?"

She hesitated. She wouldn't want him laughing at her. On the other hand, she'd had nothing to do but think while he and Hiram did their duty over at the Wells Fargo office tonight. Maybe she'd had more time to cogitate on it than either one of them had.

"Who found Milzie's body?" she asked.

"Cyrus Fennel. He'd been over to the Nugget. I saw him leave the saloon carrying a bottle. I left shortly after he did, and I saw him come out of his office all in a dither." Ethan gave a grim little smile. "I thought he was drunk. He got sick."

"So did Ned Harmon." Hiram stood and took his mug to the stove, where he refilled it with coffee.

Gert started to tell him he'd be awake all night if he kept drinking coffee, but she thought better of it. Hiram was thirty-three years old, and he could drink coffee if he wanted to. "So Cyrus was the first to see the body."

Ethan nodded. "So far as we know."

"And who found Bert Thalen's body?"

"Uh . . . I guess it was Cy — hey, you don't think —" His forehead furrowed like a plowed field. "You're not saying one of our leading citizens is going around killing folks, are you?"

"I'm not saying anything. I just think it's very interesting that we've had two murders in this town in the last six weeks, and the same person found both bodies." She looked at Hiram. "Don't you find that interesting, Hi?"

He pursed his lips and nodded.

Ethan slapped the table. "You two beat all. Cyrus was here the day Bert died, to pick up his rifle. I saw you shoot it, remember?"

"Yes. But he left here, and we started eating supper."

"He said he found Bert dead and then ran over to the Walkers', looking for the mayor."

"And at some point, he told Griffin Bane," Gert added.

"That's right. I think Cy saw him on the street. And I recollect he found the mayor in the emporium, so pretty near everyone in town heard about it."

Gert nodded. "And tonight he goes into his office alone and comes out yelling murder."

"Not exactly. But you're right that he

found both bodies." Ethan pushed back his chair. "Gert, you're almost making me believe it, and that's not good. I saw Cyrus just a few minutes before he sounded the alarm both times."

"Think on it," she said.

"I will. But right now I'm heading home to get some sleep. I'm frazzled, and there's a lot to do tomorrow." He reached for his hat and set it firmly on his head. "Wish I'd brought Scout over here instead of leaving him at the livery."

"Milzie's all covered up," Hiram said. "You won't have to see her again."

Ethan nodded without meeting his gaze. "Well, good night. Thanks for helping out, Hi. And Gert, thanks for the eats and the advice."

She watched him go out and close the back door gently behind him.

"What's the matter?"

At Hiram's question, she realized she was scowling. Just the fact that she was disappointed exasperated her. She clawed at her apron strings. "That man."

"He's a good man."

"I know it."

Hiram cocked his head to one side and waited.

"He called me Trudy last week, and I

said . . ." Still her brother waited. She wished she hadn't started. Her face was heating up, and she hated that. "Why did you tell him about that anyway?"

"Sorry."

"No, you're not."

"If you're mad, I am."

"I'm not mad. Not at you."

"At Ethan?"

She tugged the knot loose and pulled off her apron. "I told him I didn't mind, but he went back to calling me Gert."

"That bother you?"

"Yes."

"You want me to call you Trudy?"

"No."

Hiram nodded and carried his and Ethan's dishes to the worktable and set them down. He walked over to her and stooped to place a light kiss on her cheek. "Didn't mean to cause a stir. Though some folks beg to be stirred."

He took a candlestick from a shelf and lit the taper, then shuffled off through the sitting room.

"Humph." Gert lit a candle and blew out the lamp.

CHAPTER 26

Milzie's funeral drew far fewer mourners than had Bert Thalen's, though the Ladies' Shooting Club was well represented. Libby stood between Gert and Apphia in the graveyard near the schoolhouse, while Phineas Benton gave a proper sermon. The only other men present, besides Ethan and Hiram, were Griffin Bane, Micah Landry, and a half dozen old-timers who had known Frank Peart. Through gossip at the emporium, Libby had learned that the curious paid their respects at the livery stable before Hiram sealed the coffin.

Cyrus Fennel and the Walkers did not attend. Isabel maintained her father was laid out by the shock of finding Milzie's body. That seemed a bit lily-livered for a strapping big man who'd seen a great deal of life, but Libby didn't question her. Isabel stood on the other side of Gert, stiff and stony-faced.

"I'm surprised Mrs. Walker didn't come," Apphia murmured to Libby when her husband finished his homily.

"Cloudy," Libby whispered back. She didn't like stretching the truth, but she considered saying unkind things about people to be a worse trespass than covering their pride with a white lie. The truth was, Orissa Walker never admitted the existence of people like Milzie. If the old widow ever entered the emporium while she was shopping, Orissa ignored her and checked out as soon as possible with a twitching nose. Libby knew for a fact that the preacher had asked her to help lay out Milzie's body, and Orissa had made an excuse, so he'd gotten Annie Harper instead. It made Libby sad, but people don't change their ways easily. When Apphia got better acquainted with Mrs. Walker, she would probably understand why the mayor's wife didn't attend this funeral.

As the Reverend Mr. Benton began his benediction, large raindrops splatted down on the women's bonnets. Apphia ran up her black umbrella and stepped closer to Phineas to shelter him as he prayed. Libby opened her pearl gray sunshade — an extravagance she couldn't resist when it came in a shipment of new ladies' wear from St. Louis. It was a perfect match for her best gray dress. She edged closer to Gert to share its meager cover. In her gray silk, with black gloves and a hat she'd snatched off the millinery shelf this morning, she considered that she'd perhaps overdressed for Milzie's funeral. How she'd starved for places to wear pretty clothes these last few years! At least they had church now. She could wear the outfit again on Sunday and even change her gloves and hat for something less somber.

The people around her said a hearty "Amen," and she jerked her eyes open. Shame on her for letting her thoughts meander to fashions during prayer. The congregation broke ranks and swarmed toward the schoolhouse. Those who had umbrellas walked slower. The men clapped their hats on and ran, leaving the open grave for their attention after the downpour.

The mourners' state ranged from damp to drenched by the time all crowded inside, and Hiram immediately went to the stove and laid a fire. The assembly being about a third of the one at Bert's funeral, Libby judged that they would have plenty of food. All of the women had brought at least one dish, and they far outnumbered the men. The Ladies' Shooting Club had turned out to the last woman. Gert and Apphia had made sure all the ranchers' wives were notified. As a result, the luncheon dishes were nearly as varied as at the last funeral. With fewer males eager to eat it, the ladies could enjoy a leisurely feast and visit.

While the rain drummed on the roof, they dished up the food and settled in to do it justice. The men gravitated to one side of the schoolroom, and the women claimed the other side without protest.

Libby noted that Bitsy, Vashti, and Goldie wore cloaks she'd ordered in recently — black satin lined in jewel tones. They had an air of parrots in crows' feathers, as their bright skirts peeked out from beneath the somber folds of the cloaks. As the room warmed, they soon laid their wraps aside, and the saloon girls again displayed their bright plumage.

Gert wore the dark blue wool dress she wore to church on all but the hottest days. Again Libby wished she could dress the young woman in something more attractive. Apphia's two-piece lilac dress might be slightly outmoded by Boston standards but was far more stylish than the baggy cotton or woolen housedresses most of the women wore.

Libby joined in the conversation that

burgeoned around her. At first the women talked about Milzie and what a shame it was she'd died.

"Did you see the dress Mrs. Adams gave us to lay her out in?" Annie asked Starr Tinen.

"No. I'll bet it was pretty."

Libby felt her color rise. She hadn't intended for anyone else to know about that. Gert had come to her early that morning, explaining that Milzie's clothing was so caked in blood and soil that she couldn't get it clean. With hardly a second thought, Libby had drawn her to the racks of ready-made clothing and helped her choose a dark cotton dress. She wished now she'd done more for Milzie in life. Why had they all held back? Of course they'd suspected the old woman would take advantage of their kindness, and perhaps she would have. But did that matter? What did God expect of them when a neighbor lacked for decent clothes?

"Does anyone know whether the sheriff has caught the killer yet?" Starr asked.

"I don't think so," Annie said. "Gert, do you know anything new?"

Across the room, the men had talked cattle and water rights, but during the lull before Gert answered, Libby heard one of them say, "— cold-blooded killer."

Several voices rose at once.

"Sheriff, when are you going to make an arrest?" That sounded like Micah Landry.

"Folks in town are scared out of their socks," said Oscar Runnels.

Ezra Dyer jumped up off his bench, knocking Oscar's plate out of his hand.

"Sheriff, you've got to do something, and I'm not whistlin' Dixie. You got to find out who's doin' the killin' around here."

Ethan stared at the old man and held out one hand toward him. "Now, Mr. Dyer, settle down. I'm doing everything I can to find out who's responsible for this."

"Well, what about the other crimes?" Micah Landry asked. "We still don't know who killed Thalen or who attacked Griff Bane in broad daylight."

"Yeah," Oscar chimed in. "And don't forget the fire at the Paragon. Mrs. Adams could have been toasted, and you ain't found out who did that yet either."

"Hold on now," Ethan said, but half a dozen voices drowned him out.

Only Griffin was able to bring silence, when he rose from his seat and towered over them.

"All o' ya's, shut up!"

Ethan was grateful for the quiet that followed but wished he had a voice as authoritative as the blacksmith's.

"The fella who robbed me was a big man." Griffin peered around at the others from beneath his bushy brows, as though daring them to contradict. "I don't think it was anyone from in town. I'd have recognized him. If he hadn't sneaked in and got the jump on me, I'd have had him. And then Milzie would be alive." He clenched his meaty hands. "I take that kinda personal."

Ethan stood and set his tin plate down. "Gentlemen, I'm with Griffin. I take it personally, too. I think every man in Fergus needs to take this personally. Because the next person who's clobbered or robbed or burned out of his house could be any one of us." He pulled in a deep breath. Everyone in the room, including the twenty or so women, hung on his words. He made a quick decision and hooked his thumbs in his belt. "I'd like to make an announcement. I wish the mayor was here, but two members of the town council are with us, so I guess that's good enough."

"What is it?" Ezra asked.

"I'm going to deputize two or three men to help me find the killer. I'll spend my time working on it until we run him down."

"I'd be honored to help you, Sheriff," Griffin said.

"Thank you."

The others clamored to be deputized. Ethan held up both hands. "Easy, now. I need men who can help me patrol the town at various times of day and night. So far, all the crimes have taken place in town."

"Not my oatmeal cake that got stolen off the windowsill," Laura Storrey called.

Ethan winced. "There have been some smaller crimes both in town and out in the countryside." He had his ideas about that — especially since Libby had admitted she was certain Milzie had stolen from her. But the thought of Milzie bludgeoning Bert Thalen was ridiculous, and she certainly hadn't beaten herself to death. "I'm not sure those incidents are related to the more serious crimes. Folks, I'm asking you to be patient. Give me three good men to help me. The town might want to consider some small compensation for their time."

"You can't guarantee it'll do any good," Oscar said.

"That's true, I can't. But I hope we'll catch this man. And I think we have a better chance if everyone is careful. Don't go out alone at night. Lock your doors. Don't leave your womenfolk alone."

The men looked at each other. Some nodded, and others just frowned.

"I'll accept Mr. Bane's offer of help," Ethan said. He shot a quick glance toward Hiram, but his best friend shook his head almost imperceptibly. That was all right. Hiram would help him whether he wore a badge or not. "I also thought I'd ask Zachary Harper. He's not here today, but —"

Annie Harper shoved her stool back and stood. "Sheriff, maybe you'd ought to consider who's here supporting Milzie Peart today. And who came to your office not long ago offering their help."

Ethan felt an annoying tickle at the back of his neck. He took a deep breath. "That's also true, ma'am. You ladies have done a superb job of escorting the schoolchildren for the last week or so, and also of checking up on some of the widows and elderly folks. I appreciate that."

"Well, we ladies are behind you," Annie said. "But we want to see some results."

Gert stood up.

No, Ethan pleaded silently. *Not you, Gert.*

"Sheriff, we'd like to extend our offer again. The women of the Ladies' Shooting Club of Fergus will help you in any way we can. Just tell us where you can best use our assistance, and we'll be there."

"Thank you."

"Aw, now that's just foolishness," Micah Landry protested.

"Sheriff, why do you let them waste all that lead, anyway?" Ezra Dyer asked.

Across the room, Emmaline stood.

"You sit down," Micah shouted.

Emmaline glared back at him. "Sheriff, we women are not only willing; we're prepared. We all have weapons, and we've trained ourselves to use them. Which is more than we can say about some of the men in this here town."

"Ha! Most of those weapons are *our* weapons," her husband yelled.

Vashti jumped up and stood on her bench, momentarily showing a shapely leg as far up as her garters. "Sheriff, you've got more than two dozen pretty good shots right here in this room, and I'm talking about this side of the room."

The men erupted in angry shouts. Ethan wasn't sure what to do. He could pull his pistol and fire a round into the ceiling, but then they'd have to fix the leak in the schoolhouse roof. Micah lunged toward him, and Ethan tried to retreat a step but tripped over his bench and sprawled backward, taking Oscar with him. Griff took a swing at Micah. The town threatened to go to pieces without the aid of the skulking killer, until a shrill whistle pierced the air.

Everyone froze for an instant. People cringed and swiveled toward the sound. Hiram sheepishly lowered his fingers from his mouth and shrugged. Griff bent toward Ethan and offered him a hand up.

"Folks, listen to the sheriff," the blacksmith shouted.

Ethan flexed his arm and rubbed the elbow he'd hit going down. "Thanks, Griff. Hiram. Let's all settle down and talk about this reasonably."

Hiram and Griffin immediately took their seats, and the other men slowly complied, grumbling a bit as they did. Behind Ethan, the swishing of skirts told him the ladies had resumed their positions as well.

"All right. Here's the way I see it. We have the best chance of catching the killer if we're all alert and careful. Griffin, I'll deputize you, Oscar, and Zach. You all live in town and can give a few hours a day."

Oscar nodded, and Griffin said, "Sure can."

"Good. And Griff, maybe you can make some stars for the three of you. I haven't found any extras over to the jailhouse."

"I can do that."

"Now, we men can take turns patrolling

347

in town during the night, but as you all know, most of these crimes have taken place before nightfall. So be careful." He swung around to look at the women. "Ladies, we'll continue your daytime patrols in pairs." Everyone remained quiet, and he felt the pressure lift from his chest. "Thank you all. I appreciate your willingness. Mrs. Harper, will you please tell your husband I'd like his aid?"

"I surely will," Annie said. "But aren't you going to deputize any of us women?"

Ethan's adrenaline surged again. Was there any good way to answer that? His gaze met Gert's, and her gray blue eyes bored into him — eager, passionate, and expecting him to do the right thing.

"I . . . guess I could do that. Miss Dooley, we appreciate *all* you ladies' willingness, but I'll only officially deputize two of you for now. I think you and one other — whoever is your next best shooter."

Gert's eyes narrowed and she gave a slight nod. "That would be Libby Adams or Bitsy Shepard."

Libby said hastily, "Thank you, Miss Dooley, and you, too, Sheriff, but my business has kept me so busy lately that I'll have to decline."

Ethan looked at Bitsy. She wore a frothy

green dress and a black hat with unnaturally brilliant red and green feathers drooping down over one eye. She threw her shoulders back, which also thrust her bosom out — not that Ethan took special notice.

"I'd be pleased to assist in this matter, but I'll have to do my patrolling before the supper hour, due to my business commitments."

"Thank you, Miss Shepard. That should work out just fine." Ethan exhaled and looked around. "It sounds as though the rain has let up. Thank you all for your attention. Those I've named, please come over to the jail for the swearing in."

The people stirred and stood, talking over the turn of events. Women began packing up their dishes.

Ethan edged over beside Hiram. "You need me in the graveyard?"

Hiram shook his head.

"Thanks. Because I think I've got my hands full."

On the way out, Ethan caught up with Griffin and tapped him on the shoulder. "Wait up. I want to ask you something."

Griffin turned to face him in the muddy school yard.

"You never found any coins on the floor

349

after that fella robbed you, did you?" Ethan asked.

"No, he got away with my little stash."

Ethan put his hand up to the back of his neck and rubbed his damp hair. "I still can't figure out why he didn't take all your money."

"Me neither." Griffin's dark eyes flickered.

"But what I was getting at was — did you find any other coins? Ones that might not have been in your cracker tin? A penny on the floor, maybe?"

"Nope. I don't think so."

Ethan nodded and clapped him on the shoulder. "That's all right. I just wondered. Say, how do you feel about taking one of the deputized ladies with you while you patrol?"

Griffin frowned. "You were in a bit of a squeeze there, weren't you? I suppose we can't get out of it, and if they went around on their own and got hurt, you'd never hear the end of it, would you?"

"No, I wouldn't." Ethan gulped. "I was thinking of sending Bitsy Shepard out with you for a couple of hours."

"Suits me," Griffin said. "Bitsy's all right. It's a good thing you didn't pick any of those young girls though."

"Yeah, I figured Gert's position as head of

the shooting club made her a logical choice, and I let her pick the second woman. Gert's pretty levelheaded."

"She is," Griffin said.

Gert came out of the schoolhouse with Mr. and Mrs. Benton. Both ladies carried their empty dishes, and the pastor toted his big Bible and a black umbrella. Griffin's gaze lingered on them, and a protest reared up in Ethan's breast. Was Griffin looking at Gert and seeing Trudy? Naw. Griff was thirty-five — more than ten years older than Gert. Yet no one would look down on a woman in her mid-twenties who married an older man. Look at Libby Adams. Her husband must have been at least a decade older than her. Ethan did some quick mental ciphering. Near as he could tell, Gert was about five years younger than he was, and that seemed ideal to him.

He rubbed his scruffy jaw. Where had those thoughts come from, anyway? Gert had lived in Fergus for eight years, and no one had courted her. Why should he think every man got the idea at once? Maybe because his own feelings toward her had changed?

Griffin moved away. "All right, I've got to stop by the livery and make sure the team for the afternoon coach is ready, but I'll be over to the jail in a little while."

Gert walked to where Ethan stood with the mud oozing over the toes of his boots.

"Care if I walk with you, Ethan? Hiram's going to fill in the burial plot now. I told him to wait till things dry up a little, but he doesn't want to go off and leave the grave open."

"Sure, that's fine." He'd almost ridden out here this morning but left Scout in Hiram's corral after he learned his friends were walking. It wasn't all that far back to the center of town. Phineas Benton invited several of the ladies to ride back with him and his wife. The preacher had made some sort of agreement with Griffin about the regular use of a wagon and horse.

Gert waved and spoke to everyone who passed them.

"Nice sermon, Reverend," Ethan said as Pastor Benton and his wagonload of ladies lumbered by. Soon he and Gert were more or less alone, walking steadily and dodging puddles.

"Thank you for treating us womenfolk as equals," Gert said.

"Oh well . . ." No point in saying they wouldn't *quite* be equals, and he didn't want the ladies out patrolling in the middle of the night. He'd deal with that later if he had to. "You're welcome."

"I've been thinking a lot about the murders," she said.

"Still think Cy did it?" Ethan smiled at her.

"You think it's funny."

"No, I just don't think it's feasible."

"Big word for a cowboy."

"Cowboy turned lawman."

"Oh, you like it now?" Her eyes were more blue than gray as the sun struggled to put in an appearance.

Ethan shrugged. "I'm not saying I want to keep this job forever, but I don't see the city council hurrying to hold an election either."

"That's true." Gert trudged along in silence for a minute. "Well, I expect they'll wait and reelect you when they reelect Charles Walker in the fall."

A month ago, Ethan would have protested violently. Now, somehow, that didn't seem so bad. Of course, if he truly wanted to keep the office, he'd better start finding some clues to solve the murders.

He glanced at Gert from the corner of his eye. She'd worn her hair down today. Beneath her bonnet, the locks settled about her shoulders. He liked it. Of course he'd never say so.

"I have given your suggestion about Cy Fennel some thought. But we know for a fact he was at the stagecoach office at the exact time Griff was robbed at the livery. I figure that rules him out."

Gert made a soft little sound — not a snort or a sniff, but he could tell she wasn't happy with this conclusion.

"What one thing bothers you the most about these crimes?" he asked.

"You mean besides the fact that two people are dead?" She eyed him with calculation in those eyes.

Ethan nodded. "I'd like your take on the whole situation."

She held his gaze for a moment but stumbled when she stepped in a dip in the road. He reached out to steady her.

"You all right?"

"Yes, thanks."

Maybe he should offer her his arm. Something in him squirmed at the thought. Not that he'd mind touching her, but someone might see, and then the whole town would think he was courting Gert. And would that be so bad? He wasn't sure yet. His resolution never to take a wife, nearly seven years old, still bound him, though lately its grasp on his will had grown weaker. Best to keep his distance until he either hardened his resolve or decided to fling it aside.

"You know about the pennies we found." He eased away from her a bit as they walked. "Tell me what you think they mean."

"Nothing, except . . ."

"Except what?"

"You won't laugh? Because you laughed when I said maybe Cyrus did it."

"I won't laugh." He was pretty sure he hadn't actually laughed about that other idea either, but there was no point arguing over it.

"I think they mean the same person did all the crimes. At least . . . at least the two killings."

"So do I. What about the fire at the emporium?"

She nodded slowly. "Had to be."

"But with the murders, the pennies were under the bodies. After the fire, it was on the counter."

"He wanted to make sure you found it," she said. "If he'd left it with the burning stuff, he had no guarantee that the fire wouldn't grow and it would get lost in the ashes."

"Hmm. You may be right."

Her chin wrinkled as she frowned. "Or not. I mean, a store is a place where anyone could drop a penny or leave one on the counter after counting up the cash in the evening."

"Not one from the same identical year," Ethan said.

She lowered her lashes. "You said the one from Milzie's murder was the same year, too."

"That's right. All three of them."

"Well, then, the year must be significant." A cloud covered the sun, and her eyes were gray again as she looked up into his face.

"So 1866." They walked on in silence for a while, and Ethan was very conscious of Gert-Trudy beside him. Her head came just about to his shoulder. Her natural stride was nearly as long as his own, and he easily adjusted to hers.

"What happened in 1866?" she asked.

"That's what I'd like to know. My family moved here that year. I was ten years old." He sighed, thinking back. "Fergus was a boom town, full of hard-drinking miners. A lot of people lived in tents. I think there were four saloons."

"Hiram and I were just kids then, back in Maine. He was fourteen, and I was five years old."

Trudy at five. Again he pictured a little girl with blond pigtails tagging along after her big brother. He glanced over at her. "I haven't told anyone else about the pennies. Just you and Hi. Of course Libby knows about the one at her store."

"She was there when you showed the first one, too," Gert said.

"And the preacher was with Hiram and me when Hi found the one in Cy's office. I figure I won't let it be known in general though. If it really is a clue . . ."

He fell silent, wondering what one did with clues. He'd pondered this one until his head hurt.

They reached the jail and went inside. Ethan waved Gert to the chair behind the desk and brought the stool over for himself. They studied each other for a long moment in the gloom.

At last, she leaned forward, resting her hands on the desk. "Ethan, I'm sure you have the mental resources to outwit this killer. I've been thinking hard on it and even praying about it. Praying for you, that God will help you find out who did it."

A painful longing made his throat constrict. How long since someone had cared enough to pray for him? And would God really answer those prayers and make him smarter? That would be a miracle. Trudy seemed to think he had some brain power already, but he felt as stupid as a fir stump. Still, she had faith in him.

"Thank you," he said. "I appreciate that."

She untied the strings of her bonnet and pulled it off. Her hair fluttered and settled again in gentle waves. He didn't think she'd ever looked so pretty.

He cleared his throat. "One thing that really puzzles me."

"What's that?"

"Why wasn't there a penny when Griff Bane was attacked?"

"The robber left in a hurry."

"Maybe."

She inhaled and stared up at the wanted posters on the wall. "What if it fell in the straw on the floor, and you just didn't notice it?"

"I thought of that. But remember how the man we're after put the one on the counter at Libby's, to be sure we'd find it?"

She nodded. "So you're thinking he'd probably do the same at the stable — make sure it didn't get lost."

"That's right." He leaned back on the stool with his head against the wall. Again the silence stretched between them. A sliver of an idea pricked the extreme edge of his mind. He sat up. "What if the person who killed Bert and Milzie was the same person who set the fire at Libby's, but he wasn't the same person who attacked Griff?"

She sat perfectly still, holding his gaze. After about ten seconds, she nodded. "All right. You may have something there."

"Tru—" He caught himself, but her eyes had grown round. She watched him, her lips slightly parted, waiting. Ethan swallowed hard. "Your hair looks nice that way."

Now, where had that come from? He'd told himself *not* to say that. And yet he wasn't sorry. Unless she got mad again. Then he'd be plenty sorry.

In the utter silence, a voice called from the front step, "Sheriff, you in there? I'm here to take my oath."

The door opened, and Bitsy sashayed in. She wore a red dress with an abbreviated skirt. Beneath the hem, matching baggy trousers pouffed above her shoes. Ethan looked helplessly at Gert.

She smiled. "Bitsy believes the ladies should wear bloomer costumes when we go on patrol. I haven't decided what I think of the fashion. I've divided one of my skirts for when I go riding, but I have to admit this trend is practical."

Ethan opened his mouth and closed it again. Bitsy's costume was awful. More awful than her revealing saloon wear. More awful than Milzie's rags. How could any woman think such an outlandish getup was attractive? But he couldn't say any of that. Maybe sometime when he and Trudy-Gert were alone, but certainly not with Bitsy standing right there in front of them wearing it.

Behind Bitsy the door opened again. Oscar Runnels and Zach Harper entered.

"We're here," Zachary said jovially. "Thanks for picking me and not my wife, Sheriff."

Bitsy glared at Zach, and Gert hid a smile. Oh yes, dealing with deputies was going to be quite an experience.

CHAPTER 27

On Sunday morning the old haberdashery was filled for the morning service. Before Phineas Benton stood to lead the first hymn, Gert looked back toward the door. Two black-cloaked women slipped in and found a seat in the next-to-last row of benches. Gert nearly whooped for joy. She had formed a pact with Apphia and Libby to pray until Bitsy and her girls accepted their invitations to church.

A sharp intake of breath caused her to turn around. Isabel Fennel sat right in front of her and Hiram, beside her father. Isabel, too, had seen the newcomers.

"Isn't that those two girls from the saloon?" Isabel hissed.

"Yes, Goldie and Vashti. Isn't it wonderful?"

Isabel's eyes narrowed. "I . . . suppose so."

"They need the Lord," Gert whispered.

"Well, yes." Isabel faced forward.

Gert glanced at Hiram. He shook his head slightly. So, he'd heard. He knew how burdened Gert had felt lately for the ladies of the shooting club, including the saloon girls. She'd told him the overwhelming guilt she'd felt when she realized she'd been remiss all these years in not sharing God's Word with others. The Dooleys had kept up their faith, though they'd gone without church. They hadn't even owned a Bible until recently. That had bothered Gert now and then, but she'd reminded herself that, when she came west, she couldn't carry much. Besides, the children of the Dooley family had never owned their own Bibles. Their parents had one, but more would have been an extravagance. So she and her brother had gone without.

They hadn't lived as heathens. They still asked the blessing at each meal, and Gert prayed often, and she'd vaguely missed spiritual training and fellowship, but she hadn't given much thought to her neighbors' spiritual needs. Since the Bentons' arrival and Libby's procuring Bibles, Gert and Hiram had devoured the scriptures. Principles she'd learned as a child struck her with new clarity. She wanted all of the ladies of the club to learn as she was learning and to believe as she believed.

362

Most of them claimed at least a superficial faith. The saloon girls seemed the farthest from the fold, with Milzie a close second. Apphia had made Milzie her own project, hoping to win the old woman through kindness. Too late for Milzie now.

In her own heart, Gert had taken on the saloon women. They may not see their need for God, but in her new vision, their need hung out where all could see, like their brightly colored dresses flapping on a clothesline. Gert now believed she was no better than Goldie or Vashti. She lived virtuously in her brother's house instead of upstairs at the Spur & Saddle. But only her faith in Christ gave her an eternal advantage over the girls, and she longed to share it with them.

Cyrus sat in front of Hiram with his spine rigid and his shoulders unmoving during the service, except when they stood to sing a few hymns. Apparently, he had recovered from his prostration. As soon as the final song and benediction ended, he turned around and buttonholed Hiram.

"Say, Dooley, I've mentioned to the reverend that we ought to have some new pews for the church, or at least put backs on some of these benches."

Hiram nodded. "Might be able to."

"Well, an hour and a half on a rough bench with no back support is too long. I expect I'll be stiff all day."

Gert smiled at his inspiration to initiate some improvements in the sanctuary. She stole a quick look toward the doorway. Goldie was shaking hands with the Bentons, but Vashti had already disappeared through the portal.

"Now, since it's for the church, do you think you can donate your time?" Cyrus asked.

Gert's anger boiled inside her. Cyrus didn't want to do anything that would cost him a penny, but he expected other people to donate money, materials, and labor.

Hiram said, "I'll ask the pastor what he thinks."

Isabel had turned and was looking at her with her habitual sour face. Gert met her gaze and tried to smile.

"I don't expect I'll be able to come to shooting practice tomorrow," Isabel said.

"Oh? That's too bad."

Cyrus picked up his hat and said to her, "I've got to see Bane for a minute, Isabel. I'll be back."

"That's fine, Papa." After he walked away, Isabel turned her attention back to Gert. "My father wants me to start work on the old boardinghouse tomorrow."

"What for?"

"He wants to open it for business, the sooner the better."

Gert glanced over at Hiram. Her brother watched Isabel with his big gray blue eyes but said nothing.

Isabel took her gloves from her handbag and pulled them on. "He said he's gotten requests from stagecoach passengers for meals and rooms in town." She flicked a glance toward where her father stood in conversation with Griffin and leaned closer. "He's also had some sort of falling out with Mr. Bane, and he wants a place where the drivers and shotgun messengers can sleep."

Gert winced at the thought of Isabel keeping house for the likes of Ned Harmon and Bill Stout. "And he wants you to run that big place all alone?"

Isabel shrugged with a little sigh. "I told him he'll have to hire someone else before the summer term of school opens. A married couple would be best." She lowered her voice to a fierce whisper. "I will *not* give up my schoolroom to run a boardinghouse."

"I'm sorry," Gert said. "I hope it goes well for you."

"Well, I hate to give up the shooting club, too. The ladies have been . . . nice to me.

365

Of course, Papa's still furious at me for joining. He's upset with the parson, too, for letting Mrs. Benton join. Papa thinks the parson should tell all of us ladies to repent and lay our weapons on the altar."

Gert chuckled. "Pardon my saying so, but your father doesn't know much about women."

Isabel's brow creased. "I'm beginning to wonder why Mama ever married him." She clamped her lips shut as though embarrassed that the thought had escaped through them and looked over her shoulder. Cyrus was now deep in conversation with Charles Walker and Zachary Harper. "Anyway, I wanted you to know that I probably won't be able to shoot anymore."

"You could come over to my house after supper if you wanted to keep practicing."

"I wouldn't want to trouble you."

"No trouble. I shoot out behind our house for Hiram when he's fixed a gun. It won't take but ten minutes to shoot off a few rounds and keep your aim up."

A gleam of hope lit Isabel's eyes. "You'd really let me do that?"

"Sure. You've improved a lot in the few sessions you've had. I'd hate to see you give it up now. These long evenings, we may as well make use of the daylight."

A genuine smile spread over Isabel's face. "Thank you! I'll do it if I'm not too tired tomorrow."

"What will you do at the boardinghouse tomorrow?" Gert asked.

"I'm to scrub down the kitchen and dining room first, and two bedrooms. Papa wants me to start serving lunch by Thursday if I can, but I told him I won't do it unless he gets a decent cookstove in there, and tables and chairs for the diners. I can clean, but I can't make furniture, and I won't serve food on packing crates."

"Good for you. Does he have extra furniture?"

"He's got some. I think there are bedsteads and a few other pieces upstairs in the boardinghouse from when it used to be open."

"That will be a lot of work, getting the place ready."

"Yes, it will."

"Maybe I can come give you a hand in the morning."

Isabel cleared her throat and looked away for a moment. "I'm not sure Papa would pay for extra help."

"I'd come as a friend, just to help out." Gert picked up the new Dooley Bible and handed it to Hiram.

Isabel's mouth hung open for a second. "I . . . don't know what to say. Your offer is very generous."

"I don't mind helping." Gert smiled. "Could be some of the other ladies from the club will help you, too, if they have time."

Isabel stared at her as though she couldn't believe a word Gert had said. Her father strode past them toward the door and called to her without pausing. "Come along, Isabel. I'm finished."

Gert felt like blasting him, but after all, they were still in church, sort of. Isabel scurried into the aisle and followed him.

When Gert turned around to see if Hiram was ready to leave, Ethan stood next to him.

"Howdy." He nodded at Gert. "Hiram, I need to do an inventory of Millicent Peart's belongings. I wondered if you'd be free to ride out to her place with me tomorrow. From what the ladies told us, there's not much to see, but I need to make a record of it."

Hiram nodded. "If I'm not too busy putting a back on Cy Fennel's bench."

Ethan pulled back and scowled at him. "What's that about?"

Hiram waved one hand in dismissal. "I'll go with you. Come to the house when you're ready."

They walked outside together, pausing to shake Pastor Benton's hand at the door. Ethan walked with them as far as the path to the Dooley house, where he halted for a moment.

"Well, I'll head over to the livery and get Scout."

"Would you like to eat dinner with us?" Gert had debated all the way down the street whether to ask him or not. He was eating half his meals at their house now, but he'd rarely come into town on Sunday until the church services commenced. Hiram was fixing a shotgun for Augie Moore and would probably want to continue the project after dinner, but he wouldn't care if Ethan sat around while he did it.

"Thanks, but I let the boys go home over the weekend, and I'd better get out to the ranch." Ethan tipped his hat. "See you tomorrow, Hiram . . . Trudy."

Gert watched him walk across the street. Slowly she turned to her brother.

"Did you say something to him?"

Hiram touched a hand to his chest. His eyes widened, as though asking, "Me?"

"Oh, never mind." Gert slipped her hand through his arm, and they strolled around to the back door of their house.

CHAPTER 28

Ethan knocked softly on the kitchen door at Hiram's the next morning. He usually came to town later, but he had a lot to do today. Trudy opened the door and surveyed him with calm, grayish eyes.

"Morning."

"Morning yourself." He held up the dirty sack he'd brought. "Thought Hiram and I could go through this sack of things we found near Mrs. Peart's body before we go out to her place."

She nodded. "He's out in the barn."

"I'll just go on out there then." He held her gaze for a long moment, trying to think of something else to say. He didn't want the conversation to end so suddenly. She might be off who-knows-where by the time he and Hiram came back from the Pearts' homestead. "Uh . . . will you be around later, when we come back from Milzie's?"

Trudy leaned against the doorjamb. "I'm

planning to help Isabel this morning. Her father's set her to cleaning up the old boardinghouse so they can serve meals and house the stagecoach workers and passengers. But I'll come back to fix lunch, if that's what you're worried about."

"Wasn't worried."

"Oh." They stood there in silence, she at the kitchen door and he on the worn path below the bottom step. "You boys will be ready for something to eat when you get back, I expect."

"That's kind of you. I expect we will."

She nodded, and for an instant, a smile lit her features. Ethan found himself returning the smile.

"Go on," she said with a wave of her hand. She stepped inside and shut the door.

He found Hiram spreading fresh straw in the horses' stalls. Ethan sat down on the feed bin and waited for him to finish. A minute later, Hiram stood his pitchfork against the wall and walked over.

"Milzie's bag?" Hiram nodded toward the sack.

"Yup. Figured we could go through this first. I looked at it some, and I showed it to Bitsy and Oscar. I figure it's stuff Milzie picked up the day she was killed." Ethan stood and emptied the sack on top of the feed bin. He pushed the black socks and two tins of food to one side. "Libby told me Milzie came to the emporium that day, and she gave her these things. The rest of it's junk."

"You didn't put the stuff from her pockets in there, did you?" Hiram asked.

"You mean that busted egg?" Ethan wrinkled his nose. "That got thrown away with her clothes."

Hiram nodded toward the things on the feed bin.

"Well, this here" — Ethan picked up a china cup with no handle — "matches the good china Bitsy uses for the Sunday dinner. She said Milzie probably found it in her trash heap. The rest is just a tin can, a couple of nails, and an old ox shoe. Oh, and there's a piece of a mirror in that newspaper."

Hiram picked up the wad of paper.

"Careful," Ethan said. "It's sharp."

Hiram unwrapped the shard, turned it over in his hand, and laid it down with the other things.

"That's it." Ethan looked down at the meager assortment and shook his head.

"Stuff she found in the rubbish?"

"I reckon, except for what Libby gave her."

Hiram took Hoss's bridle from a peg on the wall. "I'll get my nag."

Gert carried her broom and a bucket half full of water down the street toward the old boardinghouse. She wore her oldest house-dress and had tied a linen dish towel over her hair. She still couldn't find her red kerchief, but she needed some protection from spiders and such. At her waist, a cloth bag of rags hung against her apron.

Maitland Dostie, no doubt on his way to the telegraph office, where he presided, passed her on the boardwalk. He eyed her speculatively but murmured only, "Miss Dooley."

"Good morning." Gert fought down the urge to explain why she went about so early in a patched dress carrying a pail of water. He'd hear soon enough that the boarding-house had reopened.

Her destination lay between the jail and the Nugget, but the saloon was quiet despite the early morning bustle of the town. Out front of the boardinghouse, a horse and wagon stood tied up at the hitching rail, and a rock propped open the door of the rambling building. In the wagon bed lay a mop, a broom, a small crock, a basket, and two tubs.

Gert mounted the rickety steps. Maybe Hiram could fix those — if Cyrus would pay him. He wouldn't want to do anything that would help line Cyrus's pockets unless he received compensation. Gert understood, but as she'd told him last night, she wanted to help Isabel even though she wouldn't be paid.

Isabel had never befriended other young women in the town. It was about time she learned what benefits friendship could bring. Hiram had taken that information in with his usual calm. He rarely interfered with Gert's actions and never criticized her decisions. Sometimes she wished he would say more, but usually she counted it a blessing that she lived with a quiet man.

Thumping echoed through the empty building. Stepping into the shadowy interior, she called, "Isabel?"

"Out here," came the faint reply.

Gert crossed a large, open room to a door that led into what she guessed was the kitchen. Boards covered the two windows on the outside, but the back door stood open, admitting a thin stream of light. One window's lowest board had been removed, and she saw a flash of blue through the dusty glass. She set down her broom and bucket then walked over to the back door.

374

Isabel stood outside, wielding a claw hammer. "I'm trying to get these boards off so we can see what we're doing." With a grunt, she ripped one end of a board free from the window frame.

"Let me help you." Gert stepped down into a tangle of prickly poppies and grass. Neither of them stood tall enough to reach higher than the two bottom boards on each window.

"I don't suppose you have a ladder," Gert said.

"No. There may be a stool or a bench inside."

Gert went to search for one. By the time she came back with a wooden crate, Isabel had done all she could and stood panting against the clapboards.

Gert placed her crate beneath the first window and held out her hand for the hammer.

"You really came," Isabel said.

"Sure." Gert could only manage to take down two more boards from each window.

Isabel laid them neatly by the back stoop. "It's enough for now."

"Yoo-hoo!"

Isabel jumped and stared toward the doorway. "Who can that be?"

Gert laughed.

Isabel climbed one step and called through the vacant rooms, "We're out here, in back."

A moment later, Annie Harper came through the door and stood on the stoop eyeing Gert's handiwork.

"Hope you don't mind," Gert said to Isabel. "I mentioned to Annie yesterday what you were doing, and she said she might be able to come for an hour or two."

"Myra's with me, too," Annie said. "She's lugging a pail of warm water."

Isabel blinked several times and pulled in a deep breath. "Thank you. I . . . don't know what to say."

Annie reached out and squeezed her shoulder. "This will be fun."

"Fun?" Isabel looked doubtfully up at her.

"Of course. I don't get to work with other women very often. We can sweep and scrub and talk. Let's get at it."

Isabel threw a tremulous smile in Gert's direction and followed her inside.

Myra had set down her pail of water just inside the kitchen. "What first, Mama?"

Annie looked at Isabel. "The kitchen?"

"Yes, please. Then the dining room. If we get to it, I'll want to do the hallway and stairs next, and two bedchambers for guests."

"I think it's fine that you're going to serve

meals. This town needs another decent eatery." Annie picked up Gert's broom and vigorously attacked the floor.

Gert didn't try to determine what Annie was counting as the first decent place to eat. If they got too specific, Isabel might take offense, since the Spur & Saddle was the only place Gert could think of where folks could get a good meal, and that was only at noon on Sunday, though she'd heard that lately Augie kept a stew simmering for desperate travelers.

"This is a good, big kitchen," Gert said. "Once we wash the windows and scrub down the shelves, you'll have a wonderful place to work."

"Maybe we could paint the walls a cheerful color," Annie said. "Do you like yellow?"

Isabel looked around at the drab, dark board walls. "That would be lovely, but for now, I thought I'd work on getting the place clean. Then I need to lay in supplies. Papa wants me to serve luncheon to the coach passengers on Thursday."

"Will you do all the cooking and cleaning yourself?" Myra asked, wide-eyed.

"Well, I . . ." Isabel faltered and wrung out a rag in the warm water. "I'm not sure."

"I'll bring over a couple of loaves of fresh bread Thursday morning," Annie said. "If you want, that is, so's to be sure you've got plenty for your first day or two."

Gert nodded. "And I'll bring you some dried apple pies."

Isabel stood motionless with the rag in her hand. "I . . . thank you both. It would certainly ease my mind a bit for the opening day."

Gert's mind whirled as she calculated how many of the local men might decide to drop in to taste the cooking on Thursday. When word got around, Isabel might build a regular lunchtime clientele. "I could make pies for you regular, if you'd like."

Isabel's face softened. "Would you really? I'm not so good with pastry. I suggested to Papa that we might find someone to do part of the baking."

"I'd be happy to," Gert said.

"Think about what your time is worth. I'll have Papa order all the supplies."

Gert smiled. "Sure. But for the first day, it will be my gift to help you succeed."

"Yes, my bread, too," said Annie.

"That sounds delightful. I do appreciate it." Isabel stood and headed for the nearest tier of shelves. "Oh . . . how many pies do you think we'll need, Gert?"

"Hard to say. Maybe you could start with half a dozen on Thursday and see how much you sell. If you get a lot of business, I could do six on Mondays and again on Thursday."

"Those are shooting club days," Myra called from where she wiped the first layer of grime from the windows with a dry cloth.

"That's right. But I should be able to make pies in the morning." Gert rolled up her sleeves. "We'll see how it goes, shall we?"

Annie's voice lilted out in a sudden burst of "Rock of Ages." Isabel stared at her. Myra joined in with her sweet alto, covering her mother's wobbles.

Gert smiled at Isabel. How long since she'd heard singing outside of the last few weeks' church services? She picked up a rag and hummed along as she soaked it and wrung it out.

A few minutes later, as the quartet came to the end of the third verse, a red-tinted shadow loomed in the open front doorway. Gert looked up from sweeping the hearth where the old cookstove had once stood.

"Well, Bitsy, I'm glad you could make it." She straightened and walked over to greet the newcomer. Not so long ago, she'd thought of Bitsy only as "that saloon woman." She smiled at the wonder of the changes seen in Fergus over the past six weeks. They had a church, women had been recognized as volunteer law enforcement officers, and she now claimed Bitsy Shepard as her friend.

Bitsy grinned and held up a basket. "Augie's cinnamon rolls for when you ladies need sustenance."

"Wonderful," Gert said.

Annie called, "Well, Bitsy, I must say your outfit looks very practical. And such a cheerful color."

"Why, thank you." Bitsy preened just a bit, the better to display her bloomer costume. "It's good for working without showing your garters. A bit more discreet than my usual wear, but — can you imagine — some of the gentlemen find it shocking."

Myra nodded, grinning at her. "I can imagine it. Papa said that very thing when he came home from the jailhouse on Saturday."

"Now, Myra," her mother said gently.

"But it's true, Mama." Myra stepped eagerly toward Bitsy. "He came home fussing like an old woman. 'That Bitsy Shepard was wearing pants, I tell you. Shocking. Just shocking.' Didn't he say that, Mama?"

Gert smothered a giggle at the young woman's impression of her staid father. Annie apparently found Zachary's reaction to the fashion less amusing than Myra did.

"Now, Myra, stop it. You'll embarrass Miss Shepard."

Bitsy let out a loud laugh. "Don't fret about that, Miz Harper. I haven't been embarrassed since I was twelve years old. Now, who's got an extra scrub rag? Let me at the dirt. I've only got an hour to help you, but I'll send Goldie over for a spell when I go back to the Spur & Saddle."

A small sound came from Isabel's throat. She'd stood still since Bitsy's appearance, her hands poised above the basin of water she used to scrub down the work surfaces. She hadn't moved or said a word, but her face had turned a mottled pink.

Gert sidled over to her. "Are you all right, Isabel?"

Isabel swallowed with effort. "I'm just . . . surprised. I didn't expect . . ." She darted a glance toward the vision in red.

Bitsy's painted eyebrows wriggled. "Oh, I see." Her face turned thoughtful and she set down her basket. "Well, Gert, I'll be going." She turned toward the door.

CHAPTER 29

Ethan and Hiram rode into the narrow flat spot before the site of Frank Peart's old cabin. Even though Trudy had told him the house had burned, Ethan cringed at the sight. The fieldstone chimney loomed over the charred beams and boards. He couldn't identify any large items in the ruins. No bedsprings — but then, Frank and Milzie had probably done without. There had been a stove. Trudy had mentioned seeing it in the mine above.

Hiram dismounted and let his reins trail. Hoss immediately lowered his head and began to crop the meager grass. Ethan followed him, ground tying Scout. Together they approached the burned-out square.

"You reckon the person who set the fire at the Paragon did this?" Hiram asked.

Ethan pushed his black hat back. "I dunno."

Hiram kicked at a length of charcoal that

might once have been part of the door frame. "If he did, how would we find his penny?"

"Good question." Ethan looked up the hillside. "Come on. We're not likely to find much here. We'd best check the cave."

"Milzie will have salvaged anything useful." Hiram pulled his rifle from the scabbard on his saddle. Ethan eyed him in surprise. "In case we run across a rattler."

The path to the old mine entrance held ruts and gouges. Old Milzie must have struggled to haul things up the incline. When they reached the dark opening, Ethan pulled his pistol and hesitated. Hiram fished in his shirt pocket and produced a small tobacco tin. Since he didn't smoke, Ethan's curiosity was piqued.

"Gert said to bring matches." Inside, they found a short candle, and Hiram lit it with a lucifer from his tin.

A quick sweep of the cave assured Ethan that no critters had moved in. Split and crushed rocks showed them where Frank had prospected for gold or silver, but the cave ended in a hewn niche extending not more than six feet beyond what appeared to be the back of the original cavern.

Ethan and Hiram gathered up Milzie's pitiful store of household goods and carried them out into the sunlight.

"Pins." On a flat rock, Ethan laid out fourteen safety pins, from one a half inch long to a large horse-blanket pin.

"This looks familiar." Hiram handed him a knife with a four-inch blade. The haft, about as long, was made of polished deer antler.

"Griff Bane's knife." Ethan stared at Hiram. His friend nodded. Ethan exhaled and shook his head. "How could she get this?"

Hiram cocked his head to one side. "What if she went in the livery after Griff was attacked, saw the knife, and picked it up?"

Ethan thought about that. "Don't you think she'd have tried to help him? Or told somebody he was hurt?"

Hiram drew in a deep breath and raised his shoulders. "What, then?"

"What if . . ." Ethan took his hat off and scratched his head. "What if she hit Griff?"

"Laid him out?"

Ethan nodded. "I know it sounds crazy, but . . ."

"Naw."

They stood in silence. It seemed unbelievable to Ethan that anyone would see the blacksmith injured and not try to help him. But Milzie hadn't been exactly stable.

"Griffin was sure about the knife. Said he'd pulled it out when he heard a noise. He had it in his hand when that fella jumped him. And when he came to, it was gone."

"I thought maybe Ned or Bill had swiped it when they found him out cold." Hiram turned his guileless gray blue eyes toward the cave entrance. "Doesn't seem likely Milzie would have gotten it from one of them."

"No, but she's known to have walked off with things she fancied. These pins, for instance. Libby said something about pins, and didn't Griff mention a blanket pin?" Ethan picked up the largest of the pin collection. "I'm betting this belongs to Griffin, though there's probably no way to prove it. But that knife, I'm 99 percent sure about, and Griffin can confirm it."

Hiram's Adam's apple bobbed as he looked down at the other items they'd found. "What else ya got?"

"Some shell casings. And some money. Not much." Ethan laid out a few coins. "Griffin also said some change was missing. And there's this." He laid a wrinkled but folded red kerchief on the rock beside the pins.

Hiram reached out one finger and touched it. "That bears a fair resemblance to one

Gert had. She missed it one day after their shooting club met."

"When?"

"Back along when they first started meeting. Libby came home with her one day to talk about buying ammunition. While she was there, Gert missed it."

The fact that Milzie stole from people all over town troubled Ethan, but that didn't prove anything so far as the murders and other crimes were concerned. He looked down on the burnt cabin again. "I sure wish we'd known what dire straits she was in."

Hiram nodded.

"Trudy and I —" Ethan stopped and felt the blood rush to his face. "That is, Gert and I agree that whoever hit Griffin isn't the one who did the murders. He didn't leave a penny at the livery."

"Unless Milzie picked that up, too." Hiram held the knife up and looked closely at where the tang fit into the hilt.

"Never thought of that," Ethan admitted. "She could have stolen the penny."

"Any 1866 pennies in that collection?"

Ethan examined the coins carefully. "Nope. But she could have spent it."

"Maybe so." Hiram's brow furrowed, and he picked up one of the safety pins. "Bert."

"What about him?"

"His suspenders were loose."

Ethan felt a fearsome dread in his chest. He wasn't sure he wanted to go where Hiram was leading him. "Just exactly what are you getting at?"

Hiram squeezed his lips together and very slowly writhed in a shrug.

"No, Hiram, come on. You know she can't have killed Bert."

Hiram's eyebrows shot up, and his eyes widened.

Ethan shook his head. "Because he was a lot taller than her, for one thing."

"Could have been bending over near the bunk."

"Oh, and she left the penny under his body? You think Milzie would do that? Next you'll tell me she clobbered Griff, too. Hi, think about it. She stole coins. She didn't leave them for other people to find. And she wouldn't set the Paragon Emporium on fire. Libby gave her more stuff than just about anybody."

"Not until after the fire."

Ethan frowned. "You're making my head hurt again. But there's one thing that proves Milzie wasn't the killer."

Hiram nodded slowly. "She's dead."

"That's right. And she died in a way that shows someone else killed her. And that person left the penny in her blood. The same person left the pennies when he killed Bert and when he set the fire at the emporium."

Hiram laid the knife and the safety pin on the rock. "All right. I'm with you so far. But has there got to be another killing before we learn who did it?"

"No, Bitsy, wait." Gert grabbed Isabel's forearm and squeezed, none too gently. She stared into the teacher's face, wanting to scream at her, but no suitable words found their way to her tongue.

Annie filled the silence. "Bitsy, you don't need to go. It's very kind of you to want to help. Why, any woman in our shooting club who needs a hand will get it."

"That was my understanding." Bitsy hesitated. "But if I'm not wanted . . ." She lowered her head. "I thought things were different in town now. In the club, at least."

"They are." Gert let go of Isabel's arm and walked over to Bitsy. "The club has taught us all a lot of lessons, and you, Bitsy, are one of this town's most valuable business owners. Your selflessness in patrolling and serving as a deputy sheriff to help others is exemplary."

Bitsy licked her violently red lips. "Thank

you, Gert. I was hoping I could be a neighbor, too. I've never had much chance to do that." She flashed a bitter smile. "I'll see you later at the club meeting." Again she turned away.

As she reached the door, Isabel stirred. "Miss Shepard!"

Bitsy stopped, hovering like the red sun at dawn. Slowly she turned, eyeing Isabel through narrow slits of eyes edged by thick black lashes. "Yes?"

Isabel's lips trembled. She took two steps forward and extended her right hand. "You . . . are welcome here. Thank you for coming."

Bitsy met her in the middle of the floor and took her hand for an instant then released it. "I'm glad to be here."

"Then if you'd care to assist me, I was about to begin on the dining room floor."

Gert let out her breath in a slow stream. *Thank You, Lord.*

They all fell to work and soon had both kitchen and dining room transformed. Myra took a broom to the top of the staircase and swept her way down. As she reached the bottom step, Goldie arrived carrying a coffeepot wrapped in towels.

"Hurry, Miss Bitsy! My arm's about to fall off."

Bitsy dropped her mop and dashed to take the pot from her, then faced them all with a big smile. "Wipe your hands, ladies. Time for a morsel. Then I must get back to my own work. Goldie can stay awhile and help you get those bedrooms gussied up."

They sat on the stairs, a crate, and two stools Isabel had unearthed. Bitsy poured the coffee with the dignity of a duchess, and Goldie removed the linen napkin from the roll basket and passed it to the damp, dirty women. Gert's hair had come loose and hung about her shoulders. She pushed it back and took one of Augie's cinnamon rolls. The smell of them alone set her mouth watering.

With the first bite, she closed her eyes. "Mmm. If I could make anything half this good . . ."

"What?" asked Myra.

"I'd patent it."

Gert opened her eyes in time to see Isabel take her first bite and chew slowly. A look of adoration crossed her face. Her eyes brightened. She swallowed, and her lips pursed.

"Miss Shepard . . ."

"Yes, Miss Fennel?"

"Do you . . . sell these rolls at your place of business?"

Bitsy chuckled and waved her hand. "Naw, Augie just makes them for the girls and me now and again."

"Usually for Monday breakfast," Goldie piped up.

"I was wondering." Isabel hesitated. "Do you suppose Mr. Moore would have the time or the inclination to do some baking for the boardinghouse?"

"What a novel idea," Bitsy said. "He's quite busy at the Spur & Saddle, but if you'd like, I shall ask him."

Gert pictured the brawny, bald bouncer creating fancy breads and pastries for prim and proper Isabel's clients. She took another bite of the confection. *I always knew anything was possible with You, Lord, but after this morning, I truly believe it.*

Ethan walked to the mayor's house after lunch at Hiram and Trudy's. He'd rather be anywhere else right now than on his way to Charles Walker's house. He'd as soon be with the dozen women out shooting in the ravine on Bert's ranch. But a summons from the town council could not be ignored by an employee. Since Ethan had accepted his pay at the end of May and hoped he would soon receive a full envelope for the month of June, he supposed that obligated him to go when the council summoned him.

Mrs. Walker met him at the door, and he handed over his hat to her. In the parlor, Charles and the four town councilors were enjoying coffee and cigars. Ethan's eyes watered in the blue smoke.

"Coffee, Sheriff?" the mayor asked.

"No thanks. I just had some." Ethan took the only vacant seat in the room — a horsehair-covered armchair.

"Is there any progress on this crime spree, Sheriff?" Walker got right to the point, and Ethan had a feeling the council had talked about it before he arrived.

"Well, sir, I've been working hard on making sure it doesn't happen again. Setting up patrols, checking on the —"

"Yes, yes," Walker said in his squeaky voice. "We know all about the deputies and the ladies patrolling in scandalous costumes."

Ethan eyed him for a moment. So far as he knew, only one of the women had adopted the bloomer getup, and he'd bet the council wouldn't designate her a lady. He decided to take a different approach.

"I've been able to narrow the field of suspects."

That got their attention.

Cy Fennel leaned forward and tapped the

ash from the end of his cigar into an ashtray on the side table between him and Oscar Runnels. "Care to enlighten us?"

"I have evidence that leads me to believe Bert Thalen and Milzie Peart were killed by the same person."

"What sort of evidence?" Zach Harper asked. The lopsided stars of sheet metal Griffin had made for him and Oscar were pinned to Zach's vest and Oscar's waistcoat. Griffin's was somewhat better crafted and had been burnished so that it shone a bit. He must have taken more pains on his own.

"I'm not sure I want it to get about yet," Ethan said. "If the killer knows everything I know, he might not play into my hand."

"Oh, that's good, Sheriff." Oscar held his cigar up in front of him and savored the words. "Play into your hand." He nodded.

"It's nonsense," Cyrus barked. "This isn't a poker game. Tell the council what you've found so far."

Griffin stroked his beard. "Yeah, Ethan, you might tell your deputies, too."

Ethan shoved the hair back off his forehead. Another thing this town needed, besides a bank and a doctor, was a barber. "Well, Mr. Fennel, you know your daughter was frightened by a man in the alley near your office a few nights before Millicent

Peart was killed."

Cyrus harrumphed and crossed his legs. "What's that got to do with anything?"

"Mrs. Peart was killed in that same office, only four nights later. It's my thinking that an unknown assailant waited for you on that first occasion, planning to assault you when you returned to your office that evening. Your daughter's appearance and the subsequent commotion scared him away. But on the evening Mrs. Peart was in town, he again waited for you to come and lock up for the night."

"I'd only stepped down the street for a minute." Cyrus looked around at the others as though seeking their assurance of his innocence.

"Oh, I know that," Ethan said. "I saw you myself at the Nugget."

Cyrus cleared his throat and tapped his cigar on the ashtray again, though it had hardly burned down.

"You make a habit of it?" Griffin asked. "Going out and leaving the stage office unlocked?"

Cyrus shrugged. "Occasionally I step out and leave the door unlocked, if that's what you mean. So what? Do you lock up the livery stable every time you stroll over to the post office?"

"S'pose not." Griffin sank back against the sofa cushions.

"What are you getting at, Sheriff?" Zach asked.

Ethan looked around at them. None of them was stupid, but most of them he considered a bit shortsighted. "I think that person had it in for Mr. Fennel. It's my theory that the same killer who did in Bert Thalen planned to give Mr. Fennel the same treatment. But on the second time he tried, his plan was again interrupted, this time by Milzie Peart. She wandered into the Wells Fargo office and found him lurking there, waiting to attack Mr. Fennel."

"And he attacked Milzie instead." Oscar's eyes widened in his round face. "By George, Sheriff, you may have something there."

"That's ridiculous." Cyrus straightened and glared at Ethan. "Folks thought he was hanging about Mrs. Adams's place. He did set a fire there earlier, you know."

"But this time he did his mischief in your office."

Cyrus's face reddened. "That's a lot of flapdoodle. Who would want to kill me?"

Ethan shrugged. "I haven't figured that out yet."

"Well, someone wanted to kill Bert," the mayor noted, his voice rising. "No one knew of any enemies he had either. Unless it was someone Bert put in jail back along. But that doesn't make much sense to me."

Oscar swept his cigar through the air, trailing smoke. "I figure the person who killed Bert was a lunatic who hated lawmen."

Ethan frowned and shook his head. "Then why didn't he attack me last week instead of Mrs. Peart? And why did he wait in Mr. Fennel's office, not mine?"

"Interesting questions, Sheriff, but this isn't getting us anywhere." The mayor pulled out a handkerchief and blew his nose.

The thick smoke brought tears to Ethan's eyes. He swiped at them with the back of his hand, but that made his eyes sting more. He coughed. What would they say if he opened a window to clear the smoke out?

"So you don't think the fire at the emporium is significant?" Cyrus demanded.

"On the contrary, I think it's tied in with these killings, but I'm not sure how just yet. And I don't know why he set a fire there instead of attacking Mrs. Adams, as he did Bert and Mrs. Peart. That fire was deliberately built to make a lot of smoke but not to burn the whole building. And the arsonist made enough noise to wake Mrs. Adams. He didn't intend to kill her."

"Well, our womenfolk are frightened, I

know that. We need a man who can see this job through." The mayor lifted his cup and took a sip.

Things weren't going well. Ethan clenched his teeth and wished he could get back to work. Let them call him incompetent if they wanted to. He was doing the best he knew how. But the looks on Walker's and Fennel's faces told him that his best didn't equal enough.

Zach sat forward. "Do you suppose this lunatic has set out to ruin the town? If you're right and he didn't intend to attack Mrs. Peart but was waiting for Cyrus, that would be two prominent business owners he's gone after. Bert wasn't a business owner, but he had a lot to do with town business."

"Don't forget the livery," Oscar said. "He attacked Griffin, too."

"Maybe." Poker game or not, Ethan still wanted to play it close to his vest. He didn't want to say anything about the pennies. Not yet. If he had to reveal that later, fine. For now he'd keep it to himself and the Dooleys. A few people knew some of it, but no one but Ethan, Hiram, and Trudy had all the facts. And would it hurt to let the town council think the killer also pulled off the incident at the livery? "Anyway, with my new deputies helping me patrol at night and the shooting ladies keeping their eyes peeled by day, I hope we can avoid another crime."

Zach stubbed out the end of his cigar in the ashtray. "So you think he might be planning to strike again?"

"Are you thinking he'll go after Cy?" Oscar asked.

"Yes. He failed last time — and got the wrong person. So next time he'll try to make sure he gets it right." Ethan met Cyrus's gaze. "If I were you, sir, I'd take extra precautions. Don't sit up alone late in your office. Lock the door when you go out. Take someone with you on your way home to the ranch."

Cyrus's face had taken on a grayish hue.

Zach leaned back in his chair and frowned at Ethan. "What if he attacks someone else in town?"

"It's possible he'll go after one of the other business owners. He might attack one of the saloons, or the telegraph office, or the feed store. We just don't know what's going through his head. But I don't think these attacks were random. He planned them."

"Why do you say that?" Walker asked.

"He made preparations."

"What kind of preparations?" Cyrus shifted in his chair. "It's my understanding

he used a piece of Bert's firewood to clob-
ber him with and my poker to bludgeon
Mrs. Peart. He used Mrs. Adams's merchandise to fuel his fire. Seems to me he
used what came to hand."

All of their eyes drilled into him. Ethan
wished he hadn't said so much. The men
waited. Nobody smiled.

"All of that is true," he conceded. "But if
this man who was seen loitering in the alley
is our killer, then I'd say he waited for the
right moment. He knew what he intended
to do. It happened that the wrong person
came along."

"Hmm," said Oscar. "That doesn't sound
like much preparation to me."

"Or much evidence." Cyrus looked at
Mayor Walker. "Charles, perhaps you want
to tell Chapman what we decided earlier."

Walker cleared his throat. "Certainly. Cyrus here — that is, we all decided we'd like
to see this killer apprehended, and soon."

"Of course," Ethan said. "We all would."

"Yes, well . . ." Walker glanced at Cyrus,
who nodded. "If you can't show us some
results soon — say within a couple of weeks,
why we'll just have to appoint a new sheriff,
that's all."

Ethan's heart clunked against the bottom
of his belly. They were going to take the

position away from him so soon? Who would replace him? He couldn't imagine any of the men in this room doing more than he was doing to protect the town or figuring out who had killed two citizens.

He hadn't wanted to be sheriff, but he'd done his best. It struck him all of a sudden that he liked being sheriff of Fergus. He'd wrestled with the crime issue. He'd tried to make the town safer. And he didn't want to give up now. He had to be close to solving the riddle of the pennies. If they took his badge away, would the next sheriff they picked be able to do more than he could?

He wanted to keep this job. But he couldn't let them know how much. Cyrus was mean enough to push him out sooner if he knew.

Ethan shrugged with one shoulder and put a boring drawl into his voice, which was hard since it was scratchy from the smoke. "If that's what you want to do, Mayor, it's up to you. I think I can solve these murders. I'm getting close, but I need a little more time."

"Well . . ." The mayor's high-pitched quaver grated on Ethan's nerves and made him shiver.

Cyrus struck a match and lit a fresh cigar. "Two weeks, Chapman. That's it."

CHAPTER 30

On Wednesday evening Libby waited inside the door of the emporium until she saw the Nash family walking down the street toward the church. She opened the door and called to them. Florence and her stepmother, Ellie, paused and waited for her to lock the door and hurry over to join them. When Peter realized the women lagged behind, he called to his two boys to wait. Libby was glad she didn't have to walk the short distance alone.

Together they headed for the old haberdashery and the mid-week prayer service. They'd only begun the custom three weeks ago, but already prayer meeting had become one of the highlights of Libby's week.

Florence wore the new dress she and her mother had sewn. The plaid cotton had come in Libby's last shipment of yard goods.

"Your dress came out very well, Florence,"

she said.

Florence smiled. "Thank you, ma'am. Mama likes the pattern so much, she's going to make a dress for herself after it."

Libby nodded to Ellie. "It should suit you well."

"Thank you. I've got a piece of gray flannel I thought I'd make up for fall. Oh my!" Ellie had spotted Libby's new, basket-shaped, French bag of soft leather. Idaho Territory might be a few months behind the New York fashions, but Libby refused to bypass them completely and stick to the basics.

"I saw them in the latest catalog and couldn't resist." She held it up so that Ellie could see it clearly. No need to mention the pearl-handled Smith & Wesson revolver inside. She'd decided to add it to her arsenal, leaving the heavier Peacemaker at home under her pillow except for shooting practice. The little gem of a pistol in her bag allowed her to go armed wherever she pleased and still appear dainty.

Mr. Nash held the door open for them, and the ladies entered the old store now used as a sanctuary.

Just inside, hugging the back wall and peering at the crowd with wide, frightened eyes, stood a young woman dressed in claret-colored silk. She clutched the edges of a fringed gray shawl before her bosom, but even so, the white expanse of her neck hinted at a low neckline. Rosettes caught up the skirt in front, exposing the girl's clocked stockings and shoes with scandalously high heels. Opal, the new girl from the Nugget.

Fearing she would tear out the door, Libby stepped toward the anxious young woman. Before she reached Opal's side, Apphia Benton scooted down the aisle and reached for the girl's hand.

"My dear Opal. Welcome."

Libby watched with interest. Opal had come into the emporium last week and purchased a fan and some perfume. But how did Apphia know her? The minister's wife must have expanded her outreach to Bitsy's rivals. Libby stood entranced as Peter Nash herded his family toward a bench halfway down the aisle. Ethan's ranch hands, the McDade boys, appeared, and the older one managed to end up seated beside Florence.

"Won't you come and sit with me?" Apphia asked the saloon girl.

"Oh, I . . ." Panic filled Opal's eyes as she flicked a glance toward the front of the room. Perhaps she had guessed correctly that the pastor's wife usually sat in the front row.

Libby stepped toward them and smiled. "Good evening. I'm Libby Adams, from the emporium."

Opal met her gaze and nodded slowly. "I remember you."

"Would you like to sit with me? I'm all alone tonight." Libby gestured toward a bench in the next-to-last row.

"Thank you," Opal whispered. She caught her breath and turned to look at Apphia.

"It's all right, my dear. I'll find you afterward, and we can visit for a few minutes." Apphia smiled gently at both of them, nodded, and turned toward the front of the room.

Libby entered the row and sat on the bench. Perhaps she should have suggested Opal enter first. The girl might feel the urge to bolt if Pastor Benton launched into a fiery exposition.

Two rows ahead, Libby saw Gert and Hiram sitting with the Harpers. Across the aisle, Goldie and Vashti claimed seats. Goldie glanced over at them, and her eyes widened. She elbowed Vashti, who leaned forward and stared past her. She glared at Opal and turned to face the front with a flounce of her black cloak.

Libby would have laughed if they were anywhere but church. Apparently, the competing saloons' employees harbored deep resentment toward one another.

Opal drew in a shaky breath. "I oughtn't to have come."

"I'm glad you did," Libby said.

"I have only an hour," Opal said. "Mr. Morrell says if I'm late coming back, he'll never let me go again."

"I'm surprised —" Libby stopped short and felt her face flush.

"That he let me come at all?"

"In the evening, I was going to say," Libby admitted in hushed tones.

"Well, I wanted to come Sunday morning, but I was ailing."

"Perhaps he'll let you come next Sunday."

Opal nodded judiciously. "Mostly we can do what we want Sundays. He said I've got to be back tonight by eight o'clock. It's never busy on Wednesday, but most of the traffic we get is after eight." She shot a surreptitious glance across the aisle. Goldie was staring at her malevolently. Opal caught her breath.

"Don't mind them," Libby said. "They're good girls, really. They're always well behaved when they come to the shooting club."

Opal's eyes sparked. "I heard tell about the club. I . . . I want to learn. Would they let me?"

"I expect *all* the members would welcome you."

Pastor Benton stood at the pulpit and raised both hands. "Let us pray."

As she bowed her head, Libby prayed silently, *Lord, thank You for bringing this wayward one in. You know her heart. Let her see Your love here.*

Ethan walked past the haberdashery as the opening hymn rang out. He wished he could be inside, singing along to "What a Friend We Have in Jesus." Maybe sitting next to Trudy.

He ambled along the boardwalk, past the closed telegraph office and an empty building. He hummed the hymn as the strains grew fainter and kept on until he reached the Spur & Saddle. Only two horses dozed out front at the hitching rail.

Inside, Augie was behind the bar, and a cowboy leaned on it, one foot on the brass rail below, with a mug of beer before him. Bitsy rose from the round table where she'd sat with two of Oscar's mule drivers.

"Evening, Sheriff." She wore one of her frothy dresses, but she went behind the bar and fetched a glittery silver shawl before joining him near the door.

Ethan waited, nodding to the two customers. Bitsy slung a twine bag over her shoulder as they stepped out onto the street.

"Got my piece in here," she said confidentially, patting the bag. "Not that we'll have to use 'em tonight, but I like to be prepared."

Ethan smiled. "Good of you to volunteer for this hour. I know evening's your prime business time."

She shrugged, causing the shawl to slip down over her shoulder and show a bit of white skin. "Wednesday's always slow anyhow. I let the girls go to the prayer meeting. Augie can handle what little business we'll get before that's over. But as you can see, I'm dressed for business tonight. Not a deputy sheriff's usual getup, hey?"

Ethan smiled. "Not quite. Griffin says he'll take over the patrol when church is done."

They crossed to the east side of the street. The reddish light from the setting sun reached between the buildings and glittered bright off the windows of the storefronts opposite. They walked in silence for a while, past the lane to the Harpers' farm, then the Nashes' house and post office. Ethan wished she'd worn the bloomers tonight. Would anyone see them walking together? Probably at least half the town's residents were at the prayer meeting; the novelty of church services still drew most of them in.

"Oh, I almost forgot." Bitsy stopped in front of the Walkers' house and fumbled in her bag. She pulled out a piece of brass. "Griffin finally made badges for me and Gert. Not bad, eh?" She held it out so he could see it. The word *Deputy* was engraved in block letters on the five-pointed star.

Ethan nodded. "He's getting better at it."

Bitsy drew her chin in and craned her neck as she fastened the badge near the neckline of her dress. Ethan looked away. *Please don't ask me to help you with that!* He gulped.

"There!" Bitsy moved forward, and he exhaled. They moseyed toward the emporium. "That Gert Dooley is a nice gal."

"Uh, yes she is." Ethan observed Bitsy cautiously from the corner of his eye.

"I never thought she'd mix with the likes of me, but she's been nothing but sweetness to me and my girls."

Ethan could well believe that. Ahead of them, Cyrus came out of the stagecoach office and turned to put the key into the lock.

"Evening, Mr. Fennel." Bitsy's husky

voice cut through the stillness.

Cyrus's head jerked around, and he straightened. "Well, well. The evening patrol, I assume?" He looked Bitsy up and down from her shoes, better suited to a dance floor, to the little ruffled cap that graced her curls.

Ethan winced, again wishing "Deputy Shepard" had put on more suitable clothes. "Bane will take over at nine o'clock," he said. "We're just making sure no one's doing mischief while most of the business owners are elsewhere."

Cyrus nodded. "I thought of that — everybody over to church. It's a good time to break into one of the stores."

"Well, sir, we'll take special care of your place." Bitsy laid her hand on his sleeve and gave him what some might consider an alluring smile. It made Ethan shudder.

Cyrus pulled away. "Thank you. I'm late for prayer meeting, and I told my daughter I'd meet her there."

Bitsy chuckled as he hurried across the street. "Can't stand that man, the old hypocrite."

Ethan frowned and cocked his head to one side. "Then why'd you . . ."

"Play up to him?" Bitsy smiled as they resumed their walk. "Cyrus used to spend plenty of time at my place, and I was glad for his business. His respectable friends came, too. But I'm doing well enough now that I can get along without him."

"Even with the new competition down the street?"

"I think so. I cater to a different clientele than Jamin Morrell. My place is a respectable house and nicely furnished. You've seen it."

Ethan nodded reluctantly. Bitsy's establishment had the atmosphere of a hotel lobby, with rugs, lamps, and padded chairs. Jamin's had rough furniture and a tinny piano. You could get wine in the Spur & Saddle, someone had told him. Jamin served strictly beer and whiskey.

"He's got sawdust on the floor." Bitsy shook her head. "I did that back in the day. You know, when these hills were full of miners. But as soon as I got a little money, I put it into decor. Paintings, wallpaper, a fancy chandelier. And I don't let people spit on the floor anymore."

"You've got a real homelike place. Prettier than most homes in Fergus."

"Sure I do. And gentlemen like to come there and relax. They'll spend a little more for a drink at my place because it's peaceful. They can sit and play cards for a couple hours and not worry about someone starting a brawl and upsetting their poker game." She looked up at him. "Did you know we make as much on the Sunday dinner as we do on Friday night drinks?"

"No."

"Yup. We served twenty-six chicken dinners last Sunday. Of course, Saturday night's our big night. Always has been, probably always will be."

Ethan hesitated, but his curiosity reared up. "What about the boardinghouse? I heard Miss Fennel is going to start serving meals."

"That won't hurt my Sunday traffic. I talked to her some Monday, and again this morning, when I went to help her redd up the place. She says she told Papa she wouldn't do any cooking on Sunday except breakfast, and if they have boarders, they can go over to my place or eat some crackers or something in their rooms."

Ethan arched his eyebrows. "She told him that?"

"You're darn tootin'. That gal has sprouted some backbone lately. You knew she'd joined the shooting club last week? Against Papa's will."

"Yeah. But she's taking private lessons with Tr— Gert, now that she's got to work all day."

"I told you Gert's a gem. Who else would do that for a pucker-faced schoolmarm who looks as though she was weaned on vinegar?" Bitsy shook her head. "I'm glad she's standing up to her father at last. He's got a mean streak, always has. I meant it when I said I don't like him." Bitsy looked up at Ethan and winked. "I only did that tonight to make him squirm. I don't like him, and he don't like me. We both know it." She nodded firmly.

They had passed the Wells Fargo office and an empty building and now approached the Walker Feed Company. Across the street, the singing had stopped, and all was quiet. The folks must be praying.

"So . . . if you don't mind my asking," Ethan said, "how come you don't go to church now? Seems all the other ladies from the shooting club are going, even your . . . employees."

Bitsy barked out a laugh. "They're my girls, Sheriff. No one in this town has illusions about their occupation." She shook her head. "But no, I don't see myself warming a pew. The decent folks in this town never said boo to me until lately. Now all the ladies in the shooting club treat me nice. I like it. It's kind of different, feeling as though I've got some friends. But I don't think God's ready for me yet."

Ethan looked away, trying not to register shock. "Miss Shepard," he managed, "I believe God is always ready."

Bitsy jabbed him with a sharp elbow. "Look!" She pointed down the alley between the feed store and the old building that used to be the wainwright's shop.

Ethan squinted against the dusk. Smoke poured from the big pole barn that stood a hundred feet or so behind the feed store. Charles Walker stockpiled all his grain for the store in that building. The stench of the black, roiling smoke hit Ethan's nostrils.

"Fire! Run over to the church, Bitsy! Tell the men to come quick! Bring water and blankets."

Bitsy hitched her skirt even higher and jumped off the boardwalk, wobbling on her high heels. Ethan ran for the barn.

CHAPTER 31

Gert sat with her head bowed as Bertha Runnels prayed.

"Lord, we ask that You would heal Mr. Bryce from his sciatica. Help the —"

The door crashed open, and Gert's eyes popped open. Heads swiveled toward the back as Bitsy Shepard yelled, "Fire! The mayor's barn's on fire. The sheriff says all men get to the Walker warehouse. Bring water and blankets."

Gert jumped up as the men streamed toward the door, calling to each other.

Libby struggled against the flow and came toward her. "If the buildings on Main Street catch, the whole town could go."

"Should we go over?"

"We'd just get in the way, I expect."

"We could haul buckets of water over and soak blankets for them," Gert said.

"Good idea. And I could put on a pot of coffee."

Gert looked around. "There's a back door. Come on."

She and Libby fought the tide of parishioners struggling toward the exit and gained the door near the pine pulpit Hiram had built for Pastor Benton.

Annie Harper cut them off. "You thinking what I'm thinking?"

"Bucket brigade from my place," Libby said. "And I'll donate the fixings for coffee."

Annie nodded. "I can get my big pot."

"I've got two extras in the store." Libby took her arm and steered her past the pulpit.

Behind them, Apphia Benton yelled, "Ladies, don't panic. Let us remain here and pray while the men fight the fire."

Libby hesitated, and Gert shoved her gently toward the back door. With Annie they made their escape. As soon as they got outside, she smelled it. They rounded the corner of the haberdashery, and she halted, staring at the massive column of black smoke. From their angle, it seemed to rise from the feed store itself and the vacant storefront beside it. Not until they'd crossed the street and come even with an alley could they see the barn behind that served as Charles Walker's warehouse. Dozens of men surged toward it. Bitsy, in one of her bright silk dresses, stood on the corner yelling and pointing the way.

Gert ran to her, leaving Annie and Libby to worry about coffee and other nonessentials.

"What can I do, Bitsy?"

"Water! The men can't bring it fast enough. If you can, pump water and bring it. They've got two tubs over there where they can soak their wool blankets, but we need to keep them full. And buckets of water to throw on the fire."

"Libby's pump and the Nashes' are probably closest."

Bitsy nodded. "The men are using them, and Zach Harper's gone for his wagon. He plans to haul barrels of water, but it may be too late."

Not many women had stayed at the church. Vashti and Goldie ran across the street, holding their skirts well above their knees.

"Miss Bitsy, what can we do to help?"

"Bless you, girls. Round up more buckets. Augie's already over here, but you can get pails and big pans from the kitchen. Oh, and get the wash boiler."

The two girls hiked up their dresses and charged for the Spur & Saddle.

Gert left Bitsy on the corner to direct the

people who came to help. She ran to Libby's back door and up the stairs that led directly to the apartment above the emporium. Annie answered her peremptory knock.

"Give me any buckets you won't need," Gert panted. Annie thrust a galvanized pail and a dishpan into her hands.

"Wait, Gert," Libby called. She hurried over with her keys in her hand. "I'll go downstairs and open the back door of the store. You can take anything that will help."

"I'll meet you there."

Gert pounded down the outer stairway and tossed the pail and dishpan toward the pump over Libby's well. Peter Nash already worked the handle up and down, and Griffin and Oscar, along with Jamin Morrell and two men Gert didn't know, waited to fill their own containers. Bitsy's alarm must have emptied both saloons.

At the door, Libby shoved a stack of new buckets into her hands. "Pass these out to whoever's there."

Gert hurried to the pump. "Anyone need a pail?" Augie was working the pump now, while Bill Stout and Hiram filled their buckets. She handed empty ones to Ted Hire and Cyrus. When they'd gone, Gert filled her own and hurried to the tubs where the men repeatedly brought their blankets to dunk them. Ethan met her there as she dumped two full pails into the tubs, his face and clothing black with soot. Even his badge was caked with it.

"Trudy! Keep back. You need to stay safe."

"I will." She squinted toward the barn. Her eyes stung from the smoke, and tears bathed her cheeks. Thick smoke poured from the open barn door and the spaces beneath the eaves. Inside, flames leaped among the bulging stacked feed sacks. Men soaked the siding boards on the south side of the barn. Others hurried in the big doorway with water.

"Is the whole thing going to go?"

"Maybe. A big stack of oat sacks was burning when I got here, and it's caught on the inside wall now. We're hoping we can lick it, but it will be close." As Ethan spoke, he plunged a filthy, ragged blanket into the tub. He lifted it and squeezed out enough water to keep from wasting much on his way back to the blaze. Hefting the heavy wool, he grinned at her, his teeth brilliant white in his blackened face. "Shoulda known you'd be out here helping."

"We're making coffee for all you men," she called as he turned to go.

He yelled over his shoulder, "Save me some."

"Get back!" Hiram's shout rang louder than Gert had ever heard his voice before. Men tore away from the south wall as flames ignited the siding and ripped up the height of the barn on the outside of the wall. The heat intensified, and the fire fighters couldn't approach the inferno. Suddenly the roof burst into flames.

"Mercy!" Gert turned to find Orissa beside her. Her huge eyes reflected the bright flames in her pinched face.

Gert sidled closer to her. "I'm sorry, Mrs. Walker."

Orissa turned her face into Gert's shoulder and sobbed.

"Soak the roofs of these houses," Ethan shouted. "If the empty buildings catch, the whole town will go."

A ring of men stayed as close around the barn as they could bear, smothering embers that reached the ground. The light wind favored them by sending its occasional gentle breath southward, not directly toward Main Street. The men carried bucket after bucket to the back of the feed store, the Wells Fargo office, and the vacant storefront between them. While others climbed onto the roofs to slosh the water over the vulnerable shingles, Hiram and Griffin began to carry buckets to the back of the emporium. They flooded the back porch of the store and the stairs that led to Libby's apartment.

"Think we need to do the roof?" Griffin shouted.

Hiram turned and looked toward the barn. Much of the siding had fallen away. The beams stood, outlined in flame, surrounding the high stacks of bagged corn, oats, and wheat. Without question, the whole pile had caught now.

"That fire's gonna smolder for days," Hiram said. "We can't bring enough water to drench the whole thing."

Griffin nodded. "We need to contain it."

Orissa sobbed.

Gert tightened her arm around her. "Come on, Mrs. Walker, let's go inside the emporium. You need to sit down."

At dawn all agreed the fire was mostly out. Now and then a new plume of smoke found its way out of the charred pile of grain. Ethan posted Deputies Oscar Runnels and Zach Harper to a two-hour shift to make sure the fire didn't break out again. Griffin and Hiram would relieve them for the next watch.

Ethan knelt by one of the tubs and immersed his head. Raising it, he stood and shook off the extra water. Someone handed him a towel. After he'd wiped his face, he realized it was Trudy.

"Thanks. Shoulda put apples in there so we could bob for them." He handed her the grimy towel. The skin on his face hurt as though he had a sunburn.

Mayor Walker plodded toward him and thrust out his hand. "Thanks for all you did, Sheriff."

"I'm sorry we couldn't stop it sooner." Ethan looked toward the pile of charred boards and the heaps of ruined grain.

"You did all anyone could."

Ethan nodded grudgingly. "Thank Miss Shepard, too. She spotted the smoke first. Our patrols paid off tonight. We were able to muster the men quick enough to keep the fire from ripping through town."

Walker sighed. "I had no idea anything was wrong until Pete Nash's boy ran over and hammered on my door. I stayed home last night — had a little headache." He put his hand to his temple, as though that were evidence that he'd been ill enough to dodge prayer meeting.

Ethan glanced at Trudy, who stood silently beside him holding the towel. "I hoped we could save the building and maybe some of the grain."

"I surely wish this had happened before Oscar brought in that big new shipment yesterday." Walker sighed and looked back at the ruins of the barn. "You're sure this was deliberate?"

"Pretty sure," Ethan said. "When I first got there, I could tell it started right in the front corner, not far from the door. I think he dumped oil or something like that over the full sacks on that side of the barn. I had hopes. . . ." He rubbed the back of his sore neck. "Well, no sense wishing now. But when it's cooled off, I want to poke through the ashes on that corner and see if we find any oil cans or anything like that."

Mrs. Walker came out the back door of the emporium and shrieked, "Charles! Charles, are you all right?"

The mayor gritted his teeth and staggered toward her. "I'll live, Orissa. Don't discompose yourself now."

"Oh, Charles, you've lost all your inventory."

"There, now. We've still got the store and our home. This is a great loss, but we'll get by."

Orissa's sobs rose, and he patted her shoulder.

"I'd best walk them home," Ethan said to

Gert. "The mayor may have overdone it a little tonight."

"Sure." Gert turned troubled gray eyes on him. "Libby's set up coffee and whatever the other ladies brought for breakfast inside the store: sandwiches, gingerbread, doughnuts, biscuits. All the men can go in the back door, get their eats, and head out the front. But I was hoping you'd come to our place later so we could talk about this."

Ethan smiled down at her. "I'll be there. Soon as I get the Walkers home safe."

She hesitated then said, "Look around their house, won't you, Ethan? If the killer set that fire, it's possible he did it to draw people away while he busied himself at something else."

"We think alike." He had a sudden desire to touch her, to hold her in his arms, but that was preposterous. He was covered with soot. Besides, half the town milled about, and the sun had risen and illuminated the people in all their filthy exhaustion. The light breeze whistling down the hills brought anything but romance.

"Come on." He nodded toward Libby's back door.

Fifteen minutes later, after the mayor had consumed a sandwich and listened to the commiseration of a score of people, Ethan set out with him and Orissa. As they walked up the street, Orissa said, "It's a wonder the store and the old grocery didn't catch."

"Sure is. A real nine days' wonder." Her husband's voice was threadier than usual.

"Your throat sore?" Orissa asked.

"Yes. All that smoke."

"You'd both best wash up and go to bed for a few hours," Ethan said. They came to the dooryard, and he stopped. "Did you lock up when you left the house?"

The mayor scowled at him. "Lock up? Never do."

"Well, then, just let me take a look around before you go in."

"You think —"

"I don't think anything." Ethan shot a glance at Mrs. Walker's sharp features. "I just want to be sure it's safe."

He walked slowly to the front steps. Nothing seemed amiss, and the door was shut. He mounted the steps to the porch and reached out for the knob but stopped. Something caught his eye on the mat at his feet. He bent and picked it up, running his finger along the smooth edge. He didn't take time to examine it closely. No use getting the Walkers all upset. He opened the door and went inside.

Ethan walked through the entire house,

room by room. So far as he could see, nothing was out of place. Mrs. Walker was a persnickety housekeeper. It would have been easy to see if someone had rifled the place.

At last he went out and called to them, "Seems all right. You can come in."

"Sheriff, what's the meaning of this?" Charles Walker said as he puffed up the steps. The fire had singed off half his eyebrows, and his bald spot held a sprinkling of sweat drops.

"Just checking," Ethan said.

"Do you think the same person set the fire tonight as set the one at the Paragon?" Orissa stared at him through narrowed eyes.

"I don't know, but it's possible. I wanted to be sure the arsonist wasn't up to other mischief while we were all over at the fire."

"Good thinking, son."

Ethan smiled grimly. The mayor had never called him that before. He wondered if they'd still replace him if he didn't unmask the killer in the next twelve days.

"Well, good night, folks. We'll keep watch at the warehouse, and I'll be sleeping at the jail tonight. If you need me, you'll know where to find me."

"Sure enough." The mayor wheezed in through the doorway.

"Thank you, Sheriff." Orissa followed him.

Ethan strolled slowly down the street. The stench of smoke still hovered. People exited the emporium in clusters. Through the front window, he could see Florence, Ellie Nash, and Bitsy helping Libby straighten up. Peter Nash and Augie Moore stood to one side talking with cups in their hands.

Ethan stood for a moment watching until he was reasonably sure the Dooleys weren't in there. He ambled on down the street toward their house. The Nugget was quiet, and the whole north end of the street lay subdued. No piano music, no laughter this morning. The sun eased up above the houses and the livery stable. He followed the path around to the back door of Hiram's house and knocked.

"There you are." Trudy stood in the doorway with her hair all loose about her shoulders and a spotless white apron over her blue dress. Ethan's throat ached, not from the night of breathing in fumes, but from the sight of her, so calm and content, waiting for him.

"Sorry I'm so filthy."

"Come in. I put Hiram in the bathtub, and when he's done, you can have a turn. I've got more water on the stove."

Ethan started to say there was no need but abandoned that notion. If he'd ever needed a bath in his life, it was now.

He followed her inside. She turned and leaned against her worktable with her arms folded across her chest, saying nothing but watching him. The light streamed in the window behind her, sending little glimmers off her hair. It looked almost golden, not the flat straw color he usually registered when he looked at her.

Her eyes crinkled. "What?"

"Nothing. Just . . . I appreciate it. Seems to me you hauled a lot of water in the last few hours."

"We all did."

"Well, you needn't have done more for me."

"Hiram carried most of the bathwater." She turned to the stove and picked up the steaming coffeepot. "Did you get coffee at Libby's?"

"I did, but I wouldn't be against having more. My throat still tickles."

She poured him a cup, and he took it from her. He didn't want to sit down with his trousers crusted in soot and grime, so he leaned against the edge of the sturdy pine table.

"Thank you, Trudy."

She smiled. "I'm glad I can do it."

He took a sip and savored it. "Did I ever tell you, you make good coffee?"

"Seems you might have." She waited a moment then raised her chin. "So tell me, who set the fire?"

Ethan dug his hand into his pocket and brought it out again. "Whoever left this on the Walkers' doormat."

She caught her breath and reached for the penny. "Eighteen-sixty-six?"

"You tell me. I didn't want them to see it, so I didn't look yet."

She took it over to the window and bent close. Her hair took on more golden highlights, and her face glowed. How could he ever have thought she was plain?

"That's the year, all right." She straightened and held it out to him.

Ethan took the penny, flipped it in the air, caught it, and returned it to his pocket. "Anyone could have gone over and left that on the doorstep while we were all at the fire."

She nodded slowly. "Or before he went to the fire."

Ethan raised his eyebrows. "I hadn't considered the mayor a suspect before. But you're right. He could have done it. He skipped church last night." He smiled ruefully. "I was about to embrace your theory, you know."

"Cyrus?" Her brows arched like the wings of a soaring hawk.

He nodded. "He went late to the prayer meeting."

"Yes, I saw him come in after the first couple of hymns."

"Bitsy and I met him on the street. He'd just come out of his office, and we hadn't spotted the fire yet. That fire must have been started at least several minutes before we saw it. By that time, it was putting out a lot of smoke." Ethan drained his coffee cup.

"So Cyrus could have set it and then gone back to his office." Trudy drew in a deep breath. "What now, Ethan?"

"I don't know. Most of the men in town have nearly as shaky alibis. Someone could have set that fire twenty minutes before church time. Just got it going and walked away. Or even ten minutes before time for the prayer meeting."

"And then showed up to help put it out when you and Bitsy sounded the alarm."

"Sure." He wagged his index finger at her. "So you be careful, won't you, now? I don't want anything happening to you." He touched the tip of her nose.

Her eyelids lowered as she looked at his

finger. He drew it back and winced.

"Sorry. My hands are still dirty."

She smiled. "I'll be careful."

Hiram appeared in the doorway between the kitchen and the sitting room in his stocking feet, wearing a clean plaid shirt and shabbily comfortable trousers. "Well, Eth, how's everything?" He scrubbed at his damp hair with a clean towel.

Ethan laughed. "Fine, just fine."

Hiram spread his arms, indicating his outfit. "Gert made me put on all clean clothes, even though I haven't been to bed." He shook his head. "Women."

"Oh, hush," Trudy said. "You can't sleep all day. There's too much to do. To start with, you can carry that pan of hot water into your bedroom and heat up the tub for Ethan. I didn't think it was possible, but he's even filthier than you were half an hour ago."

Hiram grinned. "Good thing I had the first bath."

Ethan picked up the potholders Trudy had left on the work counter and turned to the stove. "I'll get it. But I don't have any clean clothes to put on."

"I put out a shirt for you," Hiram said. "Don't think my britches would fit you though."

"Thanks." Ethan winced. "I've got a few things at the jail. Should have brought them."

"I can run over there for you," Hiram said.

"I appreciate that. What all do you two need to do today?"

"It's Isabel's opening day," Trudy said. "I promised her six pies by noon, and Hiram's going to take another turn on watch over at the fire."

"That's right. So you think Isabel will go ahead and open, what with all the excitement over the fire?"

Trudy shrugged. "The stagecoach will still come in at quarter to noon, fire or no fire."

"True. Well, I'll get in the tub. Meanwhile, Trudy, you tell your brother what I found over at the Walkers'." When he turned around with the steaming pan of water in his hands, Hiram was stifling his laughter, but Trudy nodded at him with a complacent, wistful smile.

"I'll do that while I make my pie crust."

Hiram winked at him. "Don't forget to wash behind your ears."

Chapter 32

Gert packed two pies in the bottom of her large carrying basket. She took a light wooden platform Hiram had built for the purpose and carefully fitted it over them, lowering the legs between the pie plates. On top of this she put two more pies.

"There. If you can carry the other two . . ."

"Oh yes." Apphia Benton put one of the remaining pies in a smaller basket and picked up the other. "Ready?"

Together they went out Gert's back door and around the path to the boardwalk.

"Thanks for helping." Gert felt a twinge of guilt at asking her morning caller to lend her a hand. "It would have taken me at least two trips alone, and I'm dead tired."

"You poor thing," Apphia said. "At least my husband and I got a few hours' sleep after the fire was out."

"Well, I'd promised Isabel, and she's just starting to act friendly to me and some of the other ladies. I didn't want to give her an excuse to back off, even if I had to hurry things up and used canned fruit for two of the pies."

"They'll be delicious, I'm sure." Apphia smiled at her. "I'm glad Isabel's venture has gone so well, but not pleased that it means even more work for her, poor woman."

Gert had to agree. Word that the boarding-house was reopening had already led to the rental of both bedrooms the women had helped renovate. Now her father demanded that she open up four more rooms. All passengers, as well as the stagecoach drivers and shotgun riders, must know that clean, comfortable rooms at a respectable lodging house were now available in Fergus.

"In the old days, folks didn't care much where they slept," she said. "Hiram told me the miners coming through town would sleep five or six to a room at the boarding-house. But nowadays people think they should have a nice room to themselves, like they would at a hotel in the city."

"And Mr. Fennel is taking advantage of that."

"No surprise to me." Gert looked over at the minister's wife. "I don't mean to speak ill of Mr. Fennel. I suppose most would say he's done a lot for this town. He's stuck around here since the boom days and through the bust. He mined for gold and ran the assay office; then he bought a ranch and got the stage line's business through these parts. He's had a hand in most of the enterprises in Fergus. Now he's just turning his hand to a new vocation. He'll make it succeed."

"He will, or his daughter?" Apphia shook her head. "Seems to me that Isabel's doing all the work."

"True. Her pa bankrolls it, but she's seen to the labor."

"And her friends have helped her." Apphia's brow furrowed. "I'm not sure we're doing Isabel a good turn. The more we help her for free, the more her father will let us."

"I know." Gert sighed. "Hiram won't do any more without being paid. Not for Isabel. She's going to pay me for my pies after today, and I know she's paying Augie for his cooking, too. I keep telling myself not to go over and help her scrub anymore, but then I think of her trying to do it all herself, and I feel sorry for her."

"She's hired Myra Harper to help serve meals and wash dishes and laundry, so don't trouble yourself anymore." Apphia paused as they came to the small street that cut between the jail and the boardinghouse. The

Bentons' new home lay a block to the east on this narrow street.

"Almost there," said Gert. "Let's take them around to the kitchen door." She led Apphia to the back of the boardinghouse. "I do think Isabel's father's coming around a little. He sent two of his coach riders to set up the bedsteads and move furniture for her. Told them they could work off the price of their rooms doing it. And yesterday he thanked Hiram for fixing the steps and offered to pay him to make a sign."

"I'm glad to hear she's getting some help," Apphia said. "I fear the women in this territory often fall into the category of forced labor."

Gert opened the door, noting that all the windows on the back of the building were now free of extra lumber and sparkling clean.

Isabel, wearing a voluminous apron over her dress, looked up from where she peeled potatoes. "Oh, Gert, bless you! I wasn't certain you'd have time."

"Sure did. And Mrs. Benton came along and offered to help me truck the pies over here."

"Set them right here on this table. I can't begin to thank you enough." Isabel indicated a small table near the door to the dining room, and Gert and Apphia set their baskets down.

Myra Harper came into the kitchen carrying a stack of ironstone plates. "These are the ones we're using for lunch, right, Miss Fennel?"

"Yes, and call me Isabel. We'll be working too closely for formality."

"All right. Shall I set the tables, or do you want the plates out here?" Myra asked.

"Go ahead and set up for six at the big table. We'll take the serving dishes out, and folks can serve themselves." When Myra had left the room, Isabel brushed back a strand of loose hair and turned to Gert and Apphia. "I don't know what I'm doing, and I have to make so many decisions. If we get a lot of customers, I suppose we should take orders and fill their plates in the kitchen as they do in restaurants. But I want people to feel that Fennel House is like a home. If they want seconds, the dish will be on the table."

"That sounds right," Apphia said. "You want your guests to feel contented and cared for, not like someone you're only out to earn money off."

Isabel nodded slowly. "Yes. That's it. Father doesn't understand. He wanted me to buy the cheapest blankets the emporium could get, but I told him that if he spends a little more and puts pretty quilts on the bed or nice, commercially milled bedspreads, the patrons will see us as more than a second-rate boardinghouse. I've been praying this venture will succeed and" — she flushed and looked down at the paring knife in her hand — "and that people will say we've made a good addition to the town."

Gert smiled. "Other folks have been praying for you, too, Isabel."

Apphia walked over to her and patted Isabel's arm. "My dear, you've put a great deal of thought and effort into this. Perhaps you have a special gift of hospitality."

"Do you think so?" Isabel sighed. "I do want to go back to teaching though. I told Father he has three weeks to find someone else to do this. When the summer term opens, I want my class back."

"Are you sure?" Apphia asked.

"Yes. I don't mind the hard work, though cooking was never my strongest talent. And Myra's been a tremendous help. But I don't like the thought of men milling around. I'll have to please the paying customers, even if they're difficult. But I told Father that if any of his stage line employees try to take liberties with me or Myra, I'm done."

"I'm sure he's instructed them to behave

as gentlemen when they come here for refreshment or for their rooms in the evening."

"Well, I'm not staying here nights." Isabel raised her chin. "There is absolutely no way I'll room here when there might be all men for guests some nights. At least Father saw the sense to that. He says he'll take me home to the ranch each evening."

"I'm glad to hear it," Apphia said. "My dear, you know I'm just around the corner. If you ever feel unsafe here, I urge you to dash out the back and come to me and Mr. Benton."

"Thank you." Isabel sniffed. "That's very kind. I don't expect to be working here long though."

Gert walked over closer. "The Ladies' Shooting Club can make this a regular stop. I'll ask the sheriff to look in evenings, too."

"Thank you. Father felt at first that someone responsible should be on the premises at night. When I suggested he might start sleeping here . . . Well, he didn't take kindly to the notion. Besides, that would leave me alone at the ranch, and I don't like the isolation of it when he's not around."

"Absolutely right," said Apphia. "If the venture pays, I hope he'll hire a trustworthy couple to live here. Meanwhile, we shall continue praying for you and sending our club members to check on you. And now . . ." She looked at Gert. "We know you and Myra have a lot to do, so we'll leave you."

Relieved they had not been pressed into doing chores, Gert followed Apphia to the back door. "Good-bye, Isabel. And do call on either of us if you need anything."

Ethan breathed deeply as he left the Nugget on Saturday evening. It was good to get out into the fresh air. He didn't know how those men could stand it in the close atmosphere of the saloon. The smoke, the smell of liquor, the bar girls' cheap perfume. Give him a clear whiff of prairie air anytime. A light breeze brought him a hint of scorched corn through the twilight, but the smells from the warehouse fire had pretty much abated over the last three days.

He ambled past the boardinghouse. Instead of a blank, echoing hulk, it now showed signs of life. The windows were no longer boarded. Soft light glowed from the dining room and parlor, and candlelight shone dimly in an upstairs front window. Cyrus had paid Hiram to make an attractive sign: FENNEL HOUSE, ROOM & BOARD. The town was mending and regaining vigor.

The little jail where Ethan presided loomed dark and silent. He walked past it toward the cozy house beyond. He smiled with anticipation. Trudy had promised to patrol with him for two hours at sunset to fulfill her commitment as a deputy. He'd looked forward to it all day. Of course, they would keep it businesslike, but he'd still get to walk with her, and no doubt they would converse. These days, talking to Trudy always left him feeling warm and hopeful that something good would happen.

He strolled around to the backyard as usual. Hiram came from the barn with a bridle slung over his shoulder.

"Evening, Hi," Ethan said.

Hiram nodded with a half smile.

"Trudy ready to go patrolling with me?"

"I expect so."

Ethan let him go up the steps first and open the door to the kitchen. The oil lamp burned low on the table, but Trudy wasn't present. Hiram looked at him and shrugged then shuffled off into the parlor. Ethan leaned against the doorjamb and waited, enjoying the snug hominess of the kitchen.

A moment later, Trudy entered. He straightened and smiled.

"Hi."

"Howdy." She wore a dark skirt and light-colored blouse with a short jacket over it. She'd tied her hair back, and while he waited, she reached for a bonnet. Frowning, she stayed her hand. "I like to be able to see, especially when I'm on watch. Those bonnets are good for keeping the sun off, but they block a good part of your vision, too."

Ethan chuckled. "Like blinders on a horse?"

"Something like." She looked over her shoulder toward the other room then snatched Hiram's sagging felt hat and popped it onto her head. "Come on. He won't miss it."

She reached for the Sharps rifle that stood in the corner between the cupboard and the door.

"You're taking his rifle, too?" Ethan asked.

"We *are* on duty."

"Well, yes, but it'll get heavy, don't you think?"

She hesitated. "I suppose I ought to get a pistol, but we haven't had much cash come in lately. I don't like to ask Hiram to lay out money for something extra."

"I thought he had a six-shooter."

"He used to, but he traded it a year or so ago."

"Well, I'm armed." Ethan patted his holster.

"What good is a deputy without a gun?"

He considered that. "Another pair of eyes."

"All right. Let's go then."

It was almost fully dark outside when they walked out to the street.

"Which way?" she asked.

"I just came from the Nugget, and things looked peaceful at the boardinghouse. Let's head down the street as far as Bitsy's place."

She fell into step beside him on the walkway. "Did you see Isabel at the boardinghouse?"

"No, I didn't go in. But I saw her father at the Nugget."

"So he hadn't picked up Isabel to take her home yet." Trudy scowled at that, and Ethan didn't blame her. Cyrus had been seeing Isabel home to the ranch every evening, and the sprinkling of boarders, which now included the coach drivers and shotgun riders, were left to have pleasant dreams on their own.

"Wonder if she had many guests tonight?"

Trudy said, "I took her two pies this morning after the Boise stage came in, and she was bustling around getting lunch. Myra Harper was helping her. She said she'd have two people staying tonight for sure, and maybe more off the Silver City coach this afternoon."

"Cyrus made a good decision to reopen the place."

"Yes, but Isabel's afraid he won't let her go back to teaching." She stepped down at the break in the boardwalk between a vacant house and the haberdashery. "This fella we're watching out for."

"What about him?" Ethan should have known her thoughts would go back to the criminal who eluded them.

"He seems to like fire."

He offered her a hand up onto the sidewalk at the other side of the alley. "I reckon that's true. That seems to be his weapon."

"That and bashing people's heads in."

"Yes." They walked on in silence to the front entrance of the building where the church services were held. Ethan paused and shook the locked door to make sure it was secure. He'd long since found cracks in most of the shutters or planks nailed over windows in town. These allowed him to peer into the interiors of the unused stores and houses to make sure no flames sputtered within. Two fires so far — at the emporium and the warehouse. And who knew but the Pearts' cabin fell to arson as well? But he tended to think that was carelessness with the stove on Milzie's part.

"Maybe we should walk around the back of these places," Trudy said.

"Sometimes I do. Let's make a circuit of Main Street. Then maybe we'll go the long way around, one street over."

"All right. We can go check the livery and go up the back of that side as far as the burned warehouse, at least." A horse nickered nearby, and Trudy turned toward the street. "Look at that. Horses lined up from the Spur & Saddle all the way down here."

"That's right. It's Saturday night. Bitsy's place will be full. It was early when I stopped in at the Nugget, but quite a few men were in there getting primed. Probably by the time we get back down to that end of the street, it'll be starting to get rough." He eyed her ruefully. "Maybe Saturday night's not the best time for a female deputy to patrol."

Trudy stepped over to the edge of the boardwalk and patted one of the horses at the haberdashery's hitching rail. "It's early, like you said. If it gets too wild, you can take me home and make Hiram go with you. I just hope Cyrus goes for Isabel before it gets noisy." She made her way down the row of horses, patting each one on the nose.

Ethan smiled as he watched her. Sometimes he forgot she was a girl. She was so competent and levelheaded. She never threw a fit of hysterics.

"Isn't this Ralph Storrey's paint?" She stroked the nose of the horse on the end of the row.

"Sure enough." The rest could have been anyone's, with all the dark colors blending into the night. The bays and chestnuts all looked black, but the flashy pinto's white patches stood out.

"I always notice him when Ralph rides down Main Street. He looks so . . . I don't know . . . happy. And eager."

"He's a good horse, all right." Ethan felt a little disloyal, comparing this animal mentally to Scout. While Scout had gotten a little long in the tooth and wasn't as fast as he used to be, he was a good horse, too, and they'd have several good years together yet.

Trudy stepped down off the boardwalk beside the paint. "Hey, fella. You tired of waiting for your master?" She rubbed his snout and slid her fingers up his broad face to scratch beneath his forelock. The gelding nickered and tried to rub his head against her arm.

"No, you don't. I don't want you slobbering all over my clean clothes."

Ethan laughed. Had she changed her clothes for him tonight? She looked good.

She rejoined him, brushing her hands together. They continued on until they reached the front of the Spur & Saddle. The place was bright with lamplight. A half dozen horses dozed at each of the two hitching rails out front. Gentle music and laughter floated out to them.

"That sounds like a piano," Trudy noted.

"Bitsy's got a nice one in there."

Trudy cocked her head toward the sound. "It sounds real pretty."

"Yes."

"Who plays it?"

"One of those bits of girls." Ethan felt his face flush. He hated to admit he even knew girls lived and worked here.

"Goldie or Vashti?"

"I dunno. The one with the blond hair."

"That's Goldie."

"Mm." He shrugged.

"She's not bad at it, is she? I wonder if she practices every day."

"I don't know. The cowboys come in on Saturday night to hear her play."

Trudy gave a little bark of a chuckle as though she doubted the music was the main attraction.

Ethan shifted his weight to his other foot. "I usually go in and ask Augie if things are peaceful."

"Let's do it."

He gulped and stood rock still. "You can't . . . you can't go in there. Not now."

"What do you mean, *Sheriff?*"

"I mean that ladies don't go in there on Saturday night." It came out louder than he'd intended.

Trudy's eyes, dark, stormy gray in this light, sparked up at him. "What's the difference? Saturday night, Sunday noon, it's the same place."

"Yeah, but . . ."

"Same people running it."

"Well, yes."

"And I'm a deputy sheriff."

"I can't deny it."

"Then let's go."

It dawned on him suddenly that she wanted to see the place. "Uh, Trudy, have you ever been inside?"

After a moment's silence, she shook her head.

"Never ate Sunday dinner here?"

"Nope. Hiram and I usually stick to home on Sunday. I don't think my brother's ever been inside either saloon."

"Uh . . . I don't think you should go in.

447

For all the reasons you never have before."

She held his gaze for a long time. At last she exhaled and reached up to settle Hiram's hat lower on her brow, shadowing her eyes. "Lots of women go there on Sunday."

"I know. And if Hiram wants to take you, he can."

She nodded, her lips tightly compressed. "All right. I'll wait here. Get going."

He patted her shoulder awkwardly. "Thanks. I won't be long."

Ethan bounded up the steps and entered the saloon, determined not to leave Trudy standing in the street more than a minute.

Two men came out of the Spur & Saddle. Gert eased back into the shadows under the overhang of the eaves. They lurched down the steps and headed for the hitching rail. After untying his horse, one couldn't seem to get the momentum he needed to bounce into the saddle. He led the horse over to the steps and mounted from the second stair. They never saw her but turned their horses toward the road that led out past Harpers' farm.

Gert left her place of concealment and walked to the hitching rail. She didn't recognize any of the horses for sure, though one compact dun looked a lot like the one

Starr Tinen rode to the shooting club. Maybe her husband had ridden into town to hear the piano music. She curled her lip and patted the dun's sleek neck. "It's not your fault if your owner has bad habits."

Across the street, a solitary figure left the boardwalk and came toward her. Gert backed up until she stood once more in the shadows beneath the saloon's eaves. With her brother's hat pulled low, she watched from beneath the brim.

The man paused and looked northward, the length of Fergus's principal street. Perhaps he considered visiting the Nugget instead of the Spur & Saddle. He faced toward her, his thin shoulders slouched. Mayor Walker. His friend Cy Fennel was down at the Nugget, by Ethan's account. Still boycotting Bitsy's establishment. As Walker approached, Gert shrank down and hoped he didn't notice her.

He reached the boardwalk before the saloon and lifted his foot to the first step. Gert noticed movement beyond him. Down the street, between the closed telegraph office and the old haberdashery, a dark figure stepped out from between the buildings. He stood still. She wondered if he was as indecisive as the mayor on where to buy his whiskey.

She saw a flash of light. The bang of a gunshot cut through the air and echoed off the fronts of the buildings on the far side of the street. Mayor Walker spun around and fell on the steps. Gert's heart squeezed, and she couldn't breathe. She wanted to duck down behind the stoop, but she couldn't take her eyes off the dark shadow that flitted toward the prone man. Would he shoot again to make sure the mayor was dead?

Without thinking of her danger, she jumped up and dashed to the front of the steps. She was a deputy sheriff. If he wanted to make sure he'd done the job right this time, he'd have to go through her.

"Leave him alone!" She threw herself to her knees beside the mayor.

The other man stopped several yards away. Light from the windows glinted off the barrel of his pistol. For a moment, Gert feared he would shoot at her. Why, oh why had she listened to Ethan and left the rifle home?

He gaped at her. His dark hat shadowed his face, and she couldn't see his features, but it looked like he'd tied a dark cloth over his mouth and chin. He raised his other hand over his head and thrust it toward her as though throwing something.

Everything happened so fast, Gert barely

noticed the men pouring out the door of the Spur & Saddle. All she could take in was the mayor lying on the steps gasping, the small *click* as a tiny object hit the stair tread beside his body, and the shadowy man fleeing down the boardwalk. He ran to the horses tied before the telegraph office. In a flash, he had unhitched Storrey's paint horse and leaped into the saddle. Gert turned her attention to the mayor. He sucked in a big breath and shut his eyes. The other man disappeared with only staccato hoofbeats testifying to his flight.

"Trudy! I heard a shot. What happened?" Ethan crouched beside her. "Is that the mayor?"

She looked up and nodded. Her eyes filled with tears, multiplying the images of a dozen men who stood above her, staring.

Augie thundered down the steps with a linen towel in his hand and knelt by Walker's other side. He pulled back the mayor's jacket.

"He's bleeding bad." Augie stuffed the towel over the wound. "I think he's breathing."

Ethan looked up at the other men and singled out Ezra Dyer. "Go get Bitsy. Ask her where we can put him."

"Sure thing, Sheriff." Ezra turned and

clumped through the throng.

Ethan slid his arm around Gert's waist. "Are you all right? What happened?"

"The penny man," she gasped.

He stared at her. "Wh— you sure?"

She nodded. His strong arm felt so warm and reassuring, she didn't want to move. But she had to, before they lost track of the evidence. She leaned across the mayor's body and picked up the small object by Augie's boot. It had bounced off the step above, spun, and lodged against the stair riser. She held it up to Ethan.

He turned his palm upward, giving her a place to drop the penny.

CHAPTER 33

Cyrus ran up the middle of the street. Long before he reached the Spur & Saddle, he was gasping. When had he gotten so out of shape? He didn't work as hard as he used to on the ranch or in his mining days. Now he mostly sat around his office all day. Suddenly the run from the Nugget to Bitsy Shepard's place was too much for him. He slowed down near the telegraph office and pressed one hand to his chest. No sense bringing on heart failure.

Parnell Oxley dashed past him. The young ranch hand had burst into the Nugget with news that the mayor had been gunned down outside the Spur & Saddle. Ted Hire, the Nugget's bartender, followed Oxley. Twenty or more men crowded around the front entrance of Bitsy Shepard's saloon. Cyrus shoved aside two at the fringe.

"Let me through." He halted, staring at the tableau on the steps. It was true. Charles

Walker lay sprawled as though he'd fallen on the steps in midstride. Augie Moore hovered over him, and on the other side, Gert Dooley sat on the bottom step with the sheriff beside her. Cyrus glared at Ethan. "What happened here?"

Ethan stood and pushed his hat back. "Mr. Fennel. We're about to move the mayor inside where we can tend him."

Cyrus pushed past another man and went to his knees by his friend's head. "Charles, can you hear me?" Walker moaned, and relief coursed through him. Cyrus wasn't prepared to lose the one man he called a true friend.

The mayor's eyes flickered open. "Wh . . . what happened?"

The sheriff leaned in close and laid a hand on his shoulder. "Someone shot you in the belly, Mr. Walker. We're going to take you into the Spur & Saddle. Miss Shepard's getting a room ready. Then we'll see if Annie Harper will come look at you." Annie not only served as a midwife, but in the absence of a doctor, she was known as the person best at sewing up knife cuts and setting bones.

Mayor Walker lifted one hand and grasped the front of Ethan's vest. "No! Don't take me in there. Orissa will have cats. Take me

454

to my own house. It's not far."

"He's right," Cyrus said. He wasn't sure Orissa would stoop to entering the saloon on a Saturday night, even to see her gravely injured husband.

Ethan looked questioningly at Augie.

"I can lug him that far," Augie said. "He don't weigh more'n a magpie."

Bitsy appeared in the doorway, and the men parted for her. "We got the room all ready, Sheriff. Did someone go for Annie? And what about Mrs. Walker?"

Ethan said, "Change of plans, Miss Shepard. The mayor's talking, and he wants to go home. Sorry we put you out."

Bitsy waved her hand. "That makes no nevermind. Did you send one of the fellas to tell his wife?"

"Yes, ma'am. And then on to the Harpers'."

Augie slid his meaty arms beneath the mayor's slight form. The lamplight gleamed off his bald head. "Hold on, Mr. Mayor. I'm going to pick you up now."

"Let me help you," Cyrus said.

Augie shook his head. "The best way to help me is to run ahead and make sure his missus knows we're bringing him over there."

As the brawny man rose with the mayor

in his arms, a wail reached them from the east side of the street.

"Not my Charles! Oh why? Why?" Orissa Walker, a black crow crying doom, swooped toward them.

Cyrus saw his duty and reached her in the middle of the street before any of the others moved.

"Orissa, calm yourself." He reached for her arm.

"Is he dead? Tell me."

"No, my dear. Far from it. Now, be quick and get his bed ready. They're bringing him home, and Annie will be here soon to help you care for him."

"Oh me!" She put both hands to her face and sobbed. "What shall we do? Is it bad?"

"I don't know." Cyrus swallowed hard, but the ache in his chest had worsened. "I think perhaps a prayer would not be amiss." He took her hand and drew it through the crook of his arm. Augie walked toward them with his burden. Ethan and Gert came behind him. "Miss Dooley," Cyrus called, "would you kindly inform my daughter of the reason for my delay?"

Gert stopped walking. "I can do that."

Cyrus nodded and turned back to Orissa. "Come," he said gently. "Let's get things ready."

■ ■ ■ ■

"You need to tell me everything you saw," Ethan said to Gert. "I'll send someone else to tell Isabel."

"Send Bitsy so she won't be frightened." Gert shivered. She reached to fasten the top button of her jacket. "You need to go after the man who did it."

"Did you see where he went?"

She lifted her hand toward the north end of the street. "He jumped on a horse and galloped off toward Mountain Road."

Ethan dashed up the steps to the Spur & Saddle and spoke to Bitsy. She ducked back inside, and he turned at the top of the steps, in the light. "Gentlemen, prepare to ride out with me. We need a posse to go after the man who did this. If you're sober and you have a horse and a weapon, prepare to leave from the livery stable in ten minutes."

As he came down the steps toward her, the men dispersed, and Bitsy and Vashti hurried out of the saloon, spreading shawls about their shoulders. They headed together down the boardwalk toward the Fennel House.

Ethan reached Gert's side. "Walk with me as far as your house, Trudy. Tell me on the way what you saw."

"He was all dressed in black. I was standing there, behind the steps." She swiveled and pointed to the spot beyond the hitching rail where a half dozen men were preparing to mount. "The mayor reached the steps, and this man came out of the alley yonder. I couldn't see him well — just that someone else was coming. Then he fired a gun, and the mayor fell." She stopped walking in front of the telegraph office. Her throat burned as she recalled the moment. "He was right about here when he did it. I don't think he saw me. He started walking toward the mayor, and I jumped up. I was afraid he'd shoot Mr. Walker again."

"Oh, Trudy." Ethan slid his arm around her and pulled her close for a moment. "You shouldn't have done that."

She leaned away from him. "I'm the law, Ethan, same as you. I wasn't going to let him do worse than he'd done. I suppose if I'd stayed put I might have seen him more clearly, but then the mayor would be dead for sure."

"I expect so."

"That's when he threw the penny. I think now he was maybe just coming closer to leave it by Mr. Walker's body, but at the time . . ."

"Hey! Where's my horse?"

They both whirled toward the hitching rail. Ralph Storrey stormed down the boardwalk toward them. "Sheriff, someone's up and stolen my horse."

"When I yelled at him, he threw the penny then grabbed the nearest horse and galloped off," Gert said to Ethan. "It was Mr. Storrey's paint. He rode that way, at least as far as the smithy. After that, I don't know."

They all turned and stared northward. Several horsemen already trotted toward the livery stable.

"I'll ask Griffin if he saw anyone ride by," Ethan said.

"I'll ask Bane to loan me another mount," Storrey said. "If I lose that horse —" He stomped off down the street.

Gert took a deep breath, certain her next request was doomed. "Ethan, I want to go with you."

"No." He kept his arm around her, pushing toward home.

"I'm a deputy. And I saw him do it."

"No."

Bitsy, Vashti, and Isabel ran up the boardwalk toward them.

"Sheriff, is the mayor going to live?" Isabel grabbed Ethan's arm and clung to it.

He cleared his throat. "Well, Miss Fennel,

I don't know. He's over at his own house, and your father's with him. You might want to go see if there's anything you can do. I'm raising a posse to go after the man who did it."

"We'll see her safely to the Walkers' house," Bitsy said. "Is the shooting club riding with the posse?" She looked eagerly to Gert.

Gert gazed at Ethan. "Please?"

"I can't let you ladies come. But you can do a lot of good here. Help Mrs. Harper with the mayor. The men riding with me can leave their women and children there so they won't be alone while we're gone. Gather the ladies in, won't you, Trudy?"

Gert felt her face flush. The whole town would know before morning that the sheriff had a nickname for her.

"Yes, we'll do it."

Bitsy, Vashti, and Isabel left them to hurry across the street and south to the Walkers' house.

"Now tell me quick," he said to Gert. "What did he look like besides dark clothes?"

She squinted her eyes almost shut, picturing the penny man in the shadows. "He wasn't as tall as you, nor as fat as Oscar Runnels." She looked up into Ethan's eyes and nodded. "He was young. At least he moved fast. I'm sorry I can't tell you who he was."

Ethan squeezed her hand as they reached the path to her house. "You've done fine."

Hiram came from the back of the house.

"Gert, is that you? What's going on? I heard a lot of commotion."

"The mayor's been shot."

"You want to join the posse?" Ethan asked. "I'll fill you in when you get to the livery with your horse and gun."

Hiram turned on his heel and bolted for his corral behind the house.

Parnell Oxley ran toward them diagonally across the street.

"You coming, Sheriff? Griff Bane says someone rode past the livery hell-for-leather on a paint horse."

"I'm right behind you." Ethan touched Gert's sleeve for a moment. "Don't stay here alone. Get over to Walkers'. If you go out to bring other women in, go by twos and threes." He hesitated a moment then pulled her to him.

His lips met hers, and fire shot through her. This was all wrong. He couldn't kiss her and then rush off to hunt down the killer. He might not return, and —

"Be safe, Trudy." He turned and ran after Parnell for the livery.

CHAPTER 34

Libby held her pearl-handled revolver in her hand when she went to open her door. Gert stood on the landing outside.

"Did you hear? The mayor's been shot."

Libby sighed and lowered the pistol. "I wondered what it was all about."

"Come over to the Walkers' with me," Gert said. "Ethan's taken a posse after the shooter, and I don't want you here alone."

"A posse? They know who did it?"

"I saw him." Gert's mouth was set in a grim line.

"Who?"

"I don't know. I was waiting outside Bitsy's for Ethan. The killer came out of the shadows over by the telegraph office and shot Mr. Walker. Then he stole Ralph Storrey's horse. Ralph's madder than a wounded grizzly. I wanted to ride with the posse, but . . ." Her face contorted in a grimace. "We may be deputies, but we're still women.

Come on. And bring your gun. I don't have one."

"Would you like to carry my Peacemaker? I've got the little Smith & Wesson now."

"I'd feel easier," Gert admitted, and Libby ran for the weapon and her cloak.

A half dozen women had gathered in the Walkers' kitchen. Apphia Benton met Gert and Libby at the door and told them in hushed tones that Mrs. Walker, Mrs. Harper, and the minister were with the mayor.

They milled about, talking quietly. Myra Harper and Ellie Nash took over the cookstove and made coffee and gingerbread for any who wanted some. Libby kept several pans of water boiling in case Annie called for it. After half an hour, Annie emerged from the bedchamber, asking for clean rags. Libby and Gert searched about but couldn't find anything that looked the least bit frayed.

"Typical of Orissa," muttered Ellie. "Here, take this." She handed Annie a clean linen towel.

"How is he?" Libby asked.

"Not good. I'm afraid the bullet's done more damage than I can undo. If we had a surgeon . . ." Annie shook her head and went back into the bedroom.

A knock sounded on the door, and Libby hurried to open it. Emmaline Landry with

Starr Tinen, her little girl, and her mother-in-law entered.

"Micah rode off with the sheriff's posse," Emmaline said as she removed her bonnet. "He told me to get the Tinen ladies and come here, as Arthur Tinen and his father were with the posse, too."

"They'd gone into town right after supper," Starr explained. She stooped to help four-year-old Hester untie her bonnet strings. "I was looking for Arthur to come home, and here came Emmaline with word to fort up at the mayor's house."

Emmaline shrugged. "I wasn't entirely sure what was going on. Micah wouldn't stop and tell me everything. Just that the killer had shot Mayor Walker, and the posse was going to ride him down. Told me to get to town and stay here until they come back."

"Did a single horseman ride past your place before that?"

"Not that I saw," Emmaline said.

"Me either." Starr gave Libby a pouty face as she stood. "We'd have been as safe at the ranch, now that Ma Tinen and I know how to shoot."

"Oh well," said Jessie Tinen, Starr's mother-in-law. "It's a chance to see the other ladies." She took her granddaughter's hand and walked with Hester toward the kitchen door. "So, tell me, is the mayor killed?"

"No." Libby nodded toward the closed door of the bedchamber. "But his condition is grave. Annie Harper and Mr. Benton are seeing to him, but it doesn't look promising."

"Dear, dear." Jessie shook her head.

As they entered the kitchen, the other women greeted Emmaline and the Tinens. Florence drew Starr into a corner for a gossip, and Ellie offered refreshments to the newcomers.

Gert paced back and forth between the wood box and the pitcher pump that loomed over one end of the cast-iron sink. The Walkers were one of the few families to have a pump in the house, and Libby tried to squelch her envy each time she looked at it.

She cornered Gert near the wood box. "Should we make a foray to the emporium? If they need more bandages . . ."

"I could go with you if you like." Gert's eagerness told Libby she chafed at the confines of Orissa's kitchen, no matter how modern the furnishings.

"Let me ask Annie if they need anything else."

Libby went to the bedroom door and tapped softly. Mr. Benton opened it. Beyond him, Orissa Walker sat stiffly at her husband's bedside, her white face more pinched than usual. Libby's heart wrenched for her. Annie's broad back bent over the swathed figure on the bed. At her feet rested a wash basin full of bloody water and drenched cloths.

Libby murmured to the pastor, "Miss Dooley and I thought we'd go together to my store and fetch anything that's needed here. I've some soft cotton Annie could use for bandages, and perhaps she could use some peroxide or salve." She shrugged, trying to think what other medicinal supplies she had in stock. She had yet to replenish some of her inventory since the fire.

Mr. Benton consulted Mrs. Harper and returned with a short list of items the nurse thought would be useful. When Libby reached the front hall, Gert waited for her. Light spilled from the door of the front room, and the gentle murmur of Apphia's voice reached them.

"They're praying," Gert whispered. "Mrs. Benton suggested it, and they've all gone into the parlor."

Libby snatched her cloak and handbag from the coat tree near the door.

"It frets me that Emmaline didn't hear anyone ride past her house before the posse came," Gert said as they went out into the cool evening. "I saw the shooter ride off, and Griff saw him go past the livery. That's the last anyone knows for sure about where he went."

"There's not much out there but a few ranches." Libby took out the key to the store.

"What if he cut off across country or circled back? He could be anywhere now."

"You mustn't worry." They reached the store, and Libby unlocked the door. They spent the next ten minutes gathering a basket full of supplies for Annie. Libby added a pound of tea and a small sack of sugar. When they left, Gert looked carefully about before they stepped out onto the boardwalk. The street was silent and dark except for lights from the two subdued saloons and the few houses on Main Street. Gert kept the Peacemaker in her hand as they walked.

"I think we should tell the others about the pennies."

Libby eyed her in surprise. "You mean the one on my counter after the fire and the one Ethan found near Bert Thalen's body?"

Gert nodded. "There was one near Milzie's body, too. My brother found that one. And . . . well, there've been others you probably don't know about."

Libby's pulse beat faster, and her throat squeezed. "When?"

"After the warehouse fire, and again tonight."

"No."

"I'm afraid so. This killer has been using the mayor for his latest target."

Libby slowed her steps. "And Ethan knew this?"

"Not specifically. Until tonight, I mean." Gert's mournful expression and ragged voice tugged at Libby's heart. "We've talked about how this outlaw seemed to be going after important people in the town. You, Bert, Cyrus. And now Mr. Walker."

Libby nodded slowly, thinking back over the last two months. "Cyrus because of Milzie being killed in his office."

"Yes. And Isabel saw a man loitering in the alley there, too."

"I remember. She and Cyrus came to tell me about it." Libby shivered. "So you think he was lying in wait for Cyrus, not for me or Isabel."

"The more I think about it, the more I believe that."

"It's almost a relief to hear you say that — it means he probably wasn't planning to do me bodily harm. Although the fires . . ."

She studied Gert's profile as they approached the Walkers' dooryard. "What would he have against Cyrus? And me and Bert and Mayor Walker, for that matter?"

"That's what we need to find out. I think it's time we brought the rest of the ladies in on this."

"How can they help?"

Gert reached to touch her arm, and they stopped walking before the front steps. "We need to figure out who's doing this. If the men don't catch up with him, he'll kill again."

Libby stared into her friend's troubled eyes. The lamplight from the window of the Walkers' front room illuminated Gert's face.

"My dear, you saw the mayor attacked tonight. You've had a shock."

"No, Libby, listen to me." Gert's voice cracked, but she went on earnestly. "I should have been able to put a name to the killer. I saw him. True, his face was hidden. I tried to help Ethan by describing the man's size and clothing and demeanor. It didn't help. Now, Ethan is a fine man, and a fairly clever one, don't you think?"

"Yes, dear, he's a very fine man."

Gert nodded and chewed her lower lip for a moment. "But if he and Hiram and I can't figure this out, we need more people. Different folks come at things from different directions."

Libby could see that nothing short of a powwow would calm her young friend. "All right, let's go in and talk to the ladies then. If the posse can't solve this case, perhaps the Ladies' Shooting Club can."

Ethan sent two men to check on the Robinsons and rode onward. Only one more homestead on this road before it petered out in the hills. Milzie Peart's. A few minutes later, he and Hiram pulled up next to the burned-out cabin. A dozen men thundered in behind them and reined in their mounts.

"When did this place burn?" Griffin asked.

"Sometime this spring." Ethan looked toward the hillside. "We'd best check the old mine, but I don't see any horse."

Hiram dismounted and dropped Hoss's reins. Ethan and Griff climbed down to join him. Ethan turned to address the other men.

"Wait here. There's a cave yonder, and we'll check it."

A minute later they stood to one side of the entrance. Hiram sniffed the air. Ethan quirked his eyebrows at him, but Hi shook his head.

"I've got matches," Griffin said. An instant

later, a small light flared up in his hands.

"There's candles inside." Before Ethan could stop him, Hiram scurried into the cave. The light flickered out, but Hiram reappeared in the entrance as Griffin lit another match. The gunsmith held out a short stub of candle, and Griffin put the match to the wick.

"If he were in there, he'd have shot us by now," Ethan noted.

"Sorry." Hiram ducked his head.

"Not the most brilliant thing you ever did."

They walked into the cave together, with Hiram holding the candle high. A quick survey told them the cave was empty, and nothing appeared disturbed.

"Let's go." Ethan led them outside again. As they descended the path to the waiting posse, the two men he'd detailed at the Robinsons' rode up.

"No one's been by there until we came," Parnell Oxley called.

Ethan bent and caught Scout's reins. He looked up at the starry sky, thinking. *Lord, show me what to do.*

"We're wasting time," Griffin said. "He could be anywhere by now."

Cyrus urged his mare over closer to Ethan.

"Suppose he cut off by my ranch and rode west."

"Could have, I guess," Ethan said. "Or he could be up in these hills."

"No sense going up there in the dark," Micah Landry growled.

"What now?" asked Zach Harper. "Head back to town?"

"Hate to do that." Ethan rubbed his scratchy chin. He looked around at the men. "How about if we split up? Half keep going this direction, and half go out the Owyhee Road?"

"He coulda lit out for Reynolds," Augie Moore put in.

"Yes, he could have." Ethan sighed. Probably the smartest thing would be to head back to Fergus. Most of the ranchers along the way had been alerted. The posse could go out in the morning and try to pick up the trail. He doubted they would. If they hadn't trampled the outlaw's tracks, they'd be mingled indistinguishably with the other hoofprints on the dusty roads.

"Gentlemen, I don't know as we have much chance of finding this fellow tonight," Ethan said.

"He's got my horse," Ralph Storrey called.

"I haven't forgotten that." Storrey's ranch was on the south side of town, in the opposite direction to the one the outlaw had taken. Ethan puzzled over what little he knew.

"Let's at least go out by my place," Cyrus said. "We can ask if anyone out that way heard a rider go past."

When no one presented a better plan, Ethan lifted his boot to the stirrup and swung onto Scout's back. "All right, let's go."

"So the sheriff's been collecting all these pennies from the crimes and trying to figure out who left them?" Starr's eyes shone with the challenge.

"That's right." Gert faced all the women in the Walkers' parlor and wondered if she'd made a wise decision. "I hoped the Ladies' Shooting Club, and you other ladies, too," she said, nodding deferentially to Bertha Runnels and Jessie Tinen, "could help us out. Seems to me, if we all put our heads together, we should be able to tell who the killer is."

"Well, he's not one of the posse," Goldie said. She'd come over from the Spur & Saddle with a bottle of whiskey. Miss Shepard thought they might need it for the mayor, she'd explained. Apphia had gingerly accepted the bottle and carried it to the bedchamber as though she held a wriggling snake between her fingers.

"Now, that's a good thought." Gert pointed her index finger at Goldie. "See? I knew this would be helpful."

"So, who was in the posse?" Ellie Nash asked.

"And who did you see at the Spur & Saddle after the outlaw rode away?" Myra added.

Libby jumped up. "Excellent! Let me get a pencil and a sheet of paper, ladies. We can make a list of men we know are innocent."

Gert exhaled, feeling as though a huge rock had rolled off her chest. It wasn't the same as naming the killer, but eliminating the better part of the town's residents might bring them closer to the truth.

She looked around at the rapt faces. "All of you be thinking while she gets it."

A minute later, Libby returned with a piece of brown wrapping paper and a pencil. She settled down on the settee next to Apphia, who handed her a book to use as a lap desk.

"All right," Libby said. "Gert, you were there. Tell us which men you're certain this infidel is *not*."

"Well, Ethan Chapman, for sure. And Ralph Storrey. His horse was stolen." Gert lowered her eyebrows, mentally counting the men who had poured out of the saloon. "Augie Moore. Ezra Dyer. Mr. Tinen — junior and senior. Uh . . . Parnell Oxley. One of the Storreys' ranch hands. Mr. Runnels . . ." Gert's gaze caught Goldie's. The girl seemed barely able to contain herself. "Of course, Goldie was there, too. She might be able to tell us who was *inside* the Spur & Saddle when the shooting took place."

Names spilled out of Goldie's mouth faster than Libby could write them down. "Mr. Colburn, Maitland Dostie, Josh Runnels, Nealy and Clem Higgins. A drummer that came in on the Boise stagecoach. That feller who's got a mine down the river. Micah Landry and the ranch hand Miss Dooley mentioned. Buck, they call him."

"Well!" Gert felt a new admiration for the girl. "Anyone else?"

"Hmm . . ." Goldie's brow furrowed. "Of course, Miss Bitsy was there, and Vashti and me."

"Do you think it could have been a woman?" Florence asked.

Everyone stared at her.

"I . . . I don't think so." Gert wished she could state emphatically that the killer was a man.

476

"All right," Libby said, scribbling the last of the names. "If anyone else can positively give someone an alibi, tell me now."

Most of the women quickly vouched for themselves and their husbands.

Isabel cleared her throat. "What about my father?"

Gert winced. "He came soon after the shooting. I believe he was . . . at the other end of town when it occurred."

"Yes, I expect you're right." Isabel's face was stricken. "I had two customers take rooms at the boardinghouse today. One was the salesman that Goldie mentioned. The other was an older gentleman who went to his room as soon as he'd had supper. Bill Stout was going to sleep there tonight, too, but he'd gone out."

"Probably to the Nugget," Gert hazarded. She wondered if the saloon girls on that end of town could give her a list of patrons.

Hester Tinen had fallen asleep on her mother's lap. Starr curled a lock of the little girl's hair around her finger as she spoke. "You know, we can't rule out anyone who was at the Nugget tonight. Unless they vouch for each other, that is."

Isabel shrank down in the corner of the sofa.

Gert pressed her lips together. She wished

she could shout out, "Your father is innocent, Isabel." But she couldn't do that. She doubted Cyrus's guilt now, but could she say that for certain? And could the shooter have ridden out of town then sneaked back to join the posse? She rejected that idea. Storrey's horse was still missing, after all.

Silence hung over them for an agonizing moment. Gert inhaled deeply. "I don't think the man I saw was Mr. Fennel. Of course, I can't be certain, but Mr. Fennel is a tall man. As is Griffin Bane. When the killer mounted Mr. Storrey's horse, I didn't have the impression of an overly large man. And I'm sure I'd have recognized Mr. Bane's build, so I've ruled him out as well."

"He's quite distinctive, isn't he?" Bertha asked. A chuckle rippled through the room.

Gert nodded. "He is."

"What was this thing you mentioned about pennies?" Myra asked. "The sheriff has found a penny after each killing?"

"Yes," Gert said. "After the fires at the emporium and the mayor's warehouse, too. There are five now. One from Sheriff Thalen's murder, one from Milzie Peart's, and the one the man threw tonight. It landed on the steps of the Spur & Saddle next to Mayor Walker." Would Ethan be upset if she revealed the rest? Gert gulped and said as calmly as she could, "All five were minted in the same year — 1866."

"That's a long time ago," Starr said.

Florence nodded. "The year I was born."

Libby cleared her throat. "They're common though. Gert and I have discussed this some. I didn't come to Fergus until a few years after that, but my husband was here then. I can't think of anything Isaac ever told me that could be connected to these crimes. We wondered if any of you older ladies can recall what went on in town that year. Did something happen that would make this person angry?"

At that moment, Annie and Orissa entered the parlor, and all the ladies fell silent.

Apphia stood and walked toward them. "How is the mayor?"

"He's resting," Annie said. "The pastor is sitting with him. I thought it would do Orissa good to have a cup of tea and something to eat."

"I'll get it." Ellie rose and hurried toward the kitchen.

Orissa's skin was stretched tight over her face. Even her hands were pale. Apphia took her arm and guided her to the spot she had vacated on the settee.

"We've been praying for your husband,

and for you, my dear." Apphia squeezed her hand.

"Thank you. Annie is optimistic."

All eyes turned to Annie for confirmation.

"Yes," she said. "It's a serious wound, but none of the vital organs seems to be hit. We've got the bleeding stopped, and he's resting easier. We'll see what a good night's sleep will do for him."

Orissa looked around at all of them. "What was it you were discussing when we came in? Something about the town's history?"

Everyone looked to Gert. She nodded. "We were saying how the people who've been attacked by this outlaw all seem to be among the town's founders. The sheriff has some clues that point to something in the past — something that perhaps happened in 1866."

"Charles and I were here then," Orissa said. "Do you think it's someone who's carried a grudge for near twenty years?"

"It could be."

Ellie came in with a tray and took tea and a few cookies to Mrs. Walker.

"That was the peak of the gold frenzy," Bertha said. "My husband and I came the next year. The mines were already starting to play out."

"Yes. Fergus was a lawless place back then." Orissa reached for the teacup. "A thousand men would come to town every weekend."

Libby said, "We've asked all the ladies to think about what the town was like then. There were several businesses that have closed since, and the boardinghouse was in its heyday."

"The stamp mill over to Booneville had begun operating," Bertha said. "A lot of ore passed through there."

"My family was here," Isabel said quietly.

Something clicked in Gert's mind. She glanced over at Libby. "Ladies, think about this. Isaac Adams was here in 1866. A few weeks ago, his widow's business was set afire. Cyrus Fennel was here that year. Milzie Peart was killed in his office. Mayor Walker was here. Both his business and his person have been attacked."

Bertha clapped her hand over her mouth. "Cyrus, Charles, Isaac . . . they were all here when we moved to town. Of course, Charles wasn't the mayor then. He started out mining, didn't he, Orissa?"

"Oh yes. They all did. Cyrus took over the assay office in '65, I think. My husband gave up mining soon after. It didn't go as well as he'd hoped. But we'd saved enough to build a decent house and start a business." She nodded and took another sip of tea.

Gert frowned, reaching for something. "What about Bert Thalen? Was he here in '66?"

"And Milzie Peart," said Ellie.

"Well . . . I'm not sure it's so important when Milzie arrived."

"But she was killed," Starr said, her brow furrowing.

"Yes, but . . ." Gert swallowed hard. "Right now my theory is that the outlaw didn't set out to kill Milzie. He only did it because she got in his way."

"In Father's office," Isabel said.

"Yes. The sheriff and I both think the killer was waiting in there to ambush Mr. Fennel. Poor Milzie went in, and he attacked her instead."

"If that's what happened," Goldie said soberly, "then the same person killed her as shot the mayor and killed the old sheriff, but not for the same reason."

Gert nodded. "That's my thinking, all right. So why did he do these things? What made him go after Bert? And the mayor and Mr. Fennel?"

"And what about Griffin Bane?" Starr asked.

"He came to town later," Libby said with

certainty. "After Isaac and I had married. He bought the smithy, and later on he took over the livery, too."

"Libby doesn't fit in," said Apphia. "From what you've told me, the killer has attacked men who were here during the town's boom years. Libby told me she came about twelve years ago and married Mr. Adams then."

"That's right," Libby said. "We were married in 1873. But Isaac had already stopped mining and established the emporium."

"That's why he didn't kill you," Emmaline said. Several jaws dropped, and she hurried to explain her thoughts. "Suppose this killer was angry at your husband. Isaac was already dead when he came, and it was too late for revenge. Maybe he thought he'd do something bad to you, his widow, but not . . ."

"Not as bad as he's done to the others," said Myra.

"If what you're saying is true, my father is in grave danger." Isabel's gray eyes pinned Gert. "That man tried to kill him and failed, perhaps more than once. He succeeded with Sheriff Thalen, and the mayor lies in grave danger under this roof. Isaac Adams is already dead. My father could be next."

Gert's mouth went dry. "That's so. And Cyrus went with the posse."

"Yes. He insisted on helping find the man who shot his old friend." Isabel's lips trembled, and she clamped them firmly shut.

Gert nodded. "I fear you're right. If anyone is in danger tonight, it's Mr. Fennel. So . . . what did those four men all do to cause such hatred?"

"There were a lot of gold strikes in the early years," Orissa said, her eyes unfocused as she looked back over the years. "The first miners came here in 1862 or '63, I think. Charles heard about it, and we got here in the fall of '63. I'm not sure if Bert Thalen was already here, or if he came the next spring — there were a lot of rough men about, and I stayed close in our lodgings that winter. But Bert and Charles met by spring and became partners."

Gert sat up straighter. "Business partners?"

"They had a claim together with . . ."

"Why, yes," Libby said. "Now that you mention that, I recall my husband telling me about it once. Isaac was in on a mining claim with the mayor and Mr. Thalen. And Cyrus, too. Isn't that right?"

Orissa nodded. "Yes. All four of them invested in a tract down the river. They thought they'd strike it rich. They sluiced out a fair amount of gold, but nowhere near as much as the few really rich claims you'd hear tell of. They each put away a stash and bought some land."

"Who owns the claim now?" Gert asked.

"I don't know." Orissa looked blankly to Libby.

"They sold it, didn't they?" Libby asked.

"Yes, I'm sure they did."

"When Isaac died, the only property I found a deed for was the emporium building and the lot it's standing on." Libby met Gert's gaze. "But if the four men owned a claim together and sold it, there must be a record of it."

"My father might have something," Isabel said, and all eyes swung her way. "He kept the assay office until business dropped so much they closed the one here. Now they go through Silver City, but he has old records in the safe at his office."

"Now, hold on just a second," Jessie Tinen said. "Arthur and I came here the year our son turned seven. Sixty-five. Right after Arthur got home from the army."

Again the ladies fell silent. The Civil War had barely touched Idaho Territory, but those who came from points east remembered it well.

"Now, there was a big to-do, I recall,

about a mining claim." Jessie sucked in her ample cheeks and frowned. "Some fella made a big fuss over it. He'd bought a claim that was supposed to be a good one, but it turned out to be worthless. Arthur decided then and there not to try mining. We bought our ranch and started working it."

A stir of excitement flickered in Gert's stomach. She turned to the mayor's wife. "Mrs. Walker, can't you remember the name —"

Orissa's face had turned ashen. She stared at the far parlor window and spoke a single word. "Morrell."

Chapter 35

"Morrell?" Libby and Gert locked gazes across the crowded parlor. Libby voiced what everyone was thinking. "There's Jamin Morrell, but he only moved here last year."

"The family . . ." Orissa spoke quietly in the stillness. "The man had a scrawny wife and a little boy thin as six o'clock."

Gert's eyes took on a resolve that made Libby shiver. "Did anyone see Jamin Morrell when the posse rode out?"

Goldie shook her head. "He could have stayed at the Nugget."

Gert leaped to her feet. "I'm going over there."

Libby gasped. "To the Nugget?"

"That's right. We need to get to the bottom of this."

"But my dear . . ." Apphia faltered.

"What will you do?" Myra asked.

"First, I'll see if he rode out with the posse."

"And if he's still there?" Libby asked. "We haven't any proof that he's mixed up in this business. The name could be a coincidence."

"I'll ask him if he has anything to do with it." Gert's eyes flashed a stormy gray.

"I'll go with you." Goldie stood and eased past the knees of the other women.

"Me, too," said Emmaline.

Myra began to rise, but her mother laid a restraining hand on her sleeve. "You'll stay here," Annie said, and Myra sank back into her chair, scowling.

Isabel stood and eyed Gert with a challenging air. "I shall come with you."

Gert nodded. Without speaking, Libby got to her feet.

"We five," Gert said. "That's enough. The rest of you stay here with Mrs. Walker."

"We shall be praying," Apphia said.

They stepped out into the yard. A chilly breeze off the mountains fluttered Gert's hair, and she regretted not grabbing her despised bonnet after she gave Hiram back his hat when he left to join the posse. She buttoned her jacket over the butt of Libby's pistol, now tucked firmly in the waistband of her skirt. Libby, Emmaline, Isabel, and Goldie followed her out of the house.

The five of them spread out and strode

side by side down the quiet street. Libby walked closest to Gert, between her and Emmaline. Uneasily, Gert wondered if they ought to have a better-defined plan.

The sound of distant hoofbeats brought her to a halt. The other women stopped and listened. As far away as she could see in the black tunnel of the street where it passed between the Nugget and the smithy, a white patch materialized.

Isabel let out a muffled squeak. They all stood still, staring and shivering.

The horse's outline became apparent as it trotted nearer. Gert relaxed and walked forward, her hand extended toward it.

"Whoa, boy." The paint horse stopped a few yards from her and snuffled. Gert walked up to him and caught one trailing rein. "There, now. Take it easy." She stroked his neck, and the horse rubbed against her shoulder.

"Where did it come from?" Libby asked.

"This is Ralph Storrey's horse," Gert said. "The one the killer stole. I don't know where he's been, but he's just moseying toward home. Good fella."

"Should we hitch him up?" Emmaline asked.

Gert considered the options. "Ralph was here when the mayor was shot. Laura's likely still at their house south of town, not knowing what happened. If the horse comes home with an empty saddle, it'll scare her."

"Let's hitch him here," Libby said. "When the posse comes back, maybe the sheriff will want to look him over for evidence."

Gert nodded. A month ago, she'd have laughed at that idea. Now it seemed very reasonable.

After she'd secured the horse at the nearest hitching rail, the five women moved on down the street, past the telegraph office, the emporium, the feed store, the jail, and the boardinghouse.

Only two horses were tied up in front of the Nugget. At the steps, Gert hesitated a moment. Someone inside plinked out a spare rendition of "I'll Take You Home Again, Kathleen." Voices murmured, and glass clinked on glass, but for a Saturday night, the Nugget seemed pretty tame.

Gert lifted her foot and marched up the stairs to the double door, with Libby close behind her. The others followed in their wake.

When Gert shoved the door open, the four people inside stared at the women. All sounds ceased.

Gert tried to see everything at once. In the lantern light, rough tables and chairs filled the sawdust-covered floor. Spittoons sat in strategic corners. A cowboy leaned on the piano, and a raven-haired girl in frothy red and silver taffeta lace sat before it, gaping at the women in the doorway. A bearded old man sitting at a table to one side froze with a glass halfway to his lips and stared.

Straight ahead was the bar. Behind it stood a girl with golden hair, resplendent in flounces of shimmery blue satin, pouring whiskey into a glass. When she saw the women enter, her flaming red lips parted.

"M–Mrs. Adams. Ladies. May I help you?"

"Hello, Opal." Libby walked toward the bar as though she habitually visited the saloon girls at the Nugget. "We wondered if Mr. Morrell is in tonight."

"No, he . . . he went out some time ago. There was a ruckus at the Spur & Saddle, I understand." Opal's eyes flicked from Libby to Gert and beyond. When her gaze rested on Goldie, her lips flattened.

Gert edged up beside Libby. The cowboy came over and leaned on the bar, watching them.

"So Mr. Morrell rode out with the posse?" Gert asked.

"Well . . ." Opal didn't meet her gaze.

Gert looked over at the girl near the piano.

"Was your boss here when you heard about the shooting?"

"Uh . . . I'm not sure." The dark-haired girl glared at Opal as though blaming her for letting these disruptive women in.

"Ted was pouring," Opal said quickly. "A cowboy came in shouting that the mayor was killed and the sheriff was raising a posse. Every man in here ran out. Including Ted."

"And Mr. Morrell?" Gert asked again, pronouncing each word distinctly.

"I . . ." Opal glanced sideways to the other girl, but she was no help. She'd come over nearer the bar and stood caressing the cowboy's mustache and smiling at him. "I'm pretty sure he went, too. I haven't seen any of them since." Opal nodded toward old Pan Rideout, the miner sitting alone in the corner, and threw another glance at the cowboy down the bar. "These two came in later. I figured we were done having customers tonight, but I guess these fellas live south of town and hadn't heard about the killing."

"The mayor's not dead," Gert said.

Opal's eyes widened. "Oh? Well, that's fine then. Guess we won't need to hold an election for a while."

Libby smiled graciously. "Rumors do get

around, don't they? Mr. Walker is very much alive."

Gert squeezed close to the bar and leaned over toward Opal. "What was Mr. Morrell wearing tonight?"

Opal blinked at her. "Wearing? You want to know what the boss was wearing?"

"That's right."

"Uh . . ."

A curtain shielding a doorway behind the bar fluttered, and Jamin Morrell stepped through it.

"Ladies. I'm speechless."

Gert straightened. Behind her, the other women caught a collective breath.

Morrell walked forward to Opal's side. "Pour me a drink, sweetheart."

Opal finished filling the glass she'd set down earlier and handed it to him. Gert wondered if she'd been fixing it for him all along. Had he been hiding in the back room, listening to every word? If so, why had Opal lied?

Morrell tossed back a big swallow of whiskey and set the glass on the bar.

"Now then, ladies. To what do I owe the dubious honor?" His dark suede waistcoat hung open, and his black shirt, unbuttoned at the neck, held wrinkles and smudges of dust. His stubbly jaw clenched as he watched them. His hard gaze slid past Gert and assessed her four companions.

Goldie stepped forward before Gert could speak. "This here's a contingent of the Ladies' Shooting Club of Fergus, mister. And Deputy Gert Dooley has a few questions for you."

Morrell's eyes narrowed, and he raised his chin a tad. "Don't you belong at the other end of the street? If you're looking for different employment, I'm not hiring."

"I ain't looking. I wouldn't work here if you paid me double."

"Hush, Goldie," said Emmaline.

Morrell's gaze shifted back to Gert. She tried not to squirm as he studied her with a bit of speculation in his dark eyes. The other club members moved in around her. She felt stronger with them at her back.

"Would you care for a drink, Miss Dooley?" he asked.

"No. I want to know why you're not with the posse."

His eyebrows shot up. "Nothing like getting to the point, is there?"

"No, sir, there's not."

"My bartender and every customer who was in the place an hour ago charged out of here to ride with the sheriff. Someone had to stay and guard my business and my . . .

other employees."

Gert's anger nearly choked her. She didn't take her eyes off him. "Opal said you went with the sheriff and the rest, but it seems she was wrong."

"She must have forgotten that I was out back going over the accounts. Or maybe she just didn't tell you." He shot a glance Opal's way. "My employees guard me from frivolous interruptions."

Libby gasped at his rudeness, but Gert let out a short chuckle. "However you want to paint the picture, my friends and I want to know where you were when Mayor Walker was shot."

"Thank you for being so concerned about my activities." Morrell tipped the bottle up and poured himself another hefty drink. "Sure you won't join me?"

"Answer the question, Mr. Morrell," Gert said stonily.

"I've already told you. I've been here since suppertime. Ask Flora." He nodded vaguely toward the dark-haired girl who still stood next to the young cowpoke.

Gert glared at him across the bar. A hot mass churned in her chest, making it hard to inhale. "You're a liar."

"Am I?" Morrell took a swallow of the whiskey.

"Your family came here twenty years ago," Gert said with certainty. "Your pa bought a claim that was worthless. You and your folks suffered. And now you've come back, aiming to hurt the people who took your pa's money and make them hurt worse than you did."

His face hardened as she spoke. Gert's pulse accelerated, and the air in the saloon thickened.

"You don't know anything about me. I came here a year ago to start a business. I've tried to be an upstanding citizen of the community. I've made contributions to the town coffers. I influenced a preacher to come here, even though I knew it might hurt my enterprise. I even offered to serve on the school board, but the town councilors didn't think I was good enough."

His voice dripped bitterness and Gert shivered, watching him toss back the rest of the whiskey.

"That upset you, didn't it? That people didn't think a saloon keeper should be on the school board. This town owes you a lot, doesn't it? You've been paying back the men who sold your father that mining claim, making them suffer."

"You have no idea how much I suffered," Morrell said in a deadly quiet voice. "My father worked himself to the bone and died of pneumonia. If my mother's heart hadn't given out, she'd have starved to death. You have no idea what we went through because of the fine leaders of this town. Now get out of here."

Gert held his stare. "No, sir. Mr. Morrell, I'm afraid we're going to have to arrest you for the murders of Bert Thalen and Millicent Peart, and the attempted murder of Charles Walker."

"And the fires," Emmaline said in her ear. "Don't forget the fires."

Gert nodded. "The fires at the Paragon Emporium and the Walker Feed Company, too."

Morrell let out a short laugh. "Oh, ladies. How exactly do you intend to take me into custody?"

Gert put her hand to her jacket's top button. She ought to have prepared for this before they set foot inside the Nugget. Seeing only the saloon girls and two customers inside had thrown her off her guard. She pulled in a deep breath as she quickly undid her jacket's buttons and reached inside for the Peacemaker. Before she had the pistol out, Morrell had stooped behind the bar and straightened again with a double-barreled shotgun in his hands.

"All right, ladies. Don't move. Miss Dooley, I suggest you put that thing on the bar and back up a few paces. This shotgun can kill you and three or four other women quicker than you can spit." His gaze roved over the women. "Uh-uh." He moved the shotgun a hair, so that his sights covered Goldie. "Just leave that peashooter alone. I must admit, that's a shapely leg it's strapped to. Maybe I could find a place for you here."

Gert caught a glimpse of Goldie's chagrined face as she let the flounce of skirt fall back over her garter with its little holster. She wouldn't be able to use her weapon either. Libby's gun was no doubt still in the bottom of her handbag. Gert doubted Emmaline or Isabel was armed tonight. It was up to her.

"I'm sure we can end this peaceably, Mr. Morrell," she said. "Put the shotgun away."

"You're the sharpshooter, aren't you? Put your gun on the bar, Miss Dooley. Let's see your hands up high."

Gert shot a sidelong glance at Libby. She stood still, her shoulders squared, but her lips trembled.

"Come on," Morrell coaxed. "If I let loose with this load of buckshot, every one of you will be killed or maimed. You know what it can do. Now all of you get your hands up where I can see them."

Gert couldn't swallow the painful lump at the back of her throat. Libby raised her hands slowly. Others stirred behind her. *Oh, Lord, what have I gotten us into? We could have done this so much better.* "Couldn't we sit down and talk about this?" Her voice quivered, and he smiled.

"I think we're beyond chitchat. Hands up."

Gert lifted her hands.

Without looking away, Morrell called, "Flora, take Miss Dooley's weapon."

The girl walked over hesitantly and squinted at Gert. She touched Gert's dark jacket, found the pistol, and yanked it out. Stepping back, she laid it on the bar before Morrell.

"Thank you. And now the one this little dove has under her skirt." He nodded toward Goldie. Flora lifted Goldie's hem and retrieved the small pistol.

Morrell walked around the end of the bar and skirted the group, still holding the shotgun pointed at them. "Get out, Pan. The Nugget's closed for the evening."

Pan Rideout stared at him. "But I ain't finished."

"Get out!"

Pan's face crumpled into his bushy beard.

He slid out of the chair and staggered toward the door, muttering, "Man can't have a few drinks . . ."

"You, too, Jake."

The cowboy turned and stalked toward the door without another word.

"All right, now." Morrell had worked his way around the group so that he stood between them and the door. He waved the gun's barrel, indicating that the women should separate. "Mrs. Adams, please step over there, near that table."

Libby hesitated and then took a few steps.

"Miss Fennel, you, too."

Isabel stood rock still for a moment. Gert was afraid she would swoon, but she took three wooden steps and stopped next to Libby, who slipped her arm around Isabel's shoulder.

"And I think I'll keep Miss Shepard's little spitfire, too. That woman's done everything she could to keep my business from succeeding." He winked at Goldie. "Over yonder, darlin'."

Goldie swept past him, her head high, and turned to stand, arms akimbo, next to Libby and Isabel.

Morrell smiled. "Oh yes. That's quite a tableau." He glared at Gert and Emmaline. "You can go. I expect the sheriff will be gone all night out in those hills, but if you see him, tell him I'm square with Fergus now. I intended to bring Cyrus Fennel down, too, but I'll take his daughter with me instead. If he comes after her, I'll deliver what I've wanted to give him for years."

Isabel's cheeks flamed, and she wobbled. Libby tightened her hold on the young woman and leaned close to whisper in her ear.

"What are you going to do?" Gert determined not to leave the other women in his power.

He only smiled, but his expression quickly turned to a snarl. "I'm going to finish what started almost twenty years ago. The men who ruined my family won't be laughing up their sleeves anymore. Now get out!"

Gert could see that standing toe to toe with him would do no good. She grabbed Emmaline's arm and pulled her toward the door.

"We can't —" Emmaline began.

"We have to," Gert hissed as she practically tossed the woman through the double door.

Emmaline caught her balance and narrowly avoided pitching down the steps into the street. Gert seized her hand and drew her down and away from the light. Pan

Rideout sat on the edge of the bottom step muttering, "I didn't finish my drink yet."

"What are we going to do?" Emmaline wailed.

Gert swallowed hard. "I'm thinking. If the men come back . . ." She glanced futilely toward the smithy and Mountain Road.

"What if they don't? We can't wait."

"You're right. It sounded like he's going somewhere. He might force them to leave town with him."

"Yes, or he might abuse them."

Gert winced. She didn't like to think that, but Emmaline was right. Every minute counted. "Come on, let's get some help."

Emmaline ran with her down the street toward the Walkers' house.

Across the way, the front door of the Spur & Saddle opened. Bitsy came out carrying a lantern. Vashti followed bearing a basket over her arm. Bitsy closed the door behind them, leaving her saloon dark and silent on a Saturday night for the first time in more than twenty years.

Gert pulled up in the middle of Main Street, panting.

"Well, Gert," Bitsy said pleasantly, walking toward her. "What are you doing out? When Goldie didn't come back, Vashti and I decided to go over to the Walkers' house and see if there's anything we can do."

"We need your help," Gert said.

Bitsy's brow wrinkled so deeply that she looked her age despite her cosmetics. "What is it?"

"Jamin Morrell is the killer, and he's holding Goldie and Isabel and Libby inside the Nugget."

"He threw Gert and me out," Emmaline said. "He says to tell the sheriff he's square with the town now."

"What did he mean by that?" Bitsy asked.

Emmaline sniffed. "He said his parents died after they left here. He blames the town of Fergus."

"I'll explain it all later," Gert said. "Right now we need to help those women."

Bitsy looked down the street, where light spilled out of the Nugget. "Yes. You can count on me."

"I don't know what he aims to do," Gert admitted. "I suspect he'll pack up and skip town before the posse gets back."

"But . . . will he take the women with him?"

"I don't know. He said to tell Cyrus they were even now. Cyrus was one of the men who cheated his father, and I'm afraid he might do something horrible to Isabel. I'm not sure about Libby and Goldie."

"We've got to act quickly; that's certain." Bitsy turned to Vashti. "Here, take the lantern and the food to the mayor's house. I'm going with Gert."

"Can't I come?" Vashti asked. "Goldie's in there."

Gert touched the girl's arm. "Go to the Walkers' and tell Mrs. Benton and the others what happened. Tell as many as have weapons to meet us down near the Nugget. But everyone has to be careful and keep quiet."

"Yes, ma'am." Vashti hurried across the street toward the mayor's house.

Bitsy turned around, hiked her skirt up, and removed her Deringer from her garter. She tucked it beneath the folds of her shawl. "Ready, Deputy Dooley."

Gert smiled grimly and nodded at her, wishing she hadn't lost Libby's pistol. "Let's go then." Her voice cracked a little, and she cleared her throat.

CHAPTER 36

Jamin Morrell watched Gert push Emmaline out the door, then swung the shotgun barrel back toward the other women. Isabel sobbed, and Libby pulled her closer.

"God is in control," she whispered to Isabel.

"Flora," Jamin said.

"Yes, Mr. Morrell?"

"You and Opal go on upstairs and pack my things for me. There's a bag in my wardrobe. I've got the wagon ready out back."

"We're leaving?" Flora asked. "Where are we going?"

"Just go do it."

The two girls hurried past him and up the stairs. Halfway up, Opal caught Libby's eye. Her face held such distress that Libby began praying silently for her. She wondered if they could somehow distract Morrell long enough for her to get her pistol out of her handbag.

Morrell laughed. "Oh yes, indeed. You ladies don't need to worry about your baggage. I'll outfit you when we reach our destination."

"Where are you taking us?" Goldie asked.

"To a new town. I've had enough of Fergus. I've purchased a business in another place, and I expect to have a much nicer saloon than this one. Better than that place down the street. And I'll have you three ladies to help me run it."

Goldie scowled at him. "You can't make us go and work for you."

"I can't?" Jamin shrugged. "In your case, I'd think you'd be glad. It will be an improvement in your station."

"I doubt it." Goldie looked about the Nugget. "This place is a pigpen."

"Oh, but I'll have a lot more to invest in the new one," Morrell said. "Mrs. Adams and Mr. Fennel are both going to kick in a significant investment in my new enterprise."

Libby found her voice at last. "You'll let us go if we do?"

"Did I say that?" He looked her over and smiled in a way that made Libby feel like a mouse that stumbled into a fox den. "Fennel will give me every cent he's got in hopes of getting his daughter back." He glanced at Isabel, and his smile faded. "Maybe I will give her back. She hasn't got the looks or the carriage you have. But you, Mrs. Adams . . ." He eyed her figure again, and Libby shuddered. "Yes, I think you'll be a nice addition to the place."

"Then why should I pay you?" she gasped.

"You don't have a choice. We'll visit the bank you patronize in Boise before we head for the new location."

Goldie tossed her head. "I ain't going with you."

He threw his head back in a laugh. "Tell me that in six months."

"The people of this town won't let you carry us away," Libby said.

"Oh, you mean the good sheriff and his friends?" Morrell scratched his head and drew his eyebrows together as though thinking hard. "Let me see, didn't every man in town ride out a couple of hours ago, looking for a phantom killer? I doubt we'll see them before morning. But just in case, we'll get moving."

Flora came down the stairs dragging a large portmanteau.

"Where's Opal?" Morrell asked.

"She's packing away a few things for her and me." When she reached the bottom of the stairs, Flora straightened. "What now, Mr. Morrell?"

"Leave that there. You get out of here, Flora."

"What . . . what do you mean?"

The double doors swung open. "Hey, what's a man gotta do to —"

Morrell swung around and fired the shotgun without hesitation. Pan Rideout flew backward out the doors.

Gert, Bitsy, and Emmaline stopped when the report of a gun echoed down the street. Pan Rideout's body catapulted off the steps of the Nugget and several yards beyond, into the dirt.

Without a word, Gert picked up her skirt and ran to the old man. Tears streamed down her face as she knelt beside him.

"Mr. Rideout! Pan!"

His eyelids lifted slowly, and he frowned up at her. "I ain't even finished my drink yet."

Emmaline slid to the ground on the other side of the miner. Bitsy stood at Gert's shoulder, aiming her Deringer at the doors of the Nugget.

"How bad is it?" Bitsy asked.

"Hit him in the leg," Gert said. "Maybe the stomach, too. There's some blood on his shirt. But I'd say two or three pellets got his leg."

Pan's mouth opened wide. He stared up at her for a moment in silence then howled. His eerie shriek reverberated off the storefronts. "Owww! He done shot me! Owww!"

Emmaline put her hands to her ears. Gert leaned over the old man and grasped his shoulders firmly. "Hush, Mr. Rideout. We'll help you, but you've got to keep quiet."

"Am I killed?"

"Not yet. Now let us get you over to my house. It isn't far." Gert looked up at Bitsy. "Think we can carry him over there?"

Bitsy nodded up the street. "Help's coming. I'll send Vashti for some blankets, and we'll get a bunch of women to lug him."

The yellow gleam of a lantern approached from the far end of Main Street. Gert peered into the dimness and made out a dozen women hurrying toward them, their skirts swirling.

Florence and Vashti reached them first, with Vashti bearing the lantern.

"What happened?" Florence asked.

"That snake Morrell shot Pan Rideout for no reason at all," Bitsy said. "He's got Mrs. Adams, Miss Fennel, and Goldie in the Nugget. Says he's keeping them."

"Not Mrs. Adams!" Florence's face paled,

and the flock of women behind her erupted in shocked exclamations.

Gert stood. "We've got to help Mr. Rideout first. He's bleeding a lot. Morrell was loaded with buckshot." She spotted Apphia in the group. "Mrs. Benton, will you take charge of him, please?"

"Of course." Apphia stepped forward.

Gert's spirits lifted. The Ladies' Shooting Club would work together as a team. "Get five or six women to help you carry him to my house and care for him there." Apphia nodded. "And Myra —"

"Yes'm?" Myra said eagerly.

"Run ahead to my house. Go in the back door. It's not locked. There's a lantern on the kitchen table with a box of lucifers beside it."

"Here, take this lantern," Vashti said.

"Good. Bring back the quilt off my bed." As Myra dashed off toward the Dooley house, Gert scanned the group. "Who can run back to the Walkers' and fetch bandages?"

"I can," said Vashti.

"All right. Ask Mrs. Harper if she can leave the mayor in the reverend's care long enough to examine Mr. Rideout. Go."

Vashti dashed off the way she had come.

"The rest of you, listen up," Gert said.

"How many of you ladies of the shooting club have your weapons?"

Several said, "I do."

"Good. I'll need you. We're not letting Morrell take Libby or Isabel or Goldie out of the Nugget. That means we need to cover the front and back doors."

"What's the plan, Gert?" Starr asked.

Gert frowned. "Mostly to keep him from leaving. If he steps foot outside, we arrest him. If he resists . . ." She hesitated, wondering how it would end and what evil Morrell might do before then. Reason told her he wouldn't stay long for fear the posse would return and trap him. Blocking his flight seemed the only good option.

Bitsy cleared her throat. "We all know that Gertrude Dooley is the best shot in the Idaho Territory."

The others murmured their assent.

Bitsy looked down at the Deringer in her hand. "My little gun isn't very good in this situation, but it's better then nothing. Gert, I suppose your brother took his Sharps rifle with him?"

"Yes, he did," Gert said.

"Who here has a rifle?"

A dark-clad figure eased through the crowd, and Gert recognized Orissa Walker.

"Mrs. Walker! I didn't realize you were here."

Orissa held out a rifle to her. "When the girl from the . . . when Miss Vashti told us there was trouble, I figured you might be needing this. My husband can't wield it tonight, but there's no one else who can use it as well as you, Miss Dooley. I'd be honored if you'd take it to defend our town."

Gert reached out and took the rifle and a box of ammunition from her. The mayor's Winchester wasn't as fine as Cyrus's Spencer rifle, but she knew she could use it to advantage. Her brother mounted a new sight on it for Walker just weeks ago. If she remembered right, it fired a little right of center.

"Thank you, ma'am." The tears rose in her eyes once more. "I appreciate it."

Orissa nodded. "Unless you feel I can be of assistance, I believe I'll go back to my husband now."

"You do that," Gert said. "Ask Mr. Benton to pray for a peaceful resolution to this."

She and Bitsy divided the armed women into two companies. Bitsy took her group around to the back of the Nugget. Gert and her troop stayed out front, aiming their weapons at the doors while Apphia and her contingent carried Pan Rideout away.

Stillness descended on Fergus. In the starlight, Gert stared at the saloon's windows. Now and then she saw movement within. What was Morrell doing? A dim light in an upstairs window went out. She moved to where she could see the stairway inside. Opal came down carrying a carpet bag, with several smaller bags slung over her shoulders.

Morrell handed the Colt Peacemaker to Flora and lowered his shotgun. He laid it on the bar and walked deliberately over to the three captives. Libby shuddered and tried not to think about what he had just done. She had no doubt he would kill her and her two companions if they made him angry. She tried to pray, but her pleas felt more like inward screams.

He stopped in front of her and studied her face for a long moment then smiled. "Oh yes, we'll have some good times together. I think you'll like California."

Libby returned his gaze with a stony glare. Isaac had told her once that her eyes could freeze the Snake River when she was angry, which wasn't often.

Morrell turned to Isabel. His expression turned thoughtful as he reached out to push back a strand of her brown hair. "Not too attractive, but I daresay with the right clothes and some lip rouge, you'll do." He laughed. "Your father is so arrogant, I think this may be the best revenge after all. I had planned to pay him one more visit before I left town, but this is much better. I can't thank you enough for coming to me tonight. He'll be so humiliated when he learns you decided to go with me."

He ran his finger down Isabel's cheek, and she cringed against Libby.

"Leave her alone," Libby said. A rush of anger crashed through her.

"Oh no. It's time for us to leave. We want to put a lot of miles between us and the men of Fergus before morning. This way, ladies." He gestured toward the curtained doorway.

Again Libby sent up a silent prayer. Her hope lay in Gert. Where was she now? Goldie caught her eye. What was she thinking? The two of them could survive rough treatment, but what about Isabel?

"Move," Morrell shouted. He grabbed Isabel's wrist and yanked her toward the doorway.

Isabel stiffened and raised her chin. "I won't go one step with you."

"I think you will."

"I'd rather die."

Morrell paused an instant then let out a soft chuckle. "Would you?" He turned and took the Peacemaker from Flora's shaky hands.

Libby no longer cared whether she emerged from the Nugget unscathed. She hauled her handbag around by the strap. As she fumbled with the clasp, Morrell deliberately raised the pistol and aimed it at Isabel. "Your father won't like this solution either. Are you sure you don't want to go?"

CHAPTER 37

Gert stood flattened against the outside wall of the saloon beside the front window. She heard Morrell's icy words. She moved cautiously so she could see through the dusty glass.

Morrell stood holding Libby's revolver aimed at Isabel. To Gert's amazement, Libby was pawing in her French handbag, no doubt going for her pistol. The dark-haired saloon girl, Flora, saw her and reached for the shotgun on the bar. Libby would be too late. And would she even pull the trigger?

Gert put the muzzle of the mayor's rifle up, almost touching the glass, and sighted.

Morrell slowly and deliberately pulled back the Peacemaker's hammer. "Last chance to come along nicely, Miss Fennel."

As Libby tugged out her Smith & Wesson, Flora hefted the shotgun and yelled, "Drop it, lady! Drop it now, or I'll shoot!"

As Morrell whirled toward Libby, Opal slung one of the bags she'd brought downstairs at Flora.

A gunshot exploded inside the saloon. Flora staggered and crashed into Goldie. Libby raised her pistol as Morrell caught his balance and focused his aim on her.

Gert aimed just a little left of his buttons and squeezed the trigger.

The column of men rode back into town just before dawn. Weary to the bone, Ethan drooped in the saddle. Several of the ranchers had dropped out and headed for home. Hoss plodded lethargically along beside Scout. Hiram sat on his back, swaying a little with Hoss's gait.

The street was quiet, and all the buildings on the north end were dark. Even the Nugget was silent.

"I wonder if the mayor's still alive," Ethan said.

Hiram nodded, his lips pressed tightly together.

Ethan pulled gently on the reins and turned Scout. The other men moved their horses up close to him. "Thank you all for trying. I'm going to catch a few hours' sleep, and I suggest you do the same. I'll head out again around noon and see if I can find anything we missed in the dark. Anyone who wants to join me, come to the jail then."

As the men said good night to each other, Hiram stiffened in his saddle. "Ethan, look."

"Hmm?"

Hiram pointed toward the Nugget.

"What is it?"

Hiram didn't answer, so Ethan studied the building's facade. The first rays of sunlight hit the front window to the right of the door, but the window on the left was a dull, dark hole.

"Someone took out the window." Ethan stared at it. "Must have gotten wild last night after we left."

"Sheriff, there's a light on at the jailhouse," Augie Moore called.

Ethan swung around to look toward the jail. Sure enough, a soft glow outlined the small window. Down the street, a horse neighed, and he stared at it for a good five seconds before he was sure his exhausted brain told him the truth. He turned and scanned the posse for Ralph Storrey.

"Ralph, looks like your horse is tied up about where you left it last night."

Ralph rode forward on his borrowed horse and stared toward the telegraph office. He put his heels to his mount's sides and trotted down the street toward the pinto.

Hiram cocked an eyebrow at Ethan. "What do you think's going on?"

"I dunno. But I intend to find out who's in my office."

Ethan swung down and tossed Scout's reins to Hiram. His back and legs were stiff with fatigue. He hadn't spent all night in the saddle since the last war. He limped to the walk before the jail, limbering up a little with each step. By the time he reached the door, he walked normally. He pulled his pistol from its holster and pushed the door open.

Trudy.

She sat slumped in his chair with her head cradled on her arms atop the desk. A rifle lay before her on the desktop, with the jail cell key beside it. The kerosene lamp burned low on its hook above her, casting a shimmer on her hair. As he crossed the threshold, she flinched, then sat up, blinking.

"Well! Sheriff Chapman." She stood with a crooked smile.

He walked over to her and stood looking down into her soft blue gray eyes. "Hey, Trudy." He wished more than anything that he had good news. He wanted to tell her they'd caught the killer, and that she and all the people in Fergus could feel safe now. He swallowed hard. "I'm sorry. We rode all night, but we lost him. Lost him early. He's just . . . gone."

A slow, shaky smile curved her lips. She put her hand up to his stubbly cheek. "You may have lost him, Ethan, but we found him."

"What?" He eyed her cautiously. "What happened? I saw Ralph's horse tied up, and the broken window at the Nugget."

"Your killer is lying on the floor over there beside the bar. It's Jamin."

Ethan drew in a slow breath. "Jamin Morrell."

Trudy nodded. "I'll tell you all about it."

A riot of questions sprang to his mind. He caught her to him and held her in his arms. "Trudy, Trudy. Are you all right?"

"Yes." She sneaked her arms around his waist, and he lowered his cheek to rest on top of her head.

In the shadows, a throat was cleared. Ethan straightened and stepped away from her, peering toward the jail cell.

"Oh, and the Ladies' Shooting Club brought you a couple of prisoners," Trudy said.

He walked over to the cell door and gazed in at the two girls from the Nugget. The dark-haired one sat on the edge of the bunk, glaring daggers at him. The light-haired one

— Opal, wasn't it? — stood with her arms folded and a put-upon air.

"You going to let us out of here, Sheriff? I helped them get their friends away from the boss."

Trudy came softly over and stood beside him. "We disarmed them and locked them up for you to deal with. I don't know how big their part was in the crimes, but they were helping Morrell get ready to leave. He was going to take Isabel, Libby, and Goldie with him."

"Take them where?"

"California, apparently. He planned to make Libby empty her bank account for him in Boise first. He was going to make them work in his new saloon. But Isabel refused to go, and he was going to shoot her." Trudy's voice cracked. "Ethan, I'm so glad you're home."

He turned and folded her in his arms again, ignoring the two women observing. She sobbed and hung on to him. "Sweet Trudy," he said. "I'm going to have to hear the whole story, but right now, we'd best go tell your brother you're all right."

"Oh, if he's gone home, he'll know." Trudy lifted her head and swiped at her eyes. "Pan Rideout's in his bed."

"What?"

"Jamin shot him, too."

"Eth?" Hiram stood in the doorway. "Well, hi, Gert. Everything all right?"

"Why don't you step outside with me and Hiram?" Ethan said to her. He kept one arm firmly about her waist as they walked to the door and out to where Scout and Hoss were hitched. The rest of the men had scattered to their homes or gone to the mayor's house for their wives. The street was quiet once again.

"The ladies caught the killer," Ethan told his friend.

"I peeked through the Nugget window," Hiram admitted. "That your shooting, Gert?"

Her eyes clouded. "Afraid so. With the mayor's rifle. It wasn't my first choice, but Morrell would have killed Libby." She gritted her teeth and looked forlornly at her brother. "It wasn't such a good idea to confront him like I did."

Hiram nodded soberly. "The mayor going to make it?"

"We think so, and Pan Rideout is, too, but they'll both be laid up awhile. He's over to our house, Hiram."

"What happened to him?"

"He got in Morrell's way."

Hiram stepped closer and touched her

shoulder. "You gonna be all right?"

She nodded and sniffed. "Yes, but I wouldn't want to go through last night again. Annie did wonders with the patients, but I'd be more hopeful if we had a doctor."

"Morrell told me last week he'd written some letters and hoped we'd get a physician to move here soon," Ethan said.

"Oh, and here we are patching up the people he shot while we wait."

Hiram said, "Well, he got us a good preacher."

"True. And do you know why he did it?" She looked from him to Ethan.

They both shook their heads.

"He wanted to be a big shot in town, like Cyrus and the mayor. But it wasn't enough. People still didn't respect him, even though he'd tried to act like a pillar of the community." Her shoulders drooped for a moment.

Ethan studied her tear-streaked face. She must feel as appalled as he had after his first battle against the Bannock. Maybe they could talk about his war experience after all. They might even be able to comfort each other. He tightened his hold on her just a little, and she looked up.

"You fellows must be hungry," she said.

"Come on. I'll make some flapjacks."

"What about the prisoners?" Ethan asked.

"Prisoners?" Hiram's eyes widened as he looked at his sister once more.

She chuckled. "I'll send Deputy Shepard over to keep an eye on them while you have breakfast."

CHAPTER 38

Church services began on time Sunday morning, though several benches were empty and many members of the congregation had eyes red from lack of sleep. Mrs. Walker stayed home with her husband, and Annie Harper sat with them. Several of the posse members were also absent.

Hiram and Ethan sat down on each side of Trudy, trying to hide their yawns behind their hands. Neither had shaved that morning, but she didn't mind.

Libby paused at the end of their row on her way in. Ethan stood stiffly.

"Good morning, Sheriff." She smiled at the Dooleys. "How's Pan doing?"

"Holding his own," Trudy said. "Bertha and Oscar Runnels volunteered to sit with him this morning. If his wound doesn't get infected, they plan to move him to their house tomorrow."

Libby nodded. "That's good. And Trudy,

you look lovely today."

As her cheeks warmed, Trudy realized she was no longer Gert. She had begun to think of herself as Trudy, too. Ethan's eyes swept over her, she could tell without looking up. She smoothed the skirt of the light blue muslin dress Libby had persuaded her to buy.

"Yes, you do," Ethan said. "Very nice."

Trudy's cheeks blazed, and she was glad when Libby turned her focus back to Ethan.

"Are you going to let the girls from the Nugget go, Sheriff?"

Ethan gritted his teeth and shrugged. "I'm not sure yet. I'd like to talk to you later about what happened last night. Trudy says Flora helped Morrell when he kidnapped you ladies, but Opal helped you escape."

"I believe she did. It happened awfully fast at the end."

"Uh, would you like to sit here?" Ethan asked, stepping into the aisle.

"Thank you, but . . ." Libby's gaze shifted toward the doorway, and she smiled. "I believe I'll sit with Bitsy and her girls. I'll speak with you later, Sheriff."

"Bitsy came?" Trudy turned her head and watched in satisfaction as Bitsy, Vashti, and Goldie settled with Libby two rows behind them. Isabel Fennel crossed the threshold with her father and clung to his arm as they walked toward their bench.

Pastor Benton stood up and walked to the pulpit. Dark shadows rimmed his eyes, and he smiled wearily.

"Greetings, brothers and sisters. Our town has endured great trials, but God has sustained us. I'm happy to report that Mayor Walker is resting this morning, with no fever. We're in hopes he'll recover from his wound in time. Mr. Rideout was also wounded, as most of you know. His injury is less severe, and we expect him to make a good recovery. One other announcement — I've placed an order for hymnbooks, and Mrs. Adams tells me they should arrive in a couple of weeks."

As the congregation sang "Amazing Grace" from memory, Trudy sent up another prayer of thanks. The pastor's sermon on love for one another touched her deeply. She'd seen the people of Fergus move from separate, self-centered households to caring individuals and families watching out for one another. As she listened, she felt blessed beyond anything she deserved, having gained a new love for the women of the town and being seated on the rustic pew between the two finest men in Fergus.

After the benediction, they filed out into

the blistering sun.

Trudy caught up with Bitsy before she could hurry away.

"I'm glad you came."

Bitsy smiled with a shrug that set the pheasant's feather in her hat bobbing. "It wasn't so bad. I may make a habit of it. Of course, I've got to hurry now and prepare for the dinner crowd. Augie's been on his own the last hour, and I expect he'll need us."

Hiram and Ethan came to stand beside Trudy as she watched Bitsy and the two brightly clad girls scurry toward the Spur & Saddle.

Hiram's gaze shifted to the south end of the street. "Looks like a rider coming in."

As others filed out of the haberdashery building behind them, they stood watching until the bay horse had brought its rider close to them. The man stopped the dusty mare in the street and gazed at the crowd of people emerging from the old store in their Sunday best. Several bags were strapped to the cantle and sides of his saddle. The man looked tired. He homed in on Ethan and smiled through a couple of days' growth of beard.

"Good morning, Sheriff. Is this the town of Fergus?"

"Yes, sir," said Ethan. "Can I help you?"

"Why, yes. I've ridden all night. Is there a hotel?"

Ethan nodded down the street toward the Fennel House. "The boardinghouse is right yonder."

He looked where Ethan pointed and smiled. "Ah. That sounds adequate. I suppose I could have waited for tomorrow's stagecoach run, but I was eager to get here. And . . . I'm looking for Mr. Morrell. He invited me to come."

"Oh?" Ethan looked at the Dooleys. Hiram shrugged, and Trudy frowned. Ethan said to the stranger, "What is your name, sir?"

He leaned down and extended his hand to Ethan. "It's Kincaid. Dr. James Kincaid."

"Praise God," Trudy murmured.

Ethan released the man's hand and shoved his hat back. "Well, Doc, you've come to the right place. I hope you're not too tired, because we can put you right to work."

Trudy laughed. "One of the patients is at my house, just a few doors down, Doctor. Would you care to take a look at him and join us for dinner?"

Hiram said, "Go on ahead with him. I'll take care of his horse."

"That sounds wonderful," the physician said.

Trudy nodded in satisfaction. "Good. And after dinner, Sheriff Chapman can take you around to meet the mayor. He's the other patient."

As Kincaid dismounted, Ethan reached for Trudy's hand. She let him hold on to it as they led the doctor toward the Dooley house.

ABOUT THE AUTHOR

Susan Page Davis is the author of more than twenty novels in the historical romance, mystery, romantic suspense, contemporary romance, and young adult genres. A history and genealogy buff, she lives in the woods in Maine with her husband Jim. They are the parents of six terrific young adults and are the grandparents of six adorable grandchildren. Visit Susan at her Web site: www.susanpagedavis.com.